THE WATER CASTLE

The
WATER CASTLE

Ingeborg Lauterstein

Boston

HOUGHTON MIFFLIN COMPANY

1980

For Miriam, Meg, Peggy,
and Professor Holcomb

Library of Congress Cataloging in Publication Data

Lauterstein, Ingeborg.
 The water castle.

 I. Title.
PZ4.L385Wat [PS3562.A845]   813'.54   80-15515
ISBN 0-395-29471-1

Printed in the United States of America

V 10 9 8 7 6 5 4 3 2 1

Contents

THE WATER CASTLE

1

The Doll

ON THIS AUTUMN DAY in Vienna, my mother allowed me to carry the candle to the altar of the Virgin for the first time. I was six years old, apple-cheeked, amber-eyed, and I held the candle proudly; the small flame flickered in the draft. Chestnuts, torn off trees by a strong south wind, hit the dome of the family chapel with a thud and rolled into the gutter, rumbling like guns I had heard on the radio in the gardener's cottage. The German station had banged and crackled with a roaring of "Sieg Heil," as if a giant whangdoodle would leap out and devour me. By the time the old chestnut trees bore their candelabra of blossoms, Austria would be part of Germany and the great whangdoodle would be let loose in our streets.

Our family chapel stood on the edge of the Vienna woods and was three hundred years old. It had come with the land when Great-Grandfather bought the farm and the breweries. I was christened here: Reyna Elizabeth Meinert. On Sunday Father Leiden read Mass here; during the week the chapel was empty. My young mother liked to bring me along when she came to pray, in much the same manner as she carried her old doll, Puppe. She preferred to come here when the chapel was empty, but she did not like to be alone.

The dank odor of old stone and incense was less noticeable this day than the acrid smell of new paint. Fritz, our gardener, an unemployed art teacher, had repainted the old carved images in the chapel while we were away in August.

"Careful with that candle. Don't burn yourself." Mama made the sign of the cross and kneeled down.

I curtsied before the Virgin and placed the candle at her pink, bare feet. She looked unfamiliar to me in her freshly painted, bright blue robe. I missed the old dark wooden image—a grandmother of heaven—as I knelt beside Mama. The now smooth and pink-faced Madonna held her naked pink doll with a smug smile, while right beside her St. Sebastian was pierced with arrows and sprinkled with newly painted blood, and St. Nepomuk hung by his heels. Infants were slaughtered in the carved relief; I counted thirteen. I had never noticed what went on, but now I could see that the mothers were not about. I naturally concluded they were all at home playing with dolls. My mama always carried her doll, Puppe, no matter what went on. And Holy Mary stood above me with a doll named Jesus.

"Make the sign of the cross," Mama whispered. I could see the outline of the doll under her cloak. Puppe not only came to the chapel but was also dressed in clothes that matched Mama's for the opera, concerts, and even the great balls during *Fasching*. Everyone flocked around Mother and Puppe at our house during parties. "Let's see Puppe! Look at that perfect copy of your dress, Ann Marie. Only one person could have done that!" They might turn to touch my curls, for I was usually allowed to stay up and greet the guests. I would be gushed over, kissed. "What fun for a little girl," they would go on. "Mama with her old doll—just like sisters. Charming and original. How you must love it all."

Now I edged away from the hateful doll, and my mother gave me a warning look from under the wide brim of her new hat. When she went back to praying, I could only see the tip of her nose. "Say your Pater Noster," she told me.

I prayed in silence and got as far as the passage on forgiveness. The thump of chestnuts rumbling down the chapel roof brought me from prayers to guns and bodies, the blood Fritz the gardener had described to me when he told me all about the First World War. Now, as I glanced around the chapel, I could see the dead and the wounded.

On the right side of the altar of the Virgin, the gigantic Christ had been painted green, one of Fritz Janicek's favorite colors. The image of the Son was three times the size of that of the Holy Mother and hung forward from a great cross. Christ was naked except for diapers and blood. A lot of red was running down the forehead from the crown of thorns; the blood on the palms and on the feet where the rusty nails stuck out was different—more orange, like my sweater and knee socks—as was the Jesus heart, which was on fire and neatly exposed. The tortured saints looked almost bored, but the Christ squinted with fury. His lips pressed together, holding back screams of pain and anguish. He looked as though he would wrench himself from the cross, rush to his mother, take the doll from her, and smash it.

I bumped against Puppe, and Mama's violet eyes reproached me from under the hat. She shifted the doll to the other side. The china head popped out from the armhole of Mama's cloak, violet-blue glass eyes glowering at me. Puppe was dressed like my mother, her green felt hat tilted at a rakish angle. I turned my back on her, but a burning lump formed deep inside me: "Dear Father and Holy Ghost, Almighty Ones, take away Puppe. Make her kaput. Break her like my china cup and take away the pieces."

The doll's tiny china hand seemed to point at me as though she were ordering me out the door like a dog. My cheeks began to glow, although it was so cold in the chapel I could see my own breath. One was supposed to pray for others first in order to get one's wishes: "God bring Otto von Habsburg back to the throne for Countess Grandmama. Dear Holy Ghost, help Papa remain chess champion. . . ." It was better not to ask for too much: "Dear Almighty, give me lots of girls' clothes, a hat and fur muff like Puppe's and Mama's." At the mere thought of the wonderful tiny ermine muff, the lump inside me burst into flames like the Jesus heart: "Holy Ghost, give Mama her Hitler, but make a hole in the doll. Let Jesus down and nail Puppe up . . ."

I raised my eyes, and all at once I realized in despair that the Holy Ghost, whom I had always considered the most powerful helper, was a mere white pigeon winging feebly against the chapel dome, as if trying to get away from the sound of chestnuts popping like guns.

"I told you to be still," Mama warned me.

"My knees hurt," I complained. I was wearing lederhosen, as usual, to please my father, and my knees were bare.

"If you were praying you wouldn't notice it. Pray like a good girl."

How could I believe that goodness would be rewarded? The chapel was ornate with misdeeds. My mother simply closed her eyes. Her smooth, full lips moved fervently. I knew she secretly prayed for Adolf Hitler's coming, a new empire, as though the Führer were a messiah. She kept her eyes closed while candlelight flickered over garish images. The messiah's domain, as I saw it, was but a slaughterhouse. I tried to finish my Pater Noster, yet I could not help wondering why there had to be victims for the power and the glory of all the almighty ones on earth, as in heaven . . .

*   *   *

Our chauffeur, Heinz, covered us with a white fur rug before he started the car. The woods, the farm, the brewery we passed all belonged to my father and were part of what Mama called the Meinert empire. Meinerts had started off as chicken farmers five generations ago; through industry and cunning they became "the Wine and Beer Meinerts."

The vineyard and the Meinert woods were separated by an old cemetery. Near the gate stood a stone funeral chapel and the sexton's cottage, and a little farther up the hill was a villa with a flower garden, the home of Father Leiden, the priest. Heinz slowed down to avoid a florist's cart. Blue patches of sky appeared like peepholes among heavy clouds. People went in and out through the cemetery gates, and their feet rustled through fallen leaves. It would soon be All Souls' Day.

Mama knocked on the glass partition: "Stop for a minute, Heinz, will you!" She jumped from the running board and rushed toward the gate; her cloak flew up, and she had to hold onto her hat against the wind. She stopped before a small woman in dark clothes and a tall fancy hat which was decorated with feathers. They greeted each other with enthusiasm. Mama held up the doll and the small woman laughed. When they began to walk side by side toward the car, I noticed that the woman wore built-up shoes with thick soles, and yet her head was no higher than Puppe's on Mama's arm.

Heinz helped them into the car. The tiny woman sat down beside me. She greeted me brusquely and examined me without the customary Viennese endearments. A veil held her fancy hat in place and covered her face like the cracks on an old portrait. "Well, here you are . . ." was all she said.

"You have not seen her since the christening," Mama remarked.

The little woman laughed and lifted the veil for a moment. Harsh cheerfulness was carved into her face, in striking contrast with eyes as dark as an overcast night sky. "I came uninvited, like the fairy godmother in the old story."

"That is not so," Mama quickly spoke up. "It was understood . . ."

"Well, half-invited perhaps, which is far less distinguished than being left out." She spoke softly, without a trace of Viennese dialect, rather like my aristocratic grandmother, Countess Reyna von Dornbach Falkenburg. "You did give the little one the right name." Her dark gaze made me uncomfortable; I had to turn away. "She has your mother's amber eyes. Those golden Falkenburg eyes, they used to call them at court."

Mama laughed. "Her father says they are the color of well-aged Meinert wine."

The little woman touched my leather trousers. Her hand, like her head, seemed too large for her body. She wore dark gloves, ornate with petit-point roses. "What is this? A daughter dressed as a son . . ."

"*Ja, ja,*" Mama said gaily. "Papa Meinert is very modern. He considers a daughter as good as a son."

We drove past vineyards, and some of the workers noticed our car and waved their hats. I stood up and waved back.

"Charming, *très charmant,*" the strange woman said softly. "Is Herr von Meinert a modern husband?"

Mama held up the doll and shook its head. "*Aber nein, ma chèrie,* you always know the answer when you ask a question. You have seen enough of him. You just want me to admit that he is a very old-fashioned husband."

The dark stumpy arm of the woman went around my shoulder, and I recognized the faint fragrance of violets. "You smell like my countess grandmama. You speak like her."

She hugged me, and I was surprised at her strength. "Children always know more than we think," she sighed. "The countess Reyna and I were at convent school together, and later we were at court. Our position was, of course, quite different."

Mama was looking out of the window rather determinedly. The car flickered through the sun, and the yellow light fell onto her hand and the ring which bore the ancient crest of Falkenburg, the falcon perched upon the sun.

"What did you do at court?" I asked the little woman.

Her mouth trembled for a moment and her bright eyes shone, perhaps with tears. "I began to make dolls' clothes at court when I was not much older than you are now, Reyna. The court hatter was a father to me, and taught me all he knew. I made hats and dresses for Puppe when she still belonged to Baroness Christina von Kortnai. *Ach,* that glorious redhead. A beauty—very much like your gracious mama. So tall. I saw her grave today." She took off Puppe's felt hat and smoothed over the wig. "Made from a cutting of those famous braids. Ja, ja."

The old doll appeared to be listening attentively, her devilish eyes staring at the woman in black.

"I still remember the first time she came to the dolls' room at the palace with Puppe. I was happiest in that room; it was my real home. All those beautiful dolls around me, each one with a name and a title, the proper clothes to go with it—and the little highnesses, when they were around, running in to keep me company. Hours passed like minutes when we played with the dollhouses. Everything was small. In walked the baroness Christina von Kortnai one day—tall, taller even than the empress, and more beautiful, full of life and mischief. Tall, blessedly tall. She was dazzling; always wore light colors or black lace."

"Did Great-Aunt Christina look exactly like Mama?"

"Well, you look at Puppe, and you look at your gracious mama. Your mama is blessed with more loveliness, more sweetness. Being a mother does that . . ."

"I did not know that you were such a flatterer, *Meisterin!*" Mama said, and put the hat back onto the doll. "You know perfectly well that my great-aunt was considered the most beautiful woman in Europe. Puppe is supposed to be her portrait."

"She looks mean," I declared. The tiny woman beside me laughed, saying that a portrait was a work of art and did not always flatter.

We were already passing the woods near our avenue. She shook her head sadly. "Poor, beautiful doll. The baroness—your great-grandmother's sister, Reyna—came to me the very day she received her. The sculptor Antonelli sent Puppe to the baroness in a wooden box lined with scarlet velvet—just like a coffin. I opened it and there she was, without a stitch of clothes."

Mama quickly interrupted this fascinating story. I had already found out by listening to grown-up talk that Antonelli had loved Great-Aunt Christina. He had made the doll and sent it to her as a parting gift when she refused to marry him. But Mama always became embarrassed by the doll's past and changed the subject. She now explained that Heinz, the chauffeur, had to drive into town after dropping us off anyway. He could easily take the Meisterin home.

"Do you still make dolls' clothes?" I quickly asked to detain her.

"Not since the fall of the empire." She meant, of course, the empire within the empire: the dolls' room where she had ruled. "I still dress Puppe, the doll without a name. But then, she is very special. I am kept busy at my hat salon with all my little highnesses—even their daughters, now." She touched my chin and looked into my Falkenburg eyes. "You wouldn't want a hat for a doll, would you?"

I shook my head. We had arrived at our gate too soon. The Meisterin lifted her veil once more. "You hate dolls. You hate Puppe," she whispered into my ear. Then she lowered her veil and quickly took Mama's hand and kissed the doll on both cheeks. She stared intently at the Meinert-Hof, our home, which retained the façade of an old farmhouse and lay half-hidden by an old willow and the rose gardens. No one would ever guess it was a mansion. In fact, the Meinert empire, with gardens, woods, vineyards, brewery, farm, and chapel, extended behind it.

The chauffeur waited, holding the door, ready to help us out, when the Meisterin pointed at the house across the street with her black-gloved hand. "That household is unfortunate, and far too close to you, gracious Ann Marie."

The house had been built by a munitions manufacturer during the First World War, in the style of a baroque castle. After the war was lost, he shot himself; the house had then stood empty most of the time, even after Eugene Romberg, my father's friend, a rich Jew, bought it for his wife Resi. Finally, during the past August, they had moved in.

"I like the Rombergs," I said. "As soon as Eli is well enough I want to go play with him. He is only a few years older than I am, even if he is so tall."

My mother edged toward the door. The Meisterin held her back by grabbing the doll's arm. "Listen to me, dear heart. Avoid the vis-à-vis. You know what I mean. And you must stay away from those horses." She turned to me. "Well, I hope it's *auf Wiedersehen*, little highness . . . We have been kept apart long enough."

I curtsied like a well-brought-up little girl. She promised me a hat. The right hat. She never would fulfill that promise.

"Now that you have met me, do you know who I am?"

"Frau Hanna Roth," I said. But in my heart, I had already named her Hanna the Dwarf.

✿   ✿   ✿

I waved enthusiastically as the car drove off. The Meisterin did not even bother to turn her head. The iridescent feather on her high hat trembled. Something was about to happen. I was to feel this each time we met. Something ended and something began. Hanna the Dwarf figured in my young life as a tiny black punctuation mark. Her warning gloved hand merely pointed my way —this time to the house across the street. As a creature of fantasy, like the Danube king, the giant Rübezahl, or Rumpelstiltskin, she merely spurred me on. I think she knew this from the beginning.

At first it seemed like any other afternoon. Fritz Janicek the gardener waylaid Mama at the yellow roses in the front garden. He always waited to be noticed by her and greeted her by whipping off his straw hat with a great show of servility. To impress her, he wore a gardener's costume fit for an operetta, with a long, green apron.

"How marvelous to have some late-blooming roses, Herr Janicek," she piped. "And it was very generous of you to devote your vacation time to brightening our old chapel." Since he had been a professor of art in a gymnasium for boys, Mama made a point of addressing him as *Herr* Janicek, and he loved it.

"*Gnädigste*," he said, too modestly. "Your gracious husband paid me handsomely, but your approval would have been more than enough."

Mama did not seem to notice his disgusting habit of squashing aphids and rubbing them into his palms. But he did make her uncomfortable. I could tell by the way she quickly held up Puppe and let her smell the roses. "We would love some for our room," she said.

The stabbing look he gave the doll while he trimmed thorns off the roses pleased me no end. Fritz had told me that his own mother had a cat she talked to and carried around wherever she went.

"What happened to your mother's cat, Herr Janicek?" I asked.

"She went to her eternal rest," he replied gravely.

Mama gave me a quick warning look and told me to carry the roses, to prevent me from asking him about the cat's departure to eternity. Fritz Janicek looked disappointed. I could tell he wanted to carry the roses to the back door for her, to get more attention and praise. His sharp nose turned white when he was angry. He thrust his hat back onto his head and walked away whistling the Horst Wessel *lied,* a song about a dead Nazi, I had been told.

Mama did not seem to hear the tune and ran ahead of me up the steps into our courtyard. Our garden, the hill with its great linden tree, chestnuts, and pines, was sweet to the eye in the autumn, with muted tones of gold, russet, and green. It extended all the way to the orchard. Mama loved this time of the year, but her mood had changed, and she rushed passed Poldi, the maid, who was letting us in. We went upstairs to the boudoir, where I usually played in the afternoon until my father returned from the vineyards or the brewery or his town office.

I inquired whether Hanna Roth was a real dwarf. Mama flared up and told me never to label anyone like that. I pointed out that everyone called me *Kleine,* little one, and this labeled me just as much. She told me to stop the back talk and said I was far too forward for my age. She filled a crystal vase in her bathroom and thrust the roses into it without arranging them or sniffing their perfume. At least the doll was out of favor, too, reclining on the window seat with one leg sticking up indecently.

I watched Mama hurl her cloak and Hanna Roth hat onto the bed, displaying her crown of braids and her redheaded temper, which everyone called her temperament. Then she sat down at her dressing table, scrutinized her own blunt features, and pouted. When she did notice me in the mirror, she turned and took off my sweater, flicked my dark curls playfully, and covered my face with little kisses. I hugged her tight. Her full figure felt soft and supple.

"Poor Puppe! Look at her still in her cloak and hat." She let me slip onto the carpet. "I must change her for the afternoon."

I only wished I could send Puppe off to her eternal rest with Frau Janicek's cat. I was too young to recognize Mama's devotion to the idol as a subterfuge. Nor could I have known how much comfort and shelter she found in performing the prescribed duties for the dead woman's doll, or how dangerous it would be to deprive my mother of the ritual. Mama had not yet been five years old when she became heir to the doll. According to the testament, only with the doll—with the brushing of the red-gold wig and the changing of her dress: white in the morning, gray in the afternoon, in the evening black—came the von Kortnai jewels and the town house on the Ring. The town house had been sold—it never interested my mother; and she let me play with the tiaras and necklaces. But I was never allowed to handle the doll. She was afraid I might break the china head. Not that I wanted to play with Puppe. I regarded the doll as a curse, an incubus.

While Mama undressed Puppe, I practiced my headstand, and everything turned upside down—the doll's little hand-painted wardrobe, the roses, Mama on the window seat. The boudoir, my mother's large bed-sitting-room, was the only fancy room in our house. Papa had had the walls lined with blue silk to match her eyes. Shirred curtains filtered the light. A wood fire crackled in the pale-blue tiled stove. Soft chairs and a sofa were covered with blue floral fabric. The rest of the Meinert-Hof retained its whitewashed walls, dark wooden beams, and the old peasant furniture from the ancestral farm.

The boudoir was always my favorite room. The soft blue carpet invited me to practice the headstand my father admired. He took credit for my robust health, because he had decided I should grow up naturally. I had been encouraged to crawl around the house before I could stand up, and he loved to see me slide down the stairs on my round stomach. No nursemaid for me! He began taking me to the farm when I was three years old. There he put me onto a pony, and when I fell off he did not allow me to cry. He preferred to see me dressed in leather pants, like himself, and I rather enjoyed this for climbing trees and doing somersaults and headstands; but secretly I adored anything fancy and female.

"Sweet little dress and bonnet," Mama was saying as she took a gray velvet costume from the doll's wardrobe. "Frau Hanna really is an artist. You know, this was the very first matching dress she made for Puppe and me. Right after she brought Puppe to Schloss Falkenburg. It was not long after the war, and food was still scarce, especially in Vienna; so was dress material. She stayed with us in the country. I loved her company."

I rolled over in a somersault and asked whether Hanna Roth had always worn a veil. Mama was not quite certain, but she did remember her in black mourning veils when she came with the doll. "She always pulled her black veils over her face when we drove around in the pony trap. The children ran after us one day shouting, 'Dwarf! Dwarf!' They pointed at me and stuck out their tongues, yelling, 'Redhead, redhead, crazy and mad head!' As soon as we got back to Falkenburg, she took me to her room, braided my hair, and began to make a bonnet for me and this matching set for Puppe from a gray velvet curtain. I still remember sitting on the floor pushing the sewing machine pedals for her, because her legs didn't reach down far enough. She talked about doll weddings, christenings, and balls. She told me the story of my life: I would grow tall and marry very young . . ."

I watched Puppe being changed with satisfaction. The joints on the neck, arms, and legs made her look like any other doll. When she was turned over, however, her head and eyes moved and took on the ill-tempered expression I had seen on my mother's face when we came in.

"I don't feel comfortable without a Roth hat," Mama admitted. "But I don't depend on her advice like the other ladies at the salon. After I was married, she said, I changed and turned away from her. She wouldn't set foot in this house after you were christened. At the salon she puts up with me for the sake of Puppe. Beautiful Puppe!" Mama kissed the china cheek. When she held the doll so lovingly, she receded into the empire within the empire where the tiny Meisterin ruled. Puppe would never have become an idol without the trimmings, the finery, the powerful encouragement of Hanna Roth.

The Biedermeier clock ticked, swinging gilded cherubs on its pendulum. Poldi, one of our twin maids, brought in a tray of coffee for Mama and hot chocolate topped with whipped cream for me. A letter on the tray attracted me because of the Hitler stamp. I reached for it.

"Don't touch," Mama said. She put the letter into her pocket, and I consoled myself with whipped cream and sugar from the bottom of my cup. The clock struck four and played its little Mozart minuet. Poldi said it was getting dark early and went to turn on the light.

"No, leave it," said Mama. "We'll turn it on later. I like the dusk." She drew me to her side on the window seat. Through the curtains I could see the brightly lit windows of the house across the street. Over there the lights were never turned off. When Eugene Romberg had moved in, everyone started calling the house the Water Castle. They said he had made his fortune by watering milk when he took over the dairies after the war. Even my father called Eugene Romberg the Splasher, for fun.

"I don't care what Frau Roth said about the Water Castle," I said. "Papa did promise I can go and see Eli Romberg because I have no one to play with."

Eli was nine years old. I had seen very little of him because he had asthma and all kinds of other problems. His parents had kept him at the Semmering, a mountain resort close to Vienna, with an excellent physician. In Vienna they had preferred to stay at Resi Romberg's apartment near the Opera. She was known as the Little Nightingale and had been a famous opera singer. When she came to our house she sang for Papa, but she had given up her career to look after Eli.

"Eli is too sickly," my mother said. "You can always play with little Herbert, the foot doctor's son. He is a healthy little fellow."

"I don't like him," I said. She knew perfectly well I did not like to play with him or any of the young children in the park. Their games bored me, and they stared at me because I talked like a grownup.

"We'd just sat down the other day when poor Eli had an attack," Mama reminded me.

"I don't care," I told her. "I loved it."

We had gone across the street for afternoon coffee. All the lights were on and even the heat, although it was warm with the sun pouring through a glass dome into the great hall. I had not minded feeling hot, because I loved all the statues there—especially the naked ones. I could not wait to explore the countless rooms filled up with furniture. But most of all I had admired Eli. I had never seen a sick person. Eli had a beautiful asthma attack as soon as we sat down to have coffee. He turned as white as his suit and gasped for air like a carp on dry land. His nurse and a doctor arrived. Maids, and even the cook in her white apron, ran around bumping into each other in a panic I much admired. Unfortunately, Mama had wanted to leave at once.

"Papa promised I could see Eli again," I said.

Mama jumped up and looked out the side window. "I think I hear his car." She ran to her dressing table and dabbed perfume behind her ears, onto her dress, and finally on the doll's braids; no matter what Mama did, Puppe retained a musty odor. "He might rake leaves before he comes up." She peered into the spyglass attached to her side window. Father did not like us to be seen at windows from the street. He considered this vulgar. We did look out into the courtyard from the alcove to watch him at work in the garden, but this was private. Meinerts liked privacy.

Soon my father would come running up the back stairs, knock at the door, and wait like a stranger. When he was admitted, he always smiled so much that his fair kaiser beard stuck out in great tufts. Mama always picked up the doll before she threw herself into his arms. I would follow. While they kissed I would look through Father's pockets for candy and little toys. "I'm a dirty old farmer," he would say. "I'll get all the beautiful dolls dirty."

Mama liked to ruffle his thick hair. "Get me dirty. I don't care." She had a way of gurgling like an infant, showing the tip of her tongue. Sometimes she even kissed soil from his hands. They were the same height, but he could pick her up like a child. The doll would be between them, the magic eyes in motion, iridescent and scheming.

This evening Mama sat with hunched shoulders, biting her full lower lip, a heritage from some Habsburg ancestor. In the mellow dusk, the autumn foliage slowly drifted to the ground. "I wish winter would not come this year," she said sadly.

"But I want the *Christkindl* and you want to go to all the balls and I want snow, lots of snow." While I spoke, Papa came striding through the courtyard in his leather breeches and a drab green loden jacket. He did not even look up to the window, and seemed intent on studying his sturdy shoes rather than throwing us kisses.

Eventually Mama turned on the lights and we heard Father coming up the stairs, slowly, as though he were tired. He did not knock on the door to play our game, but walked in and hesitated, his head almost touching the door frame. His cheeks were apple-red; his nose was fleshy; he had a straight mouth when he did not smile and a strong cleft chin. His eyes were blue-green, like the color of certain grapes. He was much admired in Vienna by both men and women—and he knew it.

"Did you bring me candy?" I shouted.

He shook his head and stepped onto the blue carpet as though entering a sickroom.

Mama picked up the doll, ready to run to him. "What's the matter, Ferdl?" she piped in her most childish voice.

"I'm sorry, Annerl, but I had to dismiss Fritz Janicek just now. He has to go without notice."

"No! It can't be! Why?"

He scratched his ear thoughtfully. "He insulted my friend Eugene Romberg. When I think of the money at Christmas, the kindness he has had from Eugene . . ."

"I know Eugene is overgenerous to our servants. But Fritz is temperamental—he's an artist."

"Eugene and I were chatting at the gate and Eugene called out to Fritz in a friendly way, congratulating him on the late roses. The scoundrel turned his back on him, did not greet us or take off his hat. I decided to have a word with him after Eugene left. Guess what? The scoundrel wears a swastika on his hatband, in the center of an edelweiss."

"Is that all?" Mama sat down on the window seat and undid Puppe's braids. "I'm sure he didn't really mean anything."

"You wanted to help this man, but I even had the police at my office asking about him last year. They know he's an illegal Nazi, and that is not all. He was accused of corrupting boys, politically and otherwise."

"They had it in for Nazis last year, that's all. Forgetting to take his hat off doesn't mean he wanted to insult Eugene."

"He hates Herr Romberg," I spoke up. "He told me so. It's because Herr Romberg is a Jew. He hates anyone who's not pure in blood; that's why he kills stray cats."

My father shook his head. "There you are, Annerl, he's even getting our little one all mixed up."

"I'm not mixed up," I said.

He pulled me onto his knee. "Now, you listen to me. He is a silly man, even if he is educated. A Czech from Prague. Janicek— is that a German name? I think he's crazy, and certainly over-educated for the job of a gardener, that Nazi professor."

"Vienna is full of Nazis," Mama said. "He is an idealist, and he tries to please, Ferdl. He gave up his vacation to restore the chapel."

"Ja, Papa; he put in all new blood."

He picked me up and turned me over. My face came level with Puppe's and I stuck out my tongue. "What have we here! A lout, a Lausbub." He kissed my cheek and smacked my leather pants. "Catch." He pretended to throw me into Mama's lap. She did not respond. He became serious again. "Eugene Romberg is my old friend."

She lifted the doll to her face. "I know. I like Eugene. Some Jews are all right."

Papa put me down and went to kiss her neck. "You just don't know what is going on in Vienna—in all of Austria—my child."

She shook him off. "I'm not your child. I do know what's going on."

I had never heard her speak that way before. I sat down at her feet, leaning against her legs. "Mama does know a lot. She even has a letter with a Hitler stamp."

"Ach, Berthold was at a riding competition in Bavaria last week. Several boys from the Theresianum went."

"I forgot about your Nazi high-school cousin. The aristocratic National Socialists at the Theresianum are so busy with politics that they flunk their exams."

Mother's young cousin came to our farm in the summertime to ride with Mama. He would pick up Puppe and swing her above his head. "I like Berthold very much," I said.

Mama flushed. She put the doll away into the little gilded rocking chair that always stood on the table. The chair rocked and the doll looked from side to side, as though she expected wild young Berthold to come rushing through the door. Mama had not finished with Puppe's hair. One side was braided, the other hung loose. This pleased me.

"A lot of young people from the first-class families are pro-*Anschluss* and German *Solidarität*," Mama said.

Papa interrupted her with a loud laugh and corrected her pronunciation of *Solidarität*. I had to laugh with him, because it sounded odd to hear my mother speak with so much stubborn authority. She frowned, and the Falkenburg line appeared between her eyebrows, right above a freckle, like an exclamation mark.

"Your boy cousin had better study for his final exam instead of riding and gambling away Austria with his friends. He might flunk again this year, and that would ruin his poor old father, the duke." He took Mama by the shoulder, but she shook him off. "Don't you realize, Annerl, that your own mother might be arrested as a Monarchist by a Nazi government? There might even be another war."

A strange, knowing smile on Mama's face made Father snatch me up as though he had to protect me from this new mother who meddled in politics.

"Even if there should be another war," she said, "you won't be called up and killed like my father."

I had never seen my parents perform quite like this. "Grandpapa von Dornbach was an *Uhlaner*," I said with Grandmama Reyna's pride. His body, she had told me, lay somewhere on the barren slopes of the Dolomites, which were covered with unmarked Austrian graves—heroes, all of them, betrayed by the Italians. They had fought for the empire.

Papa kissed the top of my head. "Ja, ja. I'm only an old cripple. Not fit to be a soldier and a hero." He had fallen from an old walnut tree in the orchard as a boy, and his broken left leg had remained slightly short after it healed; this had kept him out of the army. As he carried me to the door, his limp became a hobble.

I did not like being sent out just as things got interesting. "I met Hanna Roth today," I told him.

"*Jawohl*, Heinz told me he had the honor of driving the famous Meisterin to her salon." He chuckled. "How is the old troublemaker?"

"She said to avoid the vis-à-vis. She doesn't like the Rombergs, but I want to go and play with Eli."

"The boy is sick most of the time," Mama said with a new firmness in her voice. "She'll catch something."

"Eli is much improved. I see no reason why our little one should not have the company of such a clever and musical boy. Unless you believe in the pronouncements of the great little hatter. My sisters both did, and it ruined them."

I quickly asked how Frau Hanna had ruined the *Englischen Tanten*.

"Wearing all those hats and sitting around the salon, they became just as hoity-toity as your mama is beginning to sound. But they weren't as pretty and couldn't get away with it, so they live in England." He slapped my pants and put me outside the door like a kitten. Any other day I would have run down to the kitchen, but I knew he had something on his mind, something he didn't want me to overhear. I sat down on the landing and practiced rolling my eyes like Puppe.

"I'll get some of the vintners to work in the garden until the spring. Fritz is leaving as soon as he has packed up." He paused. "Meinerts keep out of politics and wars. Remember, you are a Meinert now."

I heard something drop and hoped it was the doll. But Mama laughed. "Now what do you think of that, Puppe?" She sounded like Grandmama Reyna. "He doesn't know about us. I, Emperor Meinert, if you remember, am a Dornbach Falkenburg—even if you did marry me."

I heard one of Father's loud kisses. A chair or table moved. "Promise. Let your noble boy cousin make a fool of himself. Promise, Annerl, to keep out of it all. For me."

They whispered, laughed.

"Will you stop pulling my imperial *kaiserlichen* beard."

2
The Web

MAMA HAD CALLED FATHER Emperor Meinert in front of the Rombergs just after they had moved into the house across the street in August. It made Resi Romberg laugh. From then on Mama often called him Emperor in public, and she always timed it well. At the end of a dinner or at the wine gardens, the *Heurigen,* this would be her cue for Papa's story of how he fell in love with her when she was a schoolgirl holding a doll. They had a sudden need to enmesh friends, family, enemies, lovers, even servants in the web of tender associations. He never tired of telling the story, and I listened so many times, I felt I had actually been with him. I loved the description of his two sisters' coming to him in the half-dark wine cellar, adorned in new fur hats like a pair of Cossacks, eyes dancing in plump faces. The Meisterin had just foreseen Ferdl's future. They had been at the hat salon to pick up their new tall hats when this glorious little girl had walked in to pick up seal hats for herself and for her doll. Ann Marie von Dornbach Falkenburg. Everyone at the salon had been enchanted. As soon as the young girl left, Frau Hanna had had a vision. She saw the girl in bridal veils under the Meinert coat of arms: the grapes and the shield.

I was fascinated by the dwarf's vision, her powers as an oracle. As I grew older, I began to wonder whether Hanna Roth had foreseen this marriage or whether she had planned it like a doll's wedding—meddled, as my father would say.

He, of course, laughed at his maiden sisters. Everyone was always trying to make a match for him. He was thirty-four years old. The next time Countess Reyna ordered wine, however, he remembered the glorious little girl and decided to make the delivery personally. He did have a good practical reason for this: the countess often forgot to pay her bills. As he walked through the open portal flanked by two rotting posts and entered the neglected old courtyard with its shrine and coach houses, he must have wondered how she could afford to give banquets. Stone walls were crumbling, and the wind rattled tall, dry weeds. He always felt sad to see the crumbling walls and missing windowpanes of the charming baroque building, even when he knew that Countess Reyna planned to restore the palace as soon as she and her fellow monarchists brought the exiled prince, Otto von Habsburg, to Austria.

The little palace had been built in 1765 by Empress Maria Theresa for her favorite lady-in-waiting, Stefanie von Dornbach. The Habsburg empress had taken her breakfast there on Sundays, after morning Mass. Her profile in marble graced the front door, and cherubs swarmed above her head. One entered a cloistered walk lined with clocks: mahogany, gilt, even Oriental clocks, with a patina of bird droppings. The Countess Reyna spent the money she had obtained from the sale of Falkenburg land and the stud farm on her conspiracy to bring Prince Otto von Habsburg to the Austrian throne and restore the monarchy. The little palace, this monument to Habsburg magnificence, stood neglected and waiting. Not a clock was allowed to tick while the prince remained in exile.

"Well, we underestimated each other, Countess Reyna and I." Papa would laugh and smack his breeches. "I didn't think I'd see a schilling, and she didn't know who she was sending down her back stairs."

Papa spurned the title *von* but spoke with pride of his great-grandfather, who had earned it by delivering excellent table wines to the court. My father was the first Meinert to attend the university. He spoke beautifully but always in Viennese dialect, which went well with his peasant dress, his tall, strong figure and cheerful face. One could well imagine him making his way down the stone steps of the little palace, stroking his side-whiskers, grinning because he had been taken for a delivery man. "I had never seen such thick walls—just like a fortress. From the outside it all looked so dainty. The empress knew what she was doing."

He did not believe in forebodings, but he never forgot how uneasy he had felt walking down those steps. He panicked, for no particular reason. His heart was beating so fast that he had to put his case of champagne down at the kitchen door. His hand trembled as he knocked on the door. There was no answer, so he walked in.

It was late afternoon. The flagstones of the courtyard, level with the kitchen window, glistened with a thin layer of new snow. He could smell something baking in the oven. "Well, there she is" was all he could say. Ann Marie von Dornbach, descendant of the Falkenburgs, seemed to be sitting there just for him. Huddled against a great tile stove, she whispered to her doll. No street sounds penetrated those thick walls and double windows, but wood crackled as it burned inside the stove. She wore a convent-school dress; her hair hung loose, shining like copper in the soft lamplight. The rounded cheeks and the bridge of her short nose were sprinkled with orange freckles. She greeted him with a smile and her eyes lit up. Then she held up her doll, who also wore a school dress, and said, "Look, Puppe! It's Kaiser Franz Joseph."

The young man with the side-whiskers could have stepped out of the kaiser's portrait in her mother's room. Flowers and candles always surrounded the picture of a smiling young kaiser in loden coat and leather breeches. My father must have looked less amiable as he stared at her, lost for words. He loved her at once.

Ann Marie had been too young to be courted as a woman, too young to accept presents. My father had courted the fourteen-year-old with gifts for her doll: a tiny diadem of pearls, a minute pair of opera glasses. Before her sixteenth birthday, he had called at Salon Roth and ordered a trousseau for the doll. Finally, during dinner, with the doll between them, she had whispered into the china ear, loud enough for him to hear, "Do you think we should marry him, Puppe?"

Hanna Roth had altered the Falkenburg wedding gown. The long train and the voluminous veils provided plenty of material to dress the doll as a bride, too. The countess had scolded my father for encouraging all of Ann Marie's whims, even the deplorable affectation of the doll, which she should have outgrown long ago.

Ann Marie von Dornbach Falkenburg became Frau von Meinert

when she was barely sixteen years old. Crowds gathered to see the wedding at St. Stephen's. Puppe was well hidden behind flowers and veils, but the notorious south wind lifted the veils when the bridal pair appeared on top of the steps as man and wife. A woman in the crowd shouted, "Look at that, she's carrying her dolly. Poor little girl. So young . . ." Mama burst into tears, fleeing to a waiting carriage. A socialist reporter hinted in the morning paper that Countess Reyna had sold her young child to a rich man, almost a commoner, just to get funds for her Monarchist cause.

My father would mimic the voice in the crowd, and he laughed when he remembered the newspaper article. Any listener who saw the look he gave Mama during this love story would know that her pleasure was his greatest victory. She always appeared to be pleased.

I had never heard a serious argument between my parents until Father dismissed Fritz the Professor. Even that quarrel didn't trouble me, they enjoyed it so much. Mama took to the new disharmony as naturally as to the change of seasons—the sharp winds and the tense political climate. She never did promise, when she pulled Father's beard and called him Emperor, that she would stay out of politics. The next morning at breakfast, however, she said, "I might as well avoid a scene with the gardener." Her haughty, nasal tone of voice dismissed Herr Janicek without my father's compunctions. "He always forced himself on me," she complained over the gold rim of her coffee cup. "I'm sorry he turned out to be such a drab little fanatic." She yawned. "I think I'll go riding. Berthold is back, and it's a fine morning."

Fritz was far too busy in the gardener's cottage to see Mama in her riding habit dash through the courtyard and toward the garage. I was hiding behind the linden tree. The cottage door was open and the curtain pulled back. A military march was playing on the German radio station while Fritz directed the three youngish men who were doing his packing. He paced about in time with the music, dressed up for Mama as a professor, an artist, in a dark suit and wide-brimmed hat. I saw him stop and study himself for the last time in the cracked mirror, then add a final touch to his costume: a yellow rose for his buttonhole.

He took his time supervising the dismantling of the tiled stove he had so carefully restored. By the time that was done, Mama must have been at the stable, being helped into the saddle by Cousin Berthold. And when Fritz Janicek finally came to look for her with a potted rose tree—his parting gift—she must already have been galloping. I stayed behind the tree while he rang the bell. Poldi appeared with the keys. A dog barked and I could not hear what was said until Fritz exclaimed, "She left! Went off without a word!"

The young men came downhill carrying three suitcases, the easel, paintings tied together with rope, and the paint box, but Fritz stayed under Mother's window, gazing up to the alcove where the doll sat in a white morning dress. Beside her stood the roses he had so carefully cut, removing the thorns, only yesterday. Only yesterday he had refused to doff his hat to Eugene Romberg, but now he swept it off and bowed low before Puppe. "Auf Wiedersehen." He sounded beautifully ominous. "She didn't even leave a message," he said to his men. "This is deliberate. She wanted to punish me."

I could have told him that she would not give him another thought. Flying over a hurdle, she would shriek and yodel, followed by a pack of Theresianer boys in dark gold-braided uniforms, Berthold in the lead. Not one of them could quite imitate her cry of delight. Fritz had heard her one night during the summer. The strange cry woke me up. All the windows were open, and I heard my parents laughing in the boudoir. Fritz was listening, too, as he stood outside his cottage in the white moonlight. I knew how he felt before I could put his dilemma into words.

Fritz led the way to the gate, carrying the potted tree. I ducked down in the rose garden. Poldi let the men out with a big grin. She had always laughed at the professor and his many self-portraits. When the wind took his wide-brimmed artist's hat and spun it down the avenue, she laughed out loud. I thought he was shaking his fist at her until I heard him shout, "I'll make him pay for this, that dirty Jew!"

An iridescent beetle was feasting on a fading pink rose. "Well, *bon appetit*, bug!" I said. "But you'd better watch out if Fritz Janicek ever comes back."

*   *   *

It rained for days after Fritz left. I did not go out into the garden. Mama refused to let me go and play with Eli Romberg in case I

caught a cold from him. When I asked to go into town with her
to see Hanna Roth, Papa was there to say it was out of the question; the hat salon with its séances was an unhealthy climate.

I would have gone to school that winter if it hadn't been for an
outbreak of diphtheria. It was Papa who got permission to keep
me at home for another year and who said I wouldn't miss a thing;
after all, I could already read and print. Now he lit his pipe and
said, "What is she going to do all winter long, our little one? She
does need other children, since she has no brother."

"What!" Mama exclaimed angrily. "I didn't think you'd ever reproach me like that!" She reached for Puppe and clutched her.
"Not after all I went through . . ."

The phrase "all I went through" reminded me of the day the
midwife had come to visit Agnes, our housekeeper, not long ago.
"I'll never forget what we went through in this house," she said
as she dunked her *Kipferl,* a crescent-shaped roll, into her coffee
cup and munched greedily. I admired her mustache. "I was at my
wit's end all right, Frau Agnes. Poor young thing in all that agony
for a night and a day. Not a word out of her, not a sound."

Agnes had been only fourteen years old when she came from
the village of Falkenburg to be my mother's nursemaid. She had
become Grandmama's housekeeper as she grew up. Now she was
in charge of the Meinert-Hof and me. Papa called her "the best
dowry." A marvelous cook, pious and righteous, she went about
in whispering skirts puffed out by white petticoats and tied her
hair in kerchiefs summer and winter. "God was good to us—that
is all that matters," she now said to the midwife in her sweet
Hungarian voice.

The midwife went on and said I was old enough and should
know what my poor mother went through for me. "All those people coming and going. I told the poor young Gnädige to let out
a good scream, just to get rid of them all. She couldn't relax. The
doctor—useless dandy—embarrassed her and the two Fräulein
Meinerts, here from England just to make a fuss. They wouldn't
leave me alone with her. The Herr himself, sitting around waiting
for a son—no help at all, with all due respect. As for the countess,
her mother, with those stories of how much trouble she and all
the Falkenburg women before her had giving birth! In the end,
that palaver at the bedroom door when the Herr didn't want the
midget to come in. A regular circus, the way she burst into the

room, dressed in black, picked up an old doll from the window seat, gave it to our poor lady, and said everything would be just fine, the lady would have a nice little girl. And there you are. I can still see our Gnädige clutching the doll. Some have their young like cats, but I guess aristocrats are not cut out for it . . ."

I formed a picture in my mind of Mama lying stiff and pale, eyes closed, clutching Puppe, whose eyes closed when she lay flat. Although I did not know how children were born until the following year, I now knew it caused pain. I could well imagine Hanna Roth presiding, in a hat and veil to hide her expression of fixed merriment.

My father did not approve of Hanna the Dwarf, and she had stayed away while he played his little games with Mama, the doll, and me. She stayed behind the scenes, like the director of a play that has run too long. Mama's seclusion at the Meinert-Hof, Papa's knock on her door—all that had become mannered, *routiniert,* as they say in Vienna. By the time I had my first encounter with the Meisterin, our roles had become obligatory. Did she really bring about a change, did she make things happen, or did she simply make me more aware of what was going on?

I know I began to watch my parents more keenly. When Father took Mama onto his knee and told her he had not meant to reproach her at all, I knew he was lying. He did want more children, especially a son. I loathed the idea of such an intruder. Mama strained away from him, but then she kissed him greedily. With new conflict came new attraction. She finally got up and pushed a fallen hairpin back into her braids. Later, when he was putting on his cloak in the hall, she was back in his arms.

"The things you do to me . . ." he said as he walked out and locked us in.

I went to her. "Why can't I go to Salon Roth with you?" I asked. Her hand trembled from Father's caress as she touched my cheek. "You never take me along, except to the chapel or to Grandmama's." At the time, I still considered the little palace dull, because I had to sit around the coffee table with old people when I was there. The countess did not take too much notice of me.

Mama picked me up and kissed me. "Why not?" she said.

She even left Puppe in the boudoir at my request. I skipped through the rain toward the gate, the waiting car. A delivery truck was parked in front of the Water Castle. I knew I would have my way before long and walk up those steps and through the high gate. For I had just discovered I had some of my father's talent for using conflict to my own advantage.

      ✿   ✿   ✿

The Salon Roth was located in the first district of Vienna, the old inner city, which had once been enclosed by city walls. The car stopped not far from the Hofburg, the imperial winter residence, a bleak, rain-streaked building guarded by bearded statues of naked heroes wrestling with mythological beasts. I had not yet been inside, but it did not look inviting. I asked where the dolls' room had been. Mama was not sure where children had played at the Hofburg, but at Schönbrunn, the summer palace, they had a sunny room. Children were brought in to play so that the empress could hear them laugh when she was in residence, but that had not been too often. No one could blame Hanna Roth for going over to the Belvedere, the archduke Ferdinand's household, after the empress died Mama told me.

"Elizabeth was murdered, stabbed by an anarchist," I said.

"Who told you that?" Mama asked angrily.

"Fritz Janicek."

"He had no business." She took a deep breath. "Anyway, Frau Hanna was invited to the Belvedere. Archduke Ferdinand had children who adored her. She took all the old imperial dolls along, without permission, and she was supposed to have added to the intrigue between the kaiser and the archduke Ferdinand. Not that it really mattered."

"The archduke was shot with his wife," I said with pride.

She bent over me. "Fritz again?"

I nodded, and she gripped my hand tightly. "Never say anything like that in front of Grandmama, and certainly not at the Salon Roth. Papa is right, you are around grownups too much."

She increased her pace as we crossed the street near the Spanish riding school and the Lippizaner stables; then we went left along a narrow street. The house was higher than those around it. My mother told me to blow my nose, and she combed my curls before we walked in. I wore my sailor coat and dress, white socks, and white gloves, as though I were going to see Grandmama. The salon was on the second floor, and I ran ahead.

I could already read printed letters, and I well remember the

polished brass sign: "Hat Salon Roth." Below it, I deciphered another sign: "School of Dance and Etiquette." That school did not
exist anymore, since etiquette was no longer necessary for those
who wished to dance, but the sign remained in place. A pale apprentice girl admitted us to the entrance room, where a chauffeur
sat waiting among racks of furs. I soon learned that even husbands
and lovers had to wait here like servants. The door of the salon
remained closed to males, much as the dolls' room must have been,
in case princelings came in to disrupt the ceremonious games. I
tried to imagine my own father seated at the modest table in the
half-dark, when he had come to order the trousseau for Puppe.
It smelled of perfumes, of mothballs, and faintly of goulash sim-
mering somewhere on a stove.

Mama lowered her voice as though we had entered chapel. She
must have been one of the youngest ladies at the salon. Some of
them dated from as far back as the dolls' room. Mama chuckled
when she warned me to be quiet, explaining that the ladies hung
on every word the Meisterin said, as if their fate were in her
hands. Yet her own visits during that winter far outnumbered
those she made to the chapel. She needed to hear what Hanna
Roth had to say, even if she did not listen to her warnings. As
long as she had her doll and her Roth hats, she felt safe.

My father had once said, women who loved hats didn't need
any psychology. (I had loved the word *psychology*). With Hanna
Roth around, who needed that "endless road of self-inquiry"?
Doctor Freud didn't have a chance in Vienna. "What's over
is over. You taste a new wine, put on a new hat, and enjoy
yourself."

We found Hanna Roth standing on a podium where a trio had
once played for the dance. A grand piano on her right displayed
hats on hat stands. The salon smelled of steamed felt and fresh
coffee. Ladies were talking in undertones, and sewing machines
rattled in the adjoining workroom. Hanna Roth seemed to study
the ladies in autumn hats she had created. The style was either
round and puffy or wide-brimmed like Mother's hat. A strip of
mirror from above multiplied these hats into a thick ring of multicolored mushrooms and toadstools.

"*Willkommen,*" she said to us. "Reyna, what a nice surprise."
She returned my formal curtsy. "Unusual child," she said. "Where
is Puppe?"

"We came without her," I quickly said.

She clapped her hand over her large mouth. "So you can do without her." She could not stifle her laughter. Then she seemed to hand me over to be greeted, passed around, and admired and marked with lipstick kisses. Mama's aunt, the duchess Hohentahler, said I looked more and more like a Falkenburg. Other ladies whom I had met at Grandmama's afternoon coffee agreed. I would be the image of Countess Reyna one day.

"I don't know why children always have to be told who they take after," said a stout woman who came in with coffee. After she had served everyone else, she came to me with coffee-flavored milk and raisin cake. She had heard how pretty I was from Frau Hanna, she said. A white surgeon's coat she wore when she assisted at the salon made her look round and puffy. While she talked to me, she ate candy and her pale eyes moved from side to side, watching the room. She gave me a candy and introduced herself as Frau Traude. Her unobtrusive presence intruded on me at once. I wanted to hear what Hanna Roth had to say.

The dwarf devoured two helpings of cake without ever sitting down, and between swallows she talked of the unruly household pets of the late empress. "Those big hounds would try and snatch my food away. I learned to eat fast. At least those monster dogs didn't bite. The little mean black boy from Africa bit ladies-in-waiting in the leg."

As soon as she had finished eating, she girded herself with a black velvet band which held a red heart-shaped pin cushion spiked with pins, needles, and hatpins. "Herzogin Helga," she called.

The duchess Helga, Cousin Berthold's mother, had a long face with a haughty nose and sweet eyes and lips. Her nervous hands fiddled with buttons on her blouse. She usually talked a great deal when she came to see Mama or Grandmother. Now she rose quietly and approached the podium, head held high, hands folded, creating for me an unforgettable picture of a condemned queen, resigned but proud. She offered, however, not her head but her hat, a great, soft, yellow chanterelle.

Before the tall duchess had mounted the podium, her hat was plucked off by Frau Hanna. The clatter of cups and spoons stopped. The ladies, on uncomfortable gilded chairs which had been designed to discourage wallflowers, communicated in whispers while the duchess took her place on the piano stool. The Meisterin came at her with a hatband and pins.

"So, our young knight has returned from his little pilgrimage," she said, giving Mama a sharp look. "Horses, cows, even pigs— a pig . . . Ja . . . I can see that no good will come of all this for the young duke or those around him." She caught my eye for an instant. "There are those I cannot reach . . ." She extended her thick arm in a formidable gesture I recognized as false.

Herzogin Helga tried to smile. "You know our Berthold has always been original and very willful, Frau Hanna. Being the only boy, the oldest among six sisters . . ."

The dwarf did not like to be interrupted, and the duchess found herself in a wild spin on the piano stool. I must have laughed out loud, for Mama pulled me onto her knee and the black gaze of the little woman now turned on me. "The child," she said softly. "Intrepid and invincible . . ."

I didn't know what she was saying, but I liked her attention and memorized the words. I could have watched her and listened to her forever. In fact, I liked her best when I sensed that she was putting everyone on. I had the advantage of being familiar with important dwarfs; Rumpelstiltskin was my favorite. I always felt sorry when he lost out in the end. I was convinced the queen's son would have had more fun in the woods with the dwarf than he could ever have had as the son of a king. Dwarfs had secret treasures and magic.

My cheeks began to glow, and I went close to the podium to watch Hanna Roth. I loved her black lace dress, patterned with woven black roses. Her hands, gloved in black lace, transformed a piece of pale gray felt into a mushroom hat on top of Duchess Helga's proud head.

I did not look around the salon too much during my first visit, but I did notice a large, ornate basket on the piano—the kind of basket that gypsies wove. I had carried one during the Easter procession at Falkenburg. My gypsy basket had been filled with flower petals, which I strewed at the altar of the Virgin and all around the village. The one on the piano, full of silk and velvet flowers, tempted me.

Hanna Roth was busy turning the piano stool and pinning. Everyone in the room listened to her as she went on about young knights who had to have their crusades, even if they came back disillusioned. Adventure was in the nature of high hope and high spirits. Her hand already held another pin, but her eyes turned to me. "So you want to play with my basket . . . You may take it, little highness."

I could not move; I felt too surprised to say a word as she handed it to me. My mother had to thank her.

A plump, faintly familiar lady in a toadstool hat bent toward me and whispered, "No one has ever been allowed to touch that basket. It has always been with the Meisterin." I read envy in her tired eyes as I touched the silk and velvet flowers. "You must be very special to her." Her old face became young as she smiled; she looked like a child who had stayed up too late. "She was found in this basket by nuns. Can you imagine how tiny she must have been as an infant?"

Hanna Roth gave her a stern look. "Pierre Roth, my guardian, as you will recall, was almost deaf and taught me to read lips." She took up a large pair of scissors, and opened and closed them several times. Before she trimmed the felt, she seemed to cut out the words which had aroused all my interest. "The children at the Belvedere always got into mischief, Baroness Gertrude, when you came to play."

Everyone laughed, and the baroness Gertrude joined in good-naturedly. Frau Hanna observed the laughing faces; then she gave the piano stool another push, and the duchess raised her trembling hands in alarm as she spun around.

One moment Hanna's black eyes were on the hat she was creating, then suddenly they returned to me. She scrutinized me as dispassionately as any of her creations. No one had ever looked at me like that before, completely without affection. The basket fell from my knee, and all the flowers tumbled out before the podium. The Meisterin turned pale and stared at the bright flowers below her feet. The assistant in the white coat was at her side at once. No one spoke. Mama took my hand.

Hanna Roth's short black arms strained up as though she had to pluck something that was out of reach. "The flowers." Her arms fell to her side. "Ach, flowers." The color returned to her face; she shook her head, and the mothlike veil danced about. "Ja, ja. All right, Frau Traude." She handed her the hat. "Take this to the workroom. A year from now, Duchess Helga, you will take this hat with you to your old Landsitz-Hohentahl."

"How is it possible? We had to sell our estate!" The duchess exclaimed.

Hanna Roth gave her an impatient push, a last spin on the piano stool. "I'm sure," she said.

Not even the tinkling of bracelets interrupted the silence. Sewing machines hummed and we could hear apprentice girls talking softly in the adjoining workroom. The Meisterin took a deep breath. "We shall be wearing small hats this spring, tilted forward, with bright flowers, a touch of tulle . . . Ja, ja." She half-closed her eyes, and her hands shaped an invisible hat. "We will be wearing our spring hats early. Adolf Hitler will be in Vienna in March. I see flowers, flags and flowers . . ."

My mother jumped up and dropped her spoon. Another lady dropped her cup, but it didn't break. They all looked bewildered, but everyone in the room believed that Hanna Roth had foreseen the future as easily as she had just predicted the new style of hat.

❋   ❋   ❋

Not long after our visit to the hat salon, Mama had her twenty-third birthday. Father surprised her with a precious painting. While she was asleep he hung an original Fragonard on the wall facing her bed: a redheaded girl on a garden swing, dangling blue slippers above daisies. I was allowed to wake Mama up with flowers and a picture I had drawn in crayons. She shed tears, she was so pleased. Later, when Papa kept inviting everyone to look at the Fragonard, they all said the picture could be a portrait of Mama. She took my picture of a dwarf riding a blue grasshopper and stuck it up beside the painting and told everyone she simply loved it. "I'm tired of this invasion," she said to her doll. "Half of Vienna is marching into my boudoir." Finally she asked my father how many more people were coming.

"Only Bertl," he said. "And not until Sunday. They are keeping him at the Theresianum this week for skipping classes."

She laughed. "That's my fault. I asked him to come riding."

The maids were out on Sunday, and Agnes took a rest after lunch. Papa himself went to the gate to let Berthold in. I stayed behind in the courtyard on my tricycle to watch "the young knight," as Hanna Roth called him. Berthold had grown to be even taller than my father; his legs were so long they looked like stilts. On this fine and mild October afternoon he wore no overcoat. Both his dark blue school uniform, with the gold on the shoulders, and his cap looked too small. The trousers were so short I could see that his dark socks did not match. As always, he held his head so high it tilted back, and this, in contrast, created the impression of exaggerated loftiness, being above it all, like a beloved harlequin. While he chatted with my father, he took off his cap and let the wind ruffle his hair.

In the past Berthold's breezy manner had irked me. He did admire me in an offhand fashion when he came to see Mama, but often I found myself ignored, rather like the doll—just another pretty plaything in the boudoir . . . Girls and dolls . . . Those six younger sisters, I now realize, must have been under his feet constantly as he grew up. If he never made me feel I was actually in the way, it was simply that no one really mattered to him when he was with his cousin Annerl.

This morning he waved to me as soon as he saw me. Then he came bounding up the steps in one big leap. "So you were at the hat salon," he called out. "And don't you believe a word little old Hanna says about me or anyone."

I left my tricycle to shake hands and felt like a dwarf beside him. "Frau Hanna said Hitler will be in Vienna in March," I reported, trying to sound grand. "And you have grown a Hitler mustache, but it's too blond."

"I'll be darned," Papa said coldly. "How come I didn't hear about all that? And how come they allow Hitler mustaches at school, my boy?"

Berthold merely laughed and crouched down beside me. "Fake," he said.

I pulled and he yelled as though I had wounded him mortally. "No use trying to train my hair to hang over one eye. It's like chicken feathers. Everyone always wants to comb it. Do you?"

I shook my head.

He smiled and I saw his mother's sweet blue eyes and dimples. "Then there is hope for us." He stood up and walked to the entrance with Papa. "She is getting to be classy," he remarked. "Not like my silly sisters. Noisy and always in droves."

To hide his pleasure at hearing me praised, Papa quickly said I was with grownups far too much and that this made me too precocious.

Berthold frowned. He could look ugly. "What's wrong with that? She takes after Annerl."

"Nonsense," Papa said sharply, "Annerl is still a little girl."

"Hardly." Berthold smiled as he disagreed. "Anyway, there's not enough precocity left in poor old Austria. I'm all for it, what?"

Soon I would try to imitate his habit of ending a clever remark with "what?"

My father changed the subject and said he had promised to take me for a walk in the woods. Berthold was used to making his way up to Mama's rooms by himself. Papa let him in, locked the door, and we left. After all, Berthold had been coming to look for Mama since she was seven, he three years old.

The duke and his family had moved into their old town house in Vienna after the sale of their country estate, the Landsitz. As a small boy Berthold could walk around the corner and cross the street to the little palace. The cousins had played together almost every day until Ann Marie met my father, and even then Berthold was often included in a ball game or a walk in the Stadt park.

Berthold was a boy of twelve when my mother married and he continued to keep her company on walks, riding in the Prater, or swimming in the Danube. After I was born and Berthold went to the Theresianum, the cousins could not meet as often. Papa did not want Mother to lose her childhood playmate, so he even arranged their meetings and sent the car to take them to the cinema when he was busy, as though Berthold had remained the boy who had attended their wedding in knee pants. And I do believe he sent him up to the boudoir at that moment, hoping this would keep him at a proper distance in time to come. My father's game was always intricate.

When we returned from our walk, Berthold was sitting on the sofa in Mama's room, his arm slung around her shoulder. They were drinking sweet wine, and she held Puppe on her lap.

"How do you like the picture, Bertl?" Papa asked at once.

"I think it's very pretty," Berthold said without enthusiasm. "I like all the blue. But I'm more for blue grasshoppers, since little old Hanna says I'll end up with horses, cows, even pigs, and cause trouble in the barnyard. Quite a future, what?"

Papa had to laugh. "She must have been in good form. She's always had it in for you, Bertl."

"That's not true," Mama spoke up. "She's always taken an interest in Bertl, but she never wanted me to play with him."

"A possessive old girl," Berthold said jauntily. "But she is entertaining. What would all our ladies do without her?"

Papa was not listening. He studied the painting. "Don't you think the picture looks a lot like Ann Marie?"

Berthold seemed more interested in the ceiling. He smiled. "To tell you the truth, I don't. It's much more what you want her to be, the way you see her . . ." He reached out; his long arms scooped me up and propped me on his knees. "What do you think of it all?"

I thought the girl in the picture looked like a sissy, although I liked her blue slippers and all the daisies under her swing; but I felt too overwhelmed by Berthold's sudden attention to speak. Yet it seemed very natural to sit on his knee. He held me gently. I accepted my new role from the beginning, and he was to reach out to me whenever he felt at a loss with Mama or anyone.

When he was ready to leave, I walked along to the gate holding onto his hand. I skipped and he hopped on one long leg. I felt his kinship and hoped it would never end.

Papa and I watched him run off. Berthold never walked away. "To think of a Fürst von Hohentahler riding a streetcar . . ." Papa shook his head. "I can still see the old duke in his carriage, in his general's uniform, always with a dachshund. So grand. Now they can hardly make ends meet."

"Frau Hanna said they'd be back at the Landsitz by next fall."

"Perhaps she can arrange for a winning ticket at the lottery."

While Papa locked the gate, I climbed up and admired the mansion across the street. All the lights were on, as usual, although the Rombergs had gone to Venice for a week and most of the servants must have been out, since it was Sunday. "Perhaps Berthold will make a lot of money like Eugene Romberg," I said.

My father looked at me with surprise. "He will need a lot of money, and I doubt that he'll ever be able to earn much."

When I asked grown-up questions, I often provoked him to

answer me as an adult. But he did not respond when I said, "Why?" like any other child. He was watching two men at the Romberg gate. "Isn't that Fritz Janicek over there, in that ridiculous get-up? I wonder what business he has with the Romberg porter. A darned nuisance, that man!"

Fritz, dressed as a professor, saw us and doffed his hat with a flourish. Papa ignored him, took my hand, and led me back to the house. "I like a quiet Sunday."

This was no time to remind him of how much I wanted to go and play at the Water Castle. His talk of other children and school did not really deceive me. In his heart he preferred to have me at home with Mama. I already knew that he was happiest when she stayed at home doing nothing at all. He wanted everything to remain the same, but Mama was changing.

Late one afternoon when I came upstairs, she did not answer my knock. I found her at the dressing table in the half-dark, facing the mirror. Her hair hung loose over her shoulders and back. I called out, but she did not bother to turn at once. I walked in, and she did not take me into her arms. I looked for the doll and did not even see it at first. Puppe had been put into a corner on her gilded chair. Again I noticed how the doll's eyes gleamed in the dark like an animal's; she had been left in her white morning dress.

"But it is evening" was all I could say. A certain foreboding kept me from enjoying the sight of the neglected doll. Mama did not hear me; she took no notice at all. My supper tray sat on the low table at the cozy window seat. I wanted this to be like other evenings, but everything was different. Even Mama's gilded clock had stopped, like the ones at the little palace.

"Can I go and play in your dressing room?" I asked.

Mama shook herself like a wet cat. "Yes, yes."

The dressing room was a haven, fragrant with flowery perfume. I stood on my toes to switch on the light. There I was in all three mirrors, in my red sweater, knee socks, and black leather breeches just like Father's. But no one who looked at my soft face with the yellow slanting eyes and fluffy hair ever mistook me for a boy.

I fondled Mama's beaver coat, then sniffed a lace evening gown which shimmered like gold and smelled like a garden. A rust-

colored winter suit with an ermine collar had been flung carelessly over a chair. The matching hat sat on the floor. I could
have helped myself to some jewelry or a satin blouse which I
often wore as a flowing gown, but the fluffy thing looked as
though it might hop away. I reached for it, put it on my head,
and slipped into the suit jacket. The fur smelled of Mama—almost too sweet. I brushed my cheek against the collar, and something scratched me. I fumbled and pulled out a gold stickpin.
A swastika no bigger than a flea was attached to the end.

Tiny things appealed to me. I ignored a drop of blood and was
about to take the pin and carry it around with me. Suddenly
Mama came up from behind in her pink robe. She loomed over
me, reflected in all the mirrors. I felt surrounded. Her mouth
hung half-open as she stared into the glass with those violet-blue
eyes. Pink spread from her neck to the roots of her hair, and all
the freckles disappeared.

"Give me that pin!" She sounded as though she had a cold.

I closed my fingers and pricked myself again. "No!" I cried,
defiant with pain. "No!" The fur hat slipped to one side of my
head, giving me a reckless, roguish air.

Mama pulled the jacket off me. "Open your fist!"

In the mirrors I saw three angry mothers strip me of finery
and reduce me to a girl in pants. I held onto the hat with one
hand and hid the swastika pin behind my back. Then I dipped
under the dresses. Mama dived after me and pulled me out by
the seat of my leather pants. She forced my hand open and I
threw the treasure down. She stooped for it eagerly. Her robe fell
apart and I saw her astonishing large white breasts, decorated
with freckles. She pulled the sash tight when she stood up, as
though she wanted to cut herself in half. I hung my head. The
fur hat slipped off and sat cowering where I had picked it up;
it seemed a long time ago.

"You are not allowed to go into my dressing room anymore!"
Mama reached up to her head with trembling hands. Tears came
into her eyes. She told me she had a migraine headache and I
should eat in the kitchen.

In her blue room, she sat down again in front of the dark looking glass. I waited, but she took no notice. Regretfully I touched
the frills of the great bed and hung around the door. The gilt

frame of the Fragonard reflected the fading light, but the girl on the swing, the idle, sweet one, was invisible. Mama had never dismissed me like that. She was holding the pin away from her like a burning match. Suddenly she jumped up, got the doll, and hugged her, comforting herself as she always did. She whispered into the deaf ear. Then she quickly stuck the pin somewhere down under the doll's petticoats, among lace and frills.

I left without a sound. My supper tray was taken to my room that evening and the next. After a week, I knew I had been banished. Mother did come downstairs to say goodnight when I was in bed, with an air of apology. She brought a doll for me one evening, an old doll with real dark ringlets. I was sitting on the edge of my bed. My hands trembled; my feet turned to ice.

"Don't you want her? She looks like your little sister."

I reached for the doll and hurled her against the wall. The head shattered.

Mama walked away. At the door she turned, and her new short skirt swirled around her long legs. She wore silver-gray shoes I admired. "You are not the same little Reyna anymore."

An odd tone of relief in her voice made me call back, "You're not the same Mama."

Now she felt free to walk away with the long easy stride of a horsewoman. Her familiar perfume lingered.

3

The Keys

I HAVE A PICTURE in my mind of our dinner table under the pink glow of the old Meinert lamp: my parents facing each other, flanked by the Meinert aunts—my father's older sisters, in Vienna for three weeks in the autumn—plump, emphatically British in their scratchy tweeds; Stephanie, the older but prettier one; Dora, the more genial. Both were much admired by the bald-headed family doctor, a staunch Monarchist, seated beside Grandmama. The Herr Doctor, a connoisseur of wines who never more than sipped from his glass, a connoisseur of women who had never married, worshipped my grandmother with watery eyes. He also took great pride in me and liked to have me on his other side, for I had been raised on Maltaline, a tonic of his own invention consisting of malt, cod-liver oil, and vitamins. "A beautiful woman is like a rose," he would say. "All her glory, her bloom is enhanced and prolonged by the right nutrients." I had to laugh because his pince-nez dropped into his wine glass or onto a cake when he got carried away by his memories of the late empress. He had been summoned to court when she became ill during one of her fasts, and he had tried to persuade her to take Maltaline, but she was afraid it might make her fat. "She would not listen," he sighed. "Her beauty was not for this world. She fainted in the imperial box at the opera. The emperor sent a court carriage for me. I had them undo her corselet at once, then I administered three large spoons of Maltaline. For one week I went to her and she continued the treatment. The improvement was miraculous. On the eighth day I came and she had gone away; it was her last journey . . ."

Could an overdose of Maltaline have driven the empress abroad and finally toward her assassin? Perhaps Maltaline, and not my wild Falkenburg blood, made me so venturesome.

"Ja, ja," the doctor would say. "Those were the days. Remember . . ." Someone else would pick him up. "Remember the time . . . ," they said to each other. A superb meal of roast fowl, or a delicate dish of veal, a frothy cake, fruit, nuts, and excellent wines seemed to create an insatiable appetite for lost power and glitter. My father, who scorned the occult, nevertheless joined into this most convivial of séances. They conjured up those good old days, and even when my eyes kept closing and I sat half-asleep on someone's lap, I could see the empress waltzing in a bejeweled gown, wearing a mask—she had secretly attended a public ball and made a commoner fall in love with her. Princes fell in love with those beneath them and commoners adored the highborn, who existed as remote as constellations. Officers pranced through my dreams on white horses, as though they were riding in a circus and not to war and to their death. I pictured the dwarf in the midst of tall regal children and hundreds of wicked dolls. Hearing my name, I opened my eyes to see Grandmama raising her glass. "Let us drink to the return of the empire —that I may live to see our Reyna waltz at her first court ball."

No wonder I rehearsed for grandeur in my mother's clothes, Great-Aunt Christina's jewels. My mother never knew how much I missed those moments of self-love in front of her mirror after she banished me from her dressing room. She was often away from home, even in the afternoon, now. When she did return, she frequently carried pamphlets in a black folder which she hid under her cloak.

It seemed as though I spent an eternity watching the house across the street, waiting for the return of the Romberg family. It could not have been more than a week or two. I was in the garden stringing chestnuts when I saw the white limousine driving up to the Water Castle. The whole family was helped out of the car. Resi, in purple, and Eli's nurse, in white, went on ahead, while maids and the chauffeur handled a pile of luggage and packages. Eugene Romberg put his arm onto Eli's shoulder, and they slowly walked up the steps and made their way in between the ornamental hedges to the great house. I believe this was the one and only time I saw Eli walking with his father.

I stood on the steps, holding onto my string of chestnuts. The splendor of their arrival, their elegant clothes, the snow-white Daimler, and the chauffeur dressed in white stunned me like those descriptions of the lost past. I could have made myself noticed, but I did not wish to spoil the picture, so I climbed the first branches of the horse chestnut tree in the front garden. There was not much to be seen. A maid shook a duster out of a side window. Since the house sat on a gentle slope I could look into the conservatory and aviary. I thought I recognized Eli's slender figure moving among birdcages and palm trees.

It began to rain. My mother came home, but I preferred to stay in hiding. Agnes opened the back door, calling my name, I stayed in my tree although I felt cold and wet, especially my feet. The rain stopped and I climbed down and lurked around the courtyard, trailing my chestnuts behind me, making them slither like a snake. I told myself I could even climb over our gate and simply walk across the street, ring the bell, if Mama wouldn't let me visit the Rombergs. She was sitting in the alcove surrounded by pamphlets, sorting and reading. When she noticed me, she picked up the doll to make her wave, but the china hand warded me off. I stuck out my tongue when my mother had returned to her reading and went back to my role of being cast out and unwanted.

The first snow, my first cold of the season, and my first direct involvement with the occult happened all at once. I had not even sneezed when an apprentice girl in spectacles arrived with a hat and a message for Mama and a music box with a pink ballerina on top for me. The note for my mother contained a warning for my father: Frau Hanna had had a dream and foresaw danger. The message I received from Hanna Roth said: "Hope this will help you get over your cold." The Meisterin had either felt my cold coming on in her bones, the way Agnes, our housekeeper, knew it would snow, or perhaps she had dreamed of my fever and love for music boxes as she had dreamed of sabotage, of red and white, milk and blood, flowing in the street.

Papa would not be warned, but I jumped out of bed many times to look out the window, anticipating snow and disaster. I also kept an eye on the Water Castle without getting a glimpse of Eli. Agnes told me to be still. I had to get rid of my temperature if I wanted to go out. It would definitely snow, she could feel it. When I asked about the blood, Agnes said Frau Hanna was a hex, quite godless, even if she had been taken in by nuns.

I went to sleep and dreamed of all the predictions. My temperature was down when I woke up in the morning, but my hopes for disaster soared. It snowed. I was not allowed to go out, but I got up, ate in the kitchen, and went upstairs to sit on the landing outside Mother's room, where I could watch large flakes drift down over a pale orange sun. I imagined white horses, white demons with wings, a squadron of albino dwarfs. Mama getting up, was moving around. I turned on my new music box and waited for "Tales from the Vienna Woods" to run down. The tiny pink ballerina on top turned haltingly until she stopped, arms raised, eyes staring.

Something was about to happen. I knew it before the telephone rang in the morning room. Poldi came thundering up the stairs, carrying a bucket with her, she was so excited. "It's urgent. It's Herr von Meinert on the phone."

I could hear Mother's loose slippers slapping her heels as she ran about frantically. "Where are those keys! Ach, Puppe, where could they be?" She had locked herself in again and managed to hide the keys.

The great bunch of Meinert keys had been my charm bracelet. I had not even noticed it had been taken from my room the other day—not until Agnes accused me of locking up the linen closet.

"Please stop that dreadful music box, Reyna," Mother now called from behind her door. "Help me. Where could I have put those keys?"

Locking up had somehow become important to her. For the last two days she had been locking everything. I could smell the essence of pine. Sometimes I put a tablet into her bath and watched it fizz. Now, hands in trouser pockets, I began to direct her search with all the authority of a Meinert and a Falkenburg. First, I called to her, she should look under the cushion of the doll's chair. And the thought of Puppe being tossed about carelessly made it all worthwhile. I ordered her to her dressing table, the armchair in the bathroom, and so on. Finally I sent her to her dressing room, the secret drawer. A shout of joy told me the keys had been left in the lock.

She flew from her room, looking like a yellow bird in a winging Chinese robe and leaving everything open. I could not resist the open door, the open drawer in her dressing room. The black folder with the pamphlets was neatly tied up, but underneath it I found a marvelous Hitler picture: the Führer in medieval armor, seated on a horse.

"Agnes! Agnes!" my mother called out.

I missed the first excitement, because I took the opportunity to pick up Puppe and shake her above my head to see the weird look of alarm on her face. Poldi, the stouter one of our maids, was shouting, "Jesus Marie! Dear heaven!" in her coarse voice. "Dear heaven!" echoed Lise, her twin. You could tell them apart by voice as well as by size. Lise sounded timid.

I ran downstairs, and Agnes, dressed for baking in her white apron and bright Hungarian scarf, caught me in her arms. She smelled of soap and vanilla. "There's nothing to be excited about now," she said. "Everything will be all right." But Poldi and Lise held onto each other.

Mama was staring out into the snow, turning the ring on her left hand. "I must go to Frau Romberg at once," she said. "They came home only yesterday and now this . . . It might be on the radio. I must get there first."

"What happened, what happened?" I cried out, jumping up and down.

"Blown into a thousand pieces, poor young fellow," Poldi said.

"Poor young fellow," Agnes repeated. "But he had a bomb in his rucksack. A godless Nazi. Every day there's something. Thank the Lord our master had left the truck when the fellow came downhill ready to smack into it."

"The brake must have gone," Mama said.

"He could have braked with his feet," Poldi said. "He must have been drunk."

"Blown into a thousand pieces," I repeated with relish.

"You shouldn't know about such things," Agnes said firmly. "But every day they are blowing something up. A godless bunch."

Agnes seldom spoke in anger. I squirmed in her arms, but she held me firm. "Why?" I asked.

"Because they are Reds," Poldi replied.

"Communists," said her twin. They had the same large hands and stocky legs and Austrian goiters. Since they had come to work for us they had begun to wear their lank, pale hair in braids around their heads, imitating my mother.

"It was just a young boy. They found schoolbooks." Mama turned to the stairs. "And there was a swastika pin . . . somewhere."

"The Reds carry swastika pins to put the blame on the Führer," Poldi said. "Our police inspector knows all about it."

"What difference does it make?" Agnes spoke up. "It's wickedness. You two girls hurry up and finish the cleaning so that you can get to church and say a prayer. We must give thanks that our Herr and his friend, and all those people who work at the Romberg dairy, went unharmed."

Mama went up the stairs as though she felt very tired. The twins went to the front rooms and turned on the vacuum cleaner so that they could talk without being overheard. They were both in love with Adolf Hitler and the Nazis, or any unmarried man in uniform. I knew they took turns going out with their favorite policeman, "the inspector." I often heard them giggle and whisper. When Agnes went shopping, they turned the radio on in the living room and sometimes they practiced dancing. I made them give me a turn and they taught me how to waltz. Poldi and Lise liked Hitler because he was an eligible bachelor.

There were many Hitlers. Grandmama's was a proletarian upstart and a criminal, Mama's a new emperor. Agnes thought of him as a godless sinner. My father thought of him as a clown and told jokes about him and his gang, laughing at Cousin Berthold with the Hitler mustache. Fritz Janicek considered Adolf Hitler an artist and therefore superior. He also sported a tiny mustache, like so many men and boys in Vienna who strutted about in boots when the party was still illegal. I was entertained by the squabbles in our house, and the idea of the Nazi boy blowing up filled me with excitement and disgust.

"Frau Hanna knew about it," I told Agnes in the kitchen. But she gave me cookies and hot chocolate rather than any more grisly information.

When Mama was ready to leave, I ran upstairs to see her in

her new dark-green winter coat. She had the doll with her; I could see the legs sticking out of the silver fox muff.

"I hope you have left the bedroom door open, Gnädigste," Agnes called from the kitchen stairs.

My mother dropped the bunch of Meinert keys into the top of the muff, which was also a bag.

Agnes confronted her. "The girls have to get in to change the bed and tidy up."

Mama snapped the top of the muff shut with the matronly dignity of a Meinert wife. "They can wait until I get home."

By locking herself into her room, she turned each outing into an escape. Hiding herself in her new town clothes—especially under those mushroom hats—she made herself conspicuous. She wore the new tight coat and her chin was buried in a high fox collar. A ruby-studded brooch adorned the most prominent part of the coat. She looked older, rich, fashionable. All you could see of her face were red, painted lips. No one would recognize her, but everyone would want to know who she was.

"I won't be home for lunch," she said. "Would you please call Stibitz and tell them to give Bertl a message? The poor boy is going to ride over on his bicycle to meet me. I will be a little late, because I do have to speak to Frau Romberg and go to the salon."

Agnes unlocked the front door, and all at once I understood that some keys were missing from the wonderful bunch in Mama's muff. Agnes kept the key for the oak door and the gate; the chauffeur had keys for the gate and the garage. I watched him help Mama into the car and carefully cover her with a white fur rug. She could never leave without being let out; when she returned, she was let in. Berthold, in his strict boys' school, was in the same position.

I watched Agnes's pink face as she locked the door. "All this locking up," she grumbled to herself. "We never used to bother with that." She was referring to the fact that as my grandmother's housekeeper, she had run a household of "the first class." Like all great servants of the old regime, Agnes was an authority on etiquette. Ladies such as my grandmother or my mother were not supposed to walk around with a great bunch of keys. They left their servants in charge.

When Father returned in the afternoon, Agnes came to meet him with tears in her eyes and wanted to kiss his hand. He grabbed her and held it clasped. "Na, na, tears? Are you sorry to see us alive?" It was his chess afternoon, and he had played at the café as usual and brought his friend Eugene home for a private game. Eugene Romberg was his strongest opponent. The rich man who now lived across the street bothered Agnes. She greeted him with the greatest formality.

I observed my father and Eugene Romberg with new interest since their lives had been in danger. Papa, with snow on whiskers and head, nose and cheeks pink, appeared excessively cheerful. Eugene Romberg peered at me from the turned-up collar of his fur-lined coat like a turtle from its shell. He looked cold and small beside Father. His face was smooth and round, and his eyes, dark and unfocused as an infant's, would haunt me. He greeted me by pinching my cheek and said he hoped I was feeling much better. There was a little surprise waiting for me from Italy. He kept watching the stairs. He was always looking for my mother.

My father slapped his shoulder. "You are too generous, Eugene. It's almost indecent."

While they stomped their feet and Father wiped his head and whiskers, Agnes led me away and told me to go upstairs for a nap. I waited until she had gone down to the kitchen before I left my room and went to sit on the stairs. My father and his friend were in the morning room. I could smell pipe smoke.

"I don't like warnings, mysterious messages. Female nonsense. It has nothing to do with the supernatural. The dwarf simply gets word. The woman will talk."

"No matter how she knew, I am indebted to both of them. I won't forget that they tried to warn us."

"Frau Traude is your mother," Father said. "Even if neither of you makes much of it. It's a fact."

I became excited at my listening post. Eugene Romberg certainly took after his mother in rotundity.

"There has not been much love lost between us. Wife or mother, no matter what went on in her life, she remained tied to her Hanna. Even when they were far apart." Eugene Romberg blew his nose very loudly; Agnes would have considered this very rude, but I loved it. "They were in convent together, orphans. You know the story. Hanna Roth never cared for me when I was a boy. She makes hats for Resi, but they don't get along too well. Still, I intend to buy the Roth house for them. I will always make sure they are well provided for. It was decent of them to show concern for my safety."

"Only in Vienna," said my father, "could such a little freak wield so much power. You must be aware of the fact that she now fancies herself a Nazi. Can you believe it! Pierre Roth was a Jew and everyone knows that. Whether he was her real father or not, what does it matter? He took her to court; he and his wife raised her and spoiled her."

"Fine people," Eugene said. "They even opened their house to my mother when she was a girl."

"So how can the dwarf fancy herself a Nazi? It doesn't make sense. She should listen to Hitler and the race theories. Dwarfs are not exactly high on the agenda in the Reich."

"Ah, but soothsayers are. I think she knows all about that. Just before we went to Italy she told Resi that Hitler would take over Austria, and she ordered her to stop flirting with the Hebrew religion. Resi was furious. She simply walked out on her."

"I wish more women would have that much sense. Ann Marie goes there at least twice a week. She even took the child along. She knows I don't approve. It all looks innocent enough. Hats, fortunetelling, dolls' clothes. As you have probably noticed, my little wife is gone most of the day. She can't possibly be trying hats all the time." He lowered his voice and I moved down a few steps. "You know she is beginning to show off—new hats, riding clothes from England, so that she can perform on horseback in style and make all those Theresianer boys, those first and second cousins, even more in love with her."

"Who can help loving her?" Eugene Romberg said with a sigh.

My father laughed. "I know, I know. You always love my girls. I have to put up with all that. After all, I married a convent-school girl. There was no one to compare me with in any way. You might consider this cynical, my friend, but I encourage the boys. She has to have her little fling. Those aristocratic school-boys, bless their hearts, are safe enough. Too high-strung and inbred to make much of a hero, or much of a lover, at that. Have you ever noticed how inbreeding makes men weak and women beautiful? Anyway, the little adventures won't last any longer than her more dangerous flirtation with Herr von Hitler."

I dropped my music box. Tears came into my eyes. Never had I heard him talk like this about Mother. He sounded as though he did not like her at all.

Eugene Romberg quickly mentioned that it had been very sweet of her to drop in on Resi this morning on her way to town.

"Annerl is too intelligent to be a true anti-Semite," Father said, "and far too well bred to be a snob."

Eugene Romberg blew his nose again. "Resi feels she doesn't really like to be around us, because we are not her class."

"Class, class," my father laughed. "She knows Resi was my girl before you stole her. She feels the competition."

I had heard my mother say Resi's taste was showy and theatrical, that it was obvious she never bothered with undergarments. This made my father laugh and remark that very few women could imitate her. Mother, of course, would not have any problem at all.

"A certain rogue, a cunning gypsy, came along and stole my little nightingale, my Resi, away," Father went on.

"Now, you know, Ferdl, I always feel like a mere stand-in."

This pleased my father. I could hear him slapping his leather breeches. "But really, you mustn't take my Annerl seriously. Hitler has a certain sinister appeal to spoiled women." I could hear him unlock the cellar door. "Just like Rasputin. Loudmouthed and fanatical, quite hateful enough to thrill their innocent little hearts. Anything freakish. I put the modiste into the same category."

"It's not all that bad, Ferdl." I always admired the way he rolled the r in "Ferdl." "The salon is simply fashionable, and so are the hats. Frau Hanna has her loyal followers."

"Just like the big little man in Germany," said my father as they went down the cellar steps. The door was shut and locked.

The two men went down to the private wine cellar—the catacomb, as my father called it. I liked the small apartment down there: two cosy rooms, wood-paneled and furnished in the Tyrolean style. Bright cushions lay about, and one, in the shape of a red heart, had been hand-embroidered with "Forever Yours" by my mother. Resi's mandolin, with its ribbons and charms, hung on a hook, but females were not often invited to go down there with Papa. Few men tasted his rare wines, talked with him in private, and played a game of chess in total seclusion. Papa liked an audience, but he insisted on privacy when it suited him.

I was left alone—much more alone than I had been when he came home. He had ignored me when I wanted to ask him many questions about the bomb and the blood. He discussed my mother coldly with his friend, and I felt as though he had torn her to pieces with his condescending words. It took me many years to come to terms with his need to deface those he loved best.

I went to look for Agnes in the kitchen. She was doing her book-keeping, and her household book and receipts lay around the kitchen table. "Who is Rasputin?" I asked her.

She looked at me over the rim of her glasses. "He is dead. He was a demon."

"Do all demons die?"

A snowdrift was framed by the kitchen window. Birds sat on shrubs, puffed up, waiting for crumbs and seeds at the feeder.

"You've been listening in again. A child your age—" she began.

"Is Hitler a demon?" I interrupted, because I knew she would be shocked.

She touched my forehead with her warm red hand. "You didn't sleep at all, did you? Look at those circles under your eyes." She took me upstairs and put me to bed.

         ✿   ✿   ✿

The sun hung low, touching the top of the slope, when I woke up. My door had been left open at my request, and I could hear my father and Eugene Romberg talking. I hurried down the stairs.

"Look at those rosy cheeks," Herr Romberg said. "The picture of health. If only my poor boy could eat properly, he would soon pick up."

"Can I play with Eli?" I asked.

"As soon as your cold is completely gone," my father promised.

I jumped up and down enthusiastically, and Eugene Romberg could not resist pinching my cheek with his soft, plump hand. He smelled of cologne and wore rings. Most of the time he looked as though he owed everyone an apology. I was sorry to see him leave, because he thought I was marvelous; but then, he admired everything belonging to my father. Even Resi Heller had belonged to my father once. I watched them leave. Eugene Romberg fell into step with Father as they walked side by side. He even took on Father's subtle limp.

Papa not only locked the front door when he returned, he also pulled the chain. He beamed when I sidled up to him. More than likely, he had won most of the chess games. Now he picked me up and threw me almost to the ceiling.

"When I go to visit Eli Romberg, will you give me my own keys, Papa?"

He kissed my face and scratched me with his beard. "That's the spirit. You couldn't be better if you were a boy."

He put me down and I snuggled up against his side. We looked out over the slope of the gardens everyone called the Meinert Park. The old brick wall which enclosed the land was topped with spikes, barbed wire, and broken glass. The Meinerts had always guarded their privacy.

It had stopped snowing, and Eli's tutor hurried from the house in his student's cap and scarf and disappeared in the labyrinth of ornamental hedges. The Romberg's front garden, as I would soon discover, was perfect for games of hide-and-seek.

"Can I have my keys now, Papa?"

He took me by the hand. "Let's see, then . . ."

Spare keys were kept in a locked case in the gallery, a long veranda facing the east. The wall was covered with portraits of Meinert men who all, it seemed to me, looked out like nosy villagers over the ever-expanding Meinert empire.

My father made a sweeping gesture with his large hand, as though he were bothered by cobwebs. "Well, here they all are, those Meinert men." Beside each portrait hung a stuffed stag's head. The Meinert men, with their protuding stomachs, pale eyes, and yellow beards, resembled one another as did the stuffed heads, their trophies. "They all ate and drank too much and died of hardening of the arteries before they were seventy years old. No great heroes here, nobody mad either, just healthy peasants."

"Except for Uncle Ernstl," I remarked.

My father chuckled. The Meinert aunts called him another Ernstl when they wanted to tease, because he liked to play chess for money and had married an aristocrat. Great-Uncle Ernstl had been considered a black sheep simply because he was different.

He had been the youngest of my father's four great-uncles. Only the older boys inherited. Ernstl did not wish to work for them and left home with a small capital, gambled and won, speculated, became rich, and caused scandals. He never worked, worried, or married. As a portly patron of music and the theater, his name was romantically linked with both actresses and ladies of the first class. He spoke French and used the *von.*

I had always loved Ernstl's portrait. He had had himself painted with a smile. His teeth were all gold, faithfully coated with eighteen carat metal—so was his watch chain, and the ring with the Meinert crest of his own design, and, most important, his fine key chain. No stag heads hung beside Uncle Ernstl—the lady killer never hunted deer.

At first, only the gold glowed in the dusk. But when Papa turned on the light, I could see the happy twinkle in my ancestor's eyes, just like Father's after he had won a game or when he played with Mama and me in the boudoir. "Can I have Uncle Ernstl's keys, if I promise not to lose them?"

Father unlocked the glass case at once. The golden keys jingled before my eyes. I jumped up and down, reaching for them. "He never came back to stay here after he grew up, but he always carried these keys and let himself in when he came to visit. A real family piece." My father crouched down beside me fastening the chain to my leather trousers when the bell rang. He straightened at once, smoothed over his hair. "Well, the lady has returned." He winked at me. "Tomorrow I'll show you how to use the keys. Never let anyone in."

I felt a pang of sadness when he left me and told me to run along. My regret did not last long. I went to show the keys to Agnes in the kitchen and told her I would be unlocking the gate by myself when I went to play with Eli.

I could see she was displeased by the way she pulled the strudel dough. "I never heard of such a thing—carrying keys at your age. It'll get you into trouble." She muttered something about sickness at that house, foreigners, and stagehands. The dough tore, and considering this unlucky, she made the sign of the cross. While I skipped around chanting "Water Castle, Water Castle," Poldi and Lise laughed. Agnes wanted me to have an early supper, but I was far too excited to eat.

While I was getting ready for bed, I heard Father ordering supper and champagne to be brought to the boudoir. My parents ate a light meal before the theater. I listened to the laughter, the scraping of the table, the popping of the cork, and the clinking glasses. My mother's voice chirped. She was no longer the same, but my father had a way of accepting change around him as he accepted a partner's move on the chessboard—with chagrin, but ultimately using it to his own advantage.

My parents came to my room when I was already tucked in, Mama dressed to go out, Father carrying her fur coat. She leaned against his shoulder, and her loose hair spilled over his vest. He came to sit on the edge of my bed, and she went to braid her hair at my little dressing table. They often came to say goodnight like this, bringing with them an air of unbearable well-being: perfume, the scent of good food, tobacco, and wine—the aroma of their pleasure filled my room. They touched my forehead and my cheeks with their delicious lips, still trembling and moist from too much kissing, laughing, and drinking sparkling wine. Their warm hands, thrilled and thrilling, made me shrink down under my quilt, for their passion overflowed and intruded on me rather than included me. I stiffened. My hand went under the pillow, reaching for the three gold keys on the long chain.

Just as I was about to go to sleep, I touched the music box Hanna Roth had sent to me, and it played the very end of "Tales from the Vienna Woods" before it stopped with a click.

4

The Water Castle

I CLIMBED UP on our wrought-iron front gate and used my keys for the first time. My father stood by and smiled. The Water Castle seemed to be waiting for me on this dazzling morning. I breathed in the sweet, icy air. All was still; no wind to send the cupid weather vane into a spin. For once the arrow aimed, ready to shatter the blue stained-glass of the winter morning sky. New snow had frosted everything, from the fancy railings and the maze of ornamental hedges to the terraces and columned balconies. The cupola had turned into a scoop of vanilla ice cream, the cupid into candy. It could all have been a masterpiece in a Viennese confectionery window. I came invited, yet I was uneasy. For a moment, I wanted to look rather than to enter. Was it a mirage, deliciously doomed; would it vanish as I set foot in it—or even disappear with me? The Water Castle stood before me as the after-image of any child's sweet nightmare.

My father stood with his legs apart in front of our gate, laughing to himself, hands deep in his inevitable leather breeches, a loden cloak slung over his shoulder. He looked ruddy, cheerful, typically Meinert—on the surface anyway. "Ja, ja," he said to himself. "Die Herren, they knew how to be grand. Castles, temples, palaces, and then—boom, bang, crash . . ."

He lit an old, carved pipe, another heirloom. Smoke blossomed into the icy air. The house before us, as far as he was concerned, served as a playhouse for Resi Romberg, and now for me—a mere extravaganza on the operetta stage, to amuse and then to vanish. Showy things were not meant to last. Lack of pretense was my father's most grandiose conceit.

"Well, there's my *Schazi!*" He threw a kiss to the room with the wrought-iron balcony. His "treasure" opened the window and leaned out, rosy and tousled. She returned his kiss merely out of old habit. She had always singled him out in this way over the heads of cheering Viennese during curtain calls. He had brought her luck. To assure success, she had to have her Ferdl at a première, just as she had needed a Hanna Roth headdress.

I already knew that Father had met Resi Heller when she was only eighteen years old, a child actress who had grown up to sing supporting roles. He had courted her as though she were a prima donna, dressed her like one. Within a year she became the darling of the Viennese—he saw to that. His Schazi, his treasure—still half-child, a mere baker's daughter from Hernals, the working-men's district of Vienna—had been as sweet as a bonbon, but he had presented her to his friend Eugene. Later on, those who were spiteful called this one of his best investments.

My father, standing beside me, took possession of the scene before us on that perfect winter's morning. He could look as smug as any Meinert, but he always laughed at himself as he allowed his contradictory feelings to create a moment of unspoiled pleasure. Pink-cheeked, eyes sparkling, he radiated well-being with a swaggering touch of self-contempt. He was a winner. Chess masters are born, not made.

He bent down and I kissed the beardless spots on both cheeks. When I began to run across the street, he held me back and said, "Always look left and right before you cross. Don't run. Walk only when it's safe, and then walk quickly." This could have been the Meinert motto . . .

Yet I did not figure as a mere pawn in the game between these friends. I could have turned back as soon as I saw the gigantic swastika drawn in the snow at the gate of the Water Castle. My father saw me hop around the sign on one leg and called me back, but I quickly jumped for the bell handle and rang. The porter came running from the lodge and raised his cap, shouting, "God's greeting!" He stepped over the swastika as he came out, picked me up, and carried me into the Water Castle.

Whenever I entered the Romberg house that winter I felt as though I had stepped into a tub full of hot water. A moment of shock preceded the luxury of sinking into the milieu Mama called unbearably stuffy and showy as a cabaret. The porter handed me over to Francine, Resi Romberg's French maid. I liked her chocolate-brown uniform with the frilly white apron and cap. She made little birdlike foreign sounds as she carefully took off my cape.

The entrance room smelled of floor wax and roses. Long-stemmed red roses in a large basket, placed between busts of Johann Strauss and Ludwig van Beethoven, had opened in the heat. Everything was rearranged here to suit Resi Romberg's mood or to make room for new furniture and art treasures. A china swan from one of Ludwig of Bavaria's castles served as an umbrella stand that morning. The furniture that did remain in place, such as Eugene Romberg's chair, the dining-room table and chairs, and the piano in the music room, remain landmarks in my memory. There was never "that dark table," placed by an ancestor two hundred years ago, or an old painted chest that could not be moved because it had "always been there." No preference for any period, style, or region could be noticed. Papa called the decor of the Water Castle a glorious mixture of original and imitation everything.

The two men who came into the house with a large painting a few minutes after my arrival knocked down an armchair and almost toppled Beethoven from his pedestal. I loved the commotion. They wore identical blue liveries with epaulets and as much gilt as the kaiser's hussars. With an air of grave importance and using mostly hand signals, they ordered Francine to hold the glass door. They urged each other on in a language of pure sound: "Ja, ja. Da. Da. Ach, na." The heat from the radiators and many light fixtures and the sun streaming in through tall windows made them perspire freely.

My own face in the hall mirror appeared foolishly pleased. A photograph of Resi Romberg holding Eli on her lap amazed me. He looked about my own age, but wore a baby dress and cap.

"Adorable, isn't it?" said Eli's nurse, Frau Schwester, as she came in. "The christening picture—it appeared in the paper. He has grown a lot since then. But he was already six when he was christened. His mama did not care to give his age to the newspaper, she never does. It keeps her young. Now the boy has to be Jewish."

Frau Schwester wore the crisp white garb of a hospital nun, and the cap made her long face appear yellow. I smelled disinfectant as she picked me up and examined my fingernails, face, and neck. "Well, well. At least we have no spots on the face and neck." Like everyone and everything else at the Water Castle, she looked completely out of place and yet fitted into the scene. "Our poor boy is waiting for you. Still at the breakfast table, too excited to eat. And we are running behind schedule." Her clipped north-German voice sounded foreign to me.

I tried to escape, but she held me firmly propped against her protruding stomach. She even supported my back, as though I were a newborn infant. I almost fell asleep, I felt so comfortable. "Ach, our Eli will be pleased," Frau Schwester muttered, as though she had to convince herself.

I soon found out that she had been angry when she was told of my visit, and much opposed to having me come frequently. She stopped at a window to inspect my leather trousers. "They can't even be washed," she said. She changed Eli three times a day and massaged him with baby oil. I seemed dangerously dirty and neglected. She even made me open my mouth so that she could look into my throat before we entered the dining room. Something made me shudder in all the heat. She touched my forehead and grumbled about her schedule. "Eli!" she shouted as she carried me into the huge, brightly lit room. "Here's Reyna von Meinert, dressed like a peasant boy."

Eli sat at a banquet table all by himself. His head hung low over a baby's bib embroidered with clover leaves. I thought he was asleep.

"Say good morning, Eli!" She sounded loud enough to stir the dead, but Eli did not look up. She placed me in a chair beside him, propped me up with cushions as though I had not learned to sit erect, and, ignoring my objections, tied a bib around my neck. A plate with a large piece of raisin cake and a steaming cup of chocolate topped with whipped cream appeared before me. The table was loaded with delicacies: platters of cold meat and sausage, smoked fish, egg dishes, fruit, and three large cakes.

Frau Schwester made her clacking sound as she refilled Eli's cup. He was breathing through his mouth and sat with hunched shoulders. "Now you must eat, my little prince. We are behind schedule and we'll be late with our morning milk. What with waiting for little guests . . ."

He did not look up, but his lashes trembled. I had never seen anyone so sad; it was like seeing him naked. He had the almond face of a storybook prince, his mother's pink lips. Black hair in a cap of silk came down to his ear lobes. He never spoke in the presence of strangers, never around anyone who bothered him. When his nurse had still ventured out into the street with him, his silence started a rumor that the Splasher's son was deaf and dumb. The little prince of the Water Castle tried to breathe, gasping like a fish washed up on dry land. His eyes remained half-closed while his nurse fussed around, and feathered eyebrows exaggerated his heavy lids. Long lashes fell over his marvelous eyes like curtains, allowing him to dream. As soon as Frau Schwester went off to the conservatory to water plants and give seeds to the birds, Eli looked up. "The gardener hates her. She feeds birds that have already been fed, overwaters tropical plants." He breathed more easily as he watched me take six lumps of sugar and a mountain of whipped cream. "Austrians and their *Schlamperei* really bother her."

I filled my mouth like a hamster. He blinked against the sun, fingering the top button of his dark blue velvet suit. All at once, his hand reached out for the sugar bowl, the whipped cream. He picked little bits off each platter. "It tastes better that way," he said. "And that way she doesn't know I've eaten."

I knew he trusted me, liked my company, and by the time we had picked the icing off an orange-flavored cake and raisins out of the *Gugelhupf*, our friendship had been sealed through a conspiracy of wild greed. The overfed birds twittered in the aviary; sparrows chirped on the windowsills, pecking at pieces of bread and cake. The bounty seemed to overflow.

Three stone Graces below the window wore nothing but little specks of melting snow and looked pleasantly cool. "Let's go out and play in the garden," I said.

"I'm not allowed to go out when it's cold, and I cannot go out without my tutor or some other man because I once had stones hurled at me over the back fence. Nazis."

"Perhaps it was only little Herbert, the foot doctor's son. He throws stones at anyone."

Eli did not believe me. When we left the table he walked cautiously, with his toes turned in, as though the carpets might either sink or take off and fly away with him. I felt the weight of the heat as I followed him through the passageway. Bright lights shone everywhere in the many rooms of the great house. Eli's mournfulness seemed as soft and mysterious as the dark. At the entrance to the great hall he stopped; his chest heaved. He held his thin hand out for me before we entered.

This room, the center of the Water Castle, resembled the Meinert chapel in size and shape, but the dome was made of glass and covered with snow. It was pleasantly cooler here. "It's so quiet," I said. "At home the maids always sing and laugh when they clean in the morning. The moment my parents are gone they turn on the radio. Sometimes they dance, and they are teaching me to waltz."

"No one is supposed to make any noise until my *Mutti* gets up," he said. But at that very moment, the two men I had seen in the entrance room appeared with a ladder and toolbox, clattering along toward the sitting corner where low divans, a large green chair, and many soft seats formed a circle in front of the main wall.

"Ja, ja, da," said the thin one, fumbling and almost toppling off the ladder as they lifted the great painting up toward a hook.

Eli whispered their names: Stauble and Pichler. They had lost their jobs at the Volks Oper because they had knocked down some stage props behind the scenes and made a lot of noise while his mother was singing at a guest performance. She had felt sorry for them and hired them to work at the villa. They remained stagehands, carrying scenery with total indifference to any drama. Stauble and Pichler belonged together; you couldn't tell them apart, and they made us laugh.

As they left, their ladder banged against a silver urn, and I heard an ominous clang. Eli's hand tightened. He led me to the picture and told me his father had bought this Titian at an auction because his mother liked Biblical things. I beheld a beggarly old giant staring wildly from a dark brown world. When Eli told me the painting was worth a fortune, I couldn't believe anyone would pay so much for such a face.

"What is 'Biblical'?" I asked.

"Well, the story of the Jews."

"How they killed Jesus?"

"They didn't kill Christ," he said. "The Romans did."

I did not know too much about the Romans, but I had seen their ruins and knew they liked to take many baths. Some people had Roman noses. The old giant in the picture had a large hooked nose and stared fiercely into the distance. "Is he Roman?" I asked.

"It's the prophet Jeremiah."

I repeated the name, because I liked the sound.

"A Jew," he explained.

"Like your father?"

Eli's eyes looked into mine. He suddenly seemed like a grown-up. "Not like my father."

I was about to remark that the prophet was much thinner than Eugene Romberg when a mass of snow slid off the glass dome with a crash. Suddenly, the sun shone down on us like a stage-light.

"What's a prophet?" I wanted to know.

Eli glanced at the painting. "Someone who can tell what is going to happen. Can't you see he looks frightened? He can foresee terrible things."

"I don't like him," I admitted. "Frau Hanna Roth foresees things, but she is funny."

Eli smiled for the first time, and he dimpled like his mother. "Frau Roth is funny-looking." He became solemn again. "She doesn't like boys, and she won't have anything to do with me."

We were interrupted at this moment by a shrilling, followed by the trills and shrieks of a bird in distress.

"Mutti practicing," Eli explained. "Frau Roth told her she had to do voice exercises every day. She came to see us after we moved in and told Mutti she should not live in this house. They both became quite angry, and they smoked so much I had to go with Frau Schwester. I could never go to the hat salon, anyway, because of the smoke. It would give me an attack."

"I have been there, and the hats looked like mushrooms," I told him.

"My mother thinks they are lucky. She's supposed to sing at a charity concert next week. She won't do it unless Frau Hanna makes her a headdress. I think she is afraid of her."

I told him I was not afraid of the dwarf, and I was about to describe my visit to the salon—especially Hanna's predictions about Adolf Hitler coming to Vienna—when Frau Schwester interrupted with two tall glasses of milk. Eli reached for his top button again and blinked. The voice exercises took on a pattern, going up and down.

"Now. We must drink our milk or Herr Papa won't be happy, my little prince. We won't be able to have little playmates if we don't start gaining strength, put on a little weight." She could never stay away from Eli for any length of time.

"Here comes Mutti," said Frau Schwester, holding the glass to Eli's lips. He sipped and choked. I could tell this was one of his tricks, but his nurse looked worried. "I don't know what she will say."

Resi Romberg always left doors open behind her when she made her morning entrance. Hundreds of crystal pendants chimed as she came tripping around the gallery above the great hall. The giant chandelier swaying on a great glass-covered chain took on the lilac color of one of her long Biblical dresses, which I would come to love. She had been teaching Eli the history of the Jews— or rather, her version of it. I always looked forward to seeing her waltz to "The Blue Danube," making her full skirt twirl around her sandaled feet. This happened each time she came to the part where the Egyptians fell into the sea and the Jewish people celebrated.

She paused at the top of the stairs. I had never looked at her too carefully. Her eyes were round and iridescent in this bright light. She had painted her lips and cheeks discreetly. Her hair fell into ringlets down to her shoulders. One hand touched the banister as she descended regally; the other remained behind her back, hiding the inevitable cigarette. The smoke rising around her head and shoulders only added to the magic of her entrance. She came down singing an aria from *Aida*, because it fitted in with her story of the chosen people. The opera, she thought, gave evidence against the cruel country by the Nile and well justified the fact that the Jews made off with Egyptian jewels when they escaped from slavery.

I could never think of Resi as a grownup. Even the most sinister men of our time became playful and irresponsible when she appeared. Resi even looked childish, because her face and curly head were large and her figure small, with a tiny waist. She sang like an angel, but she also became seductive when she sang. Her breasts rose and fell, nipples decorating her soft dress. I could see she wore nothing under it as she came down the stairs and began waving her arms like a dancer, creating smoke signals with her cigarette. I had to laugh, but she had no doubt given her appearance earnest consideration. Her notorious love for caressing silks and cashmeres transcended mere fancy. As a Jewess, she now considered nakedness under her costume authentic and Biblical.

Applause at the end of her aria came from a group of maids, Frau Schwester, Stauble and Pichler, the cook, and even the porter's wife, who had all gathered at the kitchen entrance. Resi waved to them and smiled; then she turned to me.

"Reyna," she trilled. Her kiss smelled of soap and smoke. "Good morning, Bubi!" I was surprised to see Eli enjoy her public embrace. He clung to her.

"What shall we sing for Reyna?" They always sang together as soon as Resi got up. She began the song about the birds returning in the spring. Eli became transformed. He rose and performed with his mother, tilting his head, moving his arms—he even dimpled. I loved his voice, although it was not as loud and clear as his mother's. Breathing seemed to require no effort when he sang.

There was more applause, even cheering, from the small, enthusiastic audience as the song came to an end. Frau Schwester came rustling toward us. "Gnädige," she began. "Eli has not drunk his milk."

Resi Romberg looked concerned. Eugene Romberg's "Drink Milk" posters depicted plump, rosy mothers and children. Pure milk, full of rich cream, had to be of great importance here at the Water Castle. Resi assured Frau Schwester we would finish our milk when she went on with Jewish history. She invited us to sit with her on a low divan, and leaning back among silk cushions, she began: "Remember, Eli, the Jews walked in the desert. They had no water and suffered terribly from thirst." The long description of scorching heat soon made me reach for my milk. Eli followed my example, and Frau Schwester departed.

The audience at the kitchen entrance had vanished as soon as Resi started our lesson. I found the entertainment more fasci-

nating than any of her arias. Although Resi had an excellent
memory and could learn a libretto within a week, she knew how
to forget any part of the Jewish story that did not enhance her
drama, or at least lend itself to song and dance. The bewitching
journey to the Promised Land has never quite ended for me.

One of eight children, Resi had danced as soon as she walked.
Put on song-plays with her brothers and sisters in the courtyard
of their tenement. A teacher took her to a retired singer from the
Vienna Opera. From the age of eleven on, Resi Heller sang and
was admired, entertained and was loved. She always entertained.
She could not stop herself, even with Eli and me. One could hardly
say she gave up her career for Eugene Romberg and Eli. Her
day, as I remember it, was one long performance. I came to the
Water Castle expecting drama, and one way or the other, I always
found it.

Under the stern gaze of the prophet, Resi became the pharaoh's
daughter, tripping down to the water to bathe with her maidens;
they splashed about to a seductive aria from *Carmen*. She
changed the decor, and little Moses was found under a blooming
lilac bush. Poor little Moses had difficulty in breathing and
gasped for air. She rocked him, singing Brahms's lullaby. Later,
that very same lilac bush caught fire and turned into the burning
bush. Since flames could not consume it, Brünnhilda had plenty
of time to go on with her loud song from flaming Valhalla. The
great hall came to life. Eli rose and spoke with the voice of the
Jewish God, addressing the chosen people from a mountain of
pillows.

No definite sequence ever existed. I never quite knew when the
chosen people would suddenly make off with the Egyptian jewels.
At times it became a little unclear which side Resi was on. Her
favorite earrings and a baroque necklace were missing from her
jewelry box; she described these at great length as part of the
loot. She almost forgot she had become a Jew, she felt so sorry
for the Egyptian ladies who had lost their treasures.

"Naturally, the Egyptians were very, very angry. They wanted
to get the stolen rings and pins and pearls and diamond earrings
back for their wives. But God was the god of the chosen people.
He wanted the Jews to have all those things. And after all, the
Egyptians did have a lot of gold to spare, and so many jewels that

they even put them into the pyramids with the mummies. They should not have been so angry—they were very rich . . . But they came after the Jews, and there was a great pillar of cloud, all black. But for the Jews this was a pillar of light."

Her song from Wagner's *Parsifal* was followed by thunder, which Eli produced on a gong. The Egyptians fell into the water while the chosen people walked over the waves with all the jewelry. She ended this triumph with a jolly song from *Night in Venice,* because of the water. Eli knew this song, and I learned to join in.

By this time, the last snow in the cupola had melted and sun flooded the great hall. A donkey spoke. Just as it began to rain bread, water dripped from a bullet hole in the glass dome and fell into a silver basin. Resi considered the death of the munitions manufacturer who had built the mansion to be romantic. The glass pane remained unrepaired, in his memory, as long as she was around. She was saying "Ach, poor man," when Eugene Romberg walked in.

He sat down in his green armchair. His large, dark eyes shone with pleasure as he saw us all so happy together. He complimented Resi on her gold sandals because he enjoyed seeing her perfect, tiny feet. He gave the impression of being a melancholy man, because his own large feet were always sore. A strange notion made him hide them in small shoes.

In the bright sunlight, I could admire a scar on his left cheek. He wore a suede waistcoat and gaiters to match and looked like a dandy in his well-tailored dark-green suit. "How is your beautiful mama?" he inquired.

I told him that she had gone to a committee meeting in connection with Resi's charity concert.

He smiled at Resi with satisfaction. "My little nightingale will sing for her; that's how it should be. You look charming, Reserl, but aren't you chilly in your thin dress? It's really never too warm in this part of the house. We must have the glass roof repaired."

Resi Romberg didn't say anything when she disagreed; she simply waited. Eugene Romberg's eyes fell onto our empty milk glasses. "Well, I'm certainly glad to see the children are drinking their milk. I hear you ate very well at breakfast, Eli, in Reyna's company. I spoke to Ferdl on the telephone. You can stay and have lunch with us, little one. Perhaps everyone is hungry today."

Eli sank down among cushions at the mere mention of food. His father jumped up. "I know I'm ready to eat." He offered me his arm as though I were grown up, and led the way to the dining room, taking hurried little steps on his painful feet. The heat made my cheeks glow, and he complimented me on my healthy color.

Soup waited in large, steaming tureens. The maids stood by, and Eugene Romberg was served the moment he took his seat at the head of the table. He emptied his plate before Frau Schwester had finished tying our bibs. A Jew had to be inherently hungry and thirsty after that long journey to the land of milk and honey. I could well understand how Eli's father, one of the chosen ones, would have more money and eat more than anyone I knew.

He looked up from stuffed pheasant, saying, "Eat, children, eat!" The moment we ate a few bites, a maid came up from behind ready to serve. Poor Eli was choking when his mother drew attention to him by offering him tidbits from her plate, and his father urged him to drink more milk. I again looked at the three Graces in the garden; now they had shed even their snow wraps and stood cool and naked in the winter sun.

Eugene Romberg followed my glance. "Have the birds in the garden been fed today?" he asked.

Frau Schwester assured him that it had all been done. I nudged Eli. Everyone was looking out of the window at the birds, and I quickly maneuvered his meat onto my plate and from there onto his father's. No one noticed. Eli thanked me with a smile. I felt encouraged to make a little speech.

"Some birds fly far away. All the way to the Promised Land."

Eugene Romberg looked up from eating Eli's meat in a great hurry, and beamed at my wisdom. "Just listen to this child; and look at her nice empty plate. A real Meinert."

"Von Dornbach Falkenburg," I added.

❁   ❁   ❁

"A real Meinert," Eugene Romberg repeated when my father came to take me home in the afternoon, "the way she enjoys her food. No wonder she has the mind of a grownup. You should have heard her talk."

My ability to keep quiet was somehow never appreciated half

as much by anyone. My father looked well pleased, sucking on his pipe on the way home. He wanted to know whether I had had fun with Eli. I merely told him that we had sung some songs with Resi, and I did not mention the history of the Jews and the journey to the Promised Land.

The snow had melted and the swastika at the gate had vanished. On the avenue, the large painted letters D, O, and L shone white on the wet asphalt. The word *Dollfuss* had decorated the road between the two houses as long as I could remember.

Fritz Janicek and I had been in the front garden during the summer when he was trying to teach me to wipe green bugs off the roses. I did not like to squash them, and he had explained to me that some things were better dead. Then he had pointed at the road. Those letters stood for *Dollfuss*, the chancellor had been nothing but a priest-ridden dwarf. Those letters should be scrubbed out. Fritz had filled his palm with green bugs, then clapped his hands together with a bang, like a gunshot. I wondered now whether after he was dismissed he had gone to Germany to work for Adolf Hitler, and whether the Führer had a rose garden full of bugs.

I liked to play skipping games around the letters on the road. When I asked Agnes about Chancellor Dollfuss, she told me he had been a saint and a martyr. From my experience of saints and martyrs in the Meinert chapel, I formed my own picture of the little man, lying in a raspberry-red pool while the Holy Ghost, the pigeon, was on the wing. After my lesson with Resi, I felt sorry for the chancellor for having been a mere priest-ridden dwarf, a Catholic. Had he been a Jew, he would have been protected by a stronger god, a god who spoke up and told his people how to cook and what to eat. I felt sorry for anyone who didn't have a Jewish god and Jewish angels, and I proudly looked forward to being a Jew with Eli.

Papa smiled as I clambered up and unlocked the gate with my own golden keys. He had no idea how much everything had changed for me that day. He never knew that I would cross the street—all by myself—to share not only Eli's nurse, the maids, his father and mother, but most of all, his god: God of the Jews, who guarded his children, told them what to do, and never left them to make their own way.

5

The Day of the Devil

ROWS OF CANDLE FLAMES danced in the breath of prayer. Mostly women knelt, dark before the flickering lights. Their murmured entreaties rose as one voice asking for thousands of miracles. Agnes knelt beside me, her head covered by a green kerchief, hands folded. She kept her eyes low as though she did not dare look at the saint's hand in the sealed glass case. Church bells rang out; incense rose. The white glove on the red cushion and the bishop's staff wavered before my distrustful eyes. I wondered what was inside the glove, and shuddered.

Agnes had brought me here to be saved. I had declared myself a Jew once too often in her kitchen. She considered it her duty to inform me that Jesus, Son of God, had been murdered by Jews. To be a Jew was a curse. Herr Romberg was my father's friend and a fine gentleman. Frau Romberg, poor thing, wanted to share his burden of being a Jew. To involve me was very wrong indeed.

Agnes had taken me by the hand and led me to the bus. I went to sleep, and when I woke up, she had just enough time to feed me a ham sandwich and teach me about saints and miracles. Her lesson, as I remember it, sounded quite like her recipe for salted, cured Hungarian ham: You bury a martyr or a holy person (a martyr is better); keep the body there for fifty years, and if the dead person is saintly enough—seasoned with holiness and goodness—the worms won't touch it; part of the body, at least, will be left. The pope then declares the martyr or holy person a saint. The good pieces of the remains are carved up and shipped to different parts of Christendom. A small piece of saint is called a relic and always brings about miracles among believers.

Eli had caught a cold and a slight fever—from me, Frau Schwester felt. I wanted to ask the saint to make him well so that I could go and see him again. But the hand seemed to waver, come to life, as it must have done to the horror of generations of dazed children who had been brought here for their salvation. I couldn't pray, nor could I avert my eyes from the bright dancing lights, the white glove. The finger seemed to move and point at me.

"I want to go," I said in a panic.

To Agnes this meant only one thing: "Well, you could have waited like a big girl."

Later, on the way out, when I helped myself to holy water far too liberally, she did not scold. Bending down to straighten my sailor hat, she looked as pleased as if she had just finished icing a cake. I was now supposed to be inured against Resi Romberg's sweet Judaic myth and deaf to the games and pretty songs that went with the slow progress of the Jews toward that land of milk and honey. She congratulated herself on the way to the bus for having chosen All Saints' Day for our pilgrimage. It was not only most appropriate, but the weather was fair. The next day, All Souls' Day, it traditionally rained.

She decided to change buses at the cemetery to make sure all the candles there were lit. I liked going to the graveyard, and made leaves rustle with my feet on the way downhill to the Meinert mausoleum. Agnes said it had never been a wine storage house, but it certainly looked as though it held casks, not coffins. Only an invisible wire fence separated the bottom of the grave-yard from my father's vineyard. The top of this southern slope was part of the Vienna woods.

I was not afraid of graves or the dead because I had faith in regeneration. Azaleas and rhododendrons had already formed buds for the coming spring. Everything died and grew back again. The dead seemed to be planted, rather than buried. I enjoyed looking at statues and photographs on the graves while Agnes prayed and tended to lanterns and flowers. Candles flickered everywhere. This year I was able to decipher the inscriptions. I loved "Our beloved Adelheid, loving daughter, gone from us in all her innocence to rest as an angel in the arms of God." Adelheid's photograph showed her to be such an armful that I was sure she had died of overeating.

We stopped at Great-Aunt Christina's grave. "How come she looks so much like Mama? She was old when she died."

Agnes told me that the family would like to remember her at her best. I wanted to sit down on the little wrought-iron bench and study the picture, the tiny waist and the huge hat, but Agnes took my hand and led me alongside a stone wall. Here the graves had all been dug up. Only one tall, newly polished tombstone attracted my attention. On top of it sat a tiny stone figure, just like a doll. A child in mourning black, veiled like a small bride, was kneeling in front of the mound. I recognized the feathered hat.

"It's Hannah Roth!" I called out.

Agnes wanted to turn left to get away, but Frau Hanna sprang up and came to greet us as though she had been waiting. "There you are, then," she said cheerfully as we exchanged our curtsies. "Isn't it a beautiful day here? I always enjoy All Saints' best. It isn't crowded. They all come to light candles in the morning; now we have it all to ourselves."

While she exchanged a polite greeting with Agnes and asked about her arthritis, I had time to see and dislike the marble doll who sat on the gravestone, plump and placid in a carefully detailed dress.

"And have you been to see beautiful Christina von Kortnai?" Hanna Roth inquired.

Agnes told her we had been to the family graves.

"But no one ever goes to see poor Antonelli, who made Puppe. I always do. The baroness wanted to be buried in his tomb, but they put her with her father. Strange morality. After all she did for your mother, Reyna, one would have thought the countess—"

"Well, we must go, Frau Roth," Agnes interrupted. "A little child doesn't have to know any of that."

Hanna Roth came to block our way. Her eyes level with mine, she waited until I said, "I already know. She left everything to Mama, but Mama has to take care of the doll forever."

"Forever," the dwarf repeated cheerfully. "No, no, Frau Agnes. You must not prevent this child from expressing herself. She knows more than you think." She took my hand. "She was about your age, Reyna, just as adorable, your mama. I can still see that little redhead walking into the sickroom with those yellow roses.

The baroness Christina was sitting propped up in bed with Puppe. A sorry sight: no resemblance to her doll remained. I'll never forget the way she touched her own head, nothing but gray fuzz. Then she reached out for your mama's ringlets. 'My child,' she said. 'Puppe.'"

"That doll," Agnes said impatiently. "I wish she'd kept her."

"Ach, and don't you know how much she wanted to keep her. Such a great traveler, but that journey without her doll—the final journey—terrified her. That's why she sent for me. To think, I had already made clothes for Puppe and hats for the baroness when I was a mere child! I dressed them all those years, but she left the doll—and with her everything—to that little redhead beside her deathbed. A child of fortune, your blessed mama."

Agnes examined the gravestone with a frown. "Aren't your parents buried in the Jewish cemetery, Frau Roth?"

Hanna Roth clamped a gloved hand over her mouth to stifle her laughter. "Some people have garden plots. Some go and walk in a park. I like it here. I can come here all by myself without being stared at. And one does have to have a family grave, the proper ancestors. We are expecting great things to happen," she concluded, with an unexpected little skip.

Agnes took me by the shoulder and guided me past the dwarf. "God's greeting, Frau Roth," she said curtly.

My curtsy was returned with a flourish, and the feathers on that tall hat danced in the wind. "Auf Wiedersehen, little highness," she said cheerfully. "Don't be cross, Frau Agnes. The very young like old stories and benefit from listening."

"The way she goes on!" Agnes said under her breath as we hurried toward the gate. "Godless, even if the good nuns took her in. And conceited!"

On the bus Agnes put her arm around me. Her dark Sunday coat smelled of mothballs. The bus swayed, and I closed my eyes. The white glove began to hover above me on dark wings. The pointing forefinger and thumb clinked together, forming a beak that dangled Puppe by her skirt. Like a bird of prey, the relic rose higher and higher and yet grew in size until the doll dangled, small as a mouse, upside down, the swastika on her petticoat shining like a star. The relic, perched on a blazing round sun like a gigantic falcon, turned as white as glowing cinders falling into ashes. The beak clinked open. Puppe crumbled and fell in white flakes and kept falling. I felt myself falling into fire and smoke, and woke up being held by Agnes.

Agnes asked me whether I was feeling all right. I looked white. I told her I did not like the smoke. A man behind us was puffing away on putrid-smelling tobacco. We moved to a front seat as soon as the bus came to a halt at the next stop.

I revived when I saw the window of a certain little candy shop I liked. My mother often stopped here and bought something for me on our way home from the farm or the chapel. The window was already decorated for "Krampus and Nicolo," a feast day at the beginning of December for Austrian children. I jumped up and down in my seat with delight. Krampus, a devil made of prunes, candy, and marzipan, or as a mask of papier-mâché, with lolling tongue and horns, made me laugh out loud. His bundles of switches tied with ribbons stood for boisterous fun rather than retribution. There would be roast chestnuts, tangerines, candy. I couldn't wait for the fun of running away from the switches and finally turning on Krampus, taking hold of his mask by the nose, and pulling it off. I would, of course, know all along that Poldi was the Krampus, because I'd recognize her brown felt slippers.

The bus moved on, and pink bishops' masks with white cotton beards, tall white hats, and gilded crosses came into view. "Are you going to be the Nicolo again, Agnes?"

Nicolo, a bishop, always came with Krampus and emptied a sack onto the table. Candy, fruit, nuts, and pipe-cleaner devils rewarded a good child. Agnes liked playing that part. But before she could answer me, the white-and-pink masks brought back the white glove, my dream, the relic. "I don't want the Nicolo," I said.

"Well, I never know about you." Agnes gave me a hug. "Your mother was afraid of the Krampus, even when she could tell it was really me or the laundrywoman. In the end, we just had the Nicolo at the *palais*. I didn't like to see her get all worked up."

"I like the Krampus." Agnes would not have understood how I disliked saints who suffered and admired power. It made sense to like Krampus. No Krampus had ever been dug up from a grave and declared a devil, carved up, and sent around the world in bits and pieces. "I want the Krampus. I don't want the Nicolo at all."

*   *   *

Krampus Day turned out to be mild. The *Föhn,* our south wind, came from the Dolomites and over the acres and acres of snow-covered graves from the war. My von Dornbach grandfather lay buried somewhere up there. In the high mountains, the warm wind would cause the first snowslides. In Vienna, snowbanks turned mottled and gray.

The *Föhn* made nervous people more nervous. My mother had come home from riding with a terrible headache and was re-laxing in a warm bath. I wore a dress under my loden cloak, in honor of Grandmama Reyna. She always came in a taxi, and I was waiting for her in front of the house, running back and forth and splashing my white stockings with mud. I skipped down to the gate once more, climbed up, and peered out through the wrought-iron spikes.

Strong gusts of wind fanned my cheeks and spun the cupid weather vane at the Water Castle so fast it almost vanished. The windows were all lit up over there, as usual. In the early after-noon Eli was more than likely in bed, taking a rest because of his cold. I had already rung the bell twice that morning, asking how he was. Finally Agnes had told me to stop it.

Dark clouds raced by so fast, the great house seemed to drift before my eyes, and I felt dizzy and climbed down. Something came buzzing along the quiet avenue. At first it resembled a red bug; it grew, came along under the tall birch trees with a great roar and sputtering: a red motorcycle, carrying a red rider. A Krampus, wearing a marvelous mask with a very long red tongue, stopped in front of the Romberg house. I quickly climbed the gate and waved.

"Are you coming to see Eli?" I was surprised, because I had been told by the porter's wife there would be no Krampus for Eli. Jews did not believe in such things. This Krampus kept the engine running and ignored me. Perhaps he had not heard.

"*Servus,* Krampus. Come here!"

The mask turned, tongue flying in the wind. The black boot

gave spur, and in a second the red rider vanished, roaring off toward the fields and woods.

I went, "Brrrrr, brrrrr," racing to the side of the house. Mother's bathroom window stood open, and the doll sat there surrounded by fragrant steam. I stuck out my tongue as far as I could. Then I called, "The Krampus will get you. No, the Nicolo. The white glove."

When I turned around, my grandmother's taxi had stopped at the gate. I ran down to keep her from ringing the bell. I wanted to show off my golden keys. She wore black, because she was staying for dinner, and she carried an umbrella. The little package wrapped and tied with a red ribbon, I guessed, contained pralines for me. I had been told I resembled my aristocratic grandmother, since I had inherited her amber-colored eyes and short, arched nose. I knew I resembled her greatly when it came to eating those little chocolate-covered, mint-filled sweets. She seemed to live on them, and would reach for her amethyst-studded praline box in the same manner as Resi Romberg reached for cigarettes.

I curtsied to her. She handed me the present and held out her hand. I said, "*Danke schön,*" but the white glove repelled me. She stooped and kissed my cheek. Her gold-speckled eyes regarded me with amusement as I hopped about on one leg, dangling my package. Suddenly she straightened and stared motionless into the distance. Her delicate face lost all expression as she sought refuge within herself, rigid as some terrified insect.

"I gave your pipe-cleaner Krampus away to teach someone a lesson. I don't know what made me do such a thing. I was just coming out of Demels with the pralines and von Feld came darting at me and clicked his heels. Nothing but Hitler's *Schani,* and to think he is a kinsman to our late empress! Anyway, the Krampus had fallen off, and he handed it to me. A very handsome man, I must say. I told him to keep it. A little reminder. He stared at me as if I had gone mad. Now he'll really tell the Führer that the Austrian Monarchists are senile and mad." She laughed to herself. "Safer that way . . ."

I told her I had seen a real Krampus on a red motorcycle. She sighed, took my hand, and we walked toward the house. "A lot of riffraff loose today. No one to put a stop to it."

She spoke to me as an equal, and I tried to walk tall and straight, as she did. Agnes had told me the nuns, my grandmother's foster mothers, had tied Countess Reyna to her bed at night when she was my age to make her sleep on her back; this had made her so straight, tall, and aristocratic. I tried to sleep on my back, but usually woke up on my stomach.

"I heard a loud bang this morning," I told her. "The radio said there are bombs in the second district."

"Cowards," said my grandmother with a shudder. "Of the lowest breed. Attacking helpless little Hebrew shopkeepers."

"Is 'Hebrew' the same as 'Jew'?"

"Yes, but it is more respectful, less intimate."

"What is 'intimate'?" I asked.

"To be close to someone. Hatred and violence are as much an intimacy as love—a perverse intimacy."

The window off the laundry room in the basement stood open, and a dank smell of long ago drifted up to us from old stone walls where the linen of generations of Meinerts had been boiled in huge copper kettles. I always loved this dank odor; the smell made me feel safe and quite at home. When I scrubbed handkerchiefs in deep suds on laundry day, Frau Boschke, the laundress, an authority on Falkenburg history, needed little encouragement to talk.

Her father had worked on the Falkenburg estate as a groom. She came from a family of eight, and they lived at Krummbach, where storks nested on rooftops. Near the village stood the convent of *Die Englischen Fräulein*, a teaching order of nuns who had brought up my grandmother, Frau Traude, and Hanna Roth. Frau Boschke used to stand and wait for the young ladies to come walking through the village behind a nun, who held the dwarf by the hand. Village children weren't allowed to go too close, but they loved to watch the dwarf all dressed in blue serge like the tall girls. The tiny one smiled all the time and even waved.

"We were poor, but I thought myself fortunate compared to the convent girls—mostly orphans," Frau Boschke said. "The dwarf, who was left in a basket for the nuns. . . . And your honorable grandmama—such a beauty—banished by her own father! Blaming an innocent newborn . . . It was all his fault.

He should have sent for the gypsy women; they could have saved the countess."

"Who was madder, Crown Prince Rudolf or Great-Grandpapa?" I now asked my grandmother.

Quite taken aback, she took up her lorgnon and examined my face. "The way to measure madness, I suppose, would be by the harm it does. My father, a tortured, passionate man, a warrior by nature, destroyed himself."

"I know," I spoke up. "He made his Lippizaner jump into the quarry and died. Crown Price Rudolf shot himself and Fräulein Vetsera."

"Who on earth has been talking to you?"

I said nothing. I did not want to get Frau Boschke into trouble or lose out on the fun of her stories and the soapsuds. (Before long, however, she was to be dismissed for celebrating Hitler's birthday in the laundry room with half a bottle of Father's cognac.)

Grandmama accepted my silence and said, "The death of His Imperial Highness, I feel, led straight to world war. We must pray for him."

Her words were too lofty for me. I preferred the laundry-room version of self-destruction. According to Frau Boschke, both my great-grandfather and the crown prince had died for love, the crown prince because he could not marry Fräulein Vetsera, Count Otto because he lost his beautiful redheaded wife at the birth of their first child. After her death, the count withdrew from the world, never went beyond the boundaries of his estate. For years he lived alone with a few servants, horses, and his crippled sister. When she finally died, he would not give her up; he took her body onto his horse and went riding up Falken Hill. He forced his horse to leap toward a sinking sun. The dead horse, the rider, and the corpse had lain shattered in the quarry at sunset.

My grandmother walked on to the courtyard and changed the subject by admiring the garden in the snow. She asked for my father. I told her he was very well, as always.

She laughed like a child. "Ja, ja, die Meinerts," she said. "Healthy and smart enough to stay out of trouble."

I knew she had something on her mind as soon as we walked into the entrance room. A spyglass threw the reflection of the Water Castle into the mirror, and she pointed at it with her umbrella. "Fantastic. All lit up for a *Fest* or a ball over there."

"It's always a Fest over there," I said, just as Agnes came to greet the countess, "always so much fun."

"It sounds like the Prater," my grandmother said.

Agnes kissed her hand, and their figures blotted out the reflection of the house I loved. I could not understand how Grandmama could scorn the Prater, the amusement park with the merry-go-rounds, puppet shows, balloons. At fifty-eight she seemed either much older or much younger than her years, rather like a young actress playing an older part.

"Your mother told me you went across the street to learn music."

I quickly sang "All the Birds Are Back Again." She remained unimpressed. "I also learn about the Jews—I mean, the Hebrews. Moses in his basket and the Egyptian princess and the flight from Egypt." I got carried away and quite forgot my pilgrimage with Agnes. "When I grow up, I'm going to be a Jew like Eli."

The countess interrupted my enthusiasm by beating the umbrella on the tile floor as though she had to summon a genie. "Nonsense, complete nonsense!"

I felt small beside her slender, upright figure in the black, tight-waisted dress. Her umbrella danced before my eyes. The handle was decorated with a falcon perched on a gilded orb— the Falkenburg crest. In my dream, the falcon with the doll had turned to ashes. I took a step away from the umbrella, for in the Hebrew stories dreams often preceded reality, as lightning precedes thunder in a storm.

"The Bible is not for little children." My grandmother's hand, in a white glove, waved away my fancies and turned into the bishop's hand. "You are a Catholic child, Reyna. You say your prayers and go to chapel and that is enough."

I was just about to admit that I did not like chapel when Agnes remarked on my pale face. "I hope she isn't coming down with another cold or something. The Romberg boy is always sick."

"You are quite right, Agnes. She doesn't belong over there," my grandmother concluded.

I suddenly shuddered in the cold entrance room, as I longed for the warm, bright house where it felt like summer with so many flowers, lights, songs, and games.

"What does my daughter have to say about it all?" the countess inquired of Agnes as we walked into the living room and took our place at the coffee table.

"She has a bad headache. It's the *Föhn* wind," Agnes said defensively. "Makes everyone feel on edge."

"It's all the riding. Jumping hurdles like one of the schoolboys instead of keeping an eye on things at home . . ."

I opened my pralines and quickly offered them to Grandmama and Agnes, but they were not easily distracted.

"Horses, hats, and that doll . . ." said the countess, just as we heard Mother coming down the stairs. As a girl, during her travels with Christina von Kortnai, my grandmother had always been embarrassed by Puppe. Mother never carried the doll when countess Reyna was around.

They kissed each other, and Grandmama forgot her displeasure. "Gray suits you very well, Ann Marie," she said with a lovely smile. She considered colored dresses vulgar, and my mother tried to please. They began to chat eagerly about a new shoemaker. Both Grandmama and Mother had narrow feet that were difficult to fit.

I was not allowed to interrupt this strange prattle which they could keep up endlessly. It was marvelous to watch them during this symphony of trivia. They wore their hair braided and wound around their heads, which emphasized the identical high foreheads. Their large eyes sat far apart on high cheekbones. Mother's protruded like gems, an amazing violet-blue. Yet her bright coloring, her youth and vivacity, were less extraordinary than the exacting marble beauty of the countess Reyna. And I had inherited her name and her only ornament: those deep-set amber eyes.

They were having trouble with their tailor. Grandmama was planning to go away over Christmas; her coat might not even be ready in time. She didn't mention her destination, but we all knew she was the guest of the exiled Habsburg family. Mother and daughter knew how to sustain harmony by avoiding anything that might bring about an argument. But then Mama asked, "Did Frau Hanna make a new hat for your trip?"

"It might have amused my hostess, but I cannot tolerate Hanna's presumptions. Her personal remarks are quite ill-mannered. Fortunetelling is un-Christian."

Mama laughed. "It's not that serious, Mother. Everybody meets at the salon."

"And they listen to her new interest in politics."

"They don't have to take it seriously. She's always said all kinds of things. I have listened to her most of my life. No one ever remembers half of what she says. Then, when something she predicts happens, everyone is all agog. She says anything that comes into her head. Why, she even tells me to stay away from horses!"

My grandmother laughed like a girl and sipped from her cup. "I think she has a very good point there. You don't need Frau Hanna to advise more caution and restraint. But even our beloved empress felt happiest when she was in the saddle. She shocked everyone when she took lessons from a ringmaster . . ."

While the clock ticked along to my grandmother's memory of horses and hunts, the coffeepot cast a weird shadow on the tablecloth. Agnes, who knew Mama loved the twilight, had drawn back the curtains. The clouds parted before my eyes, and a round golden orb hung low in a milky sky. The sun of my dream! I jumped up.

"Sit down, Reyna! You'll spill your cocoa." Mama dropped her bunch of keys. I picked them up, and she thanked me with a kiss on the head. The clock ticked for a few measures, and then I saw the Romberg limousine drive up quietly at the Water Castle.

"Talking about caution and restraint," my grandmother said finally, "I came to talk to you about Reyna."

My mother reached for her forehead and was about to send me away.

"No, no. I want her to stay. She knows I'm troubled about her visits to the Romberg house—"

"There is Uncle Eugene," I said quickly.

He emerged from the limousine in his dark fur-lined coat and a matching hat. The packages he carried emphasized his round shape. He faced our house and hesitated while the chauffeur put the car away.

"You don't have to worry, Mama," said my mother. "He would never come uninvited. He is very shy with me. He might only leave a package with a maid. He is always giving us little things."

My grandmother looked shocked and was about to speak when the red Krampus motorcycle came racing back.

"Krampus, Krampus!" I shouted and ran to the window.

"Come away," Mama said. "Your father might come home and see you at the front windows."

I obediently took a step back. The red motorcycle came to an abrupt stop beside Eugene Romberg, just as he had one foot on the sidewalk. The red devil did not dismount and kept the engine running; I could hear the sputtering as I admired the mask with its gilded horns and long felt tongue, which flew up in the wind.

"Someone collecting for charity, no doubt," said my mother. "He's always giving money away."

Grandmama was peering discreetly through the curtains with the aid of her lorgnon. "What next? The way he came at him, I thought he would run him down."

I laughed because the devil waved his bundle of gilded switches. Even when he grabbed Eugene Romberg's arm it looked harmless, as though he was helping him onto the sidewalk with all those packages. But he did not dismount, and he kept hold of Romberg's arm.

"If that's supposed to be a joke!" my grandmother exclaimed.

Everything happened fast but the scene was soundless. Eugene Romberg was trying to shake the masked man off. He gave him a push, and for a moment he was free. Then the black glove fastened onto his coat and jerked him back so hard his hat and parcels dropped to the ground. I cried out when the Krampus struck Eugene Romberg's bald head, again and again, streaking it red. I could see Romberg's face distorted with fury. He reached into his pocket, pulled out a bottle of baby milk he'd carried home for Eli and me. Then he swung the bottle and struck the masked assailant with a great blow. The bottle smashed; the drenched mask oozed pink. I heard myself scream. Another bottle came out of Romberg's left pocket. I ducked. He hit the mask sideways. The red rider and the steel steed fell. The Krampus lay there with the red vehicle like a fallen centaur. The wheels kept spinning.

Figures came running from the great house, in between snowbanks and ornamental hedges. Mama tried to pull me away from the window, but I struggled out of her trembling arms. The chauffeur came from the garage, then the porter's wife from her lodge, but Frau Schwester, in flying white veils, won the race. Her arms reached out to Eugene Romberg as though she would scoop him up and carry him, as she had carried me, to comfort him with her clucking sounds. She produced a clean diaper from her pocket and began to wipe his bald head, but he fended her off and cleaned his head quickly with a handkerchief, because Resi was coming down the steps. In a thin pink gown she flew toward him. His gentle plump hand went out to touch her curls, as though she had taken punishment; he dried her tears, picked up the packages, and handed them to her before he turned to the fallen man.

The two stagehands in their liveries ran to turn off the engine; they lifted the Krampus, dragged him over a pile of gray snow, and propped him against a tree. Unseated, the red rider looked pathetic, oddly dismembered. Eugene Romberg went after him. He took the mask by the nose and ripped it off the lolling head.

"Fritz!" I yelled.

Mama came to the window, and Eugene Romberg, mask in hand, bowed low to her. She sat down on the edge of a plant table, as though she were too weak to stand.

Although my grandmother despised telephones, she called the police and watched their prompt arrival with satisfaction. In heaven as on earth, she believed, there had to be an imperial law. At first, however, the arrival of police officers and then a noisy ambulance only added to the havoc in the street. Resi fainted into the arms of a young doctor and stole the scene. A tall man photographed her as she was carried toward the house on a stretcher. Behind her walked the doctor, one policeman, a man in a raincoat, the chauffeur, and the two stagehands, followed by Eugene Romberg with Frau Schwester, who insisted on taking his arm. At the gate Eugene Romberg remembered the Krampus mask and handed it over to her. She carried this piece of evidence gingerly by its rubber band and handed it over to the stoutest police officer, who seemed to be in charge.

By the time the procession had vanished among the hedges of the garden, Fritz Janicek was beginning to recover and stood up, aided by two orderlies. He wobbled on his legs like a marionette, stared at our house. One stout officer of the law and another, less imposing one were questioning him, but he waved them aside, pointed at our window, and bowed low to Mama. The men nudged each other, took off their caps, and payed homage to "the beauty," as she was called in our neighborhood. She remained seated but drew back a little behind the lace curtain, biting her full lower lip as though she had just been discovered in a theater box at the wrong kind of play.

My grandmother pulled the curtains and rang for Agnes. The cuckoo clock called the hour.

"That clock is always late," Agnes said as she walked in.

I ran to her, shouting, "Did you see it?! Did you see it?!"

She looked baffled by my wild talk of Krampus, Eugene Romberg, milk, blood, police. My grandmother had to explain. Agnes picked me up and held me. "Dear God in heaven," she said several times, looking at me as though I might have come to some bodily harm by looking on. I was getting too heavy for her, but she held onto me until the police and ambulance had departed. When I looked out again, no one was about; the avenue, deserted as an empty stage, filled me with disquiet.

"Good thing the twins were at the cinema show this afternoon. It would have been water on their mill, all this excitement and the policemen." She looked into my face. "No more Krampus," she promised.

"No Nicolo," I added, as I remembered the bishop's hand in the white glove.

She kissed my curls. "Just candy and tangerines, *nicht wahr?*"

The brightly lit window and the gleaming gold of the glass cupola beckoned. I wished I could be in the midst of all the excitement over there. Eli, in bed at the back of the house, had more than likely missed it all. For the first time I pitied him with all my heart.

"It's all over," my grandmother said.

I didn't believe it. "Hanna Roth was quite right about milk and blood," I said.

6
Children's Waltz

BY CHRISTMAS 1937 Nazis in Vienna waited for their Führer as I waited for the Christkindl. I, however, had the advantage of the very young: I could both fervently believe and disbelieve. I well remember leaning out of the window on a clear frosty night and wondering how the Christkindl could keep an eye on me and everyone, and how the Heavenly Child could decide who was good enough to have every wish fulfilled. I gazed up at a sky festive with stars and a moon round as a tree ornament. Icicles gleamed on the edge of the roof, and snow sparkled. All at once I felt I was not alone. Not the wind, but a great wing fanned my glowing cheeks, and I had visions of a huge angel in a long white gown flying through our front windows with the Christmas tree and more presents than a flock of angels could possibly have carried.

My fantasy, however, did not keep me from the reality of hidden Christmas presents. I looked in every possible hiding place. Days passed before I could get upstairs unobserved to investigate a peacock-blue peasant wardrobe near the gallery. Then, one bright afternoon, back from a walk with Agnes, I changed into felt slippers. My tread, soft as a kitten, did not announce me as I climbed the stairs. I heard Father and Resi. The gallery door stood open and I peaked from behind the wardrobe. Resi's long ermine cloak lay spread out on a wicker settee. They were hidden under it; only the legs stuck out.

"Schazi, Schazi," Father said.

A struggle began under the cloak. I knew, and yet did not

know, the sweet wild game of two hiding away. On walks
through the woods, I had never been given a chance to look
when there was rustling in the thicket or in the tall grass of the
summer fields. I had heard my parents laugh and whisper and
kiss behind locked doors and had waited for their silence and
the creaking bed. I was not supposed to be there, and felt left
out, forgotten, ashamed, and marvelously part of it all.

The amazing turmoil under the white fur made me think of
apples cooking in strudel dough. As the bubbling, boiling motion took on a rhythm, the feet went crazy. I still have to laugh
at this carrying-on under the very eyes of those staunch Meinert
men in the portraits. Uncle Ernstl grinned his golden grin as
though he could hear Resi's ghostly moans. Then the commotion
stopped—so suddenly I went stiff and hardly dared to breathe.
They lay still, Resi's fur-trimmed boot resting on Father's leg.

"I've never been able to persuade you to do anything without
making love," he said under the cloak.

Resi's head popped up, tousled, pink-cheeked. She smiled. "You
haven't persuaded me at all."

"You need more persuading!" He tried to pull her down again.
The cloak fell off her shoulders. She sat there naked, her dress
bundled around her waist. Her breasts sat up higher than Mother's and were not as large, but the nipples stuck out. I had already noticed this through her dresses. Father's shirt and tie kept
smoothing over them. She kept pushing him away. It was so hi-
larious, I wanted to pounce on them.

"You're mad, Ferdl." She held down his hands. "Crazy to smug-
gle me into the house, bring me all the way up here in broad
daylight."

"I brought you up here because it's private. I wanted to have
a little talk, that's all. See, I even left the door open. But you're
such a terrible flirt, no one is safe."

She tried to pull up her dress and he grabbed, held her, and
they kissed for a long time. Then they sat gazing at each other,
smiling, foolish. He helped her button the dress. They looked
immensely pleased with each other, she leaning against him in
the sun. "There's no need for you to run off. Stay in Vienna, Reserl; we can all go to midnight Mass the way we did last year."

She shook her head and said, "We're Jews."

"I think you've started making so much of it because you want to tease me. Eugene doesn't care. He loves Christmas music and giving presents."

I wanted to rush over to her and beg her to stay. The mere mention of all the presents from Eugene Romberg made my head spin. But most of all I wanted to be with Eli.

Resi did not give in. "How about Ann Marie? She certainly doesn't want us around, does she?"

My father, at the mention of Mother, began to fumble around, buckling his belt. "She's a little jealous," he said.

"Jealous of me?" Resi chirped. "She took you away from me!"

"All right, all right." He kissed her snub nose. "You're both jealous and I love you both."

She tilted her head like a ruffled bird. "Does Eugene love us both?"

"How can he help it? And the children have such fun. So you stay."

She jumped up and slipped away from him, taking the cloak with her. I was already inside the wardrobe when she said, "I need a change of air."

I certainly needed a change of air, for I almost suffocated with the smell of mothballs while I waited for them to be gone.

✿   ✿   ✿

People we knew often went away for "a change of air," to a spa or cure resort, when life in Vienna became complicated by love or hate, by personal or political problems. Eli left Vienna for the Semmering with his parents and his nurse before we had another chance to play or be alone together—Frau Schwester saw to that. She remained firmly planted by his side and listened to every word we exchanged.

The limousine stood waiting at our gate. My parents were persuading Eugene Romberg and Resi to come back to Vienna for their New Year's Eve celebration. "We are counting on you," Papa said. "Without you it wouldn't be the same."

"If you put it that way, Ferdl . . ." Resi laughed.

"I wish I could stay in Vienna over Christmas," Eli whispered to me. "I am feeling fine, but everyone is worrying about me. Something must be going on. Do you know anything?"

I knew much more than I could have put into words, but Frau
Schwester led him away to the door.

Eugene Romberg kissed Mama's hand twice.

"Until New Year's Eve," she said.

"Auf Wiedersehen."

Eli and I parted without another word. I simply ran from the
room.

Nothing pleased me after the Rombergs had driven away. My
father told me to stop acting up; Eli would be back in Vienna
before the end of the month. I stamped my foot and said I wanted
Eli now. He pointed out sternly that my shoelace was untied. I
said I didn't care. While he watched, I overwound my ballerina
music box, and the dancing girl stopped with a click in the middle of her waltz. Then I burst into tears. He handed me over to
Mother and said he would see about having it repaired.

Mama took me onto her lap. I cuddled against her soft blue
blouse and tried to imitate Resi's moans, until she began to wonder whether I had a stomach ache. She hoped I wasn't coming
down with something, because she was planning to take me to
Magda Hohentahler's birthday party.

"I don't like the Hohentahler girls," I said. "I like Eli."

My grandmother had taken me to the Hohentahlers' quite often. All the rooms, even the passageways, served as storage for
the antique furniture from the Landsitz-Hohentahler, the estate
that had to be sold after the First World War. During my last
visit, I had discovered a collection of chamber pots stored in the
washroom of the downstairs toilet. Magda had caught me holding a gilded pot and glared down at me from her long neck. No
one but Habsburgs had ever used the golden pot, she said. I had
put it right back onto the shelf and told her I was only looking,
but she and her sisters never stopped teasing me about using
potties.

When Mother handed me over to Agnes, my mood did not
improve. In the kitchen I complained that the cocoa was too hot.
Agnes sat down with me and poured it back and forth between
two cups. "Now you're going to stop fretting. How do you think
Eli Romberg would feel in Vienna, when his Mutti won't allow
a Christkindl to come, and you enjoy yourself with your presents?"

The cup she handed to me was decorated with little rosebuds. Fritz Janicek had often defied Agnes and drunk his coffee from one of these fine china cups. I was on the lookout for Fritz Janicek. He could not be dismissed.

Mother and I were in the car on our way to the Hohentahler party when I saw his face again.

"That was Fritz Janicek driving past us in that florist's van."

"Nonsense. He's locked up."

We arrived at the Hohentahlers' and I forgot about Fritz. Two doleful mermaids at the entrance interested me because they were stripped to the waist and their nipples protruded like Resi's. The town house was three stories high and plain. Stucco above the windows had crumbled away, leaving only a dark blemish. It had been built for an admiral Hohentahler, and the rooms felt cold and damp, summer and winter. Agnes had made me wear woolen underclothing under my blue taffeta party dress.

An old servant let us in and danced around us like a big, friendly dog. He had known Mother when she was a child, and his jowls shook with enthusiasm as he bent down to take my coat. The same old chests, tables, and dark divans stood lined up waiting for better days. While the servant spoke to my mother, I drew a devil's face on a dusty hall stand which was loaded with children's coats and hats. Just as I made a long tongue, I noticed Mama was taking Puppe out of her big muff.

"Oh, no!" I said. "What did you bring her for?"

The doll, resting on Mother's arm, eyes closed, looked harmless, quite inanimate. Canvas showed under the tightly braided hair. But I hated her with an odd sense of finality. "Ach, ja," the kind old servant exclaimed. "How I remember you with that dolly! All the little girls will love to see her."

"If she comes, I don't want to," I said.

Fortunately, Berthold came along at that moment, carrying a balloon in each hand. He had left the door open behind him, and I heard children laughing and shrieking. His arms waved; he came bounding along as though he were conducting laughter. Mama quickly pushed the doll back inside her muff and placed her carefully on top of my drawing on the hall stand.

"Too much noise, too many girls—cousins, second cousins, third cousins. Girls, girls, and more to come!" Berthold's uniform coat and pants seemed even shorter, and his hair stood up in whirls.

Mother looked at him and laughed. He put his arms around her and laughed with her. They often greeted each other this way: overcome with relief at not being apart. I wedged myself between them and joined in. Each time I met with Berthold, laughter would be spontaneous as a cry of pain.

"Come on," he said. Our voices bounced off historic walls and dark furniture; corridors flew past us as we went bounding along. His cheeks looked flushed, his eyes danced. With him I never walked. He always ran, bypassing anything that he did not consider fun. He tied his balloons to a knight's armor, then whisked us in and out of the drawing room where his mother, my grandmother, and his paternal grandmama, Her Highness, held court, flanked by Hanna Roth and some of her ladies.

He had forewarned me about his own bearded Oma, who had not shaved since Emperor Franz Joseph's funeral. She honored me with a scratchy kiss and said, "Who have we here, a pretty little doll?" I withdrew at once. Tears came into her eyes. "Ja, Hanna, as we were saying, the plundering hordes must have made off with the imperial dolls." She gave way to a little sob; her wig of curls slipped to one side. I could see she was bald. Berthold gave her a kiss, and smiling through tears, she proceeded to tell him it was high time he graduated and got married to his Annerl. He was the only one who didn't laugh.

My grandmother reminded Her Highness that she had attended my mother's wedding and told her I was a Meinert. Her Highness said, "That can't be, quite out of line." Berthold took my hand. His grandmother brightened. "If you have any sense, you rogue, you'll wait a few years. You can marry this little doll and get her back into line."

We fled. "What's 'getting in line'?" I asked in the corridor.

Berthold and Mother laughed, and they each took one of my hands, swinging me up the stairs. "*Voilà*," he said in a low voice. "Behold the general, Herzog von Hohentahler, my father and mother's uncle."

The duke general and his dachshund had come out of the study. They both wore kaiserly uniform coats that looked as short and tight as Berthold's but kept them comfortably warm and self-important. There was a unique resemblance between father and son: if the duke had gone to the house of mirrors in the

Prater to laugh at his own elongated face, he would have seen the image of cheerful Berthold.

I was glad when he ordered his dog "on guard" and made him sit up while we exchanged greetings. Not long ago I had ventured into the study to look around. Tables and desks were covered with old war maps full of tin soldiers, quite like Father's desk with its chess games that I was not allowed to touch. I had stood up on a chair to look at one of the tattered banners on the wall, when all of a sudden Radetzki, the dachshund, an old warrior, had darted out from under the desk and chased me, nipping my legs.

"It's freezing up here, *Vater*," Berthold said. "While you're winning lost battles, spooky Hanna eats up all the good pastries from Demel's. The countess Reyna is here. Why don't you go down?"

Berthold's father said, "Retreat!" and Radetzki ran into the study and vanished under the desk with a snarl. His master marched downstairs with military dignity.

"He actually asked the school to flunk me and my friends, to hold us back for a year, keep us from going to Germany. All because I refused to join the sissy Monarchists with their Otonia Club. Not a decent horseman among them."

Mother did not agree, and they argued about horses and riders as we walked along the icy corridor. I stopped at a broken window and looked down to the little palace, the enclosed courtyard with the shrine and the stone angel. Berthold and Mother used to play down there and pretend they were king and queen. The sky was milky and cast a white light onto the spires and domes of the city. Then I noticed the truck. I was sure it was the same one Fritz Janicek drove. Now it stood empty in the alley between the Hohentahler fence and the little palace wall.

Mother was not watching. She had taken down her braids. Berthold took her comb and went to work as though he were currying his horse. I opened the window and leaned out. Fritz Janicek was not down there. I felt as if an invisible hand was pushing me down; my head spun. There was a loud crash. I squealed. Berthold was beside me at once; he picked me up and closed the window.

"It's nothing. My crazy friends in the winter garden are always dancing and knocking down potted plants."

I shook my head and stared out the window.

"What did you think it was?" he whispered, rolling his eyes.

"Whangdoodle," I said into his ear.

"Ach, ja, that one. Bangs and bashes. Eyes of fire, bayonet teeth, blows mustard gas . . ."

"Nein, nein. Not a dragon," I said. "It's invisible. It's waiting. Huge and hungry."

"Ready to gobble up everything." He kissed my face. "I won't let the bad whangdoodle get you. You're my little fiancée, what?"

Mother took me from him and held me tight. "She's been on edge ever since Krampus Day."

"Naturally," Berthold said.

I wanted him to keep holding me, to have him all to myself, but he returned to Mother's hair. "Your mama always wore it in braids, under hats. When we used to play together, she let me undo it. Isn't it beautiful!"

He took my hand and hers. We rushed into the glass veranda, the winter garden which was always warm and often full of his followers, cousins, sisters, and friends, known as the "Flunkers' Club." They were dancing to a crank-up phonograph. A broken flowerpot left no doubt about the loud bang I had heard. But the moment Mother and Berthold started hopping about, I knew invisible eyes were watching Mama's hair fly about and her breasts bounce up and down under a tight, girlish dress.

I stayed behind a rubber plant. Two girls on the other side of it talked as if I were invisible.

"She's got to come here and dance with him because she married an old man," said the plump, beautiful one.

"Is he a Jew?" asked the neat-looking, plain girl.

"Not a Jew, but only a *von*. Their house is full of Jews. Bertl doesn't care. He dances with Jews as a paid partner during five-o'clock tea at the Jolly Bar. And he had the nerve to ask me to come. I had no idea what he was doing there. Can you imagine? He didn't think I'd mind watching. Told me he dances to make money to support his horse."

The music was playing a sad song, and a rasping voice, neither male nor female, sang "Blown Away by the Wind." A chair fell over without being touched. I knew the whangdoodle was about.

"Do you still see a lot of Berthold?" asked the neat girl.

"Certainly not. He is almost a gigolo. For all I know, Meinert pays him to escort his wife."

The song ended, and I wanted to ask what "gigolo" meant, but Berthold sank into a big wicker armchair, raised his hand, and yelled, "Heil Hitler!" The two girls and all the others joined in. So did Mother, and my own hand shot up as if I had no control over it. Something made me turn my head to the glass wall. Down below in the alley, a man with a sack was climbing into the truck.

Berthold came over and turned me around. "You know that was only fun, Reyna."

"What?" I asked, watching the truck drive off.

"The 'Heil Hitler.'"

*   *   *

"It wouldn't be half the fun without you," Berthold said to Hanna Roth as he led her toward the grand piano in the ballroom. Children laughed, clapped their hands. She took off her gloves and played "The Blue Danube Waltz." Her legs dangled, the puffball hat nodded close to the keys. I still believe she compelled us to dance. Couples formed—always one big person with one little person. We waltzed around the huge room, our bright images muted and multiplied in the spotted mirrors.

"Come on," Berthold said to me. "Stand on my shoes. Isn't it fun? I can make anyone waltz. Even my horse. It takes a little love, that's all."

The mirror walls gave me a picture of myself: a tiny creature in a stiff blue dress dancing with a pair of long dark legs. In the ceiling mirrors, a crack crept across the spotted glass. Cherubs swam around the edges, dark and bruised and chipped like babes that have fallen into evil hands.

"'Danube so gray, so gray, so gray,'" Berthold sang. Mother drifted past, turning a small boy in a dark sailor suit. I felt as though all this had happened before. "'Danube so gray, so gray, so gray.'" It was as if we were under water, deep down where the Danube is blue as a summer night sky and the Danube King holds court among nymphs and giant carps. The glass ceiling rippled. We turned faster and faster, spinning around as though we would never stop; the myth of our heritage held us like a whirlpool in a great river. I clung to Berthold, as if to surface was to perish.

"I will always remember the beautiful dancing," Hanna Roth said when everyone thanked her for the music. She was surrounded by little girls who were being dressed by Fräuleins. All of a sudden she stared into space, turned, and walked out into the drizzle. Lamplight made sparkling stones on her veil glitter. I watched her dip down past the mermaids and scurry off. A fiacre stood waiting. The driver doffed his bowler hat, picked her up like a child, and swung her into the carriage.

Berthold took us to the car, and I cuddled up to Mother and pretended to be asleep while they whispered. He handed her an envelope. Then he kissed her. The door banged, and the car began to move. Mother sat with her eyes closed, smiling. I did not want her to know I loved Berthold better than anyone.

The car honked three times and she sat up. We had come to an abrupt halt. Several men were running in front of the car, chasing each other. It looked like a game in the dark. Other men stood around a placard column, peeling off posters, tearing them, and throwing them to the winds. There was a heavy fine for littering in Vienna, but I saw no police.

Heinz drove on slowly; then he had to step on the brake so hard we fell forward. He called out, "Please excuse," as though it were all his fault that grown men were fighting like street boys. A struggle was going on in front of our car: one man lay on his back kicking another one, who was trying to get on top of him, shouting, "Swine-dog!" I could not understand this insult because I liked both pigs and dogs. A rock struck our windshield. Mama pulled me down and ducked just as Heinz turned the car into a side street. A white swastika gleamed on the remains of the old city wall.

"Are you frightened, Herzerl?" Mama asked, holding me tight.

Otto von Falkenburg the brave had helped to drive the heathens away from the city walls. "I'd like to throw that rock right back at them!" I said. "Why are they fighting, anyway?"

"Probably students. They are always fighting." She opened the partition and told Heinz he had been simply marvelous. I peered out into the narrow street, looking for more fights, but people walked about quietly: a pair arm in arm, heads touching, and a skinny lady being dragged past them by a demonic boxer dog.

Mama was rummaging around in her muff when we reached the Graben. She held up a doll's shoe. "Puppe! I don't know how I could forget all about her. Now she's gone!" She knocked on the glass partition with her diamond ring. "Heinz, I'm so sorry, but we must drive back at once!"

"One of the little girls must have taken her, played with her and left her lying somewhere in the house. You didn't notice her at the party, Reyna?"

I was questioned more than once. After all, I had threatened to throw Puppe out of the window on several occasions. When we went back to the hall stand, a bouquet of yellow roses stood on the devil's face I had drawn into dust. Mama laid the muff down. I think she hoped someone might slip the doll back into it while we searched the house.

We went from room to room with Berthold's hateful sisters. Magda carried her new turtle and would not allow me to touch it. The others fetched this or that old doll, pretending to be helpful. Berthold's mother came and started opening drawers and closets and looking under furniture in the hallway. The Hohentahler sisters told me to go and see whether Puppe was in one of the chamber pots I liked so much. They would never have teased me if Berthold had been at home, but he was out, dancing for his horse at the Jolly Bar.

After Mama had spoken to Father, she telephoned Berthold. I could hear music on the phone. She was kept waiting. I imagined Berthold hopping about the dance floor with someone in a fluffy dress wearing lots of lipstick and iridescent brown shoes.

He did not keep Mother waiting long after she had told him that her doll was missing. The moment he walked in the door, she wandered to the piano where the dwarf had been sitting. Running her fingers over the keys, she began to play a Clementi sonatina. She gave up from the start.

Berthold, who had always made fun of the doll, ran around anxiously. I went along as he questioned his sisters one by one, threatening them with a good smack if they were lying. "Did you break her, did you drop her by accident? It's better you tell me now." The girls stopped laughing. "We must find the old

doll for her," he said. "She's lost without it." He took my hand
and we ran back to the ballroom. "I have an idea!" he called to
Mama.

Her hands slipped from the keys.

"Old Hanna took her, I'm sure," said Berthold.

Mama began to play again. "Nonsense." She sounded tired.
"We all saw her leave. She had nothing to hide her in."

"The umbrella," I said.

"Right, *Liebstes*. Brilliant!"

"We'll speak to her on the telephone. Unless you want Heinz
to drive us over there and take her by surprise. Anyway, since
she's supposed to know everything, she should at least be able
to tell us what happened to your doll."

Mama went back to playing her sonatina and left it up to him.

"She sounds amazed," he reported after he had phoned Hanna
Roth. "Of course, she could be putting me on."

At home, after a solemn dinner, Mama went to the piano to
avoid all the sympathy and concern. I seem to remember her being at the piano for days. The telephone kept ringing. Those who
had criticized her games with Puppe now made the greatest effort to get the doll back. Agnes went to pray for the return of
the doll. Poldi and Lise took the opportunity to run to the police
station to consult their inspector. He, oddly enough, suspected a
servant. Berthold went to see the old highness, his Oma, because
he remembered she had talked about dolls. She could have picked
up Puppe without giving it a thought.

One morning when my mother was still in bed, Herr Krummerer arrived in bright green plus-fours. He was a private detective, and he took my fancy the moment he struggled out of his
minute Steyrer "baby," a small, round car. He whipped out a large
notebook and studied our house as though he were about to draw
it. I had a chance to admire his bowlegs in the white knee socks
worn by many Nazis. I listened as my father described the doll
to him as very valuable, a family piece, an original Antonelli.
Herr Krummerer kept saying, "Jawohl, indeed," licking his pencil and writing in the notebook. He took down the names of all
the children who had attended the party. My father told him
to be discreet—they were all children from first-class families.
"A child or someone irresponsible picked up the doll. Now they

are embarrassed. They didn't realize they were stealing. We have to use a little strategy," he said.

"It was not a child," I said. "It was Fritz Janicek."

Father laughed. "She is full of ideas."

7

Christkindl

UNCERTAINTY, LIKE THE ODOR of something rotten, hung over us and could not be dispelled by the fragrance of cinnamon, melting butter, vanilla. The festive season began as usual for me, in the kitchen with Agnes. I marked each day on the calendar above the sink. As Christmas approached, I stirred dough, helped to ice cakes, and licked bowls. I tasted everything, even flour, salt, and yeast. Agnes baked, prayed, and worried. When letters for Mother came from Germany she felt she should hide them so that Father wouldn't see them.

Mother went out almost every day; I hardly missed her. One evening she came home in a fierce temper. Father sat safely ensconced behind the evening paper. The headlines said: "Doctor Schuschnigg Lacks Clarity." I, on the carpet, writing my daily reminder to the Christkindl, decided to make myself quite clear with a picture of a small fuzzy dog I wanted. Mother was late and had not even bothered to take off her wet fur before she stormed in. Neither of us got up to greet her. She tore the snow-covered hat from her braids, shook it, and sprinkled me. "So, you hire a detective to find my doll and he follows me!" she shouted at Father.

"He was hired to find the doll," he said from behind the paper. "Watching you he hoped would give him a lead."

She shed her damp fur. "Now he's given up and is just watching me."

"Your courier service for the Committee of Seven is treason," Father said.

"Nonsense. The committee was formed to help make peace."

"Fine patriots, who get their orders from Adolf Hitler! I hardly need Herr Krummerer to find out what you are up to. Half of Vienna is talking about you at Café Rebhuhn." I had been there when she had handed the headwaiter a tip and a thick envelope. The room had been full of men; all of them had smoked, talked, and stared at us. I was glad we didn't stay.

"How can you and Bertl believe that the Nazis want to keep the peace when they're throwing bombs?" Father looked her up and down, from the dark, tight dress to the red boots, until she blushed. Her eyes sparkled; she faced him, hand on hip, a rebel. "You're playing around with an unsavory group, Annerl. One of these days the police will crack down—"

"So you're afraid I'm going to be arrested," she interrupted. "But that's not the only reason you have me watched, is it?"

"Will you go to jail like Fritz Janicek?" I asked.

Father put down the paper and took me on his knee. "Now, wouldn't that be a sensation? The newspapers would love it."

Mother did not like the idea. She bit her lower lip and ambled over to the piano, where she played a boring piece called "Rondo."

"Anyway, Fritz is no longer locked up; I saw him in a florist's truck," I said.

"When was that?" Father asked.

"Nonsense," Mother said. "We were driving to the Hohentahlers' and she was all excited. You know she imagines things."

"I saw him," I said.

Mother smiled as she played on. "So, Ferdl—there's something for your detective to investigate. But you'd better watch out, Herr Krummerer happens to be a National Socialist."

"I know," I said. "It's those white knee socks." Poldi had knitted a pair for me to go with my leather pants. I refused to put them on. Nazis wore them instead of swastikas. White knee socks would, I was afraid, turn me into one. I knew about spells, princes transformed into beasts. White socks, swastikas, and magic chants of Hitler slogans produced Nazis. My own mother had been bewitched all winter long.

Anger between my parents seldom lasted, but I enjoyed high favor after this quarrel. They looked embarrassed, avoided each other, and made a lot of me. The very next morning, Mama offered to take me into town, and Father said he had already planned to take me along to deliver Christmas baskets; we would end up at my grandmother's, and I could pay her a visit. I had to choose between the Committee of Seven and the police with my mother and a ride in a beer truck with Papa. When he promised to take me to the Christkindl market on the way home, I said I wanted to go with him.

Baskets each filled with a goose, wine and fruit, smelling of oranges and apples, sat on the back of the truck. I dozed off as usual and missed the vintners' village and Vlado's cottage. When I woke up, we had stopped in front of a dark tenement adorned with a brightly lit white bakery.

"You were only about two years old when I brought you here to show you off to Resi's mother. Do you remember?"

"I remember coconut kisses," I said.

When Frau Heller pushed one into my mouth and filled a paper poke, thanking Father for the wonderful basket in her Hernalser dialect, I remembered her. The smiling face reminded me of Resi, only this woman was fat and white-haired. She kept her voice low because Herr Heller, the baker, worked at night and slept during the day. "Eugene would have liked to have had a Christmas Eve dinner with us. He used to love it here. And how can our Reserl be a Jew?" She tried to take Lebkuchen hearts and chocolate Paris towers and put them all into the paper poke for me, but Father stopped her. "We're just simple people, plain Catholics," she said. She picked me up, gave me a vanilla-flavored kiss, and said she missed beautiful little Eli. "Ja, everything might have been different. You certainly were like a son to us, Herr Ferdl."

On the way to Grandmama's I ate coconut kisses. Father made a funny mouth when I pushed one between his lips. I thought of how he had kissed Resi in the gallery. "Who do you love better, Aunt Resi or Mama?'

He looked baffled. "Whatever makes you ask such a thing? Is it because I always take a basket to both the Hellers and Grandmama?"

I could hardly admit that I had heard him tell Resi he loved them both.

"You love different people in different ways," he said as he turned onto the Ring. He didn't say any more until we passed the Maria Theresa statue. The seated figure of the portly empress was enhanced by a wig of frozen snow and a lapful of ice. "You are too young to understand this, but it is easier to like someone a lot than to love them. I like Resi immensely; who wouldn't? She was the darling of Vienna. Mama belongs to me, and that is quite different."

I actually preferred the Heller bakery to the little palace. My grandmother usually had some old, formal people with her. I was never allowed to interrupt while they talked of the exiled empress Zita, the crown prince, and, inevitably, the old days of the court. Grandmama's friends ate their cakes daintily, and even their memories were polite and faded like old photographs. Not like Hanna Roth, who ate with gusto, swallowing a small cake in one bite, and whose words created pictures like a magic lantern and sent them flickering through my head.

This time, however, to my surprise, we found the countess alone in her upstairs sitting room, the famous pink salon. Two hundred years ago, Empress Maria Theresa had decided this room, where she took breakfast after Mass with her favorite, Stefanie von Dornbach, would be pink as a rosy sunrise. I pictured them sitting together at breakfast in their white wigs and beribboned dresses, listening to Mozart. The piano where he had played remained untouched in the left corner. Pink was not my grandmother's favorite color, but whenever anything had to be replaced in this room, the new had to be exactly the same as the old.

We found the countess standing on a pink padded footstool, peering out of the window through a pair of old field glasses. "Excuse me, my dears," she said. "I just had to see whether the police will round up those Nazi ruffians at the cinema. They're showing *A Song Goes Round the World*, with Joseph Schmidt. Swastikas and the word *Jew* are smeared all over the posters. Now they're blocking the box office. I like Joseph Schmidt—such a tiny man, but with the voice of a giant, and those sad eyes. They didn't stop me from going to see the film. I had escorts who cleared the entrance. I've already telephoned. I hope the police come and arrest all those useless boys."

I could have told her that Mother might be arrested with the

Committee of Seven, but Father gave me a warning look and changed the subject. "I have the pleasure of making my Christmas delivery." He grinned, reminding her of their very first meeting, when she had sent him down to the kitchen like a delivery man. "Most everything will keep until you get back from Belgium."

She jumped down from the footstool, all smiles, and thanked him with a kiss on the cheek. She had just received a marvelous note from His Serene Highness, Prince Otto himself. She showed it to Father, but I was far more interested in the Nazis and the police and the field glasses. As soon as Father left, I asked for them, but she refused. My grandmother never wanted me to see anything unpleasant.

"I only use them when I have to, myself," she said. "I prefer field glasses to spectacles. They are nice and big, and I always mislay spectacles. Perhaps one is meant to see less and remember more as one grows old. When I put on my spectacles, I see chipped plaster, flaking paint, cracked ceilings, and broken windowpanes. I also see the sadness and lines of age on the familiar faces of my devoted old friends. And I have to avoid mirrors."

She put the field glasses into one of the many drawers of her escritoire. We sat down side by side on the velvet-covered bench. "I have just realized for the first time how much your dear father has matured. What a good man he is, Reyna. How much his kind face reminds me of our kaiser." She pointed at the portrait on the pink wall. The kaiser, like my father, wore a Styrian suit with green lapels and staghorn buttons. In this picture, his whiskers were still blond. "He came to see me after your grandfather was lost in the war; he had aged shockingly. He loved this room."

She picked up an envelope and let me help her melt sealing wax and press the imprint of the falcon sitting on the sun into the wax with a ring. Then she allowed me to address the letter in careful print: "High Well-Born Frau Hanna von Roth." She told me she had written to Hanna and asked her to get Puppe back to my mother in time for Christmas. "Dolls have always been her concern. It is up to her. She has a talent for finding lost objects. It is a family piece, even if I have no fondness for such a mascot." She went on to explain how she had been troubled when Mother carried Puppe around with her even after she was married; it reminded her of Christina von Kortnai.

"Is it true that Christina von Kortnai carried Puppe even at the czar's court?" I asked.

"She caused a sensation. You can imagine my embarrassment when during a court dinner she talked to the doll and ignored her partner. I wanted to be a nun, but she whisked me away from the convent to spite my father, Count Otto, and took me into the world without the least concern for me. She never understood me . . . never forgave me when I decided to part with her and stay in Vienna. And she never came to my wedding, because I had to tell her she could not carry Puppe at St. Stephen's."

"Mother did," I said.

"That was all Hanna's fault. But your mother was still very young. When she inherited the old doll, she was about your age, and it seemed natural that she should love the toy. I'm sure the Christkindl will bring you a doll, too."

I told her I never played with dolls and wanted a dog.

She smiled. "Dogs are better than horses. Your mother ran after horses as soon as she learned to walk. To begin with, I was quite glad when Hanna brought the doll to Falkenburg and stayed on and introduced your mama to girlish games. There was no food in Vienna just after the war, and I had Hanna stay on while I went to the city to sell some of my property, just to buy food and clothing. Those were hard times. I needed money for other reasons. Austria always came first with me. By the time I returned to Falkenburg, my little girl had turned away from me to talk to the doll. This went on so much I had to forbid her to have the toy in my presence. Then she avoided me and kept company with Hanna, who encouraged those fantastic games. This made me move back to Vienna at once. Fortunately, Frau Traude had come to join Hanna. They got together and opened the hat salon. But your mother clung to the doll. The way she acted reminded me so much of Baroness Christina. I worried a lot. Your mother never made friends with girls her own age when she went to convent school. Fortunately, she began to play with young Cousin Berthold. Then your dear father came along, and he became everything to her: a brother, a father, a loving husband." A tear dropped onto the envelope in her hand. "I was not so lucky. Nor was I much of a mother, I'm afraid. I hope to be a better grandmother; I'll guard over you whenever I can."

I did not like the idea of being guarded, because I feared it might keep me away from the Water Castle when Eli came back. I began to finger her von Kortnai necklace: moonstones trembling like dewdrops on delicate chains between diamonds and emeralds. My grandmother wore this necklace on special occasions. My visit was evidently important.

"You are very quiet today. Are you all right?"

I told her I felt fine. I sat silent and awestruck as she took a rose from a vase and used the stem to wet a stamp. Her white hands had protruding blue veins which I had always suspected contained blue blood. My own hands looked insignificant and plump, but we did have the same white dots on our fingernails. Agnes said this meant good luck. Our future seemed united. For the first time, I felt at home at the little palace.

My grandmother's escritoire had many little shelves, and I noticed a beautiful dark-blue velvet box and reached for it. She stayed my hand and offered me the praline box instead; we each took three chocolates. "When we were convent girls, we did not get too many sweets. Now I never have enough."

"What is in the velvet box?" I asked.

She opened it for me and I went, "Ahhhh." A small pistol lay on white satin. The barrel was decorated with engraved ivy.

"It once belonged to our Empress Elizabeth." She pointed at the crown inside the lid of the box. "She did not wish to own this pistol after the crown prince died from a bullet wound. I asked for it." My grandmother closed the box and put it back on the shelf with finality. "She kept it loaded, and I left it that way."

"Have you ever fired it?"

"It has never been fired."

"Are you ever going to try it out?"

"I would think not. I merely keep it so that no one else will," she said quite pointedly.

She let me play with the sealing ring until Father walked in, followed by her old friend the Rittmeister. Under a long cloak, the Rittmeister wore his old Austrian uniform. His clear brown eyes sparkled, and his upright posture contradicted the age on his face. He bowed, clicked his heels. "I have the honor," he said, and kissed my grandmother's hand. I always thought he knew he was funny but didn't care.

"We'll show them, Herr Direktor," he said to Father. "We'll put an end to the disgusting carry on in our streets. There is an important meeting on the eleventh of January. I hope you will do us the honor to attend. Let them try something. We'll show them. A man like you, Herr von Meinert, belongs with us. I have high hopes now that our great ambassadress is going to confer with our prince." He bowed to Grandmama and kissed her hand again.

Father went through his usual peasant routine. The Rittmeister took him up, told him not to worry. When the Habsburg monarchy was restored, Meinert wines would be drunk at court. That was a promise. Those who worked on the land were loyal to the crown; peasant leaders had never faltered.

My father became embarrassed, and we left as soon as the old officer had admired me, the roses, the entire room. On the way out, Papa made a note in a little book so that he wouldn't forget to send a basket to Grandmama's friend. He told me that the Rittmeister refused to draw a pension from a government that he didn't recognize. He would never accept money, but a big basket full of good things and some nice wine would help.

On our way home we stopped at the Christkindl market. Father said he wanted to buy glazed fruit. The Englischen Tanten loved them. I did not love the Meinert aunts. They gave me the wrong presents, and I knew they had taken my father to court to claim control over their half of the brewery. "They're my only close relatives," Father said. "They mean well and are fine ladies. Anyway, there's a woman selling old dolls in the market. We will take a look while we are here."

He hurried along, and I followed. It was cold and almost dark. An icy wind tore at the canvas on front stalls. Gingerbread men danced on strings. A man selling chestnuts at his black stove was surrounded by stout market women. All wrapped up in knitted shawls, they stood around warming their hands and stomping their feet. They shouted to Father, in coarse voices, taunting him to buy. He answered in their dialect, and they laughed.

Sweet-smelling pine trees stood on display near the glazed-fruit stand. I munched glazed cherries. Behind me the fishman yelled, "Get one here! The most beautiful carp!" In the crowded tank, fish gasped, glaring with gold-rimmed eyes, imprisoned and waiting to be killed and cooked on Christmas Eve, when everyone ate carp. I gulped down a cherry and tried to follow Father. We became separated by a cart full of blood oranges. A man in a cap called out, "Juicy, bloody ones; juicy, bloody ones!" Women crowded around the cart, hemming me in. A pair of live chickens tied together by the legs dangled in front of me. They hung upside down, cackling and feebly flapping their wings. I smelled sweat, oranges, cheese, kerosene from lamps, and something acrid, rotten, and dead.

My father came back, lifted me up, and carried me through the crowd, and the market changed. Wooden toys danced around gilded stars, and glass angels with dragonfly wings twinkled within arm's reach. All around me, tinsel and spun glass, sugar angels, and more Christmas trees . . .

At the edge of the market he put me down. He had found the doll peddler. Red-nosed and wrapped up in a tattered fur, she greeted us with smiles. "Buy the dolls, Your Excellency, buy the dolls for the little girl."

I saw at once that Puppe was not among the insipid old dolls. Marble-eyed and harmless, they stood lined up with outstretched arms. My father examined them carefully, shook his head, and produced a picture from his wallet: Mother on their honeymoon in Venice, holding Puppe. He offered the woman a big reward if she could find the stolen doll, and handed her his card. "A wig of natural red hair. That should make it easy to find this doll."

"I'll search, I'll try to find, but mine are beautiful, Your Excellency. I will sacrifice them, I'll make you a price." She picked up a baby doll with a puffy round china face and dimpled hands. "Look at the embroidered dress. The big girl in the picture would love her, or this one here, the little one. Wouldn't you like the pretty baby?"

"No, no." I stepped back to avoid having the doll thrust into my arms. "I would rather have a pistol."

"A pistol!" the woman said with disgust.

My father laughed. "She should have been a boy."

He actually looked around for a pistol, but we could not find one I liked. I ended up with a gingerbread hussar and a bagful of hot chestnuts.

        ✵   ✵   ✵

During the war, I was to think back to Christmas 1937 as my last Christkindl. Once more we gathered on Holy Eve in a small sitting room at the rear of the house: the Meinert aunts; the doctor with his black bag (in case someone swallowed a carp bone); Pfarrer Kronz, a country priest distantly related to Father—a frail man with a powerful smile. The maids in Sunday dirndl dresses served cordials, and the laundrywoman bustled around emptying Father's ashtrays. No one could coax me from the door. I stood with my ear pressed against it, listening for the Christmas bell. Mama and Agnes had already gone to open the window and let the Christkindl fly in. My father was talking of the difficult times we all lived in, the uncertainty.

Pfarrer Kronz laughed. "Look at the child, she only thinks of the Christkindl. What a blessing." He was still recovering from an operation; his white face shone as though it had been polished. He must have been tired, but he was right beside me when I heard the bell and went bounding through the house. He witnessed my horror.

The room was dark, just as I knew it would be, with candles flickering on the tall tree, lights dancing on glass balls, silver chains, chocolate soldiers in glowing red tinfoil coats, the smell of burned sugar and a singed branch. I came to a halt, stepped back; my heart missed a beat. Row upon row of redheaded dolls confronted me; they were decked out in silk, lace, velvet—sweet and sickly, glass eyes staring at nothing, dimpled china hands held out stiff and cold as death.

"Dear me," said one of my aunts in English. "So many dolls for one little girl."

"I'm afraid," my mother said, "they're all for me." She picked up the hem of her gold lace dress, carefully stepped over the dolls, and went to the piano.

We always sang Christmas hymns before we looked at presents. My mother began to play "Holy Night," but no sound came from my lips as I surveyed the gathering of dolls. An unholy lot. Like fallen sisters of the lost Puppe. I imagined my mother gathering them all to her heart, dressing and undressing them, talking to them. There would never be even a moment for me.

Not until she began to play "A Rose Has Sprung from a Maiden Frail" did I recover enough to notice books, sweaters, boxes tied up with gold ribbons under the tree. And beside fur-trimmed boots my size, a basket. I heard faint yapping. My wish had been fulfilled. I forgot all about the dolls.

Before the song came to an end, the basket tipped over. A ball of brown fur shot out, pushing over a doll, sniffing a wig, snapping at a pink bow. It was a Pekingese. I ran to the puppy, picked it up. Soft, pug-nosed, with great dark eyes, it nipped my nose, licked my cheek, escaped, soiled the rug, tried to chew the doctor's black bag. I caught it and named it "Krampus." In a daze, I sat under the tree. I hardly noticed the maids and Mother gathering up the dolls and carrying them to a glass case. I was no longer on my own, and I whispered to Krampus the secret of the evil doll. He growled and yapped and seemed to understand. I told him Eli would soon be back.

Smiling faces surrounded me, and shiny eyes reflected the candlelight of the great tree.

"No way, no way," my father said, laughing. "I had nothing to do with this wholesale purchase. The Christkindl made a mistake, that's all."

While we sat at the table eating our Christmas carp, the telephone rang. Father answered and cried "Schazi!"

"Resi Romberg," Mother said. "I wonder what she wants."

My father took Mother aside and whispered something. He then telephoned the Romberg villa and told the porter that Herr and Frau Romberg would be back the next morning. I shouted with joy, but Mother told me something bad had happened to Resi's Hebrew teacher. They refused to discuss it in case it spoiled our Christmas.

The Rombergs did return, and came to see us the very next day. After I had introduced Eli to Krampus, I took him to the glass case and showed him the Christkindl's mistake. He stood hand on hip, examining the glass case full of unwanted dolls. A new haircut made him look older and taller. "What a great collection," he said.

"No one knows where they all came from. Mother likes only Puppe."

He blinked for a moment and regarded me as a stranger. "Collections are much better. If one gets lost or destroyed, you always have others. You know, like my kites, my birds. Birds often die." My puppy attacked his shoelace and he pushed it away, only to be attacked again.

"You mean I should have asked for more than one dog?" I asked.

He nodded, although I could tell he took a rather dim view of Krampus.

"I won't let anything happen to Krampus," I said. I picked the puppy up and held him tight. "I won't let him run away."

"David has to be helped," Resi was saying, "he wants to go to Palestine." She was sitting in the cozy corner with my parents. Eugene Romberg stood beside Mother's chair, but he was watching Eli and me at the glass case.

"Poor David was trying to save his side-locks and beard and his books from some Nazi thugs, and he lost an eye," Eli told me in a matter-of-fact tone of voice. "Now Mutti won't have a Hebrew teacher."

"Perhaps she should have more than one," I said. "A collection," I added, because I liked the word.

8

The Crystal Garden

LAUGHTER BELOW MY WINDOW woke me up on New Year's morning, 1938. The rising sun sparkled above a young silver pine like a leftover Christmas ornament. Papa stood among departing guests on top of the steps. He towered over them, flushed from the celebration. In evening clothes, he looked much more the countryman than in his peasant garb. Staying up all night only made him more animated. The leave-taking seemed endless and reluctant. Everyone talked, laughed, and Resi began to twirl over the flagstones in the courtyard, singing a popular song about glowing poppies as though it were an aria.

My father went down the steps and kissed her on the mouth just as Mama appeared in the doorway. He gathered Resi into his arms and carried her back to the others like a rescued child. Mama had flung her sable coat over her shoulders. Pale and dreamy in the bright morning light, she was passed around for hand kisses, embraces, a caress, another compliment. Eugene Romberg stayed close to her, and when her coat slipped, he carefully wrapped it around her. I could not hear any words of the chatter through the double window, but Resi said something and the kissing and laughing started all over again, as though they had only been rehearsing.

A small man in a top hat came and drew Eugene Romberg away from my mother. This was Cheese Hannes, who wanted to become Eugene's partner and merge his business with the Romberg dairies. He reached up and put his hand onto Eugene's shoulder; they spoke in confidence. Father had said that Cheese Hannes hated Eugene, yet he had invited them both.

Friends and enemies created a scene of mad conviviality that I could never forget. They sounded too loud, too gay, rather like actors in an empty theater. No one quite knew the next line; the next move depended on everyone else's uncertainty. What about Austria, Vienna? Would the curtain fall? Would it rise again? The questions were never asked. Not in polite, first-class society. I felt ashamed of all the guests, and found the wild enthusiasm embarrassing, because it involved my mother and father.

Cousin Berthold stood out in this crowd: young, proud yet unassuming in his tight school uniform, an understudy who is certain to become a star. His lack of pretense won my heart and glorified his magnificent arrogance. He did not even bother to take his turn among Mother's admirers, although he remained close to her as she flitted, turning from one to the other, so close that her green tulle skirt spilled over his dancing pumps. Her mass of hair had been gathered under a large yellow silk rose, but one strand had come loose, and the wind whipped it into Berthold's face. He did not flinch. When Papa finally escorted the guests down the steps, Berthold stayed behind.

The bustling females in their furs and long, fluffy gowns, the men in black vanished around the corner, singing, "Yes, there will be wine when we're no longer here." Resi's voice rose above all the others. Berthold was about to kiss Mama and take his leave when Eugene Romberg reappeared and came rushing toward her. I could not hear what he said; he took her hand, looking downtrodden and apologetic as he drew her away from her cousin. I suspected his feet were hurting. Berthold leaned against the door and pulled the uniform cap over his eyes. Perhaps he did not like to watch Eugene Romberg's sad performance with the little box, which no doubt contained a piece of jewelry. I had seen Eugene Romberg humiliated by Mama's refusal to accept his gifts on other occasions, but she always thanked him profusely and kissed his fat cheek.

He ran away as though he had been chased off. Mama could not see his half-smile, and she was about to run after him to make him feel better when Cousin Berthold reached out and took hold of her loose strand of hair, smiling as though he held the reins of his favorite horse. Mama stopped with surprise and turned her head. He pressed her hair to his lips, flung it away, and followed the singing guests to the gate. I threw all my pillows onto the floor and trampled on them in a sudden rage.

After my parents had gone to bed and the house became silent, I made my way downstairs in my flannel nightgown. The maids and Agnes had served a meal during the night and were asleep. On my way to the party rooms I found the yellow rose. I picked it up, held it against my face, and it stung me. I pulled the tiny swastika from its heart and put it back at once. Then I stuck the rose into my hair to make me feel like Mother. The sweetness of her perfume assailed me. She had let me sniff it when she found the bottle under the tree. "It's really too much," I said, in her voice. "But I adore it." She never found out who had given it to her, but any secret admirer should have been gratified by the way she splashed the scent onto her hair. Dressed up as a clown or a Hungarian peasant, she would hide her hair under hats, but a trail of perfume must have given her away long before the unmasking.

Doors between dining room, sitting room, and library had been flung back to create enough space for dancing. My father, as always, had turned off the lights before he went to bed. The curtains were still drawn, and I stumbled over a rolled-up carpet. Once my eyes became accustomed to the half-dark, I found a green velvet purse, took some lipstick out, and smeared my lips. A long, poison-green glove lay waiting for me in reptilian splendor. It went well with a lady who wore a swastika inside her rose and sipped champagne. I went around tasting leftover tartlets, candy, caviar, and carrying a half-empty crystal glass. When I became sick of that, I struck a match and tried to light a cigar. Then I almost dropped it. Father had come in barefooted and was laughing at me.

"Look here, Reyna Elizabeth von Meinert Dornbach Falkenburg. We don't drink stale champagne, and you should not even try to smoke a cigar—at least, not until you're over thirty. Promise!"

I promised and obediently went to wash my face and put away the glove and purse. Then I locked the rose with the swastika into the Falkenburg treasure box. I wished all the old love letters, cards from balls, and dried flowers had not been thrown away. When she had given me the box, my grandmother had said one had to be careful what one kept, but I had begun filling it up recklessly. The contents, like Meinert wine in the dark, gained potency each time I opened the box.

Mother never missed the Hitler picture, the Führer as a knight, which I had taken from her room, but when she came downstairs this morning she asked for the silk rose. When she couldn't find it, she wandered around among all the baskets and bouquets of flowers that had arrived while she was asleep. She wore a silk kimono that matched her hair. Sleeves rippled as she stooped, sniffing roses.

The bell rang again, and Poldi came in with a small bouquet wrapped up in tissue paper. "Have you seen the silk rose I wore in my hair?" Mother asked while she unwrapped the flowers. The red rose surrounded by forget-me-nots made her forget all about the lost silk flower. "A Biedermeier bouquet, how sweet! No one has ever sent me anything like this. It makes me feel like a dancing-school sweetheart." Color came into her cheeks when she read the card. Her hair hung over one shoulder in a thick braid; she flicked it back. Her lips moved, as though she were memorizing each word. Finally, she stuffed the card into her pocket.

"Who on earth sent this little bit of nonsense?" Father asked after breakfast. He took the little bouquet out of its vase, and water dripped onto the carpet. "Where is the card?"

Mother kept playing her sonatina. I sat on the floor with a collection of little New Year's trinkets she had allowed me to take off the flowers: lucky little pigs, clover leaves, chimney sweeps, toadstools. She gave me a warning look. "You know I always leave cards for you," she said to Father.

Everyone had sent flowers to Mother, as though she were ill, when they found out that she had been robbed of her doll. It was Father who had kept a list of those who sent them. When it became known that he kept a file of cards, the Viennese custom of sending great baskets or bouquets of flowers to ladies after a ball had turned into a diplomatic necessity.

"Roses to the rose of Vienna," he read to her in an affected falsetto. She kept playing while he read the cards out loud. This could go on for an hour. I went upstairs to help Poldi and Lise make Mother's bed. When they weren't looking, I took the card from the kimono pocket and ran to my room. Since I could not read the German script, I locked it into my treasure box. I looked at it often. By the time I took it to Eli, the fish and the stars on the coat of arms were smudged.

❊   ❊   ❊

We were dancing around in front of a large cracked mirror in the attic, I in a gypsy costume, waving an orange silk shawl, Eli in a trailing black cloak. Resi had given us the freedom of the attic, since Eli was confined so much. A world of adventure and intrigue became ours with a closetful of her old costumes for dress-up and plenty of un-Biblical furniture for scenery. I was supposed to be a character in *The Three Musketeers*, and Eli was directing me, when I produced the card.

"What does it say?" I asked. "I can't read script."

He held it with care. "Is it from a prince?"

"Only a duke's son. I know the coat of arms. It must be from Cousin Berthold."

"It says, 'Had to go to Germany. Wish you could have come, my love. Eternally yours, B.'" He strutted back and forth with the card and stopped again in front of the mirror. "Does your mother have a lover?" he said in his stage voice.

"What is a lover?" I asked.

"You know, in *Fledermaus* there is one, and in *Night in Venice*. Someone the soprano loves better than her husband."

"It's her horse," I said at once. "She throws her arms around it and kisses it all over the head and keeps saying, 'I love you, I love you best of all.' The horse sniffs her perfume and nips her hair."

Eli laughed and pressed a black slouch hat onto his head. "My father has a lover: Karin, the Swedish masseuse who comes to give Mama a massage. He kissed her in the car and I saw it."

We looked at each other in the mirror with mutual esteem. "It's all right for Berthold to call Mother 'my love.' He always does, in front of everyone," I explained. "He could have married her if she had waited for him. He's only four years younger, and that is all right. And if he waits he can marry me. That will get me back into line."

"What does that mean?"

"Well, aristocrats should always marry each other."

Eli had made believe he was a prince, and now his hat slipped to one side and he breathed uneasily. "I'm not a high aristocrat, but when I grow up I'll become one."

"You can't," I said in my grandmother's voice. "It has to be in the blood."

Frau Schwester interrupted with our morning milk before we could pursue the question of race and rank. She made us take off the costumes, and wiped our hands with a disinfected washcloth. I escaped to the other end of the attic while she gave Eli some cod-liver oil. Eli followed me with a look of disgust on his face.

"The canaries she takes such good care of end up stiff at the bottom of their clean cage," he said. We snickered at this ultimate conspiracy in the empire of hygiene his nurse had created at the Water Castle. "I poured half my milk into a ceramic vase when she wasn't looking."

Frau Schwester told us to stop whispering. It was rude, and secrets were unhealthy. Anyway, it was time we went downstairs; Frau Romberg was waiting.

"If you can't be an aristocrat," I said as we walked off together, "I can always be a Jew." We went to find Resi to continue our search for the Promised Land. The journey itself was our destination.

   *   *   *

Carnival 1938 ended with a great ball at the Water Castle. It must have been after eight o'clock the next morning when I managed to slip away from home and cross the street. Frost nipped my nose; I went sliding across the icy surface of the road. Sleet had begun as rain when I had gone to bed. A cruel wind had howled during the night, whipping hail against my window until I dreamed of machine guns. Now each tree, each shrub and dry blade of grass was encased in ice.

Departing guests had left the Romberg gate carelessly ajar. I entered and found myself in a crystal garden. The arched lamps shone on ice-covered bark and stalactite branches. Ornamental hedges sparkled. I must have passed a certain young silver birch each day I came to the Water Castle, but I had never really seen it. Now, in its crystalline mask, each twig revealed itself, shining against the slate-gray sky.

I had been warned not to intrude the morning after Fasching, but the garden and the great house with all its windows brightly lit invited me and filled me with expectation. My cheeks glowed, and I enjoyed the fragrant, icy air, listened to the wind rustle stiff bushes.

I could have turned back when I saw the figure draped in white, rippling sheets, but I approached, half-hidden by the ornamental hedges. A stout white person was stalking back and forth around a flowerbed, where rows of champagne bottles had been planted in the snow. I waited for the white back to turn on me at the fork of the path. Ice-crusted snow crunched like broken glass under heavy footsteps. Even the cupid weather vane had frozen, and the arrow remained fixed. I knew I should turn back. Something went *bang!* I cried out, "Help!" and sat down.

"Only a popping cork," said a familiar voice. "When bottles freeze, they sometimes pop . . . I'm sorry you were frightened, little Reyna." Eugene Romberg spoke from under the sheets.

I had to laugh, because he looked absurd and very fat in all the drapery. "What are you supposed to be, Uncle Eugene, a ghost or a nun?"

He shook his head with unexpected sadness. "Ghost, indeed . . . Ja, perhaps a ghost, who knows? I'm an Arab, Kinderl. They call me the Splasher, Rumanian thief, gypsy, dirty Jew—a joke!" He sighed deeply. His nose looked red and wet. "It's all one big masquerade. I'm an Arab, that's all . . ."

I did not know what to say. He sounded so sad that I felt I should hand him my clean handkerchief. The sheet, held onto his head by a dark cord, flapped around his kind round face. I tried not to laugh at him.

"Ach, I hate the bitter cold, but I came out to sober up. Arabs should not drink, and I drank too much." He took my hand and we walked toward the great house. As we entered, the sweltering heat, the smell of stale tobacco and perfume made him exclaim, "Ah, it smells terrible and feels wonderful!" I could laugh at the way he rolled his *r* without offending him.

In the great hall, Titian's prophet presided over the most tempting worldly debris: masks, colored glass beads, confetti, fans, a hat topped with a bird of paradise. I could have said that I wanted to stay here and wait for Eli, but I loved Eugene Romberg as an Arab and enjoyed hearing him talk to himself: "Too many people, too much food, and I drank far too much . . ."

In the conservatory, under the palm trees, stood a swing. Eugene Romberg stopped and stared at a pink, pale-haired ballerina who lay asleep in the arms of a man in sailor dress. Two masks lay on the ground. "Karin," he said softly. The pair did not stir, but the girl snored a little. Eugene Romberg smiled indulgently. "Resi's little masseuse," he explained as we walked on.

Birds chirped in their cages as we passed into the aviary, and moist drops fell onto my head. "Do you like Karin a lot?" I asked.

We had arrived at the gymnasium. "How did you guess?" He took me by the shoulder. "I suppose you could tell. I delight in her, a little bit the way I take pleasure in your company. Of course there is more, but I do find her refreshingly free of sentiment." He sighed. "I shouldn't be telling you this. I have had a little too much to drink. Good thing you don't understand."

I might have asked him about sentiments, but he took me along an unfamiliar side wing of the great house. A well-lit corridor led to a white door. He produced a key from the folds of his costume and unlocked it. The lights were on as we entered a large L-shaped room, very much like the music room on the other side of the house, only here the French windows were covered with heavy dark drapery. The urns and ceramic pots, low leather seats, and cushions could have been chosen by Resi, and seemed as Biblical as anything in the great hall.

Two large portraits, separated by a display of whips and curved daggers, caught my fancy at once. The woman and the man in the pictures sat in identical high-backed carved chairs. The faces looked to opposite corners of the room. The plump-faced young woman with the little sharp nose looked slightly familiar.

"My mama," Eugene Romberg said without pride. "Do you like her, child?" I didn't answer. "Now tell me the truth, could you love that face?"

I shook my head.

"I know you couldn't tell me why you don't care for her, but the truth is seen by children, as they used to say in Morocco."

I felt encouraged to say I didn't like her eyes.

He turned away and let himself fall onto a low, gold-embossed leather seat which sank down under his weight. He rubbed his face with both hands, as though he were washing. "Those eyes, ja, they remain the same, although she is very changed. She always tended to be plump, and now . . . Anyway, I will say this, she never meant to harm anyone."

I turned to the other portrait, the dark, soft-eyed, bearded man. "Your papa?" I asked.

He washed his face once more, making his cheeks pink. "Ach, how I wanted him to be my father, little one."

The room was hot, so I took off my loden cloak and allowed myself to sink into a soft, low chair beside Eugene Romberg. I folded my hands, tilted my head. If I had allowed myself to walk about and touch fancy enameled dishes, jingle brass bells, and interrupt him with childish prattle, he could not have given in to himself. But I made believe I was the lost doll and sat stiff and silent as soon as he began his tale. The woman seemed to taunt me with her devilish eyes as he poured something from an umber-colored crystal flask and drank it quickly. He sighed and shook his head. "Arabs should not drink," he said again, and again he filled the glass and drank. "That house, that house in Mogador . . ."

I asked where Mogador was, and he told me it was in Morocco, Africa. "A very hot land, and far away." This seemed to make him thirsty again. "What I remember most of all are the endless corridors, cool in the heat, with colorful tiles. I always liked numbers and used to play counting and hopping games. The windows were small, to keep the house cool; there was never much light, and sound carried from one end of the house to the other. I always knew who was coming. I recognized my mother's fast, clicking little heels and the slow, thoughtful steps of the man I called Father—Izaak Romberg, whose name I bear. The servants moved about on sandaled feet and made hardly any sound."

Eugene Romberg appeared so tired; his mouth drooped and his eyes had lost all luster. In the white drapery of his costume he resembled a large, listless bird. "It's all one great costume party," he said in a weary tone of voice.

Any other morning he would have asked whether I felt hungry. But I was sitting far too still. Even his direct questions became a self-inquiry. I practiced moving my eyes like Puppe's, without speaking or stirring.

"Morocco, beautiful Morocco, a land of fierce light and black shade." He refilled his little glass and raised it first to the man, then to the woman.

"Her eyes look like the doll's," I burst out.

"The doll, the doll—what doll? Oh, Puppe, of course. Well, she did not have many dolls, I'm sure, not much of anything. Raised by nuns, an orphan. I don't blame her, but she could have spared me when I was so young. I was only five years old, or perhaps six, when I discovered the truth. I will never forget that day. I had set up a game of chess on the tile floor near the stairway; it was a perfect chessboard. Izaak Romberg was very proud of my ability to play chess at such an early age, and I had a passion for the game, even then. Whenever he was away, I set up the figures of my set—they were as large as bowling pegs—and I played against myself. I was not put out by the slapping sound of soft-shod feet; there were many servants in our house. Nor was I afraid of the strange man in Arab dress. I can still see him standing there against the slanted light. He stared at me until I asked him whether he played chess; he did not smile or say one word. I remember moving a queen to take a knight; then he made a move and invaded my game, taking the place of the fallen knight. He said something I could not understand, but I recognized the angry voice.

"Did you run away?" I asked.

"No. I knew who he was, although I had never seen him before. I had often heard curses, shouted orders, and loud scolding from the kitchen quarters. The voice was usually accompanied by the banging of pots and the clatter of dishes. 'You are the cook,' I told the man, in the condescending tone of a small boy who has always had his way. 'Please get away from my game.' But he remained wordless, throwing a large shapeless shadow onto the tiles. I didn't move either, but I was glad when I heard the light footsteps of my nurse. I turned and ran to her. But as I fled, I heard the cook shouting after me, 'Boy! Come back! *Garçon!* Let me look at you, *mon fils*.'"

"What is '*mon fils*'?" I asked.

"It means 'my son.'" Eugene Romberg laughed without joy.

"They call me a Jew, a Rumanian, a gypsy, and a thief. Actually, I am a thief." He raised his glass to the dark-eyed, bearded man. "He had such sentimental eyes, Izaak Romberg. A happy man. He knew nothing. I stole his name. He thought I was his son, and I became his heir. I kept his name, all the money, mostly—I must say this in my defense—out of love. I wanted to be rich because Izaak Romberg was rich. I came away from Mogador when I was ready for boarding school in England. I never saw Izaak again; he died while I was away. Vienna was the town my mother chose. With his name, my inheritance, I came here to live as his son, as a Jew, the son of Izaak."

He rose, shivered, and wrapped the sheets more closely around his shoulders. "I feel cold; is it cold here, my child?"

I shook my head and tried to imitate the taunting gaze of the woman in the portrait.

"You are squinting. Do your eyes hurt?" He fell back into his chair. "I adore heat," he went on. "In the fiercest heat of the day, my mother would remain cool. Her arms remained cool to the touch. She never perspired, and sometimes she fainted. When Izaak Romberg noticed bruises, she could always tell him she had fainted and hurt herself. This made him want to protect her even more. He always called her 'his little white rabbit.' Resi is just as fair, and sometimes I call her 'white bunny'—ach, but Reserl is warm."

Eugene Romberg turned to the woman in the portrait, as though he had somehow guessed I was under the spell of those eyes. "This picture does not do her justice. It was painted by an artist who owed Izaak Romberg a lot of money; his heart was perhaps not in it. She was quite beautiful, in her way, when she was young. In Morocco people would stop and stare at her, she was so pale. She loved sweet things and grew plump even then. The face was not perfect—not like your mama's—but there was something about her. You wanted to be close to her and touch her. She vanished from my life. At the end of the war, when we got together again in Vienna, I was able at least to make her comfortable; but she chose a life away from me."

"I know. She is Frau Traude, Hanna Roth's assistant."

He looked at me with amazement. "Your father's daughter. Too clever, almost."

I noticed that his flask was almost empty when he refilled his glass and raised it to see the light turn its contents to liquid gold. I had always tried to figure out what my father meant when he said that in Eugene Romberg's hand, everything turned to gold.

"She came to Morocco as a young girl to be the governess at the house of Izaak Romberg's uncle, Eugene. I was named after this man. My mother had been employed at his house for less than a month. Izaak had seen her, but never took notice of her until he found her weeping in the garden. She was twenty years old, and he was almost forty. Once he had held her to comfort her, he did not want to let her go. He wished to give her everything she wanted, and he would have taken her with every one of the servants from his uncle's house if she had asked, he wanted her so much. They were married within a month, and she brought with her the cook, an Arab who had been trained at a Parisian hotel. Izaak congratulated her on having provided him with a superb chef, and he enjoyed the delicacies at the table as he enjoyed his young bride.

"He never really learned the true cause of her sorrow in the garden. While he sentimentally believed she had been a homesick little girl, I learned to listen for the slap, slap sound of the Arab's feet. The cook began to make his way upstairs more and more frequently when the master of the house was out. There was a certain secluded room, a mere garret with a low bed, a few stools, baskets." Eugene Romberg gulped his drink. "Arabs should leave alcohol alone." He shivered, rubbed his hands. "I saw them together only once. I was walking toward the garden, holding my mother's cool hand, and the Arab came along, carrying a bucket. He dropped it and she let go of my hand, hung her head with the strange look of a cringing, ingratiating dog. He went to her, and his long, dark fingers clawed her shoulder. I let out a scream. He let go of her, and she took me into her arms and held me. She felt as cold as ice."

I jumped up. "Did he hurt you, and did he hurt your mother?"

"Indeed, I think he did hurt me, child. Even if he did not lay a hand on me. 'She's mine!' he shouted in his terrible French. 'You're my son! I can kill her! I have the right to kill you! I can carve the Jew into cutlets!' I can still hear his high-pitched, hateful voice.

"A week or two later, I returned from the beach with Izaak Romberg and my mother. I remember the sand in my shoes and the outcry as we walked through the door. The cook had vanished. His belongings were left behind. He was replaced by an unobtrusive old man. The meals were less interesting. My mother replaced most of the servants. Yet I could never walk along the corridor, not even when I was a youth, without listening for the slap, slap of the Arab's running feet. Anytime I was in the house at Mogador, I felt the Arab might suddenly return to claim what was his . . . spring at me from the dark.

"I saw the dwarf, Hanna Roth, for the first time just after the cook vanished. She came on a visit to Morocco. It was odd, but around her my mother behaved with the same cringing deference she had displayed around the cook. I never trusted the dwarf. I was jealous because she took up all my mother's time for an entire month. They had been raised as orphans in the same convent. My father wanted our household to be Jewish, but the dwarf insisted on driving to church with my mother each Sunday. I still remember her hats and her great parasols. People would line up along the street to look at her, and a Moroccan dignitary wanted to buy her from Izaak for a huge sum. This made my mother angry, and she called Morocco a land of heathens without culture. I don't think Izaak quite forgave her for this."

He jumped up, drew aside the drapery, and looked out into the white garden. "I have drunk far too much, little one. You should not have let me go on like this. Good thing you don't really understand. Resi would not like this. My little white bunny. Ah, ja. Ferdl's Resi. My little phony Jew. She wants me to be a Jew, the son of Izaak. That's the way it is best." He shook his head. "Who knows? Resi has never seen this room; she thinks it's for storage. I bring Eli here to show him his grandparents. After all, there are no other family portraits in this house. This is between father and son. He has to know why I have him watched. It's not only the Nazis, but my old fears." He banged down his empty glass. "I guess I really have proved to myself that I'm the son of the Arab, one who frightens little children . . ."

"I'm not afraid," I finally said.

"You are your father's daughter," he repeated.

I stuffed my hands into my leather trousers with pompous pride. For a moment, I almost forgot I wanted to be an aristocrat with Berthold. There were, on the other hand, old tales of gyp-sies who robbed cradles and replaced a fair child with one of their own. Like most children, I spent moments in front of mirrors touching my face, saying my name. "Is Eli really your son?" I asked.

Eugene Romberg looked at me with an expression of innocent alarm. "I don't know what made me go on like this." A sun ray slanted through the curtain, making his face appear dark and hawklike against the folds of his costume. "Eli is not only my son, but he is the grandson of the cook. It's written all over him." He took the cord from his head, and the cloth fell off. He was Eugene Romberg, Uncle Eugene. "Such a wonderful child, to listen to an old man like me. Good thing you don't quite understand."

I did not understand at the time, but I had my father's famous memory. I would return to those cool passageways of the house in Mogador and reenter the strange tale of Eugene Romberg, as one can revisit a house in a legend or a place in a dream. I would forever attempt to retrace my steps in order to discover the reality of the fantastic.

❋　　❋　　❋

I could not wait to be alone with Eli again after my encounter with his father. Soon we were in the aviary, where someone had let one of the birds out of a cage during the night. It was a tiny, tame African sparrow which now perched on Eli's finger and took seeds from the palm of his hand.

"I met your father early this morning, after the ball," I told him at once. "He was an Arab."

Eli kept his eyes on the bird, but his long black eyelashes flick-ered. He did not look impressed.

"He is really an Arab," I went on. "He told me everything."

"I know all about that costume," Eli said to the bird, which kept tilting its head while it ate.

"Your father even took me to the Arab room," I bragged. "He drank a lot and told me everything."

"He always drinks in that room," Eli said quite calmly. "He takes me there when Mama goes out." Eli moved toward the cage, but the little bird flew away and perched on my curly head. I had to giggle because it pecked my ear.

Eli coaxed the bird back onto his hand and walked to the cage.

"Your father told me about Frau Traude and how he really is an Arab. I'm not sure I understand."

Eli managed to put the bird back into its cage with all the other African sparrows. There was a flurry of beating wings, and empty seedpods flew about. Eli had to sneeze, and breathed heavily. When the chirping stopped, he turned to me and said, "He makes it up."

"You mean he dresses up as an Arab and makes up the story to go with it?"

He looked at me with his large dark-brown eyes and nodded. "He makes it up because he doesn't want to be a Jew."

We looked at each other with a sympathy and understanding that would last for the rest of our lives. "But why should your mama enjoy being a Jew so much?" I wondered.

"That's because she was not born a Jew; she just took it up."

A gardener came into the aviary and began to sweep up confetti and paper coils. I went to the swing where the pink ballerina had slept in the arms of the sailor. Eli sat down with me, and I opened my palm to show him a braid I had picked up from the rug. He reached for it, and all at once it became a treasure.

"I found it," I said. In order to appease him and appear more grown-up and grand, I added, "It's all one big masquerade," rolling the r. We pushed off on our swing and laughed.

9

The Curtain Falls

AT FIRST I had learned to admire Eugene Romberg as a Jew. Resi had me convinced of Hebrew power: visitations of angels, conversations with God were a natural heritage. After my encounter with Eugene Romberg the Arab, I no longer knew who he really was. I could never imagine him as Frau Traude's son. All the same, I found myself devoted to this man who had singled me out to confide in me, who was ingenious enough to invent an identity to fit an occasion, great enough to humble himself before a child. David, Resi's Hebrew teacher, had fallen prey to Nazi thugs because he was weak. Eugene Romberg, with all the power of a chosen one, a Moses, a king, had taken the devil's mask by the nose and yanked it off Fritz Janicek. I found him generous under all circumstances, especially toward me: a king among men.

I tried hard to please my father. With Eugene Romberg, I succeeded without any effort. I often waited for him at our gate when he was expected to return and rushed across the street to meet him. He took notice of my new devotion by giving me a red leather coat lined with ocelot fur and a matching cap. Krampus received a red leather harness decorated with semiprecious stones.

Father and Eugene Romberg often got together after breakfast and went stomping through the snow with our dogs. I would run after them in my new coat, and they would take me in the middle and hold my hands. They discussed the danger of Nazis while I walked cozy and safe between them. Father usually carried an old rifle, but it wasn't loaded. Our watch dog, Frica, raced ahead and hunted without ever catching anything, and Krampus followed her, barking and leaping like a rabbit as he sank into soft snow. Eli had lessons in the morning, but he could never understand anyway why I wanted to go tagging along with our fathers. I told him I loved snow.

I romped with the dogs. Their barks and my shrieks sometimes drowned out talk about gold and getting money out of Austria. Father and Eugene Romberg talked in front of me as though I were one of the dogs. Eugene Romberg dressed, in his fur-lined coat, wrapped up in mufflers, his face gray and nose red, always fell into step with Papa. They limped side by side, and I often fell in with their rhythm.

"Your adaptability, Eugene, is sheer genius," Father said. "You adapt yourself so perfectly no one can ever get the better of you."

Eugene Romberg shook his head. "If *you* don't, Ferdl, no one else will."

They sounded too sure of themselves. I sensed fear. The contrast of danger with the safety of walking between the two friends thrilled me like the icy burn of snow melting on my tongue.

"You can't afford to hold on, Eugene, it's too risky," my father said. "That fancy Daimler limousine of yours will make an excursion to Zurich a real pleasure. I look forward to a game with our friend, Doctor Hahn; he isn't champion for nothing."

Eugene Romberg stopped and looked at my father with tears in his eyes. "Only you could put it that way. Taking me across the border for a game of chess . . ."

"Can I come, can I come, please!" I shouted.

Eugene Romberg blew his nose noisily and said he hoped that one day he would be able to invite me and my family to go on a journey around the world. My imagination soared. I saw a kaleidoscope of pleasures: rides on elephants, outlandish robes, the house in Mogador, temples with statues of many-armed goddesses. A journey for pleasure, not an exodus, where each land holds promise and each day becomes a festival. "One day, jawohl, one day," he said, "we will take a tutor and travel by yacht from land to land to give our children a sense of the past and a sense of geography. They should learn their languages by living abroad, get to know the people of other lands, and feel at home in the world."

"I want to come, I want to come," I said, taking his hand.

"Ja, we could have a wonderful time together," my father said sadly.

Eugene Romberg put his hand onto Father's shoulder. "In the meantime, I have to rely on you, my friend. If I do have a prolonged stay in Switzerland, I have to leave my dear ones in your care. You know I can't rely on my mother. She is a strange woman. Denies herself a grandson, and has no feelings for my Reserl. To think that she has the impudence to suggest that my Eli is a cuckoo's egg, an Aryan, because it suits her and her friend the modiste . . ."

"Three guesses who's supposed to be the cuckoo bird." My father laughed. "This talk comes directly from the great little old Hanna, and it's no joke; it's meant to come between us. The dwarf is a comedienne, but there's always a sting."

"My mother is mostly worried about the income she gets from me. She wants my boy to be Aryan so that I can sign everything over to him. She doesn't trust Resi."

"Hanna Roth doesn't get along with Reserl, because your wife has no interest in those phony predictions. Even Annerl came home disgusted the other day. She said the idea of Aryan certificates was crazy and heartless, insulting. One look would tell anyone whose son Eli is, with those marvelous eyes. And he has your brain."

Eugene Romberg looked up at the sky. "She really said that?" His face shone with pleasure. "I would never have Ann Marie annoyed in any way. I would give anything to spare her." He sighed. "She is right," he said. "In some ways I wish I didn't see myself in Eli quite so much. Yet it is gratifying."

"What man wouldn't be gratified at having a son?" my father said, with too much feeling for my taste.

When we turned back and walked downhill, it snowed so hard our footprints vanished. The dogs turned white as winter hares. I stayed behind and watched Father and his friend limping side by side, and imagined them making their way through the sugar-candy mountain of my storybook to the land of the Schlaraffs, Switzerland, the land of milk and honey.

"Wait for me," I called out, trying to sound like a boy, a son. "I want to come to Switzerland." My father said that I must be tired, and picked me up.

✿   ✿   ✿

One morning I woke up and found that Father and Eugene Romberg had departed at dawn. They had driven away in the white limousine, but I always imagined them afoot in a winterland of white sugar. Mother could not console me by telling me Switzerland was very dull, nor could Papa with the packages he handed me when we met his train. He had been gone about a week; it seemed much longer, even to my mother. The station was smoky and busy. Many young people with rucksacks and skis ran past us. They wore white stockings; all of them were Nazis.

I watched Father embrace Mama. They clung together. "How about Eugene Romberg?" I asked. But Father was busy telling Mama that he had almost forgotten how beautiful she was. I tugged on his cloak. "Is he coming back soon?"

Father picked me up and kissed me. Eugene Romberg sent his love to us all, he said, and presents. If things quieted down in Austria, he would come back at once.

"I want him back now!" I shouted. "It's your fault," I said to Mother. "You and all the Nazis and the Committee of Seven."

My father put me down and said it was not safe for me to go around talking like that. But Mother did not get angry. She kissed me and assured me she would miss Eugene Romberg very much. She felt uneasy and changed the subject. The new gardener would come before long and bring a little son, she promised.

On my return to the Meinert-Hof, I found not the new gardener but the old one in the kitchen. I lost my temper again at the sight of Fritz Janicek seated in his usual chair near the window, drinking coffee from a good china cup. He greeted me with condescension.

"You'd better not hurt Eli Romberg, Herr Janicek, or any Jew! I'm almost a Jew myself!" I told him.

"Well," Agnes said from the rocking chair. "What on earth brought that on?"

When Fritz was our gardener he had tolerated me because I liked to listen to him. "Things are certainly not improving since I was told to get out," he remarked in his slow, educated voice.

Just then Poldi and Lise came clattering down the stairs with the vacuum cleaner. They laughed the moment they set eyes on Fritz, and said he had grown stout during his two weeks in jail. Agnes quieted them down, comforted me with Maltaline in hot milk, and handed Fritz a piece of cake. "Now that you have picked up the few things you left behind, it's not right for you to come around anymore, Herr Gardener. We have had to have the cottage repaired after you messed it up. A new man will soon be moving in."

Fritz jumped up and left the cake. "I don't work here anymore, Frau Cook, so do me a favor and refrain from calling me 'Gardener.' Give me my proper title, if you are going to use one. I'm an *Academiker* and I'm still 'Professor'; they can't take that away from me. And don't worry, I won't return." As he was leaving, he put on his hat defiantly, and I saw the swastika in the center of the edelweiss. "Give my deep respects to your gracious mama," he said to me. "I hope she is well."

The glint in his eyes made me certain he had something up his sleeve. I volunteered to let him out with my own keys so that I could ask him whether he had been driving a florist's van. I wanted to know about jail, the Committee of Seven. Could he have taken Puppe? Unfortunately, Agnes did not give me a chance to be alone with him. She escorted him up the stairs without further delay.

After I finished my Maltaline, I went upstairs and heard Father tell Agnes that she should never let Fritz into the house again, no matter what he said. At that moment, the doorbell shrilled. "That must be Frau Romberg. I'll let her in myself. Lucky she didn't run into that scoundrel, especially today."

"I don't like it. I don't like it one bit," Resi said as soon as she walked in. "All this secrecy, this double-dealing." She could make tears come into her eyes quite easily. Now, as she turned to Father, she allowed them to run down her cheeks. "You have outdone yourself, Ferdl."

Agnes tried to take me back to the kitchen with her, but I gave her the slip.

"I think you should have told me that Eugene was leaving me, even if he didn't want to face up and did sneak off," Resi went on.

My father said, "Schazi, now, now, really," and quickly produced the cherry brandy she liked to drink. She was smoking and coughing and weeping.

"He hasn't left you at all," my mother intervened. "You know that. He loves you."

"There could have been trouble at the border," Papa interrupted. "As I told you on the phone, there was a certain risk. He's got to wait and see what's going to develop here before he takes a chance and comes back."

I was trying to console myself with a music box that Eugene Romberg had sent for me. Soldiers in bright uniforms moved around in a circle to a march. When I spoke up and asked Resi whether I could go and see Eli, to show it to him and look at his toys, she said, "Another day." Eli missed his father so much he had made himself ill. She had something to discuss with my parents. Would I please run along!

I only went as far as the stairs above the morning room and sat down close to the wall with a good view of a mirror.

"Why do you belittle yourself like that?" Father said. "He could have taken the girl along, or sent for her. Instead, he has decided to rent a villa on Lake Geneva for you and Eli. All you have to do is supervise the packing of your favorite furniture—anything at all, if we act fast. Once things stabilize here, Eugene can buy everything back from me, and we'll celebrate with a big party."

"Take my sick boy away from his doctor and move to a strange country?" Resi began, but Mother drowned her out with one of those sonatinas.

After she had finished the piece, she said, "Forgive me, Resi, but Eli is a half-Jew according to the Nuremberg law. If there is an annexation, you'd be in a bad position with him. He is far better off in Geneva. In fact, you should send him, even if for some reason you don't want to leave Austria."

"Since when, may I ask, do we have Nuremberg laws in Vienna?" Resi said. "You are giving in to wishful thinking, Ann Marie. Stooping to Nazi talk. And when it comes right down to it, Eli is not merely half a Jew. His father and his mother are both Jews, and he has the religion of his parents. No little man with vile ideas like your Hitler will prevent that or make me run."

My father interrupted and told her Mama meant well. I heard the clinking of glass and saw Resi's pert profile in the morning-room mirror. Mother appeared beside her. "You're unfair, Resi. You should join Eugene. He adores you and Eli."

Resi puffed on her cigarette. "Among others," she said. "I love Vienna. I told him so. I'd rather starve here than eat chicken in Zurich."

"You won't starve here," Father said.

"Eugene might even fool you, Ferdl. But I know about that girl. It's all very convenient."

"She is in Vienna," Father said.

"No doubt packing," Resi continued.

"Why don't you call her and ask her to give you a massage?" Mother said in her most grown-up voice. "You can go to Zurich for a few days, just to talk things over with Eugene."

"I'm not running after him, or running away. Eugene is used to moving around like a gypsy. Morocco, England, Paris, Vienna— it's his nature. I like it here."

She vanished from my view, but my father appeared in the mirror, sucking his pipe. "What it amounts to is simple. You either give in and pack your bags and get Eli out of here while there's still time, or you buy yourself a nice big swastika flag. Everyone in Vienna knows who you are. I guess we can look after you and Eli."

"Why take a chance?" Mother said quite pointedly. She actually wanted Resi and Eli to leave.

My father and Resi came through the morning-room door. I had to move up the stairs in a hurry. "There's no more to discuss," she was saying. He went to fetch her cloak. They whispered and smiled to each other and made up as he wrapped it around her. Perhaps they remembered the morning under the cloak on the gallery. "*Lieber* Ferdl," she said softly. "You don't really want me to go away, do you?" He kissed her mouth quickly and greedily, pushed her toward the door. Resi held onto his hand and pressed it to her lips.

I kept hoping Eugene Romberg would return in time for my birthday on the third of March. He did not come back to Vienna. Everyone talked so much about Adolf Hitler and what would happen to Austria, I began to fear my birthday would be forgotten. Mother was busy hiding pamphlets stenciled in Gothic letters in a novel written by Stefan Zweig, a Jew. The title of the book, *Impatient Heart*, attracted my attention. I could not read the pamphlets, but they interested her so much, I thought it would be wise to remind her of my birthday each day.

On one of these occasions, I discovered that she talked to the missing doll in her room. She had asked for me when Agnes brought her the morning mail. As I came up the stairs, I heard her say, "Who on earth would give Reyna such a present, now that Eugene is gone?" Her tone of voice horrified me, and I fully expected to find the doll presiding in the boudoir again. The door was unlocked. I peeked in. Mother, in her new gray tailored suit and wide-brimmed felt hat, stood in front of the doll's chair, hiding it from my view. Her back was turned to the door; she held her shoes in one hand and a letter in the other and wiggled her toes inside her silk stockings. A gray voile dress from the doll's wardrobe was laid out on the bed.

I shouted, "Boo!" and burst into the boudoir.

She did not turn around at once. The sun shone through the window, and a melting icicle dripped rhythmically onto the windowsill. The doll's chair was empty. "In some ways, I wish the thief would come and take away all of the doll's things and my matching dresses and hats." She wriggled her feet into her shoes. "A *corpus delicti*, that's what Puppe has become to me. All these things," she went on, with a tired gesture toward the doll's wardrobe and her own dressing room. "Like the garments of the dead. I must get rid of it all . . . Someone must really hate me."

As far as I was concerned, the theft of the doll stood out as an act of pure love. Had I not improved on the Pater Noster with "Deliver me from the doll"?

"Who knows, perhaps the person who took her also sent all those dolls at Christmas. This mystery—it's quite mad." She caught a glimpse of herself in the mirror and straightened the brim of her hat with a look of dislike I did not forget. She hated her own face. What on earth had come over her? She had always been shy, but also pleased with her looks. "Someone hates me all right," she repeated.

I ran to her and threw my arms around her and told her everyone loved her. She held me tight. "Well, someone loves you, Herzerl. It's your birthday on Saturday. *The Fairy Doll*, a ballet— the proscenium box for your birthday! Just think, that's where the kaiser used to sit! And I don't know who it's from."

"Grandmama."

"No, I already asked. She is going to Salzburg, and she won't even be here." My grandmother had told me in confidence that she was going to see the bishop at Salzburg. Austria was in grave danger, she'd said. Now that I was seven years old, I had to learn what this meant . . . But I only cared about my birthday.

Resi seemed another person likely to get ballet tickets, but when Mother telephoned the Water Castle, Resi got all excited. She had forgotten my birthday, thanked Mama for reminding her, and said she loved ballet. If Eli felt well enough, they would love to come. I jumped up and down and shrieked. Mother told me to calm down; she couldn't think. Who on earth would send tickets and say Happy Birthday without another word?

"Berthold," I said.

She kissed me because I liked him so much. "He's too poor."

She did invite Cousin Bertl, and when I found out he would come to the ballet with us, I raced through the house and danced all the way to the gate. At the Water Castle, not even Frau Schwester could restrain my enthusiasm and Eli's admiration. I practiced pirouettes and waved my arms all around the great hall, under the sad eyes of the prophet.

Eli and I had been taken to the opera during the winter by his parents, to see *The Magic Flute*. But Eli had begun to pant for breath during the second act, and we had left at once. This time Eli was fortified by Maltaline and then sedated. He was dozing in the car when we drove past demonstrators at the Hotel Bristol, shouting, *"One People, One Reich, One Führer!"* He was still drowsy at the opera and sat down in the imperial box with seeming indifference. I had no idea how he really felt until later.

Resi was angry at the demonstration, and Father tried to calm her down, explaining that the Hotel Bristol was owned by the German railroad. The Austrian police were at a loss . . .

"The Austrian police are at a total loss," Resi said in her stage voice.

Mama stayed in the recess of the box, quite ill at ease. For my birthday, Resi had given me a silk dirndl dress; I adored the sparkling buttons. Mother considered it more suitable for a costume ball. I had been allowed to put it on because Papa liked it. Resi, herself in a red Biblical costume, sported a tiara in the shape of a crown for this occasion and hardly needed to raise her voice to attract attention. She was recognized; opera glasses turned in our direction. Father was forced to exchange greetings, nod, and wave.

I felt dizzy with excitement as I bent over the velvet-padded balustrade. The seats below us were filling up. The standing room in the center back—reserved for officers during the days of the empire—was packed, mostly with young people. One older man stood out. I recognized him at once.

"Fritz! Fritz Janicek!"

"Not so loud," said Mama. "Don't point."

"Where, where?" Resi chirped. "I'd better take Eli and leave at once."

Mama took up her opera glasses. "In the standing room with some boys, probably some of his students."

"I wouldn't give it a thought," Father said. "We are in a good, safe location."

The imperial box in the old house overhung the orchestra pit on the far right. The musicians had begun tuning up. Surrounded by sound, one felt more a part of the stage and the orchestra than of the audience. Boxes all around the walls, overflowing with children in party clothes, added color to the plush red, white, and gold. *The Fairy Doll* was a traditional family evening in Vienna. Children's voices and instruments tuning up created a perfect dissonance.

"One wrong move and I'll have him thrown out," Resi went on. "I still have some influence around here."

"Now, don't get excited," Mama said. "I remember Janicek told me he has a student who became a dancer. That's why he's here." She looked through her glasses again. "You don't think, Ferdl, he could have sent us the tickets?"

"While he's only standing up?"

But Father looked relieved when Berthold came dashing in, gathered me up, and gave me a Biedermeier bouquet. This one had a pink rose in the center. He followed standard procedures with females he favored. This did not bother me when I was seven years old. I threw my arms around his neck and whispered, thanking him for giving me a bouquet exactly like the one he had sent to Mama after the ball.

He held me up high. "Just look at her! Isn't she just too much!"

When he put me down so that he could greet everyone else, I danced around him to get his attention and told him about Grandmama and the bishop and Salzburg, but he brushed me aside. "A very full house. Everyone is out celebrating one way or another. I was lucky to get away this evening."

He sat down beside Resi and told her about his job at the bar, but she was still upset about Fritz Janicek. "That man attacked Eugene," she said in a squeaky, timid voice I had never heard before.

Berthold kissed her hand. "He won't dare anything this evening, Gnädige. You have me and Ferdl and even your son to protect you." He turned to Eli. "Wait till you hear those plump Viennese ballerinas come on like a herd of elephants."

Eli had to laugh, but he did not feel at ease with my hero. I could tell by the way he blinked. Berthold noticed and said, "Your father is away, I believe. You must miss him." No one could ever be more thoughtful and less considerate.

Fortunately, at that moment the chandelier was raised. The lights dimmed. I heard Resi whisper to Berthold about David, her tutor, whom she hoped to get off to the Holy Land. Berthold did not say a word. He never faked sympathy. Jews, for him, if he had given them any thought, must have seemed like undesirable creatures of an endangered species.

Mama came to his rescue. The conductor had been applauded, and the overture began. "So, Ferdl. You might as well own up. It's your treat."

But Papa went into his usual "a peasant like me" routine. "If I had gone mad and bought all these tickets, I would certainly not keep it a secret."

The curtain rose. There was no sound of thunderous feet, only music and "ah's" from the children in the audience. I stood up. The stage below was full of dolls, propped up, stiffly seated, or reclining. The setting was the imperial dolls' room. A pink spotlight brought on a pink fairy. She tripped around on her toes, waving a magic wand. Eli touched my arm, made me jump. I had quite forgotten him and everyone else. The fairy touched a lady doll to make her dance. "Someone's coming." Eli's happy face should have told me his secret. "It must be my father." He turned around, listening intently. All evening he must have been waiting, quite certain his father had been the one who had planned the evening and would now surprise us.

"They don't usually let anyone in late," Resi said. She grabbed

Berthold's arm and with her other hand reached for Father. "What if that Nazi tries something? Eli, Eli, come here." But Eli didn't move.

"Fritz is hemmed in down there in standing room," Mama said. "He couldn't get out if he tried."

The historic reception room of the imperial box was separated from us by a padded door, but we had left this half-open. In another century, Count Metternich himself must have waited for the end of an act at the ballet in the white and gold room. Perhaps he, too, had found the door ajar, heard the music as he sat watching the silhouette of Napoleon's young son against the bright stagelights, and observed him take the bait—fall in love with ballerina Fanny Elssler. In the same room, someone was now waiting to enter. We heard soft voices.

The usher's light flickered as he held the door, and a tiny figure entered, followed by a stout one. Hanna Roth and her assistant, Eli's grandmother, came tripping into the box, making soft, apologetic sounds. "So you are the one, Frau Hanna," whispered my mother.

Hanna Roth murmured to us not to get up, but graciously responded to my curtsy, my thank-you. Resi made a sound as though someone had stepped on her toes. But the Meisterin had come to enjoy herself and beamed as she sat down in the front row with her companion. Onstage, peasant dolls performed a *Ländler*. She clapped her hands with pleasure and smiled at me.

Mama leaned toward Berthold and whispered, "Thank God Mama couldn't come!"

I saw most of the action onstage through the eyes of the dwarf, laughing when she laughed, snapping my fingers when she did. I could not take my eyes off her. She wore a dress the color of dried blood and a toadstool hat to match. Frau Traude, beside her, looked like a cook on Sunday. Sitting with an arm around the back of the dwarf's chair, she displayed that marble-white, plump arm I had liked in Eugene Romberg's tale of Mogador. I could not imagine someone fat and old being young. She had been kind to me at Salon Roth, but I hated the way she looked at Eli; even in the half-dark, I saw her eyes moving from side to side.

The dolls onstage bounded about to a loud gallop. I turned

to Eli and whispered, "Is she really your grandmother?"

"What difference does it make?" His fine fingers tapped to the music. "She never bothers with me, and she doesn't like Father. The modiste doesn't like us either, but I think she is fabulous. Those short legs!"

Hanna Roth had raised an opera glass, and her legs dangled in time to the music. Never had I seen her happier. If she had any inkling of danger, she certainly did not show it. I kept looking down to standing room, where Fritz lurked, but she never took her eyes off the stage. Suddenly, during the last waltz, she turned around and looked at my parents.

Mama sat behind me, and Father stood up by her side. At that moment, he was leaning over her with concern. Since the loss of her doll, he often treated her as though she had been injured. Hanna Roth took it all in. I did not like for her to see them this way, and I wished they were still laughing, kissing, and teasing each other—although that, too, had bothered me. I was glad when the lights came on and the dwarf jumped up to applaud. She caused quite a stir in the audience.

The Viennese are notoriously hungry in between acts and in frantic haste to get to the buffet for their little sandwiches and champagne. My father was impressed when a crowd stayed behind under our box, children waving to Hanna Roth, men in evening suits throwing kisses to Resi. She smiled, waved, threw kisses, and I imitated her. The dancers curtsied to our box during their last curtain call.

By the time the ovation ended, Mama, Frau Hanna, and her assistant had followed Eli to the reception room. He no doubt had heard male voices and still believed that his father might be there. Papa took my hand. "Let's make sure no one leaves the box." At the door, we almost collided with Fritz Janicek. "How dare you!" my father thundered at him. But Fritz held his ground and scanned the box.

Resi let out a screech and retreated toward the balustrade. Her admirers had hurried off to the buffet, and her cry, if anyone heard it, was not taken seriously.

Berthold put his arm around her and drew her away. "Don't worry," he said. "Don't be afraid. I'm here."

She leaned against him. "Call the police, Ferdl, before he attacks and murders us." Resi was never afraid of anyone. I could tell when she was putting on an act, but the tremor in her voice was real, and the accusation sent Fritz out of the box and impressed a plump man in a belted coat who was waiting in the reception room with his camera.

"I knew there was something going on," he said. "I'm Herr Watzl from the *Telegraph,* and I was waiting outside the proscenium box for the *Herrschaften,* hoping to get a picture and have a few words with Frau Resi Heller, when I saw this man brush past. I didn't like the way he tore the door open without knocking, so I took the liberty of following him."

Fritz, nose white, lips pressed together, headed for the door, but Eli stood there with his arms folded and his head low, blocking Fritz's way. Eli was in quite a temper because his father had not shown up. He ignored his mother, who shouted "Eli, come to Mutti!" in her fortissimo voice. Frau Hanna, enthroned in the largest, fanciest armchair, dangled her feet and looked on as though all this were part of the evening's entertainment. Her assistant stood by, holding a large box decorated with a pink ribbon.

Fritz, in his dark professor's suit, sparse hair combed down on one side, and the obvious little mustache, smiled and bowed to my mother. "I couldn't resist the opportunity to pay my respects, Gnädigste, in spite of the company you are in this evening," he said, with an ugly look at Hanna Roth and Resi.

"He should be in jail! He tried to kill my husband!" Resi drowned him out.

"When was that?" the reporter asked. "Why didn't the *Telegraph* know about it? And who is this man?"

Berthold said, "Enough, enough. We don't want any publicity."

"I'm Professor Janicek," Fritz spoke up. "I had the honor to serve Frau Ann Marie Meinert, Countess von Dornbach Falkenburg. I came to warn her. The countess Reyna, her mother, should not attend the legitimist meeting next Tuesday. There was another matter of interest to the Gnädige which I will not go into . . . However, I didn't come to the ballet this evening to speak with her or cause trouble—even if I might have liked to come face to face with the Jew who had me jailed. This was not my purpose. I happen to be present because Karl Winkler, the dancer, was a student of mine. I came and brought some of my boys. If you could mention Winkler's high leaps in the mazurka . . ."

"We do not want any publicity, mein Herr." Berthold sounded as snooty as his sisters.

"I should say not," Mama agreed.

Father went and opened the door and held it. Fritz left without another word.

Resi said, "If you have to write something in the *Telegraph,* Herr Watzl, just say I had an enchanting evening, and leave the rest out." The reporter hurried out as though he wanted to catch up with Fritz Janicek.

As soon as we were alone, Resi said her nerves were shattered and she needed champagne. Frau Traude came and handed me the package, a box of chocolates, and I began to pass it around. Berthold turned to Hanna Roth and thanked her for her generous invitation with so much charm that the incident with Fritz lost some of its impact.

"I merely sent the tickets," she said. "I had nothing to do with the invitations. I did not know who would be here, but as soon as I walked into this charming reception room I knew there would be trouble. Traude wouldn't let me say anything. She thought my foreboding was brought on by an old memory. The empress Elizabeth attended the ballet with a grandchild, and they insisted on bringing me to her on a cushion, dressed up as a doll. It didn't cheer her up, and I was almost dropped into the orchestra pit." She produced her pin ring and stuck a cigarette on it.

Resi went to her and let her take a light. "Let's get champagne," she said. "Let's see whether you and I, Ferdl, have a little influence."

While they were gone we ate chocolates. Berthold praised both Eli and me for our courage during the incident with Fritz. Just as Frau Hanna called me *très charmant* but my costume *un faux pas,* Resi and Father came back with an attendant in livery who carried champagne and glasses. The cork popped, and I caught it. This long intermission was to be followed by a short classical ballet which I hardly remember, for I was allowed to drink champagne when everyone toasted me and sang "Hoch soll sie Leben," "Let Her Live High." Like Hanna Roth, I drank too fast. After her second glass she became quite exalted, threw back her half-veil, and said, "How times does pass—back and forth, for some things never pass." She didn't make too much sense.

Berthold turned to her. "So what does the future hold, Frau Meisterin?" He refilled her glass.

She raised it, stared into the bubbles, and cried out like a startled jackdaw. "Ashes, ashes." She put her glass down, and her hands brushed away the vision as though it were a spider's web. "This room in flames. I must do something. Something must be done. Flames around the Führer."

Before Resi had time to react, the end-of-intermission bell rang for the third time. Berthold offered Frau Hanna his arm, but she walked past him, took my hand, and led me into the box. Her fingers felt cold and damp, even through the glove. She made me sit beside her, and when the music began I whispered to her, "How about Puppe?"

I startled her. She let go of me. "You sensed it, didn't you, *Schrecklich*? I saw these walls crumble. The Führer surrounded by flames. And the doll, the beautiful doll dismembered." Her urgent whisper was accompanied by the music of Frédéric Chopin and ballerinas drifting around on the stage below us. Her vision was far more exciting. "I will not let it happen," she promised, and with a wicked laugh she drained the champagne she had brought into the box.

We made quite a picture on the grand staircase after the performance. Hanna the Dwarf had finally accepted Berthold's arm, saying something about going unnoticed beside such a handsome young cavalier. This was not the only time she expressed the wish to go unnoticed, but she certainly made the most of being in the limelight. I came down behind her with Eli, and Father walked between Resi and Mother; Resi dressed like a queen from a children's play, Mama flushed, in pale gray, quiet and unforgettable. Frau Traude came last, carrying the dwarf's large umbrella and my half-empty box of chocolates.

A crowd gathered on each side, and children rushed forward with autograph books, handing them first to Resi, then to all of us. Father tried to wave them on, but Eli and I enjoyed giving autographs. "How sweet the little boy and girl look," people were saying as I worked on writing my long name in print.

The newspaperman popped up in front of us; his camera

flashed. Papa said, "I object," but the reporter vanished.

The picture he took of us appeared in the morning paper: "Nazi forces his way into imperial box to confront Little Nightingale . . ." My father threw the paper into a wicker basket. I gathered it up and smoothed it out and kept it in my treasure box.

In the picture, Frau Traude stands just behind my parents, her mouth full of chocolates as though she had the mumps. Berthold is unrecognizable because he has turned his head to look at Mama; she, eyes closed, looks asleep. Resi is all smiles and dimples again. You can see only the top of Eli's head because he is looking down. I stare like an owl. Many unfamiliar faces surround us, staring and pointing, children holding their books, laughing, open-mouthed. Hanna Roth has moved, turning herself into a dark blotch. Fritz Janicek's head, above her blurred shape, is a study in dark tones: watchful little eyes, a beak of a nose. He must have stood just behind her on the steps.

Every time I took the picture from the box, there we stood: a monstrous group. Violence hung over us as inevitably as an avalanche when masses of snow form in the Alps. One careless move or sound and we'd go under, all of us: Nazis and potential victims, lovers and bystanders. With time, with war, with death, who would know right from wrong, and who would know any-one apart?

10

House Without a Flag

"HOW MANY DAYS of Austria have we left?" my grandmother asked the next day. She sighed, and the lace trimming on her high-necked gray dress trembled. "Time is running out."

She was having after-lunch coffee in the sunny living-room corner with my parents. Her comment about time running out sent me running back and forth between clocks; they ticked as usual. Each time I passed the oval mirror near the cuckoo clock, I stood on tiptoes to admire myself in the old-fashioned high-necked blouse my grandmother had brought as a birthday present. She also gave me a tiny bottle of French perfume. I thought I looked very much like the countess as I craned my neck, dabbed myself with scent. That entire week rocked of lily of the valley. When the bottle was empty and it was all over, I could still smell it.

"During Carnival, everyone danced at this or that ball while the government was infiltrated by traitors," my grandmother went on. "All of you sat at *The Fairy Doll* with that misguided court dwarf while the provinces of Austria were being taken over by Nazi criminals." I particularly liked the way she pronounced "court dwarf" and repeated it to myself several times. "I know it was a special occasion." I ran to her and she pulled me onto her knee. "But I must admit, it shocked me to see that photograph in the newspaper. At a time like this—"

"Life goes on," my mother interrupted. "You can't reproach anyone for having a little fun."

"A nice platitude, Ann Marie. They are very fond of platitudes in the Reich. I do hope you don't have to reproach yourself for more than a little fun in days to come."

I did not like what she was saying, but I liked the way she spoke. The countess, like Hanna the Dwarf, always sounded as though she had rehearsed each line. I often tried to imitate her accent. She had the most beautiful voice I knew; also the most uncomfortable lap. When she went on to say that Crown Prince Otto had written to offer his services to Chancellor Schuschnigg, I slid off her knee.

"Will he come to Vienna?" I asked.

Mama started to write something on the tablecloth with her fingernail; her hands never knew what to do without the doll or the piano. Papa lit his pipe and jumped up.

"If the prince showed up in Vienna, Herr Hitler would have the best excuse to walk across the border. Not that he really needs one. I don't believe anyone will stop that man."

The countess folded her fine hands. "Except God," she said.

God did not respond to my grandmother's softly spoken words. Otto von Habsburg did not come to Vienna.

On March 11, my father and mother went to the wine gardens with a group of friends to have a little fun, while the Nazi army entered Austria and Hitler prepared to cross the border. That night loud voices woke me up. Someone had left my door ajar. I jumped out of bed and ran downstairs. Agnes in a pink robe, Poldi and Lise in white nightgowns stood in front of the radio in the living room. Only one lamp had been turned on, and a voice on the radio in the half-dark was saying, "God save Austria." I carried with me that marvelous little bottle of perfume, and dabbed myself with the stopper.

"The child," Agnes said. "No good hiding, Reyna, I can smell you." I ran to her and she opened her arms. The radio began to play the national anthem; she held me and sobbed. "The poor chancellor. Only two days ago I saw him kneeling at St. Stephen's praying to Our Lady. He kissed the gate. God protect this good man."

I listened to the loud voices on the radio and felt the excitement of the strutting marching songs.

"They are marching," Poldi cried out, and pulled her twin to the window. "The Reds, the Reds!"

"They'll murder us the way they butchered the servants of the czar," Lise wailed.

I broke away from Agnes to see the murderers. True enough, men in rows of two and three formed a procession, but it was no bigger or noisier than funeral processions returning from the graveyard after a good funeral feast. I recognized the bowlegged, smiling leader, who carried a red flag. "It's Vlado, our new gardener!"

"He won't let anyone hurt us," Poldi said. "He's been educating us about Russia."

I had not seen much of the new gardener. Father had made sure he did not hire another Nazi. Vlado, a Slovene, had to leave his family behind in Graz because he had had a fight with Nazi thugs.

Vlado was a cheerful man, and I liked the way he grinned carrying the flag. The radio was playing a Nazi marching song as the Communists passed our gate. They looked as though they had just jumped out of bed; some of them had not even bothered to button their shirts or comb their hair. I didn't care what flag they carried or what music they marched to. I wanted to rush out there and follow the flag. To see unarmed men marching had that effect on me. Once they were in uniform, they all became like the tin soldiers that Duke General von Hohentahler moved around on his old war maps. The men in pajama tops and leather pants, marching behind Vlado the Gardener, made me shout: "Bravo!"

"Shhh," said Agnes. "God preserve us from the Bolshies. Vlado is a good man, but if the master knew he's a Red, he'd get rid of him, too, even if he's the father of seven and there's one on the way."

I imagined an army of little Vlados arriving in Vienna after their farm was sold, and marched around the living room, leading them with a make-believe flag.

The next morning flags appeared like magic and danced from windows and rooftops. The day Hitler came to Vienna, my father ordered our flag to be raised. I followed Heinz, the chauffeur, to the attic, and he painted a white circle over the old imperial eagle. With my help, he drew a black swastika in the center. The double eagle still showed if you looked carefully, and the swastika looked a little shaky, but once the flag coiled out from our roof no one noticed.

The Water Castle was the only house without a flag on our

avenue. People in the street slowed down and pointed at the great house. Once the German army entered Vienna, windows, lampposts, even public facilities sported swastikas. A house without a flag, the chauffeur had told me, was marked. Anyone who walked in the streets of Vienna without a Nazi emblem was likely to be roughed up. My father had seen to the hoisting of a small but noticeable flag at the little palace. Even the countess understood that she had to protect herself in order to protect her Monarchist cause.

My father looked tired the morning he took me across the street with him to talk to Resi. It was the day of Adolf Hitler's great triumph over Vienna. We had to wait for Resi; she had slept late, as usual. When she appeared, in a gray Biblical dress, she did not sing; but she smoked.

"Naughty girl," my father exclaimed, and took her into his arms and shook her. "You'll get yourself and little Eli into trouble if you don't raise the flag I sent you yesterday."

She pushed Papa away and took me to stand with her and Eli. "This is a Jewish house."

"A Jewish house," I echoed.

"The servants can put on their swastikas outside the gate, but no anti-Semitic symbol will be worn inside these walls. There will be no flags."

"No flags," I mimicked her stage voice.

"You, at least, don't have to worry, Ferdl," she went on. "I saw Annerl and her cousin in the morning paper: 'Prominent Illegal National Socialists Welcome Their Führer.' I saw her going off to town a while ago. Weren't you invited to the great celebration?"

"Invited, jawohl, as the husband of such a celebrity." He slapped his leather pants. "A peasant like me doesn't belong among such great heroes. I tend to my wine, my beer. Not to mention the responsibility of getting the Aryans their Aryanized milk. Annerl will give our new Napoleon my humble apologies. That should be enough."

"Annerl looked elegant," Resi said.

"Thanks to me," he bragged. "I made her take off that ludicrous little flowerpot. The Meisterin must have gone berserk trying to turn Annerl into one of Hitler's flower maidens."

My father and Resi settled down in a cozy settee, turned

the radio on, drank to each other, and flirted during a good part of the Führer's first speech in Vienna. Father seemed quite to forget why he had come across the street. I did not like the way the prophet in the painting stared out into the garden at a scarecrow. The empty sleeves of the dark tattered coat flew up in the sun. Starlings pecked at the seeds in the flowerbed, and gray hunched clouds raced across the bright sky. I felt as though all this had happened before.

The loud voice of the great orator rejoiced with delectable venom at the "call of Providence." The radio crackled, masses roared their approval, but Eli reached for his storybook, *The Arabian Nights*. He had never been part of Vienna, nor would he ever be part of the new Reich. The voice shouted about the liberation of Austria, while Eli was more confined to the Water Castle than ever. I let him sniff my perfume, and he sneezed. Then I asked him how he liked the Führer's speech; he merely turned a page and gazed at a princess on a white horse. "He shouts too much," he said.

I was dabbing my scent behind each ear when I heard the voice on the radio shout, "I prove by my life that I am more competent than the dwarfs, my predecessors, who brought this country to destruction!" I wondered whether he considered all dwarfs incompetent, whether all his predecessors had really been small like Hanna. I had learned from Fritz Janicek how Engelbert Dollfuss had been put to death by Hitler because he was a priest-ridden dwarf. Perhaps Frau Hanna never listened to this speech, or, like so many, only heard what she wanted to hear.

My father was in no mood to answer my questions about dwarfs. Resi switched off the roaring, cheering noise. "Sieg Heil. What does it mean?" My father said it was utter nonsense. He got up, ready to leave, and wanted to take me home. Actually, I did not want to stay as much as I usually did. The house felt empty without the servants, who had gone to town to see the Führer. Even Frau Schwester had gone off to nurse an elderly aunt who had been knocked down in town during the frenzied welcome for Adolf Hitler. Only the porter's wife had stayed, because she was afraid of crowds. Francine, Resi's maid, was in her room with a nosebleed. Eli seemed more interested in his book than in me or Adolf Hitler.

"Ach, Ferdl, leave Reyna with me for a while. We'll have a music lesson, and later Karin is coming to give me a massage, and she has promised to do some gymnastics with Eli. That would be fun for Reyna."

My father laughed. "How about me?" he said. "It all sounds too good to miss. Especially that beautiful little Swede."

He did not look quite as carefree as he sounded that morning. At the door, he hesitated and made me promise not to cross the street by myself; there might be traffic after the parades in town. He would be back to pick me up in a few hours.

Resi had lost interest in the flight of the chosen people recently—especially after Papa had pointed out that she and Eli should go to Switzerland. The phonograph remained closed, and it was so quiet I could hear radiators ticking and birds chirping outside in the garden as we went to the music room. Not long ago, a quartet had played here, and everyone had danced during the last ball. I wished Eugene Romberg had been around for my birthday to give me something magnificent and to admire my perfume and my new aristocratic blouse.

"The maids no longer bother to dust," Resi complained, wiping the grand piano with her sleeve. "I sent them in here the other day and all they did was break the blue Dresden shepherd."

On this morning, Eli seemed as dainty and remote as the Dresden china boy, especially when he began to sing "Little Red Rose in the Meadow." While Resi played the introduction, he took on a theatrical pose. He had grown a lot this winter and towered over me. "Little red rose, I will break thee, little red rose in the meadow . . ." He moved back and forth in his velvet suit, white shirt, and patent-leather shoes, as though he were onstage. I did not bother to sing along. For the first time, the sentimentality of those words, the sorrow of a broken rose, annoyed me. I felt relieved when a dog interrupted the song with its loud barking.

"That dog, that dog again." Resi jumped up, lit a cigarette, and ran to the library window to look out to the street. "The animal has been barking and barking. He woke me up this morning. Must be homeless, or vicious. Just look at the way he goes at the gate."

We heard the bell before we saw Karin standing at the gate

in a gray suit and red beret. She was waving her briefcase to ward off the dog. Her lank, pale hair rose up in the wind.

"Mother of heaven!" Resi exclaimed, quite forgetting her Jewish religion as a black Doberman rose up on his hind legs, ready to spring at the slender girl. Just as the porter's wife came running along with a carpet beater, Karin jumped onto the gate and climbed over it. We ran to meet her, and Resi praised her gymnastics and kissed her cheeks.

"Nothing to worry about," said the girl in a shrill, foreign voice. She always sounded matter-of-fact. "The town is full of unwashed, drunken people. Millions of them." Karin had been a student of languages and gymnastics in Germany. She had not liked their exercise techniques or the food and had moved to Vienna. Her tongue was as agile as her limbs.

In the gymnasium, she provided Eli and me with soap bubbles while Resi undressed. Blowing, she explained, would help Eli's breathing. Her self-assurance made me uneasy. Resi took her place on the massage table, and Karin ordered her to put out her cigarette. "It's unhealthy," she said. I did not like to see Resi give in.

The gymnasium and the aviary were divided by a frosted-glass wall. Parakeets screeched and chirped, songbirds trilled in their cages. Eli and I climbed onto the mechanical horse with our bubbles.

"My father was going to have the electric horse repaired for me," Eli said. "I guess he forgot."

I blew a large bubble and watched it drift over lavish indoor linden, reflected in the mirror wall and the mirror on the ceiling, until it touched and was gone. I thought of the balloons at the children's party.

"Berthold is a very important Nazi. He can bring your father back later on, I'm sure. He can do anything. I would have asked him the other day when we were in Carnuntum and he showed us the Hohentahler castle, the one Hitler will give him back. I didn't have a chance to say anything because Mama got mad at him. He wanted to take me to the Roman amphitheater. She yelled at him for trying to show me this place where Romans let lions and tigers loose on Christians. She said she hated the Romans, who bullied everyone and sat there and watched human beings being torn apart by wild animals."

"Nazis are like the Romans," Eli said, and blew a number of small bubbles. "Only Romans killed Christians and the Nazis kill Jews. They would kill my father. Karin says it's always the wrong diet that makes people so mean, and also not breathing correctly."

The mirror threw a green light onto the girl's smooth, pale head. Bird sounds and her never-ending chatter had made my conversation with Eli quite private. "Did someone mention my name?" she asked without looking up from a fleshy spot just above Resi's knee. "What was I saying?" she went on. "All appetites are healthy. Only they have to be controlled." She moved the sheet without exposing more than one part of Resi's pink body.

Resi had closed her eyes, giving herself up to those anointing hands. Karin sugared her with sweet-smelling talcum powder. The parrot said, "Ha, ha, ha, *shalom*," to himself in the aviary; the steam heating hissed. In the mirror Resi appeared surrounded by leaves, a white lady in a jungle.

I no longer know what came first, the shrilling of the doorbell again and again until it stuck or the barking of the dog at the gate. Everything happened very quickly. Resi slid off the table, wrapped up in her sheet. Only minutes later, she reappeared from behind a painted screen, fully dressed in her Biblical gown. She had made a quick change, as though the scene she was about to play were familiar and only needed rehearsing.

From the conservatory we saw the dark limousine parked in front of the gate to the driveway. The headlights glowed incongruously in the sunlight and turned the hood into a toad's head. Black SS uniforms stood waiting.

Resi kissed Eli and me. "All right, Karin. You take charge of the children; take them upstairs to Eli's room and keep them there."

Karin had nothing to say.

"I want to stay with you," I cried out.

"No, no. You must keep Eli company," Resi gave me a gentle push. Karin took my hand and Eli's and pulled us along toward the dining room at a steady trot. I had to crane my neck to get a last glimpse of the toad-faced car at the gate. A black-uniform stood in the middle of the avenue looking at the white "Dollfuss" letters, as though he were saying a prayer for the dead chancellor who was a dwarf.

"You don't have to put perfume on now, Reyna," Karin scolded.

We made our way up the back stairs to the gallery. The bell kept shrilling, and a door slammed somewhere, so hard that the crystal foliage on the great chandelier chimed. A deep, growly voice began to sing "Raise High the Flags," the Horst Wessel song. We were already halfway around the gallery when the singer walked into the great hall. Karin crouched and pulled us down. We knelt beside her, peering through the banister. She put a finger to her lips, but no one could have heard us through the din of the bell and the singing.

From the gallery, the singer looked like a black spider, with his fat stomach and long, weaving arms. He wore a black SS cap back to front and walked like a sailor. Loud, high-pitched voices joined in his song. He stopped and bellowed, "*Kusch*, you drunken dogs are ruining this sacred song!" He reached for a crystal jar full of Resi's cigarettes and forced it into his pocket. "Is anyone fixing that damn bell?"

Two brown SA uniforms ambled into sight, holding onto each other. "Our professor," yelled the taller one, who was bareheaded and almost bald.

"Man of many talents," giggled his partner. "But I was always one of his best students."

The stout SS man stomped about and sang, "The SS marches with quiet and solemn tread . . ." I wondered what Resi would think of his powerful voice, and also what she would say if she saw the two other SS fellows pocketing trinkets from side tables. I could not help admiring the black spidery one as he marched back and forth in front of the prophet, bellowing the refrain. I particularly enjoyed the spooky bit about the marching honored dead. I nudged Eli, who was fingering the top button of his suit. "Ghosts," I whispered. "Ghosts . . ."

"Where is everybody?" the singer asked the prophet. "Where are you hiding, you Jews?"

"He thinks it's a portrait of your father," I whispered to Eli.

"Stop that giggling," Karin hissed. "And put that perfume away at once. It makes Eli sneeze and they'll see us. Not a word or a sound. When I say 'Now,' we go quietly along the wall to the stairs."

At that moment, Francine came into the great hall from the

servants' entrance. "Heil Hitler," shouted the black one. "Heil," echoed his brown friends, whose pockets bulged.

Francine stood below us in the middle of the rose-colored carpet. I could see the lace cap on her dark head and a few drops of blood on her little apron. The bell stopped, and the silence made me hold my breath.

The black SS man spread his long arms. "No salute, of course, ja, ja. Only a Jewish maid would stay in a Jewish house."

"I am French," Francine said, without raising her head.

"I'll soon find out about that." The bald SS man staggered as though he were at sea.

"Never mind the girl—who cares about women!" bellowed the stout, spidery one. "Let's get dirty old Grandpa off the wall."

"*Mon dieu,*" exclaimed Francine. "Is a very precious painting. Do not touch, Herr."

"You don't speak German, do you?" The girlish one giggled.

"They're all alike. Fuzzy hair, the hook nose," shouted the one in front of the prophet. He swayed, lurched forward, and held onto the back of a low chair. "Just like the old man. Can't fool me. I can spot them. Let's get dirty Grandpa, get them all."

I had to snicker. Karin pulled me back from the banister just as Resi came into the great hall. Eli looked frightened, and I took his hand. "They are terribly funny," I told him.

"Drunk and dangerous," Karin whispered. "Not another sound."

Resi stood under the glass dome; the sun shone onto her honey-colored ringlets. "*Grüss Gott,*" she said, "God's greetings." I could hear barking in the distance, it was so quiet. She held herself more upright than usual, hands folded. I noticed that she had added the gold Star of David to her costume. "You may go, Francine!" Perhaps she remembered the Marschallin in *Rosen-kavalier*; she certainly looked the part.

"Jawohl, Fräulein. Go and come back at once with a bucket of hot, soapy water and a scrub brush," said a familiar, slow, didactic voice. "We are doing a little cleaning up today in honor of the Führer." I hardly recognized Fritz in his tight black SS uniform with its belts and buckles. A death emblem on his cap had been polished to a high gleam.

Eli whispered, "It's only Fritz." He seemed relieved. We both knew Fritz as a gardener, and we had seen him defeated, struck down with a milk bottle by Eugene Romberg.

Francine said something to Resi.

"I understand French, mademoiselle, and I have good ears. You'd better hurry with that hot water." His beak nose pecked, almost touching her cheek. She fled, and the men all laughed.

Karin said, "Now," and slid to the wall, but Eli clung to the banister and held onto my hand. Karin came back, looking unhappy. I did not see why she should be worried, when Resi stood down there as though she were onstage, waiting for the welcoming applause to pass before she sang.

More brownshirts came in and wandered around the room, staring at her and pocketing little knickknacks in passing. Resi was not smoking. The spidery SS officer walked around her in circles. She pulled herself up, relaxed her shoulders as though she were about to sing an aria.

"Your name?" he barked into her face.

She did not flinch. "Ach, pardon. I was sure Herr Janicek had told you who I am, if you have never seen me onstage." Her voice sounded amused, as though she were smiling, but we could not see her expression from the gallery. "You have not introduced yourselves. I don't know who has honored me with this surprise visit."

The bald SA man went a few steps in her direction, reeling as though he were on the deck of a Danube steamboat on a windy day. "Are you a Jew?"

"Shouting has become very fashionable, but my hearing, as a musician, is quite perfect. I am a Jew." Her clear, lilting voice could have been heard in the top row of the balcony at the Opera. Then she spoke softly. "Are you a Christian?"

Karin squeezed my hand, and it hurt, because I held my perfume bottle. "If you come, Eli will follow."

But Eli shook his head and clung to the banister.

"At this point, Frau Romberg," Fritz Janicek said, "we do the questioning. My men have celebrated with a little champagne at the Schongross villa. You know, those boys are still celebrating. High-spirited lads . . ."

"We would like a word with Herr Romberg." The stout SS man waved his arms about as though he were trying to catch an invisible Eugene Romberg in a great net.

"My husband has left Austria," Resi said. "Everyone knows that!"

The stout one turned his attention to the prophet Jeremiah and shouted, "The old Jew, where is he hiding?"

"Mein Herr, this is an original Titian. His *Prophet Jeremiah.*"

"I know a Jew when I see one," roared the bloated black uniform.

Fritz grabbed Aunt Resi's sleeve and held onto it. Somewhere a clock struck, and I thought of Grandmama's "Time is running out."

"Your husband beat me over the head and had me arrested, but I tell you, yours is the greater insult. You think you can embarrass me in front of my boys, my former students. Ja, I know paintings. I was a professor of art and Latin at a gymnasium for boys when you were still among the proletarians at Hernals and had never heard of Titian."

"Kusch, Professor," the black one yelled, and stumbled. "I might not know as much as you do, but you can't fool me. That's Grandpa on the wall—spitting image of the Splasher, except for the beard. I have an eye for them. They're all hiding in the cellar. Come, boys, forward march!"

"None of that. No cellars, Hensler. You've had enough." Fritz Janicek spoke as a pedagogue. "My oldest pupil . . . he celebrated a little too much. My students are very much attached to me; they always were. Anyway, we won't keep you standing here, Frau Romberg. I see our mademoiselle has obliged."

We did not see Francine until the group began to move toward the door. She was carrying a steaming bucket in one hand and a large scrub brush in the other.

Fritz held her back. "The French are not as handy as the Jews, nicht wahr? You, Frau Romberg, all decked out with a Jewish star, will be the one to assist us in our good work." His eyes scanned the gallery at this moment. Karin gripped my arm; we ducked. "Close your perfume bottle, Reyna," she whispered angrily. "They'll smell us if they don't see us. Be still. They are leaving."

Francine dropped the bucket and brush and fled to the kitchen entrance. The men laughed. "After her!" yelled Hensler, clinging to Fritz, the professor. "She'll lead us to the old Jew. Off to the cellar, *Burschen,* that's where they are, with all the money."

Fritz shook him off. "No more cellars for you, boy. You two, Karl and Loisl, take a look around the house. See who's here, who should be out there with us." He turned his attention to an Egyptian cat, stroked the stone head, picked it up. "You don't mind," he said to Resi. "Just a little souvenir from this beautiful house. Who knows?" She turned her back on him, and he forced the stone cat into a rucksack which had been left out of sight under a table when he first came in.

"May I ask you to take up this bucket and brush, Frau Romberg? My rucksack is rather heavy, as you can see—otherwise I would have the honor to assist you."

Resi was looking around for a cigarette, her crystal jar. Fritz went through a lot of bowing and scraping to produce one and light it with a gold cigarette lighter which he found in his rucksack. When he finally handed her the bucket, she took it up as though it were filled with liquid gold. I could see the steam rising. A circle of dust marked the spot where the beautiful cat had stood. Resi went back to the pedestal with the bucket and dusted it with her sleeve.

I gave way to a sound, half sob, half guffaw, as the pantomime reached its anticlimax. But no one heard me. Hensler was again bellowing "Raise High the Flags," repeating the first line with a lolling tongue. Fritz Janicek took Resi's elbow, like a dinner partner, and steered her out. Several uniforms followed. Only the SA men remained.

Hensler turned to the prophet. "Rip off your beard when I find you," he yelled. His two comrades were busy looking around for more souvenirs rather than hidden Jews. They ignored him as he staggered toward the wall. He clung to the massive frame as though he were about to crawl up and attack the canvas. It came down on Hensler with a great crash. The frame struck him on the neck, and he vanished under it. A blackbird sang somewhere near the gallery window. The glossy boots protruding from the frame jerked twice. Everything was still. I screamed.

The two SA men pulled out revolvers and looked around. "Who's there? Come out, or we shoot!"

Karin had already pushed us back against the wall. Eli took me by the shoulders and with unexpected calmness pointed at our favorite hiding place, the tapestry with the unicorn.

"It came from upstairs," said the one who sounded like a girl. "Let's go."

"How about Hensler?"

"Idiot. Let him sleep it off under there."

"*Also, Los marsch!*"

The tapestry hung to the floor and hid us completely. But Fritz Janicek's boys had had art lessons and stopped to discuss whether it was an original French piece and whether they should take it off the wall before anyone else got hold of it. I became terrified, and in my panic opened my perfume bottle and dabbed my face with scent.

Eli sneezed three times. They tore the tapestry aside and came at us with guns and clubs. "Out, *raus*, Jews, or we shoot!"

Eli was panting for breath and had to sneeze again, because I had spilled some of the lily-of-the-valley perfume on his suit.

"You can't hurt these children," Karin said in a very small voice. "They belong across the street, to Ferdinand von Meinert, and I'm the nursemaid. We were visiting Frau Romberg."

"Visiting a Jew-house?" the one called Loisl asked, buffing his manicured fingernails on his uniform.

"We came to see the birds," I said, and I lost all fear at the sound of my own pert voice.

The one named Karl grinned into Karin's face. "So you work for the old Meinert fox, little blonde. He took the milk away from the Jew; guess he's trying to make himself at home here, too . . . Well, you tell him from us that our professor has other plans."

Loisl was eyeing us with curiosity. "No need to hide," he said with an ugly smile. "The professor likes little boys." His huge Adam's apple bobbed up and down above me. "You look around, Karl. I'll take them to the professor. Might be something fishy."

He herded us ahead of him through the empty house and out the gate. The headlights of the toad-faced limousine still glared at the locked car-gate. Loisl waved his arms when we reached the top of the steps and yelled something about the car lights, but no one listened.

A holiday crowd had gathered between the Water Castle and the Meinert-Hof. I had never seen so many people on our street. Herbert, the five-year-old son of the foot doctor, lived nearby and had come to the park several times with his round-faced nurse to play with me. I disliked his baby talk and whining. He called me "Boy" and was afraid of me. Now I saw him fidgeting around, pulling his nurse by the hand like a dog on a leash. He held a red balloon, decorated with a swastika, on a long string.

Fritz Janicek and Resi were separated from the crowd when a large truck drove up. Fritz talked to the driver. Resi put down her bucket and looked around. She greeted a mother and daughter, neighbors. They wore their Sunday hats and gloves. The chimney sweep, right next to them, had been at work, was all black, and carried his coiled brush over his shoulder. He was grinning. His teeth shone white in his blackened face.

We did not see the ladies kneeling on the road in fur coats until the truck moved forward. Five or six of them were scrubbing away at those white "Dollfuss" letters, which had resisted rain and snow for most of my lifetime. The vehicle came to a halt so close to them that they had to crawl aside. Men in white shirts and swastika armbands tumbled out. They did not seem to feel the cold March wind. Their coarse faces glowed with excitement; they staggered about, nudging each other, laughing, and pointing at the women. "Scrubbing day. Scrubbing day. Spring cleaning for the Führer."

Schoolboys had climbed the steps in front of us to get a better view, and Loisl could not get us past them. They clapped their hands, whistled, and jeered, waving swastika flags. In the middle of all the confusion, little Herbert broke away from his nurse and danced around in front of the men, shouting, "Hurray, hurray, Hitler scrubbing . . ." until the nurse lunged forward and grabbed him by the seat of his pants.

Resi stood on tiptoes, trying to see over the heads of the men; Fritz seemed to be having an argument with the driver. The ladies with their buckets remained on their knees in their beautiful coats, as though they were in a trance.

"Back to work, there! Come now," yelled the leader of the whiteshirts, a rosy-cheeked youth. The other whiteshirts pushed in front of the SS and yelled, "Work, Jews, work," as though they had to make up for their lack of rank.

The ladies began to scrub again, in accord. They did not raise their heads, took no notice of each other. Each one worked alone, scrubbing with soft hands at those indelible letters.

The chorus "Jews! Jews!" brought more people along. Workingmen in Sunday clothes carried flags; a baby nurse in uniform, with a lace-trimmed carriage, craned her neck; an old couple out for a spring walk came to see what was going on. The old lady carried a bouquet of yellow primroses.

"Professor! Professor!" shouted Loisl. Eli put both hands over his ears. We had been allowed to wear our coats, but he shivered. Dread, like bliss, could not be measured in seconds, minutes, or years. Time was running out.

It all began when a skinny fellow in a white shirt and horn-rimmed spectacles spat at a lady in a beaver coat, shouting, "Dirty Jew whores!" Everything happened very fast, and seemed to go on endlessly. Fritz's boys joined the whiteshirts, and they circled around the women as though at a playground, enjoying a new game. "*Pfui!*" they shouted and spat at the ladies. "*Pfui!*" Someone kicked a stooping back. The schoolboys in front of us shouted, "*Pfui, Teufel!*" buffeting each other and sticking out their pink tongues. They laughed.

To outdo the SS men, the round-faced, innocent-looking young leader of the whiteshirts stepped forward into the middle of the circle. He was It. Standing above the cowering women, he grinned, fumbling with his pants; the gesture looked boyish and natural. He bent his knees, leaned back, and cupped his most private parts as though he held a tulip bud. As he stood, poised like an oversized stone urchin making water in some ancient fountain, the men nudged each other, laughed, and staggered forward. They lined up with him, street boys at play. The smiling boy directed his stream onto a well-coiffed white head, and it ran down into her fur collar.

I had seen the lady driving past our house. Her hands trembled; she drew her head into her coat like a turtle.

"Filthy pigs," Karin hissed through her teeth. She tried to cover our eyes.

I saw the performance through her fingers. Men danced around in circles, one by one, competing, goading. Loisl, beside us, clapped his hands. Workingmen, the chimney sweep, looked on as though they were at the circus. They watched the Nazis make water on heads and hands and silk stockings.

By the time Fritz, with Resi, pushed his way through the crowd, the men were buttoning their trousers, though little Herbert had broken loose and pulled down his own trousers, ready to urinate on anyone nearby. The competition was over. Participants and onlookers, shamefaced, excited, frightened, or entertained—none of us would ever forget this scene.

Memory of evil works like one of those clockwork automats in the amusement park, the Prater, where figures stand rigid until a coin sets them into motion, to move about and perform the same scene over and over again as long as the mechanism lasts. In my dreams, the white-haired lady in the soiled beaver coat floated on a green barge, dressed up in black boots and a swastika armband and a Hanna Roth hat loaded with yellow primroses. I can still see her sitting on her heels, wiping her soiled face with her gloves. Then she tossed the gloves away gracefully and returned to her scrubbing.

Her beautiful white hands, her large ruby ring, must have caught Fritz Janicek's attention. He had been left out, but now he stepped forward. "*Also,* Frau Romberg. We seem to have missed some of the action. Now, I think these ladies need some help." He stepped on the beautiful hand with the ruby ring. The lady leaped up with a scream.

I yelled, "Stop it, Fritz Janicek!"

Karin's hand closed over my mouth, and in my confusion I bit her finger. I wanted to run to Resi, but Karin wouldn't let go of me.

The woman was rubbing her hand, and suddenly the black dog came through the crowd with a yelp and pounced on her with his front paws, licking her face, her hands, with frantic barks of joy. Sympathy passed through the crowd like the rustling of leaves in the wind. "Poor dog, chased away from home. They say the men kicked him." The woman clung to the dog, weeping.

"Order!" yelled Fritz the Professor, as though he were confronted with an unruly class of boys. "Let's go back to work at once. We are not finished. No more nonsense, or I'll shoot the beast."

The woman said, "Go home, Rolfi," and began to cry even harder.

"They arrested her husband," said a boy in front of me. "They took a lot of things—that's her car over there."

The crowd murmured, "Poor dog . . ." Helpful hands urged the animal out of the circle. The chimney sweep said, "Here, Rolfi," and led him away by the collar. At that moment, Resi came forward to confront Fritz and glowered at him.

"Well, are we ready?" he said.

She stepped on her cigarette and carefully put it out. Then she gathered herself up as she did before she sang. She grew in stature. A loose cloak hung dramatically over her gray dress, exposing the Star of David. Her blonde, soft, dimpled prettiness, like the whipped cream on a chocolate cake, was typically Viennese. This would be her scene; she captivated the onlookers.

"Nonsense," she said in her Viennese stage voice. "This filth, this insanity, is criminal."

Fritz pressed his thin lips together and gave her an angry push, but she was accustomed to taking a firm stand, to help project her voice, and he hardly moved her.

"Mutti! Mutti!" yelled Eli before Karin could stifle him in her arms.

Fritz grinned. "You go to work at once, Frau Romberg." He waved to Loisl. "If this lady doesn't do as she is told, bring me that Jew kid."

Resi turned, facing the onlookers out of sheer habit. "You leave the children alone," she said, as though Fritz were a stage villain. "I'll go to work; I'll clean up." She reached for her bucket, and in the swift motion of one trained to dance, she turned and emptied the hot water over Fritz, splashing some of the whiteshirts who had been closing in on her.

He shrieked, and his boys pushed forward with clubs and drawn guns. I was knocked down, but one of the schoolboys helped me up. Then the drunk ones, the sober ones, the uniforms and half-uniforms, the workers, even the baby nurse and the old couple gave way and roared with laughter. The crowd liked to be entertained; they were ready to be amused at anyone's expense. They laughed as though they were at a show in the amusement park.

A garbage truck drove up, and the men in their official streetcleaners' uniforms leaned over the top. "What's going on here? What's with Frau Reserl Heller?"

"Ja, that's the Little Nightingale," someone called out. "From the State Opera."

Loisl managed to get us through the throng of boys. "Make way, make way," he shouted, waving his club.

The old lady with the primroses took him by the elbow. "Don't you hurt those children," she said.

"That's the Meinert child," Herbert's nurse called out. "Don't you bother her."

During a moment of confusion, the mood of the crowd began to change. The professor's boys put their guns away. Whiteshirts went back to the truck. The ladies rose, tembling, to their feet, and everyone made way for them. They followed the dog and his mistress, walking hurriedly alongside the garbage truck. Only the buckets and brushes were left behind.

"And grown men, too," a woman's voice said behind me. "They'll say anyone is a Jew if it suits them."

"Who forced her to marry one?"

Karin pulled us toward the Meinert gate.

"Professor! Professor!" The bald SS man who had stayed in the Water Castle came running down the steps, dived through the remaining boys. "Let me through! Murder!" he yelled. "Hensler is dead!"

Fritz Janicek looked as though he had been stung by a bee in the rose garden. "Who's dead? What are you saying? Not my own student, not Freddie?" He finally stood in the limelight. He, too, was used to performing, for his students. A cunning look came over his face. He forgot his dripping uniform as he paced back and forth.

"Murder," he said. "Murder of a young hero, one of Adolf Hitler's *Schutzstaffeln.*"

Some of the whiteshirts came back and stood around him.

"Who did it? Who?" they demanded.

Loisl, who could have given the answer, sat with a bottle on the running board of the black car.

"Murder," Fritz said again. "For a moment I thought history was repeating itself." His voice sounded as full of excitement as Hitler's. "Right here, in front of this Jew castle, I was struck down by the Jew himself. Now the Jew wife got the better of me. But not quite—no! SS man Hensler is lying dead in there." His voice broke, just like the one I had heard on the radio. He wiped his face in a clever dramatic gesture. "My oldest student is murdered, a martyr. Killed by Jews."

He pointed at Resi. A circle of his boys formed around her. Karin made me open the gate, but I heard Resi say, "I was not in the house."

"Don't you believe it," Fritz said. "There'll be plenty of witnesses."

Nazi logic and justice was still new. His educated voice might have had its effect, but he was interrupted at this moment by a shriek of agony, a loud wailing. Little Herbert screamed with unbelievable power. Everyone turned and flocked around him. We were already inside the gate. Agnes was coming to meet us.

"Has he been hurt?" people asked, hovering over the blue-eyed boy in his matching blue knitted suit. "Sweet little fellow. What happened?"

Little Herbert made the most of his scene; sobbing loudly, he pointed up to a diminishing speck in the sky.

"It's nothing, nothing at all," the nurse said in a Slavic voice. "The balloon, it got away and flew off. He let go of the string in all the excitement."

Herbert was yelling, "I want it back! I want it!"

"Now, now, little angel. You'll get another one."

"Don't cry. Here's some candy."

Men and women turned to him in their great need to comfort. Catering to his futile grief helped them to feel they were kind, after all.

11

Glass Walls

THE CROWD MOVED OFF like well-directed extras. Whiteshirts leaped into the truck and sped toward town. I can't remember how we got inside the gate and up the steps. Eli didn't move; he looked stunned, and Karin half-carried him to the door. He was spared a last glimpse of his mother. She was standing stock still as Fritz minced his way toward her. He picked her up, and she smiled as he carried her with visible effort. The boys lined up like guards of honor at a wedding. She threw them kisses as she was lifted into the black limousine, and then she burst into song. Agnes came running from the back of the house, swinging a carpet beater. The new gardener followed. Before they understood what had happened, the limousine had turned around to drive off. For a moment it looked as though the new gardener would run after them, but Poldi and Lise had come out and they held him back.

✿   ✿   ✿

No one could find out where Resi had been taken. The search for her began at once. Nazis and anti-Nazis, everyone, tried to find her and bring her back—except Mama. She gave up on Resi as she had given up on the doll, never taking part in the effort to find her, never accepting the fact that she had been taken. Herr Krummerer reappeared in our living room with his notebook. A lawyer came and went. Cheese Hannes, Eugene Romberg's partner, had reluctantly accepted my father as new director of the Romberg dairies. Now he turned up in our living room as a puny SA man. "I had nothing to do with it, Ferdl," he said at once.

My father had decided to keep Eli in the *Stüberl*, the catacombs, next to his wine cellar. Frau Schwester took charge and was told to keep out of sight. Just as Cheese Hannes asked where Eli was, she came bustling through the morning room making her clacking sound. Mama never left the piano and kept on with one of her sonatinas.

"It's kind of you to worry about the boy, Hannes, but he does have Aryan relatives," Father said.

Mother played to his words, her hands dancing over the piano. No one listened to the fluency of her music. Only the stiff, expressionless dolls inside their glass case formed a captive audience. She caught my note of satisfaction at once when I told her those dolls were all in jail. A line formed between her brows. She allowed her head to drop back, as though her braids had turned to metal. Her eyes filled with tears. "Who isn't!"

Father had gone to the door with Cheese Hannes. He came back into the room, upset by his visitor. "Will you please stop practicing the piano and act as though you cared! You are no longer fifteen, Annerl." Her fingers slipped off the keys and she watched him with her violet-blue eyes. He paced back and forth, and his reflection fitted over the unwanted dolls in the glass case.

"I'm forced to work behind the scenes," he said. "If I show I want Resi back, they'll suspect me of double-dealing. They like the idea that I took over the dairies and Aryanized Romberg Industries. Imagine, Hannes had the nerve to ask me whether I put Janicek up to the whole thing, since he was my gardener. With Resi out of the way, Hannes said, we wouldn't have to worry about her interest." He went to Mama and took both her hands and pulled her toward him. I got between them.

"I'm sorry, children." He caressed us absent-mindedly. "I'm in a state. Eli is a worry. It isn't safe to keep him here."

I said I wanted Eli to stay. Mother took my side. "The doctor says he should rest until he feels better. He's only half-Jewish. Mixlings will get passports."

"The borders are closed. He is my responsibility. The twins know he's here. They'll never keep their mouths shut." The new gardener knew, too, for he had carried a cot down to the cellar room.

I had to wait until Eli had rested and eaten something before my father unlocked the cellar door and allowed me to go down. I could hear the fan of the ventilating system and a clicking sound. I carried a music box Resi had given to me down to Eli. When I started it off, Frau Schwester tore open the door and shouted, "Who is it?," holding her knitting needles out in front of her, ready to defend Eli. She was knitting something baby-blue for him and put it away to examine my hands to make sure I was clean enough to come in.

Eli sat propped up by too many pillows in the little peasant bed which usually served as a settee. Frau Schwester's cot had been made up on the other side, under Resi's old mandolin with all the gay ribbons and charms. Eli's eyes remained half-closed when I handed him the music box and told him he could keep it. He wound it up and listened to the "Merry Widow Waltz," tilting his dark head. We both remembered how Resi had sung it for us during the journey to the Promised Land.

Frau Schwester had brought books and toys from Eli's room, and they were lined up on shelves close to his bed. But the collection of fancy toy soldiers, stuffed animals, gilded carriages, and kites from India looked out of place in the little peasant room. So did Eli, in his dark green silk pajamas with embroidered initials. His flawless almond-shaped face, the velvety dark eyes and hair outlined by blond wood and white pillows, startled me. He even smelled exotic, foreign, as he sat there, perfumed and sad-eyed, like an exiled prince.

For the first time I did not know what to say to him. We had seen things we could not talk about. He wound up the music box again; the music played. Outrage hung between us like a glass wall. I felt dull, disappointed. His half-smile as he listened to the music box bothered me. I had come to comfort him, to make myself feel better. His sadness at the Water Castle often hid contentment. Now he smiled. I had been determined to keep him there at my home and never let him leave. Now I looked at him in wonder and knew this could not be.

He never asked for anything; he was above all that. He did not even ask for his mother. We listened to the music box play its waltz tune while Frau Schwester clicked her knitting needles. She peeled a red apple for us, and we shared it. Then she decided we were tired and insisted on picking me up and carrying me upstairs.

As soon as she put me down, I heard Berthold's voice. I ran into the living room and threw myself into his open arms, shivering as though I had come in from the cold. My mother was saying I was really all right, that there was bound to be a delayed reaction. I clung to him, and he rocked me as he laughed. I breathed in the fragrance of his fair skin. He smelled like Mother. A delicious feeling of safety came over me, although he was talking about Resi's being in danger. I buried my face against his neck and gave him a secret kiss.

"You certainly have a way with little girls, Bertl." My father sounded more like himself.

"Sisters, cousins, girls, girls . . . Ja, ja . . ."

I felt as though I had just found Berthold again. All during my early years it would be like that, particularly when he was away. I would almost forget what he was like, then he would return and I would feel as though he had never left me at all. His laughing mouth, that funny hair, made me gurgle like an infant.

He threw me up toward a carved light fixture, caught me, threw me once more, almost too high. I had seen only him—suddenly, I saw only the uniform. Not blue anymore—black, new, with gleaming epaulets, death's head, eagle with swastika—the uniform of hate. I heard myself scream. "Put me down. Get away!"

"It's the uniform." Mother picked me up, her cheeks red and her eyes angry. "Ferdl's fault. Why did he have to take our child over there? If Resi wants to play the part of a Jew, that's her lookout. She never once thought of her child. Ours shouldn't have been there."

She took me upstairs into the boudoir, shut the door and locked it. Father had to knock to be admitted when he came upstairs later on. He stayed with us. I sat on Mother's lap, and she fed me. Krampus was there, too, and he sat on Father's knee, trying to get some of my food and licking everyone. I knew they were worried. We sat together in a huddle, forced together, and I sensed danger, especially when Mama said I could sleep in her bed. I knew she was afraid men in uniform might come through our locked gate and burst into the Meinert-Hof and take not only Eli but me, too.

My father said, "I'm a man who loves his family and his work, a little glass of wine, a game of chess. I'm a simple fellow. I just want to be left alone. Politics are not for me."

Mama shook her head, took hold of his kaiser beard with both hands, and kissed his mouth. I pushed between them. Krampus started to nip. Mama even tolerated him. Not long ago, she had gone as far as locking herself in and hiding the keys when she was really anxious to leave. Now we clung together within new boundaries. We seemed to be encased like unwanted dolls behind glass walls that both forced us together and kept us apart from a utopia of obscenity where even little Herbert could get into the act and pull down his pants. Who could blame him, or blame us? Innocence knows no guilt. We could do nothing.

✻   ✻   ✻

I was supposed to be asleep under Mother's down-filled quilt. My parents sat at the little round table, eating a light supper. Mother was saying, "Anyway, Ferdl, Resi has you where she wants you. Now that she's vanished, all you can think of is how to get her back."

"This sounds as though she had herself accused of murder just to get my attention. Do you think I'm worth it, Annerl?" I was glad to hear him tease.

"Not exactly, but—"

He closed her mouth with a long kiss. "Let's go to my room, or we'll wake the little one . . ."

The Biedermeier clock ticked me to sleep, swinging its cherubs. Mother was snoring softly beside me when I woke up. It was beginning to get light. She was lying on her back, a braid coiled on the pillow. I touched it. The room smelled of her perfume. I sucked my thumb, although I hadn't done this for some time. Agnes forbade it sternly. She was afraid it would push my front teeth forward—as though the Falkenburgs had gotten their crooked teeth from sucking their thumbs! My eyes wanted to close, and I half-dreamed of Grandmother, the little pistol. Then

I saw the doll's chair rocking back and forth in the twilight to the ticking of the clock.

I sat up and stared at an invisible doll rocking back and forth, impervious and stiff. Once more I listened to the girlish laughter of the imperial keeper of the dolls. I jumped from the bed, went to the chair, and stopped it. A window had been left open, and the draft had set the delicate chair into motion. I looked out. After all that had happened, the Water Castle remained lit up as it had been the morning after the last ball. I knelt on the window seat and sucked my thumb, listening to birdsongs. One by one, the windows across the street went dark.

A group of men stood in front of the gate, stomping their feet to keep warm; their cigarettes glowed. A wagon and a black horse waited under the linden tree where Fritz Janicek had been unmasked. The driver on the front seat was drinking from a bottle. Then I saw Stauble and Pichler come through the gate, their fancy liveries spruced up with swastika armbands. They carried a long wooden box, also decorated with a swastika. I could almost hear their "Ja, ja, da, da. Na," as they came down the steps and dropped the box to salute the men in the street, shooting their right arms up. The men returned the salute and took off their hats. The box was then carried to the wagon. When it slipped from Pichler, one of the men came forward, gave it a swift kick, and booted it up.

Stauble and Pichler joined the driver on the front seat. He offered them the bottle and they all drank. Then he cracked his whip, and the horse began to trot. Streetlights went out at that moment, and the wagon swayed over the white letters which the kneeling women had not been able to erase with soap and water. The men on the sidewalk saluted each other with a "Heil" and took off in a car.

Where were the musicians playing the funeral march, and why didn't the horse wear black plumes? Why didn't the relatives in black clothes walk behind the dead man, followed by tradesmen, street urchins, dogs? I liked to see the mourners return after the funeral feast, stepping along behind the prancing horse, to the jolly "Deutschmeister" march, the horse trotting, ready for the stable. I took comfort in sucking my thumb and went back to sleep.

I did ask Father why there had been no funeral celebration for Hensler. He became angry. "We'll just have to dig him up. To prove that little Resi could never have broken his neck."

"Then will there be a procession?"

My father did not seem that concerned. Neither was I after he told me that Eli and Frau Schwester had already left the Meinert-Hof for an unknown safe place. My father promised I could speak with Eli on the telephone after he settled in, and one day we might even go to visit him. I had one of my outbursts, because I knew I could get away with it.

"An unknown place! How can you take me?"

He smiled and said Eli's hiding place was known only to himself, no one else. While I listened, my hand reached into my pocket for the golden keys. At night I slept with them under my pillow. I kept an eye on the house across the street and waited for the lights to come on again.

I tried to strike a bargain with the Holy Ghost at the chapel: "If you bring back all the Rombergs, I'll sing you 'All the Birds Are Back Again' ten times." I think I turned to the wooden bird among the rafters because that image had remained untouched by Fritz Janicek's brush.

On the way home, Mama told Heinz to stop at the candy shop. The vintners' village was bright with flags and Hitler posters. But the movie house still advertised an Austrian kaiser film, and the familiar face with the side-whiskers smiled down on children carrying flowers. The poster was marked up with black swastikas.

When we stopped at the candy shop, the windows, which had been full of devils and devils' masks when I passed on the bus with Agnes before Krampus, were all boarded up. A Jewish star and swastikas patterned the boards, and "Jude" was printed on the wall.

"How could this be? Poor old people. They were so kind to you." Mother banged on the glass partition, and Heinz drove on at once.

"I hate Nazis," I said.

"You must not say that. We're not all like that. It's just the riffraff." She kissed me and held my hand.

I remember the days that followed as unusually bright and chilly. I was fed more Maltaline than usual and put out into the garden to play. The new gardener, Vlado, even brought along his small son, Gusti, a curly-haired towhead with a dirty face, a runny nose, and a bad smell. Fortunately, he vanished up into a tree almost as soon as he came through the gate, and his father could not coax him down. I look up my vigil on the steps, with a few music boxes, some cookies, and my dog. Krampus ran back and forth between the gardener, who was busy painting the cottage, the tree with Gusti, two squirrels, and me, barking, growling, scratching up. When the servants from the Romberg villa came across the street to see my father, Krampus snapped and was spanked. He should have been rewarded.

They came to be paid by Father and to say goodbye. Francine was dressed up in one of Resi's fur-trimmed coats. All of them wore Sunday clothes, and they brought more of Eli's toys, clothing, and his books. The cook wanted to know how he was doing, whether he was eating well, where he was. My father told them he believed Eli was quite well, and lit his pipe. Francine gave me a little kiss, then she handed Father a small patent-leather case. Resi's room had been searched by the Gestapo and sealed, but she had managed to get the jewel case out in time. She was lost for German words, faltered. Some of the pieces, she said, were missing . . . *"Quelle domage."*

They all kissed me and went back to the Water Castle to collect their belongings. My father stayed in the front garden after he saw them to the gate, and he began digging, turning the soil at the flowerbeds beside the garage. He spat into his palms and worked as though his life depended on it. I took up a spade and jumped on it with both feet, a trick which usually made him laugh. He didn't notice me and kept watching the house across the street.

"Damn them all!" he exclaimed when he saw the procession of servants come down the steps, led by the cook in one of Resi's fur coats. They went back and forth, carrying not only suitcases and rucksacks but lamps, little tables, and radios. A truck came and was loaded very quickly. Two taxis drove up. When I saw Francine walk away with a cage full of Eli's African sparrows, I ran to the gate shaking my fists.

The new gardener had come to watch, his round, smiling face distorted by rage. He shouted something in Slovene and shook our locked gate, begging Father to let him go after them. Father told him it was no use. If the servants didn't take the stuff, someone else would. "I know, I know," Vlado said. "I got away from those dirty dogs, but they plundered my farm." His son sounded off like a tom turkey from the top of a birch tree. "I'll murder you if you break that branch," Vlado yelled. His wife had stayed behind with the rest of the children to sell the farm, then she would join him. Father had made inquiries; they were good people. I might have told him that Vlado had marched carrying a red flag, but the telephone rang just as we came into the house.

It was Frau Schwester, and after Father had made a list of things she needed, he handed me the receiver. I heard Eli say my name. He asked me what I had been doing. His voice rose and fell like his mother's, and he rolled his *r* like his father. I did not tell him that Francine had taken some of his African sparrows, but talked about Vlado to make him laugh. Eli said he was glad Father was going to bring his stamp collection; he had a friend where he was who liked stamps. When he mentioned his friend, Frau Schwester interrupted our conversation. I never did get to tell Eli I had learned to climb trees with dirty Gusti. There was no better way of watching what went on across the street.

A day or so later, I had perched like a bird when Stauble and Pichler came bungling down the steps. They bumped into the gate, and the burlap slipped off the big painting. I saw the prophet. Although they no longer worked for Resi, they still wore the operatic liveries. Trousers stuffed into black boots and swastikas hardly brought them up to date. They went back into the house after they had loaded the painting, and I climbed as high as I dared. Dirty Gusti swayed above my head. Krampus almost gave us away, since the tree was not in leaf and he was barking and clawing and leaping at the trunk. As soon as the men reached the gate with Resi's four-poster bed, he raced to the front railing, stuck his head out like a frantic gargoyle, and yelped at them.

Resi's great carved bed swayed between the two men, organdy curtains and frills dancing in the wind. I yelled, "Stop, thief! Stop, thief!" From above me came wild guttural sounds. Dirty Gusti did not communicate with words, but his meaning was always clear. Emitting an unearthly shriek, he startled the two men.

The bed slid away from them down the steps. "It's all your fault that the prophet fell down!" I think I added something like "Traitors to the crown!" because I had heard the expression in a story on the radio. This set them into a panic. They didn't look at the tree; instead, they scanned the cloudless sky for an accuser. They picked up their burden in a frenzy and made it to the truck. Never had I seen them move so fast or heave so hard. As the truck drove off they jumped in the back, fell onto Resi's bed, all arms and legs, tumbling like June bugs.

Forsythia—gold rain, as we call it—decorated our slopes and lit up the wrought-iron railings across the street as though nothing had happened. The grass turned green, and crocuses sprang up. Snowdrops lingered in the shade, touching my heart as they began to wilt. Where was Resi? Eli never mentioned his mother when we spoke on the telephone, Agnes or Mother, someone, was always listening to what I said to him. Once, after I heard a cock crow and asked Eli whether he was staying at the farm, Frau Schwester cut us off. I annoyed my father with that question, and I reminded him constantly of his promise to take me to Eli's hiding place.

On one of those bright afternoons I was swaying on the lower branches of a chestnut tree near the gate when a taxi stopped in front of the Water Castle. Frau Traude and Hanna Roth got out and walked up to the great house. Eli's grandmother was hatless, round and light on her feet. Hanna, adorned with a hat full of flowers, rang the bell by pressing it with her umbrella. The porter's wife came, wiping her hands on her apron. There seemed to be an argument. Hanna Roth swung around on her platform shoes and came down the steps in a fury. Frau Traude followed. It looked as though they had tried to get in and the porter's wife had turned them away.

I called to them and climbed down so quickly I broke a few twigs and scratched my legs. Then I opened the gate and exchanged a curtsy with Hanna Roth. Gusti slid down and made himself heard with unseemly sounds at the Meisterin.

"In trousers, playing with dirty boys, climbing trees . . ." She shook her head. "In our new Austria, the Ostmark, girls will be girls, playing with dolls. Motherhood is important to our Führer."

I refused to believe that playing with a doll had anything to do with being a mother, but before I could say anything, she had turned her back on me to concentrate on the great house. "I hope you take heed, my little highness. Listen to old Hanna who can see things that frighten her. Never go across the street again unless I'm around."

Before I could ask her any questions, Frau Traude produced chocolates for Gusti and me. After taking two, Gusti scampered off, as though all his brothers and sisters might come after him.

The Meisterin was about to leave when Father came around the corner, walking toward the garage with Heinz. He saw us, handed his briefcase to the chauffeur, and came toward the gate in great strides that minimized his limp. The wind ruffled his thick, fair hair; his cheeks glowed. I knew something was on his mind because he pulled on his right ear.

Hanna Roth greeted him with a brisk "Heil Hitler," eyes sparkling behind the veil and dark tulips dancing on her hat. Frau Traude mimicked the salute and hung back. Only now did I notice they wore identical swastika pins on their coats, on the left side, near the heart.

My father laughed and responded with a flourish. "Here I am, carried away by your great enthusiasm, Frau Meisterin. Although unspeakable things have taken place, witnessed by my little one and your Eli, Frau Traude. Nevertheless . . ."

"You must not blame our Führer," Hanna Roth interrupted. "Just think of it—can you imagine, they have plundered the villa." She pointed at the cupid weather vane which was spinning around in the wind. "God knows who has the keys. The porter can only get into the conservatory and the aviary. We'll soon see about that. Frau Traude has a right to take charge of her son's house. I'm going to speak to Frau Gauleiter Brinkl at once."

My father laughed and said nothing had changed in Vienna. Everyone still had the right connections.

"It's not in the interest of the Führer to let those unworthy men loot and take over the great houses in Vienna."

Father was trying to hide his amusement. "You certainly have the interest of the Führer at heart." He sent Heinz to pay the waiting taxi and insisted that the ladies come into the house to see my mother. I was delighted and walked side by side with Hanna Roth. Her step had a new springiness. Even her complexion, behind the delicate veil, looked less sallow. She entered the Meinert-Hof as though she had been coming and going every day, and greeted my mother with an even more dashing Hitler salute.

"It's years since I have been here." She settled down at the coffee table. "Nothing has changed."

Mama poured coffee and gave Hanna Roth a quick glance. "We have changed. But not you. You never change at all."

"True, true," Frau Traude spoke up. "I'm old and fat, but Hanna remains the same."

"Our youth is in our hearts. It seems only yesterday since I was called here and our little Reyna was born." The dwarf reached under the table for a doll's fan. She opened it playfully and fanned herself. As soon as she laid it down, Mama snatched it up and put it into her pocket.

"Run along, little love," Father said to me. I went no farther than my listening post.

"Let me take this opportunity . . ." he began. "Since you are interested in your son's house, Frau Traude, I presume you have your documents in order. An Aryan certificate."

"I told her months ago, when I was preparing for the great changes, to come to the convent with me and get things straightened out," Hanna Roth said.

My father laughed. "There's something to be said for that kind of foresight, after all."

I could not see the group from the stairs, but I imagined Frau Traude stuffing herself with the vanilla crescents I loved. She did not say a word.

"*Liebe* Frau Traude," Father went on. "I must ask you, as the grandmother, to help us get the boy to Switzerland. We must prove that he is only a mixling. I have done my bit by approaching the Hellers—poor people, so worried about their daughter and the boy. They have obliged. Once he is safe, I have more freedom to do something about his mother."

"How about the house? We have to have Traude's papers to make her claim," the dwarf spoke up.

"People come first," my mother said with the firmness I had seen in my grandmother. She kept surprising me. One moment she seemed helpless and lost, even to herself, affixed to the piano, then she'd speak her mind as never before. But she would be clutching the doll's fan inside her pocket.

"The house is important," Hanna Roth said sternly. "I see trouble unless we act at once."

"In this case your inspiration can serve everyone," my father said, with irony she seemed to miss, for she went right on.

"Traude must take over the house at once."

"How about the milk business; are you and Frau Traude going to make a claim on that?" he asked. Hanna Roth did not like to be teased. I heard only the clinking of china, and I wished I could go and get some of those vanilla crescents. Krampus came up the kitchen stairs, pushed open the door, and found me.

"I never wanted to look into my background," Frau Traude finally spoke up. "A country doctor gave me to the nuns. No mother ever came my way. I didn't care who she was, since she didn't even give me a name. The sisters named me after the founding mother, Gertrude von Kortnai. They left out the title, of course. Most of us at the convent had been abandoned, but we were loved and sheltered by the nuns—perhaps too much. The name they gave me is hateful, like a borrowed dress. I always preferred to be known as Traude by everyone."

"These are old sorrows," said Hanna Roth. "We are now thinking of the future." I imagined her gazing out of the window at the house she wished to enter.

"All right." Frau Traude sounded as though she had her mouth full. "I will go to the convent."

I should have known Father had made a good move even before he persuaded Frau Traude to go to Falkenburg. His mood had changed during the last few days. When our visitors got up to leave, he offered to drive them into town.

"You had better watch over our little highness," Hanna Roth said to him. "I sense danger. Too much boy stuff, too venturesome, up on all the trees. Comes from wearing leather pants."

He merely laughed and helped the ladies into the car.

I went back to climbing as soon as they drove off. No one stopped me; no one at my house believed Hanna Roth. I didn't fall off the tree, but I fell into disgrace with my father later on. He caught me leaning out of the window on the landing. I was watching Fritz Janicek and his boys drive up to the Water Castle and get in, using their own keys. It was late afternoon. Mother was playing the piano. I did not hear Papa come at me. He took hold of me by my leather pants. Had I been dressed like a girl, I might have been treated differently.

"Get away from the window, you *Fratz*. I would think you've seen enough." He smelled of cologne and schnapps, and he spanked me. I ran off to my room and sobbed. When I heard him come upstairs, I hid under the bed. I had never received more than a little slap on the wrist before that day.

When Father got down on his hands and knees and coaxed me, I called him a Nazi. He pulled me out from my hiding place and sat down with me and held me on his knee. Tears rolled over his pink cheeks into his side-whiskers. I quickly told him he was not a Nazi. He kissed me, and I said I hadn't really felt the spanking through my leather pants.

"Even if it didn't hurt, *Putzi*, you felt the insult." He shook his head. "Believe me, it's all one enormous insult. Someday you'll understand." He must have just learned where Resi was. He had spanked me because he was in a fury. When everything came out in the open later on, he showed no trace of anger.

It began to sleet and rain. Howling winds put an end to the early spring. I complained to Agnes when I couldn't go out to play in the garden. She said the wrath of God was upon us. Vlado was having coffee in the kitchen and said it had nothing to do with God, it was simply April.

The first phase of the *Umschwung* had created high hopes and dread in our house and all over Vienna and Austria. My father had always been addressed as "Herr Director." Since his empire had expanded, he had become "Herr General Director." He gained a more imposing title and lost the unhurried joviality which had dominated our household and made it safe.

I asked him almost every day to take me to Eli. Finally I gave up. I told Eli on the phone that I didn't think we'd ever meet. At that very moment Father came back into the room and told me to get my cloak. It was pouring. He said we would pick up Frau Traude in town and take her along to visit Eli this afternoon. He saw me looking at his chauffeur's cap and the swastika pin in the center of an edelweiss.

"That's what we've come to. Your old father dressed up in this masquerade in order to get around."

Mama, it seemed, had taken the car into town. I was delighted to ride in the beer truck, wrapped up in a scratchy blanket. Broken branches littered the avenue, and Papa drove slowly; rain beat against the windshield. Flags dangled, wet and heavy. Hitler posters hung loose from columns and board walls. My father lit his pipe. I didn't like the smell. The windshield wiper ticked and ticked like the metronome on Resi's piano which had kept time to Eli's song of the little red rose. Drops of rain trickled down the windshield. I closed my eyes.

In my dream it poured as though rain would never end; water streamed where the streets had been and flowed between the Water Castle and the Meinert-Hof like the Danube in spring. The flood rose and rose, as high as our house, flowing into the boudoir window, gurgling over the blue carpet, sweeping Puppe from her golden chair, floating her off into a whirlpool to sink down, down to her china fingertips and down into oblivion. Eli was crossing the torrent on a narrow plank, led by a figure in white—not his nurse, but the guardian angel, the man in the flowing white gown from the picture above my bed.

"Heil Hitler," chanted a young man, and woke me up. It sounded more like a benediction than a salute. A flashlight shone on my face. I could not open my eyes to look at the man in the rain.

"Heil," Father bellowed.

Frau Traude was holding me. "Heil Hitler," she said in a ladylike voice, not quite her own.

"Heil Hitler," I said, trying to sound dashing like Hanna Roth. A Hitler salute could tell you a great deal, if you listened.

A man showed my father some kind of a card. "Where are you going?" he demanded, shining his light on Papa. His own face was lit up from below, and I thought of him as a beautiful frog in a slouch hat—watchful, expressionless, from another world. Father told him we were driving to Grinzing to get some eggs. "In this weather?" he said softly. Rain dripped from his pale green hat. He had high cheekbones, smooth skin, and pale, large eyes. He had stopped us in the rain, questioned us with authority, yet he did not frighten me.

"Ja, in the Ostmark we have a lot of rain, Herr Inspector," Father said in his worst dialect.

"Captain," said the stranger. "Our car broke down, but we can't fit into your truck. Drive on. Heil Hitler!" The flashlight played over me once more. We all said "Heil" again, and I tried to sound fancy like Mother and make my eyes big. The wet German seemed to appreciate this variation and kept watching me as we drove off.

Frau Traude thought he had frightened me and put a raspberry-flavored candy into my mouth, told me to go back to sleep. She smelled of vanilla and caramels and felt soft but never quite comfortable.

The truck swooshed through water, came to a halt. Father said, "*Verdammt!* Those *Pifkas* must be drunk." German uniforms came tumbling out of an inn and staggered on the road. "God forbid one get under my wheels. Is the Meisterin as enthusiastic about the Nazis as ever?" he asked as we drove on.

Frau Traude gave me a slanting glance. I closed my eyes as though I were asleep and tried to remember the beautiful frog face. "Hanna adores Adolf Hitler," she said. "She came with me to the convent, you know. She decided to pay the mother superior a visit. But the nun is now almost ninety years old and could not understand the swastikas on our coats."

"I'm not sure I understand your friend," Father said. "Doesn't she know about the Reich's philosophers and their master-race theories? Someone should enlighten her. Between you and me, dwarfs are not going to be popular."

"But clairvoyants are, Herr Ferdl. Hanna is famous—not just in Austria. She has more inquiries than you would believe, direct from Berlin."

"Well, I hope her predictions are palatable; she's not always known for her tact."

I heard Frau Traude's teeth crack a hard candy. She changed the subject. "It's all done. I have the Aryan certificate. I don't understand my son. Ever since he was a small boy he's had this obsession that he was not Romberg's son. I've had to live with that insult. Then, at the worst time, he decides he's a Jew."

Father stopped and blew his horn twice, muttered something, and said he didn't know what she was talking about. Eugene Romberg had never mentioned any of it to him in all these years. "This is no time for old family quarrels," he concluded.

"I know one shouldn't look back. Hanna always says that. I certainly never wanted to find out who my parents were."

"Well, you don't have to be ashamed of Christina von Kortnai, though she was eccentric and traveled around the world like one possessed. My two sisters are travelers too. Rich, unmarried women are often a little crazy when they get to be a certain age. I was frankly amazed. So was Ann Marie. Wait till Eugene hears he is actually related to her."

"She likes cousins." One could always tell when she quoted Hanna Roth, because her voice changed and she even sounded like her.

I got all excited, especially when Father said something about blood being thicker than water. No wonder Eli and I took to each other.

I felt Frau Traude stiffen. "The nuns should have investigated long ago. It was not easy for me to make my way. Apart from unsuitable clothes, toys that didn't interest me, I never had anything. They could have questioned Pierre Roth, who brought me those things. Perhaps the sisters didn't even want me to find out who I was. A homeless girl like me usually took the veil. I guess that from their point of view, Antonelli, the sculptor, would not have been a suitable father."

"From what I know of him, I think you were better off with the nuns."

"But to think that she would snatch Reyna von Falkenburg, who was only her niece, away from the nuns, and leave me." Frau Traude rustled a paper bag out of her pocket, popped another candy into my mouth. I had closed my eyes again and was all ears. "No matter what kind of a man Antonelli was, he would have provided for me. Instead I had to make my way as a governess."

The truck slowed down. I could smell smoke from Father's pipe. Frau Traude touched my head and snapped a curl. "Hanna says the baroness had regrets when she was dying. You see, Hanna was there when your wife, no older than your little one, was brought to her bedside. A von Kortnai redhead. The baroness's mind was no longer clear. They had her on morphine; but she must have remembered her own child, even if she was too far gone to know that time had passed and I would be grown up . . ." She shifted me and went on. "Hanna believes that the estate and the doll went to the little girl beside her bed, who should have been me."

"I guess you could still make that claim," my father said sharply. "Is that the idea?"

"I no longer care about it all. I caused enough trouble in my day."

"You must have been quite a woman."

"I made mistakes. But I don't want those who don't want me. Christina von Kortnai didn't want me, and I don't want her to be known as my mother. It's as simple as that. Eugene turned against me with some crazy notions . . . said things no child should say to a mother, and didn't want me. When Izaak Romberg died, I sent Eugene away to boarding school in England and let strangers bring him up, just the way I was raised. Sometimes parents are worse than strangers, Herr Ferdl."

He did not respond.

"He even turned his poor sickly boy against me with those old grudges. He certainly knows how to make money, but he doesn't have much sense."

"Eugene talks about you with great fondness and concern."

I knew better, for I had heard Eugene Romberg call his mother a strange woman. And to me she would always remain just that. I never could think of her as a relation. None of us could.

When we arrived at the farm and stopped in front of the Tanten-Haus, which looked like a barn from the outside, it was still raining hard. She reached into her pocketbook and brought out a large envelope. "Here are the papers—a certified copy of my Aryan certificate."

"Please do thank Frau Hanna for going with you." Papa carefully put the documents into an inside pocket. "She has the knack of getting things done. It's an art."

"She is an artist," Frau Traude agreed. Perhaps she did not want to get my father's meaning. At the time, everyone was running around getting Aryan ancestors.

12

The Big Game

ELI CAME TO MEET US in the dark entrance to the Tanten-Haus. His velvet jacket glittered with his mother's diamond pins.

"You sparkle," I said.

Frau Schwester stood behind him in her starched uniform. "Poor boy decorated himself all up. What else is there to do on a nasty day like this? We cleaned his mother's jewelry. This was always my job. I was the only one she could trust."

Eli grinned like an urchin, not at all like "poor Eli." I noticed the change at once. At the Water Castle he had fallen into the habit of keeping everyone happy and busy with his sadness; if he gasped for air, he sent everyone into a tizzy and upstaged his Mutti. Here, in exile, he breathed easily.

Frau Traude, after exchanging a handshake with him and his nurse, appraised his decoration with her shrewd eyes. "Those pins are worth a fortune," she said to my father. "I think they belong in the safe at Salon Roth."

"They belong to Mutti," Eli said, before Father could intervene. "They are mine until she comes back."

"Certainly not as toys," his grandmother said unpleasantly.

"Everyone else is wearing swastikas," Eli said, eyeing the one she wore on a prominent part of her blue coat. "I think brooches are much prettier." He reached for my hand and led me off without any further ado. When we were out of hearing, he said, "My father gave them to Mutti and they are priceless. I will never give them up."

"You wear the pins because you want to. Poor Papa has to wear a swastika, and that's no fun," I said.

Eli hummed to himself as he led me through the Tanten-Haus. It always smelled a little musty, but he didn't stop to catch his breath on the stairs. "I guess you already know that Mutti is all right. Having to stay at the Hotel Metropole isn't that bad. Your father told me they are keeping her there for her own safety."

I had heard something about the hotel and "internment." For once I refrained from showing off with a new word. After all, Eli was interned, although he looked perfectly at home at the Tanten-Haus. My aunts had collected trinkets and furniture with the lack of taste he was accustomed to.

He had chosen the largest one of the five upstairs bedrooms because he liked the Venetian canopy bed that once had belonged to my flamboyant ancestor, Uncle Ernstl. The canopy was decorated with naked cherubs and plump beauties of both sexes surrounded by flowers, peacocks, and wild animals. French windows led onto a balcony overlooking the farm. A slow-burning wood stove kept the room almost as warm as the Water Castle, and all the light fixtures had been turned on.

I could hear the cows mooing in the barn, waiting to be milked. Usually I liked to go and see the animals as soon as I got out of the car. This day, I was happy with Eli's toy animals. We lined them up for a journey to the Promised Land. Not childish fantasy, but a quest for reality in the wild dream our world had become led us back into our old games. Without Resi's direction, her scenario, songs, and dance, the light touch was missing.

"And they shall know I am the Lorrrd." Eli sounded exactly like his father. When the Lord hardened the heart of the pharaoh, Eli, on a chair, turned into the Egyptian ruler. "After them, boys!" He urged his soldiers to go after the Jews as though Fritz Janicek had entered his very being; his mouth took on a pinched expression. I got the cue and staggered about singing the Horst Wessel song, but Eli's transformation impressed me so much I muddled my favorite part, "We march in spirit with the honored dead," and sang, "And all the ghosts march with the honored dead."

"I am the Lorrrd God," Eli thundered. "Depart and go up hence!"

I sang, "The SS march with quiet and solemn tread."

I remember turning myself into a seraphic messenger so that

I could get up on the high bed and fly down onto the furry rug. Eli climbed a brown velvet-covered chair and as Moses conversed with God. According to Resi, Moses, a great orator, talked with God all the time. "We, the chosen ones, will never be slaves. Never will we scrub and have our enemies do wee-wee on us."

After that we sat side by side on the rug and listened to the rain. Neither of us mentioned Eli's mother, but the game came to an end because we missed her so much. I took his hand and whispered, "Guess what, you are really in my family." He thought I made it up, and I had to give him my *Ehrenwort*, my word of honor. I told him about my mad great-aunt, Christina, her lover, Antonelli, the doll she adored, and the daugher, Frau Traude, whom she gave to the nuns.

"This makes me an aristocrat," he said. "At least, a bit of one." He closed his eyes so that he could dream it to believe it. I fingered a square emerald on his jacket.

"A mixling," I could not help saying, because I liked the word. He looked shocked, and I put my arm around him. He smelled of baby lotion, and his shirt had been dried in the garden; I could smell the sun. "You're a kind of cousin. Like Berthold, only not as much."

He turned into Resi when he smiled and dimpled. We got up and started to jump and bounce on the bed, reaching up to touch a monkey, a tiger, a naked leg, a peacock's tail on the canopy. In the end we fell down, helpless with laughter. After a minute, our eyes met; we had been too noisy to listen. Men were talking downstairs. Then we heard footsteps.

"Someone's coming; let's hide," Eli said.

"Only Father. I can tell by his limp."

He came in quickly and closed the door behind him. "Don't be afraid, but I've got to take Eli to the steward's house. Frau Schwester is already there."

"Can I go?" I asked.

He said I couldn't. The men who had stopped us on the way to the farm had followed us. They thought I was Eli because I wore pants. There was nothing to worry about. I would go down with Papa and he would show me off. His smile worried me. I didn't like the way his mouth twitched. But before I could ask any questions, he wrapped Eli into the bedspread, told me to open the French window. I saw him leap, fall, and recover at once, holding onto his heavy bundle. He rushed toward the stables and around the corner to the steward's house.

I shut the window and hid in a closet full of old skirts and winter coats. My aunts saved everything, even a pink silk cloak I couldn't imagine they'd ever worn. The odor of mothballs made me pant as though I had asthma, like Eli, until I remembered that other time when I had to hide in a wardrobe, the blue one, after I had seen Father with Resi. The moment I heard steps and scuffling, I shrank back and dipped under the cloak. Floorboards creaked.

"Reyna?" I heard panic in Father's voice. I burst out of hiding and grabbed his leg. He told me to be careful, and put a basket full of eggs onto the bed. Everything would be all right, he said, holding me so tightly that I could feel his heart beating fast. The men down there had a picture of Eli, and they would see in a minute that I was much younger and didn't look like him at all.

The picture they held up when I walked into the living room turned out to be one of Resi in a negligee, holding an Eli about my age who was dressed up like a baby in a long skirt. I had seen it before. Father and I had walked out a side door and come in with the eggs at the front, as though I had been at the farm. The room with the oak beams and polished floorboards seemed to be crowded with men in raincoats and SA uniforms. They all stood up, studying the picture, and kept looking at my face. Neither Fritz Janicek nor any of his SA boys was among them, but I recognized the man who had stopped us. He wore a beautiful gray suit with a discreet swastika. Without the hat, he had a few sand-colored curls on top of his head; the side was shaved.

When my father invited the men to sit down, the group divided naturally. Comfort-loving Austrians settled into soft chairs and sofas. The captain and all the other Germans remained standing. There were no more than six or seven men. My father put his basket down and with pride held me up for inspection. He asked them whether I wasn't far too pretty to be taken for a boy. "Good breeding, good eggs, good chicks." He sounded as though he were delivering a lecture at the autumn fair. "Even the Führer himself admires my lovely wife. Old stock, you know. Dornbach Falkenburg," he added. Then he proceeded to explain how he believed in letting chicks and children run wild. He took a risk, but he produced quality. He put me down and showed off the basket full of beautiful large eggs. "You can imagine my fascination with the race theory!" he concluded, with a smirk I had never seen before.

Frau Traude had been engrossed in the Tanten water colors: Greek temples and Scottish ponds. Now she came and offered the men her candy. The Austrians could not refuse. The Germans thanked her politely, but only the captain took one. Then he came toward me, holding it on the palm of his hand. His forehead bulged at each temple like a frog's. I admired his slanting nostrils. He held the candy out for me; I accepted with a *Knicks*, a girlish curtsy.

"Come now," he said sternly. "If you're not Eli Romberg, where is he?"

He sounded so much like Father's imitation of German officials that I had to laugh. Besides, I liked his monster face with the slanting pale eyes to match the nostrils.

"What's the matter? Am I so funny?"

I had a fit of the giggles. He even looked shiny, like a wet frog: skin, shoes, fingernails. I kept on giggling because I was no longer afraid.

"Now do you believe she's a girl?" my father asked.

A seated SA man stopped sucking his candy and said, "We Austrians know a pullet from a cockerel all right, Herr General Director." He turned to my amusing assailant. "I've five of them at home. Boys and girls. I wouldn't believe a word they say at that age."

I took time peeling the paper off my candy, popping it into my mouth. Everyone in the room seemed more at ease. Father teased Frau Traude and told her she wouldn't get any eggs if she didn't give him a candy too. He craved sweets when he played a serious game of chess, and now he sucked it with relish. I knew that twinkle in his eyes; he was winning.

"I don't know whether the Herrn from the Reich know what I have had to put up with. The papers hinted that I kidnaped the Romberg boy to protect myself from any claim he might make."

The captain was staring at the Tanten water colors with a look of disgust.

"The boy is only a mixling. As it turns out, three-quarters Aryan," Father went on.

The motionless captain, half broomstick and half frog, stood over me like one of those oversized statues that make one feel like a dwarf. "Eugene Romberg," he yelled. "Where is he, child?"

"In Switzerland."

"Frau Romberg?"

"Lost or stolen."

His eyes sparkled like Resi's sapphire pin. "Eli—your friend. Where is he? Answer at once!"

I held my ground, hands in leather pants like Father. "Gone." I sounded every bit the trusty Meinert.

"I guess the Herr Kapitän doubts my word," my father said to the Austrians. Some of them looked uneasy and lit cigarettes.

The SA father of children who lied said, "Herr von Meinert must excuse. We from Vienna know who we are dealing with here. The captain has only been in the Ostmark for a week."

"I just don't want to have it said I got rid of the Rombergs or hold the boy prisoner to protect my interests. This is not in keeping with Führer idealism." Father lifted his pipe from his pocket and lit it. With the best show of peasant sincerity, he asked whether he could offer the gentlemen a glass of his superb Spätlese, a wine he was proud of. The German civilians refused politely before the Austrians had a chance to accept.

"The Herr von Meinert does not have to worry," said an Austrian in tweeds. "After all, Frau Romberg is wanted for killing an SS man. Romberg is a Jew, the boy a half-Jew. That's a known fact."

"That's right, you don't have to give it a thought," said the family man. "No matter what arrangements you've had to make."

My captain stood as though he were carved of stone. I knew he was not finished with me. His eyes turned on me, ready to pounce. I held my ground.

He grabbed my arm. "Eugene Romberg is right here—in Vienna —your house—speak!"

There was a boy who once fooled a giant by throwing a bird instead of a stone . . . "In Morocco," I said. "There's that house with tiles and Arabs. He loves it there. He told me so."

The Austrians laughed and said I was terribly smart. Was I really only seven years old? "Breeding, breeding," said the Viennese in tweeds. "It tells." He gave the captain an angry look and took his place with Father and me. "The Gestapo does have evidence that Herr Romberg has left Switzerland. His wife, it seems, has been taken from her internment by force. One naturally suspects . . ."

"I can't believe you," Father said. "I have had a letter from him not long ago from Geneva."

I became overexcited and repeated the word *internment* six times, because it had become a favorite. I danced about chanting, "Exodus, exodus"—another word I enjoyed. The captain veered around in my direction. A grin across his face. He tried to turn his laughter into a cough. He never did deceive me. I knew him to be a friendly monster. Of all the men in the room, he was the only one who liked me. He became young when he smiled, much closer to my age than the others. I took his giant hand.

"*Du*," I said, because it was proper to address monsters as familiars. "You have been teasing, haven't you? You know where Eugene Romberg is, don't you?"

His face turned back to stone. Fabulous, but still a monster. If he believed I was Eli, he would grab me and take me away and have me interned. But I was safe. My father, well pleased with my convenient impudence, told the men I had been reading since I was four years old. I could do additions in my head. He told me to add eight to four and then to add six. I performed—not for him, but only for my captain, who didn't blink an eyelid.

After that, a German civilian with a small red face introduced himself to my father as a lawyer from München. "We have lots of experience in dealing with cases like this one in the Reich. If the Rombergs turn up to make a claim—the boy—if you have any problem at all . . . Doctor Grebber at your service." He clicked his heels and handed my father a card.

"At the Ministerium!" Papa managed to sound as though he had never known anyone in such a high place. He shook hands with the man and said it was an honor.

"You don't have to go to the Ministerium, Herr General Director," said the family man. "We handle these things in our own informal fashion here in Vienna. Mixlings and Jews are not wanted in our city." He handed Father his card, too.

"Well, look at that," Father said. "The Golden Boar. A good customer of mine. Next time you order wine or beer, you come and see me at my office and we'll have a glass of wine together."

The SA man was all smiles, and told my father to come and

have dinner at his inn and taste the roast sucking pig, a specialty.

"So," Father smiled, "this turned out to be a pleasure. Gentlemen, feel free to search the house, the farm. If you wish, the vintners' village. I've nothing to hide, and the Herrn from the Reich might find it interesting. We handle wine and beer the old-fashioned way, just like poultry, cattle, horses, and children. Simple folks, that's what we are." They stepped outside to confer, and he closed the door and said, "They won't search."

"Has Eugene really left Geneva?" Frau Traude asked. "Has he come back to get Resi?"

"Never!" Father laughed. "They were trying to see my reaction, get the child to talk. I've heard of their methods. They deliberately ask you silly questions to get you to talk." He turned to me a little too suddenly and gave me a big kiss. "No one can get the better of this adorable rogue."

Frau Traude rummaged around in her paper bag for a last candy. She was not entirely on our side. Father knew it. The men came back. Father was right; they took their leave. He shook hands with them all, shouted "Heil," and I joined in with all my might to impress the captain, who pretended to ignore my performance. The innkeeper stayed behind. "You mustn't be put out by the captain," he said to Father. "He's quite young. A German prince of the old blood. Doesn't unbend. Typical."

I ran out to see them get into two cars. The Germans had the bigger one. The rain had ended, and it smelled of grass and cow dung. The prince sat in the front. I jumped into a puddle with both feet for him. He yielded, with a look of affection warm as the sun.

Father made a lot of me after they drove away. I was much impressed by the way he had played his game, and began to model my Nazi salute on his deafening "Heil." I learned to shoot my hand under the nose of this or that important Nazi.

Those in power competed from the beginning and watched each other with distrust, but they relied on my father, confided in him, and praised his good sense, even after the war began and went on to disaster. The beer was to become more watery, there was always plenty of wine, year after year—and milk whenever possible. Father kept the big game going. Officially he appeared to be one of those men who had gained through the losses of others. The

Nazis liked that. He beat them at chess, gave them a taste of his good wine (never the best). The high and mighty came, went down to the catacombs for a private talk. I imagine he laughed, claimed he was a mere peasant, when it suited him. "I live from day to day, barrel to barrel, milking to milking" was his refrain. While he spoke, he always believed what he was saying. But the joking, bantering tone in his voice was not the same without the deep belly laugh. Nazi *Bonzen* came and went at our house, and generals ate at our table. If one of them vanished, or went away to war, died, fell out of favor with the regime, Papa shrugged it off. It was all a game of chess to him, and he was a winner.

Herr Verwalter Schopenauer, as a youth, had worked for my grandfather. Now he worked as steward for my English aunts; but at all times he served my father. He was widowed, childless, a short, stocky man, bowlegged and strong. He believed in a united Europe and collected stamps. He and Eli sat at a round table with Eli's albums, the white head and the black one side by side. Eli still wore the glittering pins. A large mirror expanded and repeated the scene. I could see myself enter in leather pants, white shirt embroidered at the lapels with edelweiss, green knee socks, cape slung over my shoulder. I had my grandmother's wide-awake expression, her large amber eyes and fine features, and Father's rosy coloring; my dark ringlets made me look like a doll. I did not like that one bit. I felt I had saved Eli, but no one who looked at me would believe it.

I wanted to tell Eli how heroic I had been, and especially about the captain. If I didn't look like a hero, the captain certainly did not look like a real prince. I walked around the table and stood behind Eli. He pointed at his collection of old imperial stamps. "That's Empress Elizabeth," I said.

"They murdered her," he said, looking calm and pleased with himself. Father and Herr Schopenauer talked in the corner of the room. Eli's power of concentration, my father was saying, reminded him of Eugene Romberg, a chess master. Eli certainly had his father's white hands and deft fingers. I watched him pick up the empress stamp with a pair of tweezers and place it beside a soft-faced man with a respectable, non-Hitler mustache. "Engelbert Dollfuss," he said. "They murdered him . . ." In Eli's game, the tall, magnificent empress and the tiny Dollfuss belonged together.

Eli raised a magnifying glass from the stamps to his grand-mother, as though he had to place her in his album. "So you are a von Kortnai," he said in his collector's voice. "Reyna told me. Did Hanna Roth keep you from telling me?"

"You sound just like your father," she said. "And to think I came especially to tell you all about it! You are quite wrong about my friend Hanna. She urged me for years to find out who I really was. I was the one who didn't want to know." She bent over him to touch his hand, but her eyes scanned over the gems on his velvet jacket. "It's certainly not Hanna's fault that we are es-tranged, Eli; your father saw to that . . ." She fumbled around in her large handbag. Perhaps she craved something sweet; but the candy had all been eaten. "Hanna Roth was taken to court as a child. I became a governess and later a wife. We never lost touch. I hope you will grow up to have a friend like that."

"Me," I said in a nasty tone of voice. She ignored this and went on to say she wanted to know him better; but her eyes moved from side to side, contradicting those kind words.

"So I am a von Kortnai," Eli said, and the glance he gave my father, batting his long lashes, showed that indeed he had inher-ited the furtiveness portrayed in the old doll. Did he know that my father and his Mutti liked to lie naked in each other's arms? I never talked about it with him, but he certainly knew about his father and Karin.

A boy decked out in diamonds puzzled Father. He never under-stood Eli, but now he became fascinated as he watched Eli at the table with those stamps. He recognized the game. Sometimes he played by himself, both winning and losing. Eli had begun with the murdered empress and the little chancellor: victim with vic-tim. He was learning to categorize, like those who called him a mixling. While Father looked on, he placed a Hitler stamp beside a Schuschnigg: assailant and victim. Without losers there were no winners—not in a real game.

❊　　❊　　❊

I caught the measles from dirty Gusti. Easter bells rang out for Resurrection Mass, and I had to stay in bed. When I sat up, the sun, behind closed shutters, made zebra stripes on my arms. In the dressing-table mirror a monster face spotted like a ladybug stared back at me. If you dipped a finger into ink it turned black, and if you saw ugly things you turned into a spotted monster with gold-striped arms, and you itched.

I pitied myself with all my heart and was about to cry, to ring the bell, or to flee to the kitchen when I saw the sugar-coated egg on my night table. I held it into a bar of sunlight, looked through the peephole, and forgot my misery. A girl in white stood by a lake, holding flowers. The figure, willows, swans on the water, and turrets of a castle were cutouts and gave a sense of distance, the remoteness of a daydream. I began to invent stories from this scene, and anyone who would put up with me heard about the girl with the magic flowers who entered the castle to free her best friend from a spotted monster.

Agnes had bought the egg for me at the candy store in the vintners' village. The old owners had vanished; the new one had hung a Hitler portrait on the wall. The Führer would have liked this, because he practically lived on sweets. Agnes missed the kind old couple who had welcomed us as friends, but she could not resist buying the egg with the vista of the pretty landscape and the little girl with flowers—the sort of girl she wanted me to be.

My grandmother came to visit and held the egg to her eye. The little girl, she said, would marry a prince and live in a castle. This reminded her of a prince who'd simply walked into her courtyard the other day. "I was sitting on my garden bench, writing a note. In walks this tall young man. I knew he had breeding as soon as I set eyes on him. A Prince Lütensteg. German *Uradel.*" She explained to me that this meant a heredity dating back to the thirteenth century. "He knew my family history and asked politely to take a picture of the Palais Dornbach. I took him inside and showed him around. Guess what, he spotted a picture of you, Reyna. It turns out he met you with your father."

"Captain Frog Prince," I said. "He and some Nazis came to the farm."

"All right, all right," Mother interrupted. "We don't have to bore Grandmama with all that." She grabbed up a white doll's shoe. "You didn't say anything political to him, Mama?"

"No, we didn't get into that."

"That's good. You see, Ferdl told me about that young German. Prince or no prince, he works for the Gestapo."

"He thought I was Eli Romberg because I was wearing pants," I said.

Grandmama said something in angry French. Then she continued. "He impressed me as a remarkable young man, but the way he walked into my courtyard unannounced did give me second thoughts. I guess we have to get used to intruders. I must say I took to him."

Of all the German intruders, Captain Frog Prince would always be my favorite. The most hateful intruders remained invisible, spied on you, and listened in to telephone conversations. One day Father thought he heard something on the line when he was on the telephone with Frau Schwester. He hung up at once. I was no longer allowed to speak to Eli on the telephone. Most of my spots had gone, and I begged my father to take me to Eli; he became evasive.

Soon after that he came home one evening and threw an envelope into Mama's lap. It was Eli's passport. I was allowed to look at the photograph: a poor Eli, younger and thinner and sadder than he was now. The passport was gray and decorated with a swastika—quite German and official. It gave me a sinking feeling.

Mama shouted with joy and said Father was a genius to obtain a Swiss visa. My heart sank when he announced that he was only waiting for the right moment to whisk Eli out of Austria.

"When you take Eli, can I come along?" I asked.

"Never," said Mother.

Father was far too pleased with himself to notice my disappointment. "You'll never know what I went through. Our pen-pushers and the German Bonzen, what a combination! Fortunately I have a few good connections. Most of all, I know how to cover my tracks." I had visions of papers falling like snow did during our winter walks, hiding his progress.

Mother was all smiles. As a Nazi conspirator she had defied the Austrian authorities. Hitler himself had honored her for that. Now she enjoyed getting the better of the new regime. "It would be wonderful if you could get Resi out of the country as well."

"She may not wish to go to Eugene. In fact, in order to become free she might have to divorce him."

"A mere formality. Eugene would understand. They can remarry. I am sure I can get in to see her. They won't turn me away. I'll talk to her."

Father changed the subject, to Berthold. "I guess a lot has happened to your cousin. He wants to talk to me."

"I don't see much of him these days," Mother said. "He knows I don't like the idea that he got his *Matura* without taking a single exam. He never even bothered to let me know that the Hohentahlers have Aryanized their old estate. Hanna Roth told me. It's a disgrace."

"They bought the Landsitz back," Father said.

"With what?"

"Jewelry. The old highness, Oma, helped out. After all, she lives in a cottage on the estate."

"I'm sure they got a bargain."

"But they did pay. Most Jews get nothing, or a few useless marks."

Mother wore a delicately embroidered white blouse which brought out the bright coloring in her face. "It's all very shady," she said and bit her lower lip.

"I took over the Romberg dairies," Father said.

"But you paid in full and got Eugene across the border with all his money."

A cuckoo called somewhere in the Meinert woods. Father said he loved those crazy birds. "Well, Annerl, I guess I set a good example. Bertl did the same thing. He got the Greenbaums into Croatia with the Hohentahler jewels and some of their own valuables. Don't ask me how. But it was quite heroic of him to take such a risk."

"Don't they have a beautiful young daughter?"

My father laughed and said he hoped Berthold had some reward.

"He should have taken his exams," Mother said.

*　　*　　*

A few days later, Berthold arrived unannounced. Mother and I were in the rose garden when he drove up in an orange-colored cabriolet and screeched to a halt between the trees in front of our gate. He honked his horn, swung his legs over the door without bothering to open it, and hopped out. The weather was as sunny as his mood. I ran to open the gate with my own keys and jumped into his arms. This time I ignored the black uniform and only saw his smiling face; an emblem scratched my arm, but I ignored it. "Father says you are a hero," I told him.

"A reluctant hero, what?"

He kissed Mother, and they laughed together. "You took quite a risk getting the Greenbaums out of the country," she said.

"No risk at all. I got the estate back, so it all looks like healthy self-interest. Quite safe. I learned it from Ferdl."

I climbed into the fancy car and sat at the steering wheel, making believe I was driving to the farm to see Eli.

Mother asked him where he got that car. He said he earned it. "You probably wore your uniform when you took the test," she said in a nasal voice.

"I had to pass so that I could take the Greenbaums to Yugoslavia. The car was their parting gift. Come, come, Annerl, I think I deserve it, don't you?"

She didn't say anything.

"A carrot-colored car goes well with your hair. Come, children. We'll look beautiful in my equipage. Let's go to the Prater and eat ice cream."

I clamored for a ride on the merry-go-round and for the Kasperl theater, a puppet show. He promised me anything I wanted, but I must have ogled his death's-head emblem. He twirled me around and said, "Don't look at me like that, Liebstes; uniforms are always embarrassing to me, but they do come in handy, and at least this one isn't too small."

The day burst into color and light in his company. Vienna whizzed past the orange-colored car. Wind tore at my blouse, my curls.

"Careful," Mother cried. "You're going too fast."

He went even faster. I asked why the streets were so empty when we raced through the second district with its boarded-up shop windows, the word *Jude* smeared on boards, on walls. Neither Mother nor Berthold answered my question. "Poldi and Lise said the Jews were all rounded up, locked into synagogues, made to stand up like cattle," I said. "They had nothing to eat, couldn't go to the toilet and had to sing Jewish songs."

"Poldi and Lise? I wouldn't believe a word of it," Mother said without conviction.

"I'm glad Resi is at a hotel," I said. But in my dream, cows had stood crowded together in our chapel; one of them opened its mouth and sang the Hebrew songs that Resi rehearsed and never sang at her concert. When we stopped in the Wurstel Prater, our amusement park, I could hear those cows singing to me. Mama said I looked white; going so fast had made me sick. Berthold bought a red balloon for me. I remembered Herbert, the foot doctor's son, holding one while the men urinated on the kneeling women. The string slipped from my hand, and I burst into tears.

Berthold said: "Don't cry, my sweet. I'll buy you another one." I shook my head.

We sat under the trees at Eissvogel's, and the musicians played "Tales from the Vienna Woods." A German soldier waltzed with a girl in a pink dress, and she was laughing. "Not so stiff," she called out for everyone to hear. "Let go of yourself. Like this, like this." She took the lead and he stumbled. They sat down. Mama was telling Berthold I had had the measles and had been quite sick. He said I was adorable and took me onto his knee; the cow in my head stopped singing Hebrew songs. Berthold said life could be beautiful in such a convincing way that I hardly noticed the storm troopers at a nearby shooting gallery.

Berthold thought the Kasperl would make me laugh. At the puppet theater, the Kasperl hit a crocodile on the head with a broomstick, then he smacked a policeman. The stage, decorated with mirrors, showed Berthold kissing Mother's mouth three times. The crocodile came back, roared with huge red jaws, white pointed teeth: rapacious, as unappeasable as everyone else that spring. I heard myself howl.

"Poor little girl; she doesn't like the crocodile and the bad Kasperl. There, there's your Herr Papa, don't worry." A good-natured countrywoman handed me over to Berthold.

He gathered me up with little kisses, refused to accept my tears. He laughed, loved me—tender, pleased with himself, a reluctant hero out to celebrate recklessly. Everything was his for the taking and his to give, that day of all days. "Papa indeed," he said, showing his white teeth. "Why not? There's nothing like family."

"Your mustache is gone," I said.

"I don't need it anymore."

We had a ride on the *Riesenrad*, the giant wheel. "Silly old Vienna," Berthold said, as we looked down over the hazy city, the many church steeples and green patches of parks. "Too old, too much history, just too beautiful, and quite impossible." I did not like heights and closed my eyes to the Lilliputian world of trouble below. He went on to tell Mother that he was riding in a big parade on Sunday—quite a circus. There would be huge, ugly papier-mâché figures of famous Jews. "You'd better invite your mama to your house. She doesn't approve and might get herself and some of her friends into trouble."

Back in the car, we drove slowly past riders on the bridle path. Berthold waved to a girl who rode sidesaddle. At the Prater, Stern Hitler Youth marched. I heard the ghost of a march, the rolling of drums. In the deserted streets of the second district a newspaper drifted past us in the wind like a headless eagle. Empty streets flew past me. I stared at Berthold to keep myself from getting dizzy. He was smiling to himself.

"You have something up your sleeve," Mother said when he helped us out at our gate. "Aren't you going to tell?"

He kissed us, leaped into the cabriolet, and sped away.

       ✿   ✿   ✿

My grandmother could not come the day of the parade; she had invited her old friend the Rittmeister for coffee and asked us to join her instead. Mother could not understand why the countess had put her maid to all the trouble of setting the table on the balcony outside the pink room. It threatened rain, and the sky looked like an unwashed window. But the parade went on without the sun. Now and again the wind carried the sound of bands and cheering voices. My grandmother got up several times and leaned over the balcony to look up at the sky.

I had insisted on wearing an old white dress that made me feel like the girl inside the Easter egg. I had a beetle in my pocket and decided to let it go in the courtyard. While I looked around for a good spot among weeds near the stone angel, I heard my grandmother cry out, "I see it, I see it!" I looked up and there was a glider, silent as a dove.

"It's snowing, it's snowing," I shouted. Leaflets snowed down from the sky. Usually they carried Hitler messages, slogans of sorts. One landed near the old shrine in the tall, uncut grass, and I picked up a piece of paper decorated with the Austrian double eagle—a message without words. When my grandmother saw it she said, "*Gott erhalte*, God protect."

The Rittmeister added, "Our kaiser." He promised to teach me all the words of the old Austrian anthem. His uniform was well hidden under a raincoat.

"You got rid of the printing press, I hope?" Mama asked the countess.

"It is well concealed; no one will find it. I wish I could see our Berthold's face when the double eagle comes snowing down on him." She laughed like a girl, clapped her hands. But she did not relax until the phone rang about an hour later. "Our pilot is safe. God bless him."

❀   ❀   ❀

The almond trees in bloom, the grass so green outside our garden pavilion, early Maybells nodding in the shade, and late crocuses bright as confetti on the slope—all suited Berthold's mood. He had come to play chess with Father a few days after our outing to the Prater. They had carried wine and glasses up the hill to the pavilion. Mother and I brought sweet things to nibble, in a basket. She and I sat on the window bench. Father and Berthold leaned over the chess table in the middle of the little wood-paneled room. After a while Father poured some wine and handed a glass to Mama. I took a sip.

"Don't you like Annerl's dress, Bertl? The Führer did. It would have been a good picture of him kissing her hand in the *Illustrierte*, but that darned hat hid her face."

Berthold looked at Mother's embarrassed face as though he were seated on a cloud. His eyes shifted from her hand-embroidered linen dress, the tight, fitted bodice, to the blossoming trees in our orchard. "Beautiful," he said.

My talent for chess was never great, but I could tell Father was giving the game away. When he played with me, he did this out of affection. Berthold was in the mood to win and didn't even notice that Father was making fun of him. A tweed jacket with leather patches at the elbow, new riding breeches, brown glossy boots, made him look like a country squire on a spree. His eyes danced, and he kept combing his hair with his fingers, which did not improve it. He shouted with joy when Father let him take a knight.

Mother was reading, using a purple sash from Puppe's ball dress as a bookmark. She followed each line with her fingertip, like a schoolgirl. Her braids hung over each ear. Father eyed her as he eyed his chess figures, and sometimes me.

"What are you reading, Annerl?" Berthold asked.

"*Mein Kampf*," Mother said girlishly.

"I don't know anyone else who's actually reading the book," Father said with a smirk.

I looked over her shoulder, deciphered the words, and said aloud, " 'Nation and race. Further Aryan influences on Japan.' "

Berthold laughed. "Too much for me. Aryan influence in Japan. Far-fetched. But then, I'm quite dumb, what?"

"You got your Matura," Mother said.

"I didn't deserve to pass. I don't deserve any of my luck." He raised his glass and toasted us all. "Everything seems to fall into my lap these days."

He returned to his game with Father, and Mother continued reading. Berthold had given up the illusions he had shared with her when they had acted as illegal Nazis. Excitement and blatant desire had come to an end with the arrival of Adolf Hitler and left them uneasy, like a couple after a hasty, artless act of love. There had been no fulfillment. Berthold was too young and impatient to relish disappointment. He made the most of his opportunities. Whenever his attention wandered from the chessboard, Berthold lifted his glass and over the rim, drank in, the little spring flowers on Mother's décolleté. She read on. Untouched by admiration and unimpressed by phrases in a book which beguiled millions, she bent over the seductive page, exposing her charming, freckled nape.

I popped two cream-filled, chocolate-covered towers into my mouth imitating Hanna Roth. No one noticed. The game went on. It was so quiet I could hear Krampus barking somewhere in the garden. A fly buzzed in a spider's web up on the rafters. A black spider sat lifeless on the net, then darted forward to the kill.

"*Schach Matt*," Berthold cried out.

Father raised his glass. "*Prost* to the winner!" He had managed to give the game away. "Guess what, Annerl?" A tremor in his voice caught my attention. "You might as well know that your clever cousin snatched Resi out of the Metropole; he's keeping her hidden away all to himself. And don't think he doesn't love it."

The book fell from Mama's lap with a smack. "You're joking!"

"You weren't supposed to tell," Berthold said with a silly grin.

"Want her to read about it in the paper? It's all going to come out when the opera gets into the act. They want her free to sing *The Merry Widow* for our great leader."

I jumped up and down and asked when Resi would come back to the villa, and about Eli. Father told me to calm down and leave Eli out of it. "I had almost succeeded in getting Reserl released when our hero came along," he said. "The Romberg cook was ready to swear that Resi was not even in the house when the SS man was killed."

Berthold looked sheepish. "How should I have known? I made a bet with some of my old school friends, a few of the Flunkers. We all got a little drunk celebrating our graduation."

Mother picked up the book and threw it onto the bench. "You let me go to the hotel with a box of chocolates and cherry brandy, Ferdl. There I was, waving my Hitler letter under the nose of the Gestapo. I even made a fool of myself and lost my temper when they told me she had left their safekeeping; I told them they were lying."

Father smiled and kissed her hand. "You did me a big favor. They might have come to search here or at the farm. It would have suited them fine to nab the boy and hold him hostage."

"But why didn't you tell me? Why, you've acted as though you had hidden her away yourself ever since!" she shouted, red with anger.

I asked about Eli being a hostage, but no one even heard me.

"You'd better watch out, Bertl," my father laughed. "I really got the cold shoulder. Led the life of a dog."

"You both think you're so funny." She wrinkled her nose in disgust. "You'll end up getting my mother into trouble."

"What does Resi have to do with your mother?"

"It's your fault that a German Gestapo man came snooping around the little palace. Looking for Resi or Eli, no doubt."

"Captain Frog," I said, "prince of the old blood."

"Someone she would be inclined to trust," Mother said.

"Well, it seems you've been holding back, too," Father said, and refilled the glasses.

"How did you do it, Berthold? How did you snatch her?" I asked.

"It was all luck. And it started off as a big joke. I ran into Krummerer."

"*Puppen* detective," I said.

"He now works for the Gestapo, but he's still for hire. He goes in and out of the Metropole. Knew all about Resi. He is in charge of moving out the best furniture and rugs. It turned out those two bunglers, Stauble and Pichler, Resi's handymen, do some of the moving. Perfect. The rest was easy. A little costume party. Money no object. I wish I could have smuggled poor old Schuschnigg out at the same time. They keep him locked up at the hotel and make him clean toilets, I hear."

"Can you imagine our Bertl in a skimpy SA uniform, wearing a black wig?" Father chuckled, and I laughed and clapped my hands.

"I don't think it's all that funny," Mother said in her convent-school voice. "Those two stagehands can't be trusted. They'll inform on Bertl."

"They didn't know me," Berthold said. "That's what made it such a farce. If they had been caught, they would have been highly suspect. They worked for Resi, and she was very good to them."

"How about Krummerer, that opportunist?" Mother asked.

"He had been employed by your husband, Annerl, and he might have thrown suspicion on all of you. Not that they would get a straight word out of him. Great at picking locks. We heard Reserl singing in her room like a canary. Had her out of there in a minute. The guards had received a gift of champagne—Krummerer saw to that. Most of them were drunk; the others were busy with all the official papers we presented to them. They had to fill out forms by the meter. Krummerer and I rolled Resi up in a rug. Our only worry was that those two fools would drop her on the way out. I promised them a fat bonus if they got the rug out fast. It worked. The Flunkers were waiting in a truck."

I wished he would go on with the wild story, but there was a silence. "It could have gone wrong," Mother said. "How on earth did you get her out of Vienna? They must have been after you?"

"Two other Flunkers followed in an old Fiat. We changed over at the Belvedere gardens. It was raining and no one was around. Reserl was full of mischief. Sang *Salome* for us all the way to the Landsitz. I think she's mixed up; it wasn't Salome who had herself rolled into a rug. Wasn't it Cleopatra?"

"Salome or Cleopatra, I'm glad to know she's singing. It will help her case."

"She must be very grateful to you, Berthold," Mother said.

He laughed foolishly. "Ach, ja, she says it was almost worth being locked up, just to be rescued by me."

"I still find it unbelievable. Why didn't you tell me that she was as free as a lark?" Mother said. "When you took us to the Prater, Bertl, she was waiting for you to come back . . ."

Berthold got up, glass in hand, and faced the brick wall, the top of our gardens, where barbed wire and spikes and broken glass secured privacy. A tiny fat robin left a nest on a nearby apple tree and flew over it. Father opened another bottle. I quickly passed the basket of tartlets around. No one wanted any.

"He didn't tell me right away, either," Father said. "The day I was followed to the farm, I fortunately knew nothing. I didn't believe them when they said she had escaped. I thought it was a trick to test me. And when Bertl showed up at the café and told me everything, I was the one who suggested he should wait for the right moment. I wasn't sure you were ready to share your cousin with anyone, my love." He went to refill glasses and gave Mother a smacking kiss.

She got up and stood beside Berthold. They had the same strong, slightly bent legs, full, smooth lips. Never did they look better together, and never had they been more distant. Father proposed a toast and they all drank.

"Now that you've played your prank and won the bet, Bertl, are you still pro-Hitler as much as ever?" Father asked. "Or is Reserl teaching you Hebrew?"

I ate another two chocolate towers. No one paid any attention.

Berthold threw back his head and showed his fine teeth, like a stallion impatient with his bit. "I got myself into it. Now I either sink or swim." The wind played with his hair. I can still see him standing there. Not quite twenty years old, far too available, vulnerable—a young knight, as Hanna Roth called him. He flushed from neck to forehead, the way Mother often did. "She really wants to stay with me."

Papa hummed "Vienna Only You," the song Resi had often sung for him. He put his arms around Mother. She was about to push him away, changed her mind, and snuggled up against him.

"It's all quite mad," Berthold said, and looked out the window.

"Is it now? Is it, my young hero? It's always my girls you're after, nicht wahr?" Never had I seen my father drink so fast.

"Especially this little sweetheart." Berthold snatched me up. He had wine on his breath.

I threw my arms around him, nuzzled, and found a trace of lavender on his shirt collar. "Did Resi hug you?" I asked.

"What's that buzzing? Do you have a fly in your hand?"

"Saving it from the spider," I told him.

We left my parents to gather the chess set, glasses, everything into the basket, and went into the garden to let the fly go. Father and Mother walked through the orchard. He was carrying the basket, and she had her arm around his shoulder and was leaning against him, and her hips wiggled.

"Well, it's spring," Berthold said. "For flies, for spiders, for everyone." Then we went to the shed, found a long-handled broom, and swept the webs and insects—dead and alive—out into the damp grass.

*   *   *

At lunchtime the next day, Father told us he had seen Resi and Berthold, that it was a great romance. Mother pushed her plate away, and I stuffed myself. Resi Romberg was free and safe. We should have felt jubilant. I felt sick. Mother frowned. Father said they would not last.

Agnes looked at the dark circles under my eyes when I came down to the kitchen, and thought I had caught a spring cold. Perhaps jealousy is catching. She asked no questions and simply put cushions down for me on the window seat and made me comfortable. The window above me was almost level with the ground. Rain drizzled on daffodils, and the air smelled of newly cut grass. Vlado was whistling and chopping wood at his cottage. Agnes sat beside me in a crisp green dirndl dress. Her fair hair, streaked with white, was gathered into a tight bun behind the ears. She stroked my hair and cheeks with red hands; they felt rough as a kitten's tongue.

She told me about storks returning to the village of Falkenburg, how they would collect glittering things in their nests. The villagers kept their windows closed against the birds and their doors locked against gypsies, who, like storks, took things they fancied in the spring. It was unlucky to touch a stork's nest. No one dared to enter a gypsy's dwelling to look for lost things, either, for they would put a spell on you.

"Tell me about my great-grandmother Anne-Marie and the gypsy child who ate a diamond," I asked.

"The laundress has been talking to you again."

Agnes was right. I had been helping Frau Boschke on Monday by ironing handkerchiefs while she starched and ironed Father's shirts, and I had gotten her onto the subject of my great-grandmother. "She married the brother because she loved the sister." Frau Boschke had vanished behind steam as her iron came down heavily. "They said she fled to the sister on her wedding night. But after a while they all settled down. She was with child, taking a stroll with her sister-in-law, Countess Anna Gitta. There was a dirty little gypsy child sitting in the grass, and the lovely Anne-Marie picked it up and fondled it. The little one took a fancy to a diamond she wore on a thin chain. Playfully, she put it around the dirty little neck. The brat tore the chain and swallowed the stone. Two days later it died of bleeding." Frau Boschke had folded a shirt and flattened it with the iron. I had loved her rasping voice when she had said, "*Schrecklich*, the dreadful curse of the gypsies." I had spat on my iron to test it and listened to the horror of my great-grandmother's untimely death in childbed.

Agnes had a way of censoring family history, and she never quite came to the point. "They called her the angel, your beautiful grandmother. She looked like one, and she was so kind she'd give anything away. They still talk about the way she attended to her sister-in-law, poor crippled little thing. And to think she'd take a diamond and give it to a little gypsy child. She was just too good for this world."

Agnes sang me the gypsy song I liked. The melody often drifts through my mind, caressing like the touch of those rough hands, like a kitten's tongue:

> *What's mine is thine, you own all you desire.*
> *You own all of me,*

Let the sun be your diamond, the hay our bed,
Violins sing of castles where we will dwell,
Until eternity.

I liked the "eternity" part when houses and people began to change hands around me. I put my head onto Agnes's lap, closed my eyes. "Again, please; sing it again!"

The blackbirds trilled as Agnes repeated the song. I might have dozed off, but Poldi and Lise came scampering downstairs with some dirty towels and sheets. Agnes went, "Shhhh." I heard them whisper and kept my eyes closed, sucking my thumb.

"It's true, it's true," Lise said in a muffled voice. "The porter's wife knows. She's had a letter. Just imagine. That skinny little Swede and fat Herr Romberg living it up in Switzerland."

Agnes must have become interested. She didn't stop Poldi when she said, "That's why Frau Romberg didn't want to go to Switzerland. She knew about those two."

Agnes said, "Enough, enough," and sent the girls upstairs with a bucket to scrub the tiles in the entrance.

Soon the kitchen was empty. I bit the inside of my cheek in silent rage. Why couldn't Resi and Eugene Romberg have stayed together until eternity? I jumped up and stuffed my mouth full of baking chocolate that Agnes kept in a jar; it tasted bitter. When I went upstairs, Agnes had gone out. The twins were laughing and talking, and their scrub brushes sounded like snakes hissing a waltz. I ran to the telephone, and when I picked up the receiver something went thump right above me on the ceiling, as if the great whangdoodle had hit it as it stood over me. I called Eli. Frau Schwester answered, and for once she was quite careless.

"So you're allowed to speak to me again." Eli sounded pleased, but not for long. I told him the news fast: his Mutti was staying with Fürst Hohentahler and would divorce his father. She was going to sing at the Opera for Adolf Hitler before long. Eli did not say a word. "Karin is in Switzerland with your father, living it up." I heard a crackling sound on the line.

"How about me?" Eli asked.

The whangdoodle had made me do something terrible. I kept talking wildly, because I should not have talked at all, about my great-grandmother who loved the sister and married the brother. A von Kortnai. Eli did not seem impressed by our mutual ancestor.

I went on to the lurid tale of the diamond, the gypsy child. He did not respond when I said, "Well, where there's love, there's jealousy," in a Frau Boschke voice. I waited, listened to his silence, and heard him gasping for breath.

"What have you said to the poor boy!" Frau Schwester yelled into my ear. "What have you done? He's having an attack!"

An hour later Father came home. I stayed out of sight. He opened and shut drawers, throwing things into a suitcase. He caught sight of me on the stairs and gave me a hurried kiss. He would have left without explanation, but Mother came in. She was taking piano lessons in our neighborhood. The music sheets fell from her arm when Father told her that I had been lonely and had called Eli, and someone had listened in.

"Fortunately, Frau Schwester called me at once and told me that Eli was having an attack. I put Eli into a big empty barrel on the back of a truck, the nurse came along, and we took him to the doctor. The attack saved him. Fritz Janicek and some of his men came out and searched the Tanten-Haus."

"They'll arrest you. They'll find poor Eli," Mother sobbed.

"Fritz will exterminate him," I yelled.

Father put his arm around us both. "Don't worry. I turned to the upper echelon, the German authorities, explained my position —how Janicek had been my gardener and I would get the blame if they took the boy hostage. I presented Eli's Aryan certificates, the passport, asked for an escort to the border. I got one. The captain, von Lütensteg. He's taking us in his own car."

"No, no," Mother cried out. "It's a trap. They'll arrest you."

"For a fervent Nazi, Annerl, you have little faith. It's not a trap. It's a deal. The boy is being extradited. It is safest that way for all of us. You'll read about it in the paper tomorrow: 'Ferdinand Meinert protects Aryanized milk industry. Son of Jew evicted.' How does that sound to your innocent ears?" He took her into his arms, kissed the tears from her eyes. Ever since Resi's rescue they had turned to each other, spent evenings together in the boudoir drinking champagne.

I did not shed a tear until Father returned safely and handed me a tiny diamond-studded watch from Eugene Romberg. To MY LITTLE FRIEND was engraved on the back. I howled like an infant, and Papa picked me up and said I should not cry, I should laugh.

All had gone well. Eli had been medicated and slept most of the way to the border. "He thought he was going to see his mother. Poor boy. When he did wake up, I had to tell him everything. He didn't even act surprised. Not even when Karin was at the border to meet him. You never know about children."

Eli had not given me away. I imagined him sitting in a black limousine with yellow headlights like the eyes of a tiger. Perhaps he had nodded from Father's shoulder to Captain Frog Prince.

My parents celebrated with champagne, Mother in a pink negligee Eugene Romberg had sent to her. Father liked the way it clashed with her hair. "There I was, with all these presents and nothing for the young captain. There was some chocolate. I gave it to him. He's just a boy, really. I think the world of him. He made me stay behind the barrier with Eli. Karin with her Swedish passport came to get him and brought the package, took Eli by the hand, and led him into Switzerland. She looks quite the lady, and she really likes the boy. He did not mind going with her. Eugene was waiting, waving on the other side. Eli ran to him."

Poldi brought up some Wiener schnitzel; I was allowed to have supper in the boudoir. Suddenly I felt terribly hungry. Mother had no appetite and picked away at her salad. "What will Resi say?" she asked.

No one spoke. Her clock ticked. I almost choked, I swallowed so fast.

"You didn't send the boy off to punish Resi?" Mother asked.

Father looked at her with amazement. She was not supposed to be clever. "What are you trying to say?"

"You know what I mean."

"Never mind. The main thing is that the boy is safe."

"He wanted his Mutti," I yelled. I picked up my little watch in one hand, the breaded meat in the other, and fled. It was getting dark. I let myself out into the garden. A black kitten I had never seen before sat at the fountain, batting the water. I called, "Mitzi, Mitzi, Mitzi-cat." It came to bat my watch. I gave it the rest of my meat, although I still felt hungry. This made me feel generous, like Eugene Romberg. Then I strapped his sparkling watch around my wrist.

Its hands stayed at five o'clock through all the years my grandmother and her clocks waited for the return of the empire. I never wound up my watch, yet whenever I wore it, time was marked without the ticking away of minutes: a time of envy. And one day it would pass. I would wind up my watch and bring back the good old days of the Water Castle.

13

Hitler's Cousin

I HAD CLIMBED the main branch of the chestnut tree in our front garden. Gusti, the gardener's son, swayed high above me, his dirty face and curls gray against white clouds, like one of those dust-covered cherubs on the façade of the little palace.

"Now, don't you break any of those branches and damage the tree by falling off," Vlado called from the rose garden. Trees took ages to grow; children, for Vlado, just came along.

I perched like a bird. Had I spread wings, I could have flown through the candelabras of chestnut blossoms in one straight line to Resi's balcony. I was so close to the clouds it was easy to transcend reality. I wrote a letter in my head: "Dear Führer, please let Eugene Romberg and Resi and Eli come back to the Water Castle. He is not a Jew. He is an Arab and he will give you many presents. Respectfully yours, Reyna von Meinert Dornbach Falkenburg." As soon as I learned to write properly—in school this September—I would write this letter. If I could only tell Adolf Hitler how much I wanted the lights of the great house to come on again, I was certain he would relent. Many such pleas for mercy were composed and never written, or written and never read.

From the tree I saw the porter's wife at the Water Castle come out of her cottage and put down dishes, calling, "Kitty, kitty. Here Mitzi-cats, here!" Cats came running to her—Persians, Siamese, tiger cats, white cats, black cats, and an orange one. During the cool and rainy weather they had sheltered in the pavilions and sheds of the Water Castle. Unlike their Jewish owners, the cats had remained free.

Vlado put down his tools and laughed out loud. "Now if that isn't subversion, feeding the Jew cats. There they go, committing race shame in broad daylight." He laughed so hard at his own joke that he had to wipe his eyes.

I slid down from the tree at once and asked him about race shame. He merely tweaked my nose. "Who's purebred in Vienna anyway, and who wants to be German?"

I laughed with him; I myself was part Hungarian, from the von Kortnais.

Before long cats began to cross the street, and I fed them behind the gardener's cottage. They had mated, and by the time the yellow roses grew large as cabbages, mother cats transported kittens by the scruff of the neck and nursed under shrubs. Those mixlings—multicolored evidence of race shame—enjoyed the splendid warm days and played undisturbed while Eli was forced to flee from the land of his birth.

Under the very eyes of a black-and-white self-portrait Fritz Janicek had left hanging on the board wall of the cottage, cats and mice, spiders and flies made themselves at home. I put bread crumbs into a maze Fritz had invented for mice, but removed the trap at the end. Vlado threw out the flypapers. "Let nature do the work," he said when the twins came to the cottage. He was educating them, and read aloud from the forbidden works of Karl Marx. Cats purred to the incomprehensible words, and the Janicek self-portrait flapped in the Föhn wind. There was a slapping sound of the swastika flag hitting the roof of the Meinert-Hof.

Vlado looked a bit like a seasoned tomcat himself with his round head, tufts of curls sticking up like ears; he certainly sounded like one when he yawled one of his Slavonic love songs for the twins one rainy Sunday. They were off to town, ready for adventure, dressed in blue under a large red umbrella. Vlado came out of his cottage and serenaded them with his song and invited them in for a glass of slivovitz. Gusti and I went into the adjoining shed. Glasses clinked in the cottage, chairs were pushed around in a skirmish, and the girls giggled. "I give it to you straight, girls. You stay away from those uniforms. You hear me? You're too ignorant for your own good." Through knotholes Gusti and I saw the two girls sitting on Vlado's knee. Fritz Janicek's green gardener's apron lent Vlado an odd, matronly dignity. "I give it to you straight, girls. The Huns are capitalists. They've taken our schillings. They come here and buy everything with their lousy marks. That includes girls." He emptied his glass in one gulp. "It's always the same. They have all the money and we do all the work."

The girls laughed at him and said he wasn't exactly straining himself.

"Impudence!" Vlado said. "When I'm trying to educate you and teach you a little about politics and love!"

Dirty Gusti gave us away by yelling: "Vater pinch, Vater pinch!" Vlado chased us out, and a kitten came racing along with us.

When the twins finally tumbled out the door, laughing and tidying their dresses, Vlado shouted, "You'd better come back. Wait, you two! After all, it's not every day you can have the company of Adolf Hitler's cousin."

They opened their red umbrella defiantly.

"Listen to this, you two pets, and don't breathe a word, or we'll all end up in the Danube with a rock around our necks." He came out and pushed between them, holding them captive. "My grandmother—God rest her soul—a wild girl when she was young, did the laundry at the house of a Jew in Graz. Guess who was the cook and general maid—you know what I mean, the girl who does everything? The granny of the Herr Führer. God rest her soul, too."

He tried to draw the twins back into the cottage. Lise shouted, "Stop it, Vlado!"

"I don't have to force myself on any girl, believe me," he went on. "Not with my looks and my relatives. My old man and Adolf's were born a year apart. My granny, the laundress, and the *Schicklgruber* woman, the general maid, both got money to raise their little bastards. Who knows whether it was the old Jew or the son who did it, or both of them? Now, isn't that a story for you, girls? Hitler's old man a half-Jew! Keep it under your hat. Ja, Adolf is a mixling all right, swarthy devil. I'm a mixling too, but you can't tell except that I'm smart and bookish and wild for girls."

Only a few days later Vlado's wife, who was also his niece, arrived in Vienna and brought the rest of the children. Father took me to see them in their vintner's cottage. They all looked like

Vlado and Gusti; only the oldest girl had dark hair. None of those children came to our garden, but Olga, Vlado's wife, often sat in an old wicker chair in front of the cottage to keep an eye on Vlado and shoo away the twins, the cats, Gusti, and me.

"Now you leave Vlado to do his work or he'll be in trouble. He talks too much," she said in a squeaky voice that didn't go with her enormous swollen body. I liked her much better after her child was born. She fed her infant and even let Gusti suck from her great breasts. A fluffy gray mother cat usually sat among the rosemary bushes nursing her striped mixlings. I missed the excitement of Karl Marx and the twins. It was quiet in the garden and in the house.

Mother had been resting for almost a week, feeling slightly indisposed and refusing to see a doctor. Agnes went up and down the stairs with camomile tea, rice dishes, egg yolks beaten with white wine and steamed into one of my favorite desserts. I found a wicker doll carriage in the attic. My favorite black kitten submitted to being dressed up in my old baby clothes and purred itself to sleep as I wheeled it about.

No one had time to shorten a new dirndl dress my grandmother had consoled me with after Eli left. "Eli has gone," I said to my Mitzi-cat as I changed its clothes. "But even our imperial family is in exile." My grandmother's voice was easy to imitate; so was Olga, as she suckled, cuffed, scolded, and loved her young. I lost myself in the fragrant garden. My new role, old as the world, kept me busy, bossy, and happy. I enjoyed myself so much I quite forgot that women in Mama's family regarded motherhood with dread.

The kitten had gone to sleep in the carriage, wearing a Falkenburg baby cap. I left the carriage in the shade and twirled around the splashing fountain in my long dress, to feel the spray on my face and make the skirt fly up.

"Reyna, Reyna," Mother called, leaning out of her alcove window in a fantastic straw hat trimmed with poppies, cherries, daisies, and cornflowers. "A surprise from Frau Hanna—isn't it mad, isn't it marvelous!"

I ran upstairs and tried it on. Mama was all excited and laughing. She had been looking pale for some time, but now her cheeks glowed. Only her laughter sounded a little too shrill, especially when she showed me the old doll's hat.

"This was the original straw hat with fruit and flowers. Frau Hanna told me she made it for Great-Aunt Christina and Puppe when the baroness was indisposed."

"I know about that. Christina von Kortnai gave birth to a baby, Frau Traude, and she gave her away to the nuns because she preferred the doll."

"You know too much and you talk too much," Mama said sternly. "And your dress has to be taken up; you'll trip over it." She took the hat away from me and put it on, dancing around in her flimsy robe. "I feel so much better," she said, hopping on one leg in her chemise as she stepped into the dress she had worn to the Hitler reception. "But I am getting fat, lying around. I can hardly button this dress. Frau Hanna is a genius. She knew I needed something to cheer me up."

Her hectic flush and those trembling hands made me uncomfortable. I left her and went back into the garden. The wicker carriage stood beside the fountain where I had left it. The baby cap and shirt lay neatly folded on the pillow.

"My Mitzi-cat is gone!" I cried.

"What is the matter?" Mama called from her window.

"My kitten."

"It's run off," she said.

"But it can't undress!"

I howled like a mother robbed of her young when I found out that Vlado had given the kitten away. The apprentice girl who had brought the hat was leaving when she saw the cat in the doll carriage and fell in love with it. Vlado, who was there to let her out, gave it to her. He liked giving presents to girls: fruit, flowers from our garden—anything that, strictly speaking, did not belong to him. As a Communist, he felt he had the right to take —not to keep and enrich himself in any way, like a Nazi, but to distribute from the rich, who had too much, to those who had not. He thought he had done a good thing. After all, there were too many cats, too many homeless kittens, and more to come.

To console me, Mama, in her new straw hat, took me to town to the Stadt park on the ring. The band played Strauss waltzes, and men in German uniforms paraded around with Austrian girls. While Mama and I sat on Huebner's terrace eating sour-cherry ice cream topped with *Schlag*, a van drove up in front of the

Water Castle. The cats and kittens, tame and guileless, were rounded up as easily as their owners had been.

When we returned home, not a cat remained. The twins told me that they had all been exterminated and could not be recovered. Everything had been taken away from me. I could no longer be consoled. Papa came home, and I crawled under my bed. He tried to reason with me. Meinerts never did tolerate stray animals on their land. And what would have happened when winter came? The cats could never have survived.

"Don't tell me they were murdered for their own good," I yelled, "like the czar and his family by the Bolsheviks!"

He told me I didn't know what I was talking about and asked me whom I had been listening to. He said worse things could happen.

I banged my head against the wall, and he gave up and called Agnes. After he left, she took me onto the sofa and held me while I cried for the Jews, the cats, the czar, the dead emperor, even the mice who had been lured into the Fritz Janicek maze and decapitated. Agnes rocked me to sleep like an infant.

It was beginning to get dark when I woke up. Mama was sitting beside my bed in her new hat. She told me she had telephoned Frau Hanna; the kitten had taken a great fancy to the Meisterin, and the girls had named it "Dolfi." If it had stayed with me, it might no longer be around. This way it had a good home. It turned out to be a tomcat and would soon be noisy and troublesome in a garden.

"I want to go and get my Mitzi-cat back," I said.

Mama pointed out that cats made her sneeze. When I suggested the cat could stay in the kitchen, she said we would see about that.

14

Annunciation à la Mode

"KITTY, MITZI, kitty cat," I called as soon as Mother and I walked into the salon. My black kitten was stalking back and forth over the keyboard of the great piano. A tinkling, discordant rhythm accompanied the Meisterin's inspirational "Heil Hitler." I responded heartily in the hope she would let me take my kitten back. Anything seemed possible as she exchanged the usual curtsy with me.

Then she turned to a framed Hitler poster which hung between high windows, and she genuflected with the utmost devotion. Now I had no doubt who my kitten had been renamed after. Not a stern Hitler, who had wiped Austria off the map and allowed his men to ransack the Water Castle and steal Resi; the Hitler in the poster, dressed like my father in an Austrian suit, looked like an Austrian patriot and created the impression that he had made Germany part of Austria.

Hanna Roth acted as though she had brought it all about. She seemed younger in her triumph. Her dress was the color of a summer night sky, and the sleeve danced when she reached up to the Führer's green hat decorated with a chamois beard brush. "Ach, that terrible brim. Such an unfortunate hat."

Everyone was watching her. Mother and the ladies I knew sat on the right side of the piano, tilting their floral hats. Hatless newcomers on the left side of the podium looked baffled. Here was my chance. I grabbed my Mitzi. The cat growled and leaped onto the piano top.

I had another chance during Hanna Roth's roll call of new

ladies. She picked up a dark appointment book and read, "Frau Gauleiter from Salzburg, or Frau Gruppenführer from Frankfurt." They raised their hands, displaying brilliants. Lips smooth and pink as though they had just been kissed, they shouted, "Here!" when they heard their husband's title in the hierarchy. Only one rather imposing lady got up to introduce herself.

"No, no," said Hanna Roth. "We all have titles and important names of the past, the present, or," she concluded with a sharp look at me, "the future." The cat jumped down and followed behind her as she went back and forth to finish her roll call. I sidled up to the podium, and I could have caught him by the tail.

"The cat and the child," she suddenly said. "Those yellow Falkenburg eyes."

Everyone was looking at me, and I withdrew to a corner.

"I woke up and could not get gold and yellow out of my mind. Then I looked at the calendar and saw it was the twenty-eighth of June. The anniversary of Sarajevo." She scooped up the cat, and he allowed himself to be draped over her shoulders like a fur piece; he hung there while she went on and on about the beautiful yellow hat she had created for Archduchess Sophie. "I implored her to wear it during her visit to the Balkans. If she had only listened to me, she would have worn a crown!" The cat came to and batted blue flowers on her little hat. She put him down and went on in a loud Hitler voice: "Believe me, that murderous weapon would have dropped from the assassin's hand." Dolfi fled under the piano. "You can't blame men for everything. It was the ignorance of a woman—one woman—that brought about the disaster." She made it clear that she had been crossed and world disaster had been the consequence.

Everyone seemed impressed, but I only cared about catching my cat. I did get to hold him briefly when Mama was on the podium having her hat adjusted. Dolfi came out to rub against her silk stockings, and she sneezed. I snatched him, holding on too tight. He hissed and scratched me, but I held on.

The Meisterin said, "Strange that bearing life should always cause indisposition among the highborn."

Mama grabbed the dwarf's thick arm. "You're teasing me. It can't be." All the color drained from her face. Freckles stood out in spots.

Frau Traude, who had been busy with cups and saucers, came to me at that moment and asked me whether I wanted a brother or a sister. I was so shocked I loosened my grip, and Dolfi escaped. "I don't like babies," I said. "I want my kitten." No one else heard me because Hanna Roth began to entertain them all with stories of weddings and christenings in the dolls' room.

None of this was fun for Mother. While everyone else was having coffee and cake, she sat on a sofa, folding her hands over her stomach in a protective gesture, very much like the Madonna with the angel in my children's prayer book. I had shocked Agnes once when I asked her whether the fancy angel was Mary's lover. She explained to me that the angel was God's messenger. I concluded that the angel was a bit of a prankster. After all, Mary should have known what was going on by the sign of her own round stomach.

The annunciation by Hanna Roth seemed equally unnecessary, and certainly unkind, since she had made it in public. I overheard one of the hatless ladies whispering, "I wonder who the father is?" I became impressed, since Agnes had assured me that a father could be heavenly.

"I have never been wrong about life and death," Hanna Roth said. "That's why I sent you the hat. Fruit and blossoms. A veritable crown of fertility. Wear it. Wear it and stay away from those horses!" These were her final words. To prevent any desperate effort on my part to repossess the cat, she snatched him into her arms and waved to me with his paw.

Once we were outside the door, Mama took my hand, and we fled as though we were pursued. "I had no idea. Agnes must know. She just didn't want to worry me. Perhaps your father knows, too. They all treat me like a child. I am terrified. Hanna Roth is well aware of that. She was there when you were born."

"I know; she came and handed you Puppe," I said. "Who knows, perhaps she'll bring her back if you have another baby." The idea appalled me. Neither of us could consider Mama's state a blessing.

She tried to be cheerful when Father kissed her, full of pride. He had no idea she felt God had punished her for being a Nazi with Berthold. She went along with plans to prepare a nursery. I kept close to her. We read together in the alcove of the boudoir.

Physically she improved; she felt far less tired and enjoyed food. One evening, after a downpour, we opened the window and listened to the evening song of blackbirds. She turned to me. "It won't happen. She knows it won't happen." She was talking about Hanna Roth, and from that moment on she became restless.

*   *   *

On a warm evening in late June or early July, a bonded messenger carried an envelope marked "Private and Urgent" in purple ink from the Meinert-Hof to the Meinert Heurigen, the wine garden. I had forgotten all about this. Now, all at once I see the old blank face, the trusty hand with the sealed envelope for Mama. A weathered hand, waiting humbly for a few coins, a tip, "drink money," as we call it.

This could have been the last *Dienstmann* I saw deliver a message. Around the time when Austria turned into the Ostmark and became a mere *Gau,* a province of the Third Reich, the bonded messenger who had carried gold, love poems, or wicked notes to my mother vanished. So did the lavender-women who had sung their way down our avenue, baskets on hips, and the *Handle* who had come chanting and coaxing for old clothes, with his cart and an old, sugar-crazy nag.

The Schrammel quartet was playing old songs of new wine, love, and passing happiness. Mother handled the envelope as if it were burning hot. A flickering frenzy came over her as she read the short note, carefully holding it under the table. It was not like her to keep the old Dienstmann waiting.

The plump vintner's widow who now had the concession for the Meinert wine garden gave the old man a glass of wine. He raised his glass. "Your health, Herrschaft." He drank, holding his red cap clamped under his arm. "I thank you, Herr Baron," he said when Father paid him. A good tip always deserved a good title. "I hope the honored lady has not had bad news."

"No, no," Mother said, and stuffed the letter into the pocket of her loose dress. Her shape was beginning to change.

Father waited until the old man had left and turned to the guests at our table with a smile. There was our old doctor, two reporters, the German lawyer I remembered from the Tanten-Haus, and Herr Gruber, the pot-bellied wine *Biter,* who could tell with a sniff and a sip what was wrong with a wine. "Bad news, indeed," Father said. "She is always making everyone fall in love with her, and they send her poems, flowers, declarations of never-ending love. I have to keep a file of her admirers. She could never remember them all." He raised his glass, and it turned gold in the light. "We have good news!"

They all drank to Mother. The musicians came to our table, and I sat on Father's knee while we all sang, "There will be a wine when we're no longer here." The garden was crowded. Families with friends, children, and some dogs sat at those long pine tables with their sausage, bread, ham, and chicken, to sample new Meinert wines. All around, everyone was singing. Herr Gruber's sad spaniel raised his head and howled. Lamps strung between the old trees seemed to sway with the song.

Mother was not singing. She stared at the moths dancing around the light. When Father got up to refill glasses, she took the letter out of her pocket. I looked over her shoulder: GRACIOUS LADY, IF YOU WANT TO SEE YOUR DOLL AGAIN, COME TO THE MEINERT CHAPEL ON THURSDAY AT NOON. COME ALONE WITHOUT CAR. It was printed in large purple letters.

"Will you go?" I asked.

She tore the note up in anger and called me a snoop.

＊　　＊　　＊

Thursday was a sunny day. "I don't think you should go to the chapel," I said to my mother, with all of the dwarf's authority. She had tied a kerchief over her head and was wheeling Poldi's bicycle to the gate. "Never go without your hat," I said, while she arranged a pillow in the basket to keep Puppe from breaking. I did not want her to go to the Meinert chapel. She might find the doll and have twins. Her doctor had mentioned twins.

She had taken me along when she had gone to see the specialist. The waiting room had been full of pregnant ladies, and the table loaded with a display of frolicking china babies. Mother came out of the examining room in a state. The doctor kissed her hand and assured her that he had only teased her, it had been a joke. He had never heard more than one heartbeat. But she was convinced that she would die giving birth to twins unless she had the doll.

She made me hold the bicycle, ran into the house, and came back with both her straw hat and the doll's, which she tied to the handlebar. "Unlock the gate," she said.

"Father will be mad."

"Don't tell him." She started off wobbly because she had not been on a bicycle for a long time, and she laughed at herself in the fancy hat. Soon she pedaled smoothly with her strong legs.

"Come back!" I cried.

When Father came home, he found her gone, and he questioned me. "On a bicycle—what madness is this!" He took me by the shoulder and shook me as though it were all my fault. I had to tell him about the purple note. "An ugly hoax, no doubt. She might be in danger. There's so much envy. God knows what's waiting for her. She might fall . . ." He ran back to the car. I jumped in, and he allowed me to come. Heinz had gone to lunch; Father drove himself. I had to hold on, he took the corners so fast. At the chapel, he stopped so suddenly I fell forward.

Mother sat on a bench under the chestnut trees, her hat askew. The bicycle leaned against the chapel wall. I saw no doll in the basket. We ran to her, and she burst into tears. "Why did you follow me? If they see the car they won't bring me Puppe."

No one ever knew how many notes written in purple ink Mama eventually received. Judging by the way she ran around, they might have been delivered to her each hour of the day and night. The picture of a smiling Resi in the newspaper one day did not help her mood. Mother showed the article to my grandmother when we were having coffee.

" 'Little Nightingale free of charges and free of Jew who deserted her.' " Grandmother put the paper away and said she didn't know what the press was coming to. "I guess it's better to be considered an eccentric than to be locked up. I can't figure out whether von Feld wanted to pay me back for handing him a Krampus and telling him off last winter, or whether he thought he was doing the Monarchists a favor by telling a reporter that we are dotty and old. Anyway, if Hitler hadn't sent von Feld to Turkey, my Rittmeister would have challenged him to a duel." She knew I was listening in and gave me a kiss. "I am so glad to know Frau Romberg is going to be back at the Opera. What a delightful voice she has. She'll be leaving the Landsitz."

"Ferdl would like to have her come back to the villa so that she can amuse him while I get more and more unsightly every day."

My grandmother looked cool and beautiful in a pale gray crepe de chine dress. A soft breeze rippled the ruffles at the wrist and hem. "You look your best, Ann Marie. Ferdinand is no fool. He is merely polite. He knows perfectly well she wouldn't move back to the house by herself. Rooms in town near the Opera will be more convenient for her when rehearsals start."

"Not for Bertl," said Mama. "He likes big houses."

"I doubt that he will go that far," my grandmother said. "He is a terrible flirt. Young officers have always had their *Libelei*."

15

Hidden Laughter,
Hidden Tears

"WELL, THE ROMANS built excellent roads," Mother said as we drove by the first aqueduct near Carnuntum.

"And they built the amphitheater," I said.

"That's right, I brought you along last year."

"You got mad at Berthold," I reminded her.

She took out a compact, powdered her nose, and said that it had been hot. Today was a perfect day.

"He took us to the arena," I said.

She dabbed my nose with her powder puff. "How well you remember words."

I also remembered her red face when she had had her temper fit and yelled, "Love—love! How can you talk of love here, where those vile bullies sat and watched Christians being torn apart by wild animals?"

Berthold had laughed at her and said, "Forget the nasty old Romans. Circus for the people and all that. A vulgar lot, dead and gone. Now we are here, and love is more fun than history, what?"

Lately, however, Berthold was having his fun with Resi. They were sitting at a round table in the garden of the old inn as we drove up. He had his arm around her, and they were sipping wine from the same glass. She had let her hair grow, and it hung down her back in ringlets like a girl's.

Elderly people from the nearby Roman spa put down their

newspapers to look at Mother in her new hat and me in a starched white dress. Mother reached for my hand. She had brought me along for self-protection and as an ornament, the way she used to carry Puppe. For a moment I thought she might turn around and get back into the car, leaving Berthold and Resi under the apple tree. I let go of her hand and ran to them.

Resi jumped up and caught me in her arms, calling me an adorable sweetheart. She greeted Mama without letting go of me. Suddenly she burst into tears. "Eli, ach, my Eli." Berthold dried her face with his handkerchief. It was embroidered with his crest, the fish and the stars. Resi took it from him and kept it in her hand. She wore a simple gingham dress, not her style. I could see the Star of David under the thin fabric. On her left shoulder I noticed a small silver swastika. Berthold stroked her hair, kissed her cheek.

"We shouldn't have come," Mother said. "It's making Resi un-happpy. I feel we're intruding."

Berthold kissed her hand. "How could you ever intrude?" He waved to a waitress and ordered cake, strawberries, and whipped cream. "How about champagne? We're celebrating."

Mother said she couldn't drink it. I felt disappointed, for I was certain he would include me in the celebration.

"I just don't want to lose a minute of all this . . ." Berthold waved his wonderful long hand. The gesture included the Roman ruins and the gentle valley below the inn where his white horses grazed in a fenced-in field. Resi leaned against his shoulder. "She'll soon be too busy for me," he said. "Rehearsals start next week."

"I'm not in the least interested," Resi said. "I'd just as soon keep singing for you at the Landsitz."

I got away from the cloying, clinging Resi to play with unripe apples the wind had stripped from the old tree. "Will you ever come back to the villa?" I asked.

Resi shook her head. "I'll never set foot in that place again."

"Then why on earth do you have Ferdl fight for it?" Mama asked in a nasal, convent-school voice.

Resi smiled knowingly. "He has his own reasons. He always has. I suspect he would like to choose his neighbors."

I spoke up on behalf of Frau Traude, Hanna Roth, and my cat.

Berthold laughed. "Old Hanna. That's right, she wants a mansion to go with her fantastic American car. Did you know that she's taken up driving? You should see her. She's a menace."

"She did not Aryanize the car," Mother said. "A Rothschild or someone like that gave it to her for sewing diamonds into a hatband. Hanna is no anti-Semite; she was raised by a Jew. But she is a snob. Besides, like many of us, she is convinced that Hitler would let Jews take their property."

"I still don't trust her," Berthold said. "She's a snoop, a busybody, and a menace in that car. Carnuntum is her favorite run. Those predictions are bunk. She's a mischief-maker."

"Well, she said the Opera is going to burn," Resi laughed. "I'd better watch out. But she did bring me luck with those hats when my career began."

"You had other backers," Berthold said. She pouted, and he quickly kissed her hand and said everyone adored her, sounding a lot like my father. He must have felt at a loss in public with the Little Nightingale, and took his cue from Father, who had a lighthearted way with his ladies.

"I think Hannah Roth does know what is going to happen," I said.

Berthold picked me up and hugged me. "She has no idea you're my little fiancée, what?"

"There he goes. Leaving me for a young girl," Resi cried out.

Berthold ran off with me into the field behind the inn to show me some piglets. They lay nestled together, sleeping inside the pen. One of them twitched and squeaked. "It's dreaming," he said. "I wonder of what."

"Of being eaten," I told him. He did not laugh, but took my hand and led me to a wooden bench. We sat and dangled our legs; he smoked. The land before us stretched toward the Danube in flat meadows with field flowers. The Roman aqueduct looked blue in the sun.

"Why are you sad?" I asked.

He put a finger to his lips; his eyes twinkled blue like the flowers in the field. "Nobody must know." The piglets nudged each other awake and began to totter about their pen. "I never used to worry at all. Now I worry a lot—about everyone and everything. I shouldn't have to at my age." He stamped out his cigarette and put his arm around me. I wanted to sit there with him forever.

"Do you worry about me?" I asked.

"You and Annerl?" He laughed. "No more than I worry about myself. You're part of me. Do you understand? Just like my left arm."

"Why not your right arm?"

This made him laugh out loud. The piglets scampered to the far end of the pen. "Now you're no longer sad," I said.

He kissed me on both cheeks and said I cheered him up no end and called me his Liebling, making me feel important, happy, so much his favorite that I didn't even mind it when he returned to the table and to Resi. He spoon-fed her with strawberries, whipped cream, and cake, pushing food into her mouth and kissing sugar off her cheek. When I became tired of their performance, I said, "Mama is going to have a baby."

Berthold let go of Resi and reached for Mother's hand, turned it over, and kissed the palm. "Ferdl told me. I wasn't sure you wanted to have it mentioned."

Mama gave me an angry look. "I don't want to have it mentioned!"

"But you could have told me, Bertl!" Resi cried. "I'm so happy. No wonder Herr von Meinert is so smug these days. I can't believe it! Let me look at you. Of course, of course. You look great." She leaned her rosy face against Berthold's shoulder dreamily. "The most wonderful thing that can happen to anyone."

"Not to me," he said.

Mama laughed and could not stop laughing, the way she often did when he was around. Resi drew me aside. "Just think, you'll have a playmate, a brother, like Eli." I shook her off. How could she mention Eli so carelessly? Her hand on my arm sported a signet ring with the crest of the fish and stars.

"I won't have a brother." I hoped I sounded like Hanna Roth. "And babies are no playmates."

"It's a confusing time for children," Mother said. It was easier to think of children in general than to think of me, just as it was more comfortable to think of Jews and not of Eugene Romberg or the old couple who had sold us candy.

I ran back into the field. In the days before the Anschluss, my outbursts and abrupt departures would not have been tolerated. Now everyone made allowances. I walked about decapitating flowers. Eli's Mutti was leaning against Berthold in the garden of the inn, free to wear his ring, dream of motherhood. The Water Castle stood empty, and she would not return. I sat alone on the bench, and for the first time I wished my grandmother had come with us. She was always the same.

Suddenly Berthold ran out onto the road and waved his arms. A dark-blue motorcar came around the field where his white horses had been grazing in the shade of trees, flicking their long white tails. Now they galloped about in the sun, rearing up and neighing. The car circled around the field a second time. I ran out to Berthold. He waved his arms and we both shouted: "*Halt, halt!*"

"I told old Hanna to stop driving around the field. It stirs up my horses." As the car moved toward the inn, he jumped onto the running board; the car came to a jolting halt. "You are very wicked, Frau Hanna," he said.

She smiled, sitting tall and magnificent in the shiny dark-blue car with yellow spokes. No one could tell she was a dwarf when she was driving. She must have loved that. A red-faced driving teacher with a white mustache sat beside her. "I told Frau Roth she must slow down when there are cows, horses, or sheep."

Hanna Roth shouted, "Heil Hitler!"

I curtsied and yelled "Heil!" like Father.

"Let's leave the Führer out of this," Berthold said. "There are lots of roads—you don't have to drive around that field."

Gold-rimmed spectacles enlarged Hanna's fierce dark eyes. "Something draws me here," she said, and stared into the distance. "I can't explain it."

The man beside her made her excuses again. Mama interrupted, "Frau Hanna, what a magnificent car." The inside was upholstered in gray velvet, and attached to the side there was a crystal vase with a deep-red rose. "And your hat—sensational." It was a white straw bowler with some dark-blue feathers. I tried to look into the back of the car, but the partition was closed, the curtains drawn.

"I'm glad you are wearing your hat," Hanna Roth said. "You look splendid; and what a charming idea to wear Puppe's sapphire necklace around your wrist."

I had not noticed the doll's necklace under Mother's long, ruffled sleeves; the dwarf, in her new driving glasses, saw everything. Berthold, with his usual charm, invited her to join us for some refreshments. She refused. Just seeing us, she said, was refreshing enough. Her eyes rested on Resi, who had come sauntering over, smoking, smiling to people in the garden who recognized her.

"Well, well," Hanna Roth said without pleasure. "There you are —free, ready to spread your wings, Frau Resi."

"Now, now, Frau Meisterin," Berthold interrupted, waving his finger. "No warnings, no predictions for our Resi. She's gone through quite enough. You've already upset my Lippizaners."

"Horses," she said, starting her engine, "are unpredictable. Dangerous to you, Frau Ann Marie. Wear your hat in good health." She began to turn her car; Berthold jumped aside, and we all stood back as she bumped into the fence.

"I knew there'd be a warning," he said.

The driving teacher puffed up his cheeks and looked nervous. "Easy on the gas!"

"Don't worry," she said with unexpected gentleness, "I have Frau Traude asleep in the back. The warm weather and all the to-do over the Romberg mansion . . . She's exhausted, poor darling."

"Why doesn't she stay out of it?" Resi flared up. "It's my home!"

The car jolted to a halt, blocking the road. Guests at the inn stood up, stared, and listened. Hanna Roth and Resi both thrived on an audience. "It's never been your house, meine Liebe. But artists like you don't have to worry. You have a way of making yourself at home anywhere." The dwarf raised her arm in another arrogant Hitler salute, honked her horn, swerved toward Berthold. "Watch out, young knight. Enjoy yourself. Soon you will be called away to serve our Führer." She deliberately gathered speed at the field. The horses galloped about.

"She's a devil," Berthold said. "Ruining my horses. Now they'll shy as soon as they hear a car. Worse than ever, isn't she? Quite impossible, what?"

"I think she's terrific," I said. "But she did take my cat." As the car completed the turn and moved away, I saw Dolfi stretched out by the back window like a toy.

❀   ❀   ❀

Hanna Roth must have made a hat for the wife of the new chief of police in order to pass her driver's test, and surely her psychic powers alone got her safely up the winding road to the spa Bad Gastein, the fountain of everlasting youth. She took Frau Traude, the cat, and no doubt many hats. Everyone I knew left Vienna between the end of July and the beginning of August. The struggle for the Water Castle was interrupted.

Grass grew tall across the street; one could no longer see flowerbeds, and the ornamental hedges looked straggly. Rambling weeds climbed up statues' legs; foxgloves and wild daisies sprang up like magic. No one disturbed the enchantment of the neglected garden. The house remained dark, but the porter's wife kept the gate light on all night. Moths danced around it. I hooted at owls when I passed by, walking with Agnes; the owls hooted back. The first fireflies twinkled among weeds. "Do you remember the cats?" I asked.

Agnes and I never talked about the Rombergs or the women kneeling in the street, but when we stepped over the spot where the letters had been painted out, she made the sign of the cross. "Soon you'll be on the Grundlsee, splashing around," she said. "And I know how your grandmama is looking forward to your staying at Ischl with her." My parents always made Bad Ischl their first stop, to please the countess, who stayed there every summer, surrounded by followers.

Monarchists came to the old kaiser resort as pilgrims. In the afternoon when we sat at Zauner's eating Zauner torte, the river rushed by and water gurgled to the tune of a little orchestra playing Strauss waltzes and operetta tunes. I was entertained with stories of the eighteen-year-old Franz Joseph's falling in love with his fifteen-year-old cousin, Elizabeth, younger sister of the cousin he was supposed to marry. I knew the church where they had announced their engagement, the ballroom where they had danced. Ischl had never recovered from that romance.

The kaiser villa did not impress me. My grandmother and the Rittmeister showed me all the rooms one morning when it was rainy and cold. The Rittmeister was glad everything was preserved. My grandmother wanted to renovate and get things ready for Prince Otto. "It needs decent heating, modern bathrooms. Why not renovate? There is no sense in preserving this place. The empress and the kaiser were never happy here. He preferred shooting to poetry. There was no real understanding. One should make a shrine of the Schratt villa instead. She was his true friend and knew how to comfort. A fine actress, too."

I hoped we would take the shadowy path the kaiser had taken when he went to see Frau Schratt at the nearby villa, but Father came to look for me. Mother had decided she wanted to go back to Vienna to consult a doctor. We returned to Vienna at once. She vanished for one entire day, came home despondent, terribly hungry, and laughed too much during dinner. I found the envelope addressed to her in purple ink, in her wastepaper basket.

The next morning she took me for a walk in the midmorning heat; in the afternoon she made the chauffeur drive us to the Danube for a swim. She held me in her strong arms, and we drifted gently downstream. Heinz, stiff and worried, followed along the bank with towels and her bathrobe, swatting midges. I could have floated on the water all afternoon, but the baby kicked Mama for the first time, and this spoiled the fun.

"I know it's supposed to be thrilling," she said to me on the way home, "but I feel as though I have been invaded." There was a lot of talk about invasion that year.

She did not want Father to know of our swim, or of the baby's kicking. He worried about her, came home with a string of pink pearls one day, a silk shawl the next. He was always giving her things; when I checked his pockets, I found them empty—he had forgotten my candy. He indulged her. We had only been back a few days when she suddenly decided to go away again, not to the lake and to the music festival, as planned, but to the Semmering. She had avoided the fashionable mountain resort when the Rombergs and Eli had stayed there. Now she decided she loved the mountains, so close to Vienna that Father could go back and forth. I somehow knew she had a note telling her Puppe was at the Semmering. Someone was teasing her.

I dozed among hatboxes in the back of the car until we had left Vienna behind. I never tired of the fairy-tale landscape of our country: green fields, dark forests, mountain peaks, and rushing rivers; farms with windowboxes full of begonias; haywagons; castles on lakes, fortresses on mountains, ruins overgrown with rambling roses. Cows grazed lazily. Clouds traveled quickly ahead. A giant might step over the tiny hamlets, using leftover Maypoles as toothpicks. Elves might loll about on water lilies or ride on the backs of dragonflies. And Eli, dressed in white, might come down the steps of the Hotel Pannhans to welcome me. We would walk through the woods to waterfalls, gather wild berries, sail nutshell boats in brooks—all the way to the Promised Land.

The Grand Hotel sported swastika flags. The manager, not Eli, came to welcome us. He showed me the swimming pool in the basement, with artificial waves; voices reverberated from stone walls. One night when noise in the corridor woke me up, I went downstairs in my pajamas. Mama, I saw from a window overlooking the terrace room, sat with a group of hotel acquaintances watching the dancers.

I took a slide on the long banister down to the pool. Never had I heard such shrieks and laughter. The door had glass panels; I stood on my toes. Never had I seen such fearsome fun. The wave machine, in full force, splashed water against the walls. Five or six SS men in full uniform dove around each other in the water, yelling and splashing. Their hats had been stacked up on each side of the pool. One fat man wore a uniform hat and nothing else, and he was trying to push a thin man under water; only the head stuck out, and an arm in a black sleeve. I knew Fritz Janicek by the nose, even before he threw water at the smiling fat man and shouted, "Take this, my wicked angel!"

Two nights later I had a chance to go sliding down the long banister again. No one was at the pool. The smooth water reflected a small child in striped pajamas.

I did, however, see Fritz Janicek again. Mama and I were walking through the woods one morning, and I fed squirrels while she rested on a bench. An artist had set up an easel below the path and was painting. I went halfway down the hill to look at the picture. There was Fritz Janicek, in his artist's hat, brush in hand. His back was turned to me; the fat-faced man, smiling and dimpled, sat on a tree stump, all dressed up in pale blue. The painting captured his look of infantile wickedness and those dreamy blue eyes perfectly. Fritz was adding some purple swirls in the background, although everything was green. "You inspire me," he said.

I went back to Mama and told her to look. She grabbed my hand, and we turned around and ran back to the hotel as though we were pursued.

"Fritz Janicek writes those notes in purple ink," I said.

"What do you know about it?" Mother asked sternly. I could not say any more without giving myself away. "Do you know the fat man he's painting?"

"A wicked angel," I said.

❁   ❁   ❁

We returned to Vienna, and I could not wait to go to school. Three new dresses hung in my closet, one of them blue, with a pleated skirt, a present from Resi. She had moved into an apartment near the Opera. The owners, a Jewish family, had fled abroad. My father was busy moving her and saw to all the formalities. Berthold came to see Mother and took her to show riding or lunch at the Cobenzl, a mountain with a pleasant restaurant overlooking the city. I remember her being helped into Berthold's little car in one of her soft, full dresses. The wind whipped the skirt around her. With that big belly she would have been more comfortable on all fours, like the cats. I had seen a cat have her young behind the gardener's cottage and could not imagine this could happen to my mother.

The weather remained unusually warm, excellent for the early grape harvest. On the first day of the harvest, Mother rested comfortably in a hammock near the fountain, and my father took me to the vineyard to allow her some quiet. He had not noticed the envelope, addressed in purple ink, sticking out of her pocket. As soon as we left, she must have dropped her magazine. By the time I met with Gusti and some of his brothers and sisters at the back of the winepress, she must have been on her way to the top of the Hoch-Haus, the only high modern building in the inner city.

At harvest time the Meinert vineyard was patterned with baskets, wheelbarrows, wagons, stooping men, all the way up to the cemetery. Father always worked with his vintners for an hour or more each day. They loved him for it. The men worked side by side, grumbling in dialect, cursing, joking, whistling, and singing. The ritual dated back to the time of the Romans. Wives and older children went up the hill with ceramic jugs of fresh, cool grape juice and a basket full of rolls filled with ham or sausage. The men took a swig and yelled, "Herr Gott, that's good! What a wine we're going to have!"

Sometimes I helped to pick grapes, but this time I chased around the pressing house with Gusti and his brothers and sisters. Afterwards I felt that I should have stayed with Mama. She might not have gone to town in a taxi. I would think of the way I was spitting grape seeds with the Vlado brats while she sat waiting on the Hoch-Haus terrace café, watching the door.

We were still spitting grape seeds at each other when Nadica, the brats' grown-up pretty sister, came and chased them home. She told me this was no way for a Herrschaft's child to behave. Later I felt my name-calling and spitting had been wicked enough to make bad things happen. I found out that Mother had called Berthold from the Hoch-Haus and burst into tears, told him no one understood how she felt about the lost Puppe. Berthold must have felt guilty too. He left everything and went to pick her up. I formed a picture of her leaning against him in his car, weeping as he sped to the Landsitz.

At the moment, however, I had no idea anything was wrong. Left alone, I settled on a barrel in the shade and breathed in the fragrance of grape skins, watched the grape juice flow from the mill into vats. The men worked hard and perspired. They all had a smile or a kind word for me as they passed by. Some of them wore brown shirts and boots, as though they couldn't quite part with their storm trooper's uniforms. I watched the friendly faces. "Did you hit the Jewish candy man, Herr Josep?" I asked one who wore an oversized swastika. He handed me some grapes, patted my head, and went on.

Father came down the hill and gave me a sip of cool grape juice. "You're as dirty as the Vlado brats," he said. He was ready to take me home. "Agnes had better stick you right into the tub."

We drove up to the house and Agnes stood waiting, holding one of Mother's leather suitcases. She wore her raincoat over a housedress, as though she had to go somewhere in a hurry. Her eyes looked red, and she was blowing her nose. I jumped down and hugged her.

"What's the matter?" Father asked.

"Would the Herr please drive to the hospital at once? I must go there with the suitcase. Our Gnädigste has had an accident. A fall. God has spared her, but she is hurt."

"What are you trying to tell me?" Father yelled. "What are you trying to tell me!" he shouted again when he spoke to the doctor on the telephone.

Poldi told me I had a dead brother.

I was not allowed to go to the funeral. Father returned in an unfamiliar dark suit, limped into the courtyard and around the fountain. He did not say a word, and I followed him as he made his way uphill. The empty hammock swung in the September breeze. Some of Mother's nightgowns danced in the wind on the line behind the rose trellis. I tried to take his hand, but he shook me off. His head hung forward. I limped alongside him to the washing line. He reached up as though he were sinking and grasped a white lace-trimmed gown, thrusting his face into the silk. I heard him sob, and it sounded like a cough. He was choking. I felt an icy claw fasten to the back of my neck. Chestnuts pelted the roof of the gardener's cottage, going *bang, bang, bang.*

16

Blame It on the Wind

MY MOTHER HAD FALLEN off a young mare at Landsitz Hohentahler, lost her child, injured her spine, and suffered a concussion; her brain was shaken up, as we say in Austria. At first only Countess Reyna and my father went to visit her at the hospital. The details of the accident were not discussed, but all of Vienna knew of the misfortune and prayed for Mother, sent flowers; some, perhaps, rejoiced that even the most privileged met with disaster.

A huge bouquet from the Führer himself was brought to Mother's bedside. "You who have been destined to serve my cause so well must recover on the brink of yet another victory. Sieg Heil! Your Adolf Hitler." This message sounded so much like a command, my father had Mama moved to a sanatorium at once. The newspaper said: "Beauty Greatly Improved After Führer Message."

The delivery of the Hitler bouquet, my first day of school, and Hitler's meeting with Mr. Chamberlain all happened around the same time. It rained. Agnes allowed me to put on the new pleated dress Resi had given me. We walked under her green umbrella, green as mountain spirits. I did not cry or hang back like some of the other girls, who clung to their mothers, but I hated the indignity of being one of many as we were led upstairs. The ugly smells of disinfectant, ink, and urine permeated the old building. In the classroom we were sorted out and lined up according to size and given a number. I, number seven, saw Agnes standing in a small park below the window, green under her green umbrella. I waved, but she didn't see me.

The teacher, a faded woman who wore her dull hair in a sausage around her head, patted me and made me sit in front. A Hitler picture behind her desk showed us a Führer wearing a dark suit and tie and holding a large book, like a stern teacher. When our Fräulein Teacher turned and led us in a Hitler salute, he seemed to squint. I felt as well disposed toward our leader as I ever would, since he had sent my mama a huge bouquet and made her well enough to be moved into a sanatorium.

The Fräulein Teacher gave us paper and said we should draw a picture and as many letters as we knew. I drew an Adolf Hitler who grinned, squinted, and held a bouquet; then I printed all the letters of the alphabet. It did not take me long. I had time to look around. Most of the other girls wore their hair in two plaits tied with ribbons. A big one behind me, with straw-colored hair braided with red ribbons, stuck out her tongue. I returned the insult. A bell shrilled. We had to line up in pairs at once to go downstairs and hear the Führer speak on the radio.

The teacher collected our papers, put numbers on them, and went to the back of the room where a girl had remained in her seat. I had noticed her when we lined up the first time because she was close to my size, dressed in black mourning, with a cross on a long gold chain but no swastika. Her brown hair hung loose to her shoulders. The teacher handed her a second piece of paper and spoke to her in undertones. When the girl raised her head, her dark eyes were filled with tears. I thought of Eli, although I'd never seen him weep.

"A Jew," said the girl in red, who stood at the end of the line because she was so big.

"Only half," said her partner.

The girl in the back seat lowered her head over the paper; only the quiver of her long eyelashes showed she had heard. She was trying to draw.

"Go home, Jew!" shouted the girl in red, stepping out of line.

"Back with your partner," the teacher said mildly.

The girl made an ugly grimace. "Jew, drop dead!" she shouted.

The pencil fell from the child's hand. I ran to her and picked it up. The teacher told me to get back into line, but the one in red barred my way. I sprang up against her, dizzy with hate, and struck her face. She slapped me back, and I kicked her as hard as

I could. She yelled, and the teacher came along shouting, "Stop, stop at once!" But the big girl grabbed my dress just as I lashed out, and it ripped down the front.

"Ach," the girls cried, "the beautiful dress!"

I ran away from the room, down the stairs, and out to the park. Agnes was still there, and she caught me in her arms. In the principal's office, she said I was upset. There was a little boy, a half-Jew, who lived near us . . . But at that moment, the teacher walked in and put my Hitler picture on the desk.

The Frau Direktor of our school wore a gray smock and smelled of lard. "I see you can write the letters of the alphabet, and I imagine you can read." I did not quite trust her smile. The dark hair under her thick nose looked as though she were trying to grow a Hitler mustache. She held my picture up. "Is this supposed to be our Führer?" I nodded. "Not a pleasant image, is it now?" The schoolroom Hitler hung behind her desk, too. My Hitler had the same fierce squint, but at least he held flowers and he grinned, showing his teeth.

Agnes explained that my mother was in the hospital and the Führer himself had sent a large bouquet and a note to make her well. I was trying to show this in my picture. The Frau Director looked impressed. I was excused, sent home to change my dress.

I never did go back to school. My grandmother came and took me to the little palace—away from it all, as she put it. That, of course, was an illusion. She told me I would begin lessons again in October, share a French governess with the Hohentahler girls. I said I didn't like the girls, that they were Nazis. "They are girls of your own class," she told me. "At least they are housebroken." I did not agree.

She gave me Mother's old room, but a Madonna Mama had drawn in convent school kept staring at me with those wide-set eyes I knew so well. Mother had really drawn herself. On the headboard perched two fat wooden babes with wings, giving me bad dreams. One night I saw a baby doll in a glass box being carried down the steps of the Water Castle. I cried out "Don't drop it!" to the two handymen. I woke up, and Grandmother was holding me. I slept in her bed, and it smelled of violets.

We had breakfast in the alcove of the pink salon, under the eyes of the smiling kaiser portrait. The windows had been thrown open on this fine autumn morning. Grandmama and I settled down in the alcove to a game of dominoes. Autumn leaves flew past our window in gusts of wind. The trees and shrubs had changed to russet and yellow. An old man was raking fallen foliage into heaps. The moist, loamy odor, the scraping sound, and the golden light of autumn, my grandmother said, made her feel at peace. I was winning the game because she kept looking out, enjoying her favorite season. "Ach, the swallows have flown away early this year. I do miss them. Just think, for hundreds of years they have come back here to nest. Of course, they weren't always accommodated in the passageway. I learned that on my travels as a young girl, when I stayed in Italy with Aunt Christina. There, swallows nest in churches, in *castellos*, everywhere."

"And the Italians eat them, and they roast nightingales, and they eat cats."

"Who told you that?"

"Fritz Janicek."

"A questionable authority, and I would say a poor educator. Now he's collecting other people's paintings. 'League for the Protection of German Culture,' indeed! An opportunist and a thief."

"He has collected the doll. I'm sure."

"Nonsense." She gave me a sharp look, and we continued our game. "He was indebted to your mother—why should he steal from her, when he is collecting paintings worth millions? As far as eating birds and other animals is concerned, people will eat anything if they are hungry."

"They'll eat each other," I said.

"He told you that?" I nodded. "Where on earth did your mother find such a terrible man?"

"In the soup kitchen for the unemployed," I said.

Our conversation was interrupted by a car horn honking three times. I leaned out of the window and saw the heavy oak portal to the courtyard open to the dark hood of Hanna Roth's car. The Meisterin drove through a pile of leaves, and the old gardener swung his rake, shouting, "*Halt, halt!*" She jolted to a stop at the front door, slid from her high seat, and entered in a great hurry. Her platform shoes stomped up the marble steps. She knocked, stormed into the room before the countess could say *herein*, and stopped in front of us as though she had stepped on her brakes too late, too hard.

"*Guten Morgen.*" She was breathing fast, not so much from running upstairs, as from the effort of holding back her inimitable "Heil Hitler" in front of the countess Reyna. Excitement came with her at all times. I jumped up to welcome her, but her eyes measured me sternly as we exchanged the usual curtsy. "You've grown a lot."

She looked smaller, but ever so stylish in a gray suit; russet-colored feathers on her gray felt toque trembled from inner vibrations. "You must get rid of that Doctor Habinger, Countess. He can do your daughter harm. He refused to let me see her, snatched my flowers from me, and blamed me for her accident. I am not to blame."

"If you don't feel responsible for making the horse shy with your car, why bother to burst in here like this?" My grandmother did not offer her a seat. "The harm has been done. The Herr Doktor keeps most visitors away."

"But how can anyone blame me? Had I not warned her again and again to stay away from horses? Why, even this child knows that. I would put a hat on her head and hear the thunder of hoofs. And I had a vision of a tiny infant lying stiff and still inside her hatbox. I thought only of the doll." Her gloved hand went to her heart, but she kept looking at me. Did she know her vision had entered my dream? "I should have made her listen," she went on. "I did not trust myself enough."

"You certainly trust yourself enough to go racing around in an automobile—at your age! You could well afford a chauffeur."

Hanna Roth stared into the courtyard, listening not to the reprimand but to—"Horses' hoofs! *Clomp, clomp*," she cried out. "On and on, *clomp* and *bang, bang*. Explosions in my ears." She let herself fall into a pink chair, threw back her fine veil, and covered her ears with both hands.

My grandmother went to fetch brandy and poured a little for the Meisterin. During this rare confrontation with the dwarf, she held back the old sympathy of their convent days as orphans. Their perfume of violets, their fine way with words revealed a bond they both fought against.

Hanna Roth sipped from her glass and beckoned me. I sat down beside her on a footstool, to make myself small. "I don't know what you have been told of that accident, little highness."

"Nothing," I said. "Only that Mama fell off a horse."

"An untrained animal, but that foolish singer bragged that she could make any Lippizaner waltz if she sang. They provoked the young mare beyond endurance before I ever drove up. I had not even turned the corner when I heard Frau Resi shrieking away at 'Tales from the Vienna Woods' and your mother in hysterics, laughing, giggling. No wonder she couldn't control the horse when it balked. Her cousin came running from the stable, but she refused to dismount for him, chose to ignore all my warnings. By the time I came along, the Lippizaner was acting like a billy goat."

"Not so fast, Hanna," the countess said. "My daughter, seated on a Lippizaner in a flowing dress, wearing one of your wild hats, should have been conspicuous and absurd enough to bring your car to a stop at once. Ann Marie was asking for trouble on that horse. It doesn't take a clairvoyant to know that. But your driving up to the young mare, knowing that you had made those horses hate your car, was even worse." She was so upset she took three pralines without offering any to us. Her face remained smooth and calm, but her eyes lit up like polished gold. "Unless, Hanna—unless you were so angry with my daughter for ignoring your warnings and predictions—you just had to teach her a lesson."

"Blame me if you must, and my car. But the owner of the horse can tell you: it was the wind. She would not have fallen. He had managed to get hold of the reins; from my car I was able to fix the horse with my eyes, make it stand. I can do that. The stupid singer, of course, felt she had mesmerized the Lippizaner with her "Tales from the Vienna Woods" and started to shriek all over again. At that moment, the wind tore the straw hat from Frau Ann Marie's head; it struck the horse on the nose. Frau Resi yelled, 'Dance, Liebchen, dance!' No wonder the horse went mad."

Grandmama had to smile in spite of herself. "Ach, ja, it's best to leave it like that. Let's blame it on the wind." She shaded her eyes from the bright autumn light; perhaps she had to hide tears. "My father died falling from a white horse—or rather, with it. But there was no doubt he alone drove it to leap into that quarry."

"Not he alone," Hanna Roth said in a deep voice. "On horseback your father turned into a demon. Remember?"

The countess withdrew into silence. Hanna Roth took a footstool, carried it to a mirror, stood on it to put on her driving glasses, adjust her hat, and stare.

"Frau Hanna, where is Mama's doll?" I asked.

She did not flinch and kept facing the mirror. "Unloved, in darkness," she said in that special deep voice. "Among cobwebs and spiders, dust."

"Will Mama get her back? And will Mama walk again?"

"She will not get her back. She will more than recover, but she won't walk for a long, long time."

The dwarf's departure was abrupt. In the courtyard she tipped the old gardener, and he held the gate as she drove off into the street. Grandmama called out of the window and asked the old gardener to please bolt the portal. "Not that it could really keep anyone out," she said to me. "This place was built to welcome, not to shut out." We both ate pralines, and she said she would speak to Father. After church on Sunday we could all go and see Mother at the sanatorium. "Every time I see her she asks for you. She longs for you. The doctor thinks this will make her get up and walk. I think he is quite wrong. In fact, I believe she'd be far better off at home."

*   *   *

St. Stephen's was full of worshipers these days, Grandmama explained as we walked up the steps. Good Catholic Austrians came to attest their faith and pray against evil. Everyone who had any sense feared war.

She slowed down as we entered church. A countryman in a loden cape brushed past her without any sign of recognition. I soon found out she received important letters that way, in case the Gestapo opened her mail. Most of those letters were sealed with the imprint of a crest; their language, veiled and archaic, made little sense.

We did not stay for the entire Mass because I began to fidget when we kneeled at the Schutz Madonna, whose miraculous protective cloak was lined with dolls half the size of her Baby Jesus. I felt the weight of that cloak, those pallid dolls, multitudes of stillborn brothers, for I had wished away the doll and she had vanished, the brother I did not want had been born dead. I meant to ask the Madonna to forgive me, but to my astonishment I saw a gold chain wound around one of the many flickering candles; from it dangled a Star of David exactly like Resi's. I wanted to show it to my grandmother and tugged on her sleeve, but she raised her finger to her lips, finished her prayer, and made the sign of the cross. I hardly had time to ask the Madonna to make Mother walk.

I had learned from Vlado that the rich were born and died in private sanatoriums and stayed sick in lonely private rooms because doctors wanted their money. From the outside Mama's sanatorium looked like a barracks. I followed my grandmother through two glass doors, and we walked down a white corridor. It smelled of ether and roasting meat. Nuns in long white habits and winged caps went gliding by with trays and flowers. White walls seemed to move toward us until we came face-to-face with the sanatorium Hitler picture: a Führer in a belted coat, exuding stifled exhilaration, like a debonair surgeon.

Mother's room was full of flowers; the blinds were drawn. She lay, eyes closed, rosy, half-smiling, and all decked out in lace, on a large pillow embroidered with the crest of Falkenburg—an enchantress resting, as though she had danced all night, celebrated with champagne. I woke her with a kiss; she raised herself, grabbed me; her eyes lit up with pleasure. "Good evening, little heart."

Grandmother gave her a kiss. "It's morning, Ann Marie."

Mother laughed with a little hiccup. "What difference does it make?"

One side of her hair was braided, the other had come undone. This bothered me and reminded me of Puppe when she had been put aside. I tried to braid Mama's hair. Grandmama pulled a chair close to the bed and admired all the fresh flowers. I had heard about the Hitler bouquet, and there it was at the foot of the bed, half-wilted.

Mama did not feel like chatting when the countess talked about the old gardener who had such a bad cough, about the trouble with her roof. She held me close to her. Then suddenly she let go, and her hands searched under her covers. She bent over the guard rail of her bed. "She must have fallen out of bed," she said. "Thank God, there's a rug."

Grandmama stood up and took Mama's trembling, restless hands between her own. "Someone took the doll when you had her at the Hohentahlers a long time ago. The Herr Doktor wants you to remember those things."

As soon as Mother's hands were free, she started feeling around the bed again, staring at the wall like a blind person. She looked unhappy, and I kissed her cheek. My grandmother was trying to divert her by telling her about my lessons and how wonderful I was, but Mama leaned over the railing and told me to look under the bed. I found the Hitler note, not the doll.

Father walked in, and I quickly stuffed the note into my pocket. He brought a huge box of candy and a French fashion magazine.

"Ach, there you are!" Mama sounded relieved and pleased. He ran to her, all smiles. "Give me the box." She reached for it. "You brought me Puppe."

"I can't bring you Puppe. Doctor Habinger wants you to remember that she was stolen. But I brought you candy and a magazine. You can look at new styles. How about a new fur coat for this winter?"

She burst into tears. He took her into his arms. She clung to him frantically and could not stop sobbing. Grandmama pulled a bell rope, took me by the hand, and we walked out into the white corridor. Two sisters came along, smiled at me, and whispered to Grandmama that the Herr Doktor would be stopping in later. They went into the room. Father emerged, looking very tired. He lit a pipe and said he had spoken to the doctor. Berthold was allowed to visit Mama later; this should cheer her up. It cheered me up, and I kept looking down the long corridor while we waited.

Soon the nurses came out, and we went back into the room. Mother sat up among her flowers. The sisters had pinned up her braids, and she wore a soft blue satin bed jacket. "Good evening," she said again and hugged me, kissed everyone.

"The Herr Doktor wants you to remember things, Annerl," Father said. "We have already been here."

My grandmother let up the blinds. "Now you can see the sun. We come in the morning on Sundays. I will bring you a calendar."

Mama nodded, all smiles, and proceeded to direct Papa as he tended to her flowers. She admired him at his task, threw kisses as though he were gardening below her boudoir window. He played the game, collecting little white cards from fresh bouquets and baskets for his file box. "I guess you have the Führer note under your pillow?"

"Ja, ja," she said. Her eyes looked enormous, and she had to yawn. "I love those yellow roses. Who sent that dear little tree?"

"I don't know," Father said.

"And the orchids." Mama twittered. "I feel they'll fly away, turn into butterflies."

A nun knocked and came in with coffee and cake. My grandmother got up. It was time to go.

Mother and I held onto each other. "Remember," she whispered, "look for Puppe."

Father kissed her hand. "The doll is gone, Annerl. The Herr Doktor wants you to face facts."

"Facts, facts. What are facts?" Mama said in her new, dreamy voice, and lay back on her pillows.

In the corridor, Grandmama took Father's arm. They had come to rely on each other. "A shame that all the great nerve specialists have either left Austria or are locked up."

"Just when they are really needed. And I don't mean just for our Annerl."

"I'm glad she doesn't remember that she lost a child," my grandmother said. They weren't really listening to each other. Nor had they listened to Mother's "Facts, facts. What are facts?"

"I'm trying to give this doctor a chance, but I can't go along with his ideas. Do you know that he told me I should scold her, tell her to get up at once and give me another son?"

"Barbaric," my grandmother said. "He should start by trying to get her mind off the old doll."

"She does have daily therapy and massage. They keep trying. And she is well guarded since that scoundrel Janicek burst into her room with the rose tree."

"She doesn't remember that either," Grandmother said.

"Half of Vienna would come and bring her flowers," Father said. "The orchids came from Eugene Romberg, with a note saying he would come to visit her soon. I was stunned. He can't mean it."

They talked in low voices. A hush lay over the corridor. Nuns opened and closed doors. I saw one old woman with a yellow face and bushy white hair, sitting up in bed. She had no flowers.

If Eugene Romberg came along and saw her, he would send her orchids, too. All the way down the steps I kept saying, "He will, he won't, he will," and at the last one, "He's coming!"

At that very moment Berthold drove up in his little car. Resi was with him, hatless, her hair tied back with a long purple chiffon scarf which streamed behind her in the wind. Berthold, in his black uniform and black riding breeches of the Reiter SS, waited with open arms. I ran to him, although my grandmother had told me she disliked the SS cavalry just as much as the rest. Berthold held me to comfort himself.

I was in great demand. As soon as he let go of me, Resi reached for me. She seemed ill at ease around my grandmother. The frivolity of her dress did not go with her mood.

At least she cheered up Father. He was smiling, young, and well pleased with the world as soon as Resi appeared. "It does my heart good to see you, Schazi," he said. "Doesn't she look good enough to eat, Countess? Nothing like a sweet Vienna girl!"

Grandmother did not have a chance either to agree or to disagree. Berthold was twirling her around, kissing her. You could see her weakness for dashing young officers. "You are a young rascal, Berthold." Romance with actresses, gambling, horses—all went with the life a young officer, like the one she had married.

"How is our Annerl?" Berthold asked.

"She has been sedated," Father said. "This morning I spoke to her doctor. You can go and see her, but only for a few minutes. Reserl, you'd better stay with me."

As soon as Berthold had gone through the door, Resi's face fell. "He's got to wear his uniform now," she said. "He's dead tired from drilling. They're sending him to the Czech border. Got his orders this morning."

"Terrible!" my grandmother exclaimed. "A Herzog von Hohentahler in Hitler's army."

Resi blew her nose on her scarf, and tears ran down her cheeks, streaking her rouge. "Perhaps he wants to get away from me. He blames himself and me for what happened to Annerl. But she was already upset when he brought her to the Landsitz. If anyone is to blame, it's me. You must believe me—I was only trying to cheer her up. She looked so adorable sitting on the horse in her hat. We laughed so much. And we had never had more fun

together." I put my arm around Resi, and she wet my white cloak
with pink tears. "I feel God punished me for renouncing my own
religion. I sinned. Now I know it, and I went to church this morning, lit a candle, and gave the Madonna my Star of David, if
she'll only make our Annerl well and keep Berthold safe."

My father was about to comfort her when Berthold came
through the door. He stood there just staring into space. "Ferdl,
you'd better come back at once."

"What happened?" Resi cried.

"The doctor told her I had come to see her and she had to
get up or he wouldn't let me into the room. I heard him yell,
'Stand, stand for the Führer, walk, march.' A minute later I
opened the door and she was lying on the floor unconscious. He
frightened her and made her fall. I'm going right back to slap
his face, that idiot."

I unfortunately missed the row with the Herr Doktor. The
countess and I went to the Meinert-Hof in a taxi to prepare for
Mother's return. I helped to fluff pillows and arrange flowers in a
crystal vase. Father gave all the flowers at the sanatorium to
other patients, and I imagined the yellow-faced old woman with
the rose tree or the orchids. Mother arrived by ambulance with
a private nurse. Our own doctor came at once and administered
a large dose of Maltaline.

       ❋   ❋   ❋

The day the first snow fell that year, Frau Schwester arrived from
Germany. Her Frau Mutter had died in spite of all efforts. I had
a picture of Mutter, stiff as a bird at the bottom of a cage. Frau
Schwester took over Mother's care and tended her day and night.

I stayed with my grandmother until Christmas that year. After
that, my father took me into town to have my lessons with the
Hohentahler girls. The moment I came home, Frau Schwester
made me take a bath. My dog, Krampus, subjected to Frau
Schwester's suds, fled uphill and rolled on the compost heap.
Dirty Gusti came to climb trees with me and ended up in the
laundry tub. When he emerged, scrubbed, combed, and clean,
he hid from me.

Vlado called her Frau Bath Schwester and asked when it would
be his turn. But he was ever willing to carry Mother's wheelchair

out into the garden when the nurse called him. To him she expressed her worries about the birds in the aviary across the street, the beautiful plants in the greenhouse. The Water Castle remained mysteriously empty, German property, and there was a rumor that Adolf Hitler himself had taken it over, because Rudolf Hess, his deputy, came to look at it several times and sat on a garden bench. According to the porter's wife, he didn't want to have anything touched. Just as well, she'd said, who would do the work with her husband away in the war? By this time Hitler's army had invaded Czechoslovakia and Poland. Berthold sent me a Polish costume, but it was too small. I was growing fast.

Mother did not talk about war. She just changed the subject when anyone mentioned it. The household routine revolved around her. It was always time for her Maltaline, her bath, her hairdresser, her massage, her piano lesson. She had to have rest and quiet and peace to get back on her feet. Father certainly left her alone, but military men with jingling medals and other important Nazis came to pay her homage while she sat in a corner chaise of our living room, beautifully dressed, perfumed, and bejeweled. They came with furs from Poland and later with lace from Belgium and fancy china. She thanked them, flirted with them, made them sit close to her, even held hands with a shy, fat German Feldmarschall. "War, war? What war?" I heard her ask. As so often, she went on to talk about a beautiful old doll. Then she asked to be carried to the piano, and she played for him. He listened and tears came into his eyes. "Frau von Meinert, I can never thank you enough for an hour of such perfect peace," said the man of war.

I followed the war with Berthold's father, General Herzog von Hohentahler. His old war maps were all marked up with red pencil as we drew the new borders and placed the troops—his tin soldiers in glorious kaiser uniforms, his cavalry and horse-drawn cannons. I picked an officer in blue uniform on a prancing white horse and moved him to the head of all the troops carrying the old Austrian banner: Berthold, our hero. I gladly put up with the school hours with Madame and the Hohentahler girls for the sake of those lessons in strategy from the general. He looked like Berthold, talked in the same cheerful, breathless tone of voice. He told my grandmother that I had more sense than any of his girls put together. Even Radetzki, his old dachshund, sat at attention when I walked in.

The duke and I often listened to the radio in his cold study. The day we heard that the German army had crossed into France, where he had once been defeated, he gave both me and Radetzki a resounding kiss. We went to Berthold's room and sat on his bed with the dog and looked through a box full of photos of Berthold and his school friends, some showing him on horseback, taking hurdles. I often went to Berthold's room, under the pretext of reading his Karl May adventure books, tales of the American Wild West that were invented and written by a German in a prison cell. The hero, Old Shatterhand, wrestled with bears. Chief Wineto, an Indian, was his best friend. The wars they fought were honorable, won by cunning, not force. I found drawings of horses and Indians between the pages. Sometimes I opened Berthold's wardrobe and touched his old Theresianer uniform. I felt close to him, although he was far away.

The day Paris fell, I was in the Hohentahler ballroom, turning cartwheels from one end of the mirrored wall to the other just to annoy the Hohentahler sisters, who had no talent for acrobatics. Our lessons were about to end. It was the middle of June 1940.

Madame, our teacher, came to look for us and gave me a hard slap. "To think you would show your derrière on a day like this!" As though my flying legs in lace-trimmed knickers had caused the humiliation of her hometown. She had forgotten to perfume her tailored suit, and she smelled of garlic. I tried to cheer her up by telling her that Napoleon had marched into Austria with the French army, and I gave her an account of the battle of Austerlitz, the Napoleonic trick of leaving a flank unprotected as a trap.

Her pale, jagged face seldom smiled, but she tittered when I pleased her by learning fast. She liked it when I remembered dates and names in history. She never knew of my lessons in war strategy with the duke. Her lessons were in French. To begin with the Hohentahler sisters had laughed at my pronunciation, but soon I spoke French well, while they never learned to do cartwheels. I used strategy in the schoolroom, pretending I did not know an answer until they gave the wrong one. I fancied myself a Napoleon.

"If this war goes on," said the general, "I'll have to get more soldiers." We were locking up his study for the summer. Victorious tin soldiers in old Austrian uniforms, capes, tassels, finely detailed braids, occupied Holland, Belgium, Denmark, Norway, and France. "The next move should be across the Channel. We'll keep winning as long as we stay out of Russia." On our map, Blitzkrieg was won as fast as a slow game of chess. "There might be all kinds of changes to be made when we get back together again." The duke looked worried.

Austria, with Germany, had been fighting a victorious war now for two winters; food was rationed, but this hardly affected us— anything could be bought, although the coffee was ersatz. Heavy curtains had been put up to keep the streets of Vienna dark. But the lilacs bloomed, and the moon, round as a Chinese lantern, shone down on the Water Castle, defying the blackout. Owls began to hoot to each other again.

Somewhere planes flew toward London to drop bombs. Father had received a letter from the Englishen Tanten: " . . . visiting our friends in Sussex." This meant they had moved to safety. I was handed a letter from Eli by my grandmother. She would not tell me how she got it. He said he missed me and he was fine, going to school, playing tennis with Karin, and learning to ski. "Do you ski?" he asked. And this foolish question hung between us for years. Letter could be dangerous if they fell into the wrong hands, but I would have preferred total silence to "Do you ski? Love, Eli." I did not even ask whether I could send a reply.

My grandmother watched me tear up the letter and said nothing. We saw each other almost every day during the school year; she had come to know me well. I had my secrets, and she had hers. She often withdrew to the pink salon with a visitor and locked the double door.

I went to the Romberg villa with Frau Schwester every morning that June. The porter and his wife had gone away to the country, because she had been unwell. They had entrusted Frau Schwester with the key to the gate. The door to the aviary remained unlocked. You could hardly see the door, for the shrubs around the glass houses had grown high as trees. We went to feed the birds and water the plants in the conservatory. I usually left the work to Frau Schwester. While she tended to the birds and told them to take a nice bath in clean water, I went to the glass door that separated the dining room from the greenhouse. It was locked, but I could peer into the gold and crimson splendor, the long table covered with ecru-colored lace. I thought of those days when it was spread with white damask, full of delicacies Eli didn't want and I loved.

My grandmother was getting ready to go to Bad Ischl. Soon we would be going away to the Styrian mountains. My father's barrel-maker had written to him from the town of Schladming. A nice big mountain farm was for sale; the farmer's only son had been killed in France. Father had been looking for a place far from any large town. "I don't believe they will bomb beautiful Vienna, even if they had a chance," he said to Grandmama, "but I want a safe place for my family. There'll always be a room for you, Mama." This was the first time he ever called the countess "Mama." She liked it, took his hand, thanked him, and said she would never leave the little palace, no matter what went on. "We just don't want you to be alone if there's any trouble," Father said, lowering his voice, for this could have been considered subversive talk.

"I'll stay with you, Grandmama," I said. This pleased her and made her laugh.

The weather had turned chilly and gray, and Father postponed our departure. I went with Frau Schwester to the Water Castle one morning, as usual. She carried a bag of seeds. It had been raining. I ran ahead eagerly, up the steps. "The gate is open!" I said.

"I am sure I locked it," Frau Schwester said. "The porter must be back." But the porter's cottage was locked up, and no one answered the bell. The main path had been cleared of weeds and the gravel raked not long ago. Frau Schwester in her white uniform, cradling the seed bag like an infant, strode along and called, "Hallo! Anyone here?" She stopped and told me to go home. Instead I turned left onto the overgrown path to the greenhouse. It smelled of jasmine and of wartime cigarettes. Beside a statue of a naked youth with wings, an Icarus, sat a man in a leather coat and pilot's helmet, smoking a cigarette. I hid behind a bush. He was mumbling to himself, something like, "It's up to me. I know that . . ." when Frau Schwester came strutting along.

"How did you get in, mein Herr?" she exclaimed.

"A German nurse? What are you doing here, in my garden?" he asked with unquestionable authority, which somehow did not go with the dazed look on his face. He was quite young; his heavy eyebrows formed a thick line above deep-set light eyes. A square jaw and tight mouth spoiled his handsome face. He looked unhappy.

"The porter is away, and I take care of the greenhouse and the poor birds in the aviary."

"Ach, the birds," he sighed. "In 1923 I found them all dead in their cages. I felt like a ghost in the empty house, but at least I was not shut away like my Führer, or wounded. No one knew I was here, except for the friend who had the key. It was November, and I used to come to sit out here to think . . ." He stared in my direction but did not see me, then he turned to Frau Schwester. "Jawohl, Frau, that is good. You must feed those winged creatures." He gazed at the statue beside him. "Ach, to have wings!"

"I have the responsibility," Frau Schwester persisted. She had not listened to him. "How did you get in?"

He reached into his pocket, brought out a bunch of keys, and held them up. "I come here when I fly into Vienna, just to sit on this bench and think. Don't you know who I am?"

She called out, "Lieber Himmel," looked up to the sky, clutching the seed bag to her heart. "So it is true?"

"Rudolf Hess," he said with gravity. "You have my permission to go and feed the birds. Our Führer loves birds." He waved her away, and she hurried on toward the aviary, making her clacking sound. The strange man laughed to himself. "He loves canaries singing in cages, but it is better to spread wings and take to the sky." He stared up to the clouds. The weather vane spun around in the warm wind. Like the roulette wheel an admirer had brought for Mama from France, it came to a stop. The arrow pointed down the avenue. I heard a car, the screech of brakes. The man jumped up in his secluded corner. Through the bushes I saw the yellow spokes, the dark blue glossy hood. "There she is, finally," Rudolf Hess said to himself.

I hardly ever saw Hanna Roth anymore. She spent much time in Berlin. Her smiling picture appeared in the newspaper every time the victory she predicted was celebrated. She had become too popular to have much time for Mama, it seemed. On Mama's birthday and on mine she came with presents, obviously in a big hurry to leave. At the Hohentahlers' she did not single me out. Now I was thrilled to hear her rapid footsteps on the gravel path, and as she turned and passed my hiding place, I had a whiff of that violet perfume, a glimpse of midnight-blue elegance which matched her car. The famous seer did not see me.

It had begun to drizzle, and she walked under a large umbrella. Rudolf Hess jumped up, stepped on a cigarette, and tore off his pilot's helmet. "What news from Berlin, Frau Roth?" He shook her hand, and in her dark cloak she looked minute beside him.

"I should not have gone," she cried.

Like a lover, he fell down on one knee and touched her arm. "Did you see him? Did you speak with my Führer?"

I could not see her face, but I saw her stiffen inside the cloak. "I went to plead for peace, but it was not meant to be."

He tore at his thick hair. "Did you see him?"

"Not in person," she said sadly. "I was waylaid by a gang of hecklers on the steps to the chancellery."

"But my letter—my letter should have helped you get past anyone!"

She lowered her man-sized black umbrella like a shield. "Get me past the worst insults I have ever heard, threats to my person? Louts in uniform, and they had come from our Führer, carried a painting to him, it seemed. One of them picked me up, swung me. I thought he might hurl me to my death down those stone steps. There was one they called Professor, from Vienna; he knew who I was, all right, but he let them have their fun before he stopped them. He will pay for this!"

"Janicek," Rudolf Hess said. "That devil has wormed his way into the chancellery through Hermann Göring. He looks for paintings for him and brings some to the Führer. A hateful fellow."

I fell over in the bushes with excitement.

"What was that rustling—is there anyone around?" Hanna asked.

"Birds, just birds and a nurse in the aviary, feeding those in cages." Rudolf Hess allowed himself to fall back onto the bench. "Ever since you told me you see me flying into a cage, I dream of being a bird."

She went to him, and he stared at her with those deep-set pale eyes. "You are forewarned," she said. "Stay on the ground. Stay beside the Führer. He is in terrible danger . . . Taunted and threatened, I fell into a trance. When I came to, that professor with the mean eyes had me in his clutch. I was at the entrance to the chancellery, surrounded by guards. 'When is his favorite canary going to die, when, *when*?!' he yelled at me. Those louts surrounded us, and before my eyes their grinning faces turned into skulls. I yelled and they dispersed. 'When is his favorite canary going to die?' asked that professor. 'Tell me more!' I must have said something in the trance. They had not allowed me to come to. I closed my eyes and saw the chancellery crumble like marzipan, I heard unearthly thunder and the famous balcony lay shattered. I thought it was all part of my vision when I saw Hermann Göring standing over me holding your letter. 'Rudolf Hess has sent you to the Führer, it seems. Too late. I just came from him. His canary Siegfried keeled over suddenly. My Führer sees this as a bad omen. Thinks the bird was poisoned. He has gone into seclusion. Go back to Vienna at once, little woman, before you are accused of killing the bird.'"

"You must try again. I will take you to my Führer. We will fly to Berlin at once. He must be made to listen, to make peace with England. He will hear what you have to say."

"I will never return to Berlin," said the dwarf, and closed her umbrella. "I have trouble sleeping now, and am haunted by a vision of Adolf Hitler holding a dead canary in the palm of his hand while bodies of soldiers lie piled up in snowy fields."

"He is my brother. Just like me, he has faith in the stars. He believes in seers. The generals, the Reichsmarschal, those warmongers have him hemmed in. We must go to him!" He was by her side, nudging her on—not merely along the path, but straight to Berlin and his Adolf Hitler.

She held onto a branch of dark-purple lilac. "Nein, *niemals!*" she called out. "He will never listen to any woman on this earth —that will be his downfall." They stood side by side, she no taller than Hess's legs. The wind ruffled an ornament on her soft hat. Cock sparrows chirped in the bushes in a chorus of eternal irreverence and never-ending discord. She raised her head and peered through the trees at the Meinert-Hof. "That damnable

Föhn wind!" I heard her say. She had a way of blaming the elements and never herself.

I crouched low as they walked by, but they would not have seen me. She was staring ahead, and his vision was blurred by tears. He pulled on his pilot's helmet. "Now it's all up to me." He hurried toward the main path. Hanna Roth followed. He hoisted her into the car, took the wheel, and they drove away.

17

Language of Intrigue

I FILLED a candy box full of Rudolf Hess paper dolls that I made from newspaper pictures during the summer of 1940. A leather button I picked up in front of the bench where he had sat talking to himself went into my treasure box. In those days, I used to practice his dogged expression in front of mirrors. He was unique, like Hanna Roth, and I could not forget him.

On Mother's birthday, in October, the doorbell rang. Hanna stood at the gate, half-hidden by a huge bouquet of dark dahlias. I relieved her of the flowers when I let her in; they did not go with her costume. Although she professed to hate war, she wore a dark coat with frogging, brass, tassels, and the fur hat of one of the duke's tin hussars; only the saber was missing.

"*Bonjour,*" I said with a curtsy.

"Heil Hitler," she said with military dash. "French words are not in keeping with the Führer's plan to purify the language. He considers our Viennese mishmash of foreign words a language of intrigue, a Schlamperei."

"Rudolf Hess doesn't care about the Schlamperei. He likes to come here," I said.

She turned her head like a bird of prey. "You saw him?"

"I saw him with you at the Water Castle."

"You adore him. I can tell. You are a discreet child, aren't you? Keep it to yourself."

"Will he come again?" I asked hopefully.

She walked ahead of me. "I wouldn't be surprised. Years ago, when the Führer was put into prison, Rudolf Hess fled to Austria.

Someone gave him the keys to this house. It had stood empty; the owner had died."

"Shot himself and made a hole in cupola."

"Something draws the deputy Führer back to that house. If you ever see him over there again, you must telephone me at the salon. Just say that Herr Vogel is back in Vienna." She turned to look at the Water Castle. The sky above was overcast and gray. The air smelled of dead leaves. "One day I am going to live over there," she said.

"Why don't you ask Rudolf Hess for the keys?"

"Ach, he will never let go of those keys. The lock was never changed; he has kept them all these years. And he'll return. He soars like a frantic bird."

"Does he really want to make peace with England?"

She turned her head sharply, "Never breathe a word of that to anyone. He has faith in my visions, you know. He wants to save the Führer. He loves him."

"Why do you love the Führer so much?" I asked.

She hurried into the house to wish my mother a happy birthday, and never answered my question.

Mother sat on the chocolate-brown velvet chaise, bathed, massaged, perfumed, and surrounded by flowers. She wore the birthday sweater Frau Schwester had knitted with wool unraveled from my old dress; good yarn could no longer be found. Nurse had had to use a lacy pattern to make it go further, and she styled the sweater like a baby's, with ruffles at the neck and cuffs. The ice-blue color set off Mother's violet eyes as water sets off the sky. Contrast and harmony created an indescribable appeal: at the age of twenty-six, she was the picture of both pampered innocence and voluptuousness.

The second anniversary of her accident had come and she remained an invalid. She had improved at the piano, and a teacher came several times a week. I found *The Brothers Karamazov* under her pillow. She read Dostoevski secretly. Although she depended on others completely, she became quite independent in her thinking. She liked to have me near her when I came home, just as it pleased her to have flowers. I usually settled down to do my homework while she read her Dostoevski. "All these people are obsessed and mad," I heard her say to herself. "But they are never bored."

Father brought important men to amuse Mother. Hanna Roth seemed to know all about that. They exchanged "Heil Hitler's," and Mama said she loved Frau Hanna's costume and the magnificent fur hat.

"You should wear hats and dress more formally, meine Liebe," Frau Hanna said at once. "You are bewitching all kinds of men, and that can be dangerous." She cast a quick, knowing glance at the letters in Mother's lap. Sometimes Father read them aloud. Most of the men wrote of undying, hopeless love, and they declared that they would fight the war and would die for Mother. "They have a need to talk about themselves, and that puts their lives into your hands, as an ultimate tribute. Your husband should not allow you to become an idol."

When men came, I was never allowed to stay and watch. Frau Schwester carefully removed me. I had listened in once, outside the open window. I never saw the visitor's face, only a powerful back in a tweed jacket. He had half-knelt beside Mother's chaise. His hoarse whisper sounded like a voice in a confessional: "I had power to take the girl from the camp. She was a Polish Jew from a small village, beautiful as a Madonna. How could I think there was anything shameful about saving her? Was not the Madonna a Jew? I had to hide her. Kept her locked up in my country house. One night she tried to jump out of the window and run away. I beat her up. The next time I came to her, I discovered she preferred death to me." I heard a deep sob. "I have no right to sit here at your feet, Gnädigste. You should have me thrown out."

Frau Schwester had come into the room, rattling a tray with Mother's Maltaline; perhaps she had listened in, too. Minutes later, she escorted the sinner to the gate. Left to herself, Mother said, "It sounds just like Dostoevski. He must have made it all up to shock me." I never saw his face.

"And we all know you have become an oracle, dear Frau Meisterin," Mama said now, with the most winning smile. "Look, I brought down Puppe's jewel box. I had almost forgotten all these lovely things." Mother knew how to lure anyone to stay with her.

"What a nice little pin," I said, imitating the hoarse whisper of the sinner.

"Do you have a sore throat?" Mother asked. "Should I call Frau Schwester?" I shook my head. "That little pin," she said, and took it from me. "Remember, Frau Hanna, when you dressed me and Puppe for the Art Ball as little girls? She wore this darling little clover pin made of emeralds."

The dwarf sat down beside Mama and unbuttoned her coat. "I made bonnets and pantaloons, and we ordered patent-leather slippers."

"I danced all night . . ." Tears came into Mother's eyes.

"You will dance again one day; you're young. But remember what I told you. Do not encourage admirers. Be more formal with them, wear hats when you receive, and be less formal with Herr von Meinert. I hear he eats at The Golden Stag quite frequently with the Opera crowd."

"Ach, don't worry so much about me," Mother said. "I have no idea where my doll is this afternoon. I want you to accept this little pin." She would not listen to any objections.

The doorbell rang. Mother quickly pinned the brooch onto the military coat. Flowers and visitors had been coming all day. Now a thin man in a black uniform came rushing in as though someone had given him a push. He clicked his heels and produced a Biedermeier bouquet.

Mother opened her arms to him. "Berthold!"

A long-legged stranger stood and stared at us. "I can't believe I'm really here," he said in the laughing voice I loved. On his way to Mother he kissed the top of my head. "I used to feel I could put you into my pocket. How you have grown." It sounded like a reproach. He lay the bouquet down on Mother as if she were a monument, greeted Frau Hanna, and said, "At least my Annerl is the same. Only more magnificent." He sank into Mother's arms, crushing the flowers. When he came up for air from a long kiss, he said, "I was actually afraid to come here. Stayed away for a hundred years." He reached out for me and hugged me. I clung to him, and motes in the lamplight spun around, waltzing to his heartbeat. "It's so good to be home."

He got up suddenly and bowed to Hanna Roth. "Meisterin, here I am. You didn't succeed in having me bumped off at the front." She was about to protest, but he raised his hand. "Your famous predictions for victories as long as the German princes fought on the front, you know. I was there, too. I have to thank you, what?"

"What are you talking about?" Mother asked. "Where have you been?"

"To hell and back," he said.

"I believe the Führer should rely on the sons of peers rather than those of the lower classes," Hanna Roth began.

"Hitler is very much of the lower class," Berthold interrupted. "He doesn't trust us. I almost gave my life to learn the truth. It is dangerous to distinguish yourself in this war if your father is a duke and a general. The Führer hates it when any of my kind earn the Iron Cross. Prince Helmut, the kaiser's grandson, died a hero, and Hitler rolled on his carpet in a fury when he heard of the hero's funeral and the Monarchist demonstration. Three guesses who was there shouting 'God save the Kaiser'?"

"Grandmama and the Rittmeister and all the rest," I said.

"This is dangerous," Hanna Roth said, and left us immediately without formality.

"What are you all talking about? Come back, Frau Hanna. What's dangerous?" Mother called out.

Berthold knelt down beside her. "I shouldn't talk like this. Poor Annerl. Everything's all right. The countess Reyna is back in Vienna. I'm not allowed to be a hero anymore and am stuck in an office. No hero's funeral, what?" The skin of his cheek looked too tight; a muscle twitched. I tried to stroke the frown from his forehead. "Damn the war."

She just sat there on the brown velvet chaise and folded her hands. In her stillness, she rivaled all the flowers around her; only her eyes moved. I had to think of the doll. She did not say a word while he went on about how much he had missed her, loved her, and how guilty he felt about the accident, blaming himself during the years he was away.

"I almost forgot how beautiful you are. Are you unhappy, Annerl? Tell me." He did not really expect a reply. No one expected anything from her in those days—except love. First he kneeled beside her as a penitent, then his arm went around her waist, and he annoyed me by caressing her hair, her shoulders and breasts. "Your doctor says you're better and you could try to get up and walk. But you won't let yourself." He kissed her face. "You're not just going to sit there and tempt your susceptible cousin. Come, you don't have to feel guilty. Anything between us is always just fun."

Her expression remained serene; she did not stir.

"That day when you cried on the telephone and told me to come to the Hoch-Haus, I came so fast I didn't even unsaddle my horse. If I had only . . ." In his mind he must have unsaddled that horse and prevented the accident a thousand times.

He had come to make her walk, but ended up lying beside her among cushions and love letters and on top of *The Brothers Karamazov*. A hat would certainly have been in the way.

Frau Schwester came in, well accustomed to ending such tête-à-têtes. She led me away. I knew at once I would end up in the tub, as though soap and water could wash away what I had seen. I picked up Krampus and said, "You're more magnificent than ever," in Berthold's voice. Expression mattered much more than language or words when the intrigue was love.

*   *   *

During my ninth year I enjoyed myself as a Catholic, a Jew, a Nazi German, a Monarchist, a military strategist, an occultist, and a Bolshevik. It was like trying on different dresses in order to select one and ending up with them all. Anyone with a strong belief won me over—but not for long.

The day after Mother's birthday, Madame sent me out of the schoolroom for a breath of air. She thought I felt sick. Actually I had been holding my breath and staring, trying to go into a trance while she was dictating poetry. Out in the hall, I skipped to the mirror and did my Hess scowl and "*mein* Führer loves birds." Berthold must have heard me speak. He came in very quietly and caught me practicing Vlado's Communist fist, sticking out my chin like Mussolini.

"What on earth are you doing?" He kissed the tip of my cold nose.

I laughed and he laughed with me. "So, why did you make the fist?"

"For fun."

He became sad. "For fun. Ja, I used to do my 'Heil Hitler' for fun, until it became compulsory." He hung up his leather coat. I sniffed it and touched it. He wore black breeches and glossy boots and told me he had been riding. "I miss all the old junk in the hallway; I grew up with it. Now it's cold and empty." He took my hand and we went down to the kitchen to eat bread and lard. We settled down on a woodbin. "It's as though I had never been away. Only this is real. I don't believe I have to go back to that nightmare. Don't tell my father—it's a dark secret—I'm no soldier. I used to play war with him up there, the way you do now, but I detest being moved around by nitwits, like a tin soldier. They could all profit from studying lost battles up there with our general."

"The chancellery will crumble like marzipan," I said in a dark voice.

"You've been listening to the great Hanna von Roth. But she didn't teach you the Bolshevik fist." He cut thick slices of bread and dipped into the lard pot with gusto. A kettle hissed on the old stove, and he made herbal tea, sweetened it with honey for me, and even stirred my cup. "Now, you might as well tell me about the Communists in your life."

"Vlado. He used to be only the gardener. Now he's in charge of the milk-bottling plant. When Father is busy he brings me here by streetcar."

"How come he is not in the army?" Berthold asked.

"He pretends he has the shakes when they try to recruit him. He practices in the kitchen and makes Agnes laugh. He tells them he can't control his bladder."

Berthold said they would find out he was a shirker and this was very dangerous. I assured him no harm could come to Vlado because he was Hitler's cousin. He laughed so hard he almost spilled his tea. "It's so good to be back in Vienna," he said. Then he became serious again. "I bet you never told any of this to your father, Reyna?" I shook my head. "Does your grandmother know about this Bolshevik?"

"She wouldn't like Vlado if she knew he reads Karl Marx. And she might tell Father. I know you won't tell."

He kissed me on both cheeks. "I understand you and the countess go to Café Wiesner twice a week. What's going on there these days?"

"Grandmama hobbles on a cane when we go there, as if she were very old. Herr Wiesner is a Monarchist. He bows and scrapes and we sit in the back room. He brings us good things to eat. There's a piano in the back room and someone plays while they talk in French, English, Hungarian. That way no one can figure out what they're saying. It's a language of intrigue."

"Sometimes you sound exactly like Hanna Roth," he said.

Heady with my success, I told him I knew that Tante Dita had escaped to Italy. Grandmother wanted us all to say she had vanished into the Gestapo "night fog." "Grandmama hobbled to the Gestapo to beg for the Tante's life. This way they'll think some other branch of the secret police has taken Tante Dita away from under their noses. They all compete in snatching people."

Berthold was refilling the cups. "I bet the Gestapo are watching the café."

"Only Krummerer."

"Not *the* Krummerer?" He was laughing again.

"He's all right. He sits in a fur-lined coat outside the Palais Dornbach on a folding chair and reads the newspaper. Father tips him and gives him presents. Sometimes he goes and stands in line at the bakery for us."

"I bet he doesn't stand in line. A nifty rogue. The way he picked the lock and got Resi out . . . You can't trust him. Does he ever ask you anything?"

"He writes a report, and he wanted to know who Tante Hermine and Uncle Colo are. I didn't know."

Berthold put his arm around me, and we sipped our tea. I felt warm, and my cheeks glowed with self-importance. "It was the same when your mother and I were children. We knew all of your grandmother's friends as uncles and aunts, as intimates. Never their names. That was long before it was dangerous to be a Monarchist. She wanted us to know her friends as people and was afraid we might show off at school and go around name-dropping."

"Grandmother wants me to know them so that I will be grand, too, and a Monarchist."

Berthold leaned against brightly patterned Portuguese tiles that dated back to the days of the admiral. "Has your grandmother succeeded?" he asked.

"Naturally," I bragged.

"You're a Monarchist?"

"Sometimes," I told him.

He laughed so much he dropped his spoon. "A sometime Monarchist who does the Bolshevik salute because it's fun. With you I can forget the thousands of kilometers of our front."

"Bad strategy." I made myself heard.

"We won't conquer the world, what?"

I cuddled up against him like a sleepy child on a journey. We didn't talk anymore and sat peacefully, like travelers who know their destination. Across from us on the bright tiled wall hung a framed proverb embroidered in blue cross-stitch by Berthold's sister Magda. The embroidery set had been given to her by my mother at the great birthday party. It was just like Magda to present the cook with that silly proverb: "Salt and bread make your cheeks red." After Berthold went away, I would say it out loud to myself as a magic chant to bring him back.

18

Rondo of Hate and Love

By spring 1941 the general and I no longer had enough imperial troops to place on our war map. We used knights from the days of the Crusades to occupy Yugoslavia and Greece. When he asked me what I thought Hitler's next move would be, I picked up my favorite officer on the white horse, closed my eyes to concentrate, and, without looking, placed Berthold in Russia. The general, who had not noticed my antics, thought I had followed the old Bonaparte road. "I can see them moving north until the snow falls," I said, to further impress him. My imitations of Hanna Roth kept improving. No one noticed, now that Berthold was far away.

We took victories for granted, and I was getting a little tired of war games. My father gave me a bicycle for my birthday and I learned to ride it by rolling downhill— a personal victory, a joy equaled only by my success as a hypnotist when I immobilized a chicken on the farm. The subject, according to my book, had to be willing. I had found the book, *Power and Magic*, at the Tanten-Haus, brought it home, and sat at the living-room window ready to go into "Mass Hypnotism." It started to hail. I looked up and saw a man standing in the middle of our avenue. Hail beat down on him; he stayed there like a tree. I only saw his back. The wind pelted him, tearing at his black and glistening-wet cloak. He stood staring at the Water Castle, bewitched as though he had sprung from the pages of my book, hypnotized by the cupid weather vane. Water ran down the windowpanes and the great house; the man in black swam before my eyes.

Mother's hairdresser was in the house. The buzz I heard sounded like the dryer until it turned into a drone. I spotted the plane and leaned out of the window. It circled in and out of dark clouds above the Water Castle like a bird of prey. Buffeted by the wind, it rose, fell, and went on circling above the cupola. Once more it rose, then it vanished, and finally it swooped down, landing in a large field behind the porter's house.

The man in black came to life, turned around: Fritz Janicek, pale and wild, cold water running down his face. He reached out in an involuntary gesture. Then he dipped out of sight into the bushes. A second later he emerged on his red motorcycle and buzzed away in devilish haste.

I ran to Mother's room. It smelled sweet. The hairdresser and Agnes were combing Mama's mantle of bright hair, talking softly. The radio played soothing music. I darted in, asked for the opera glasses, and ran upstairs to a little sewing room for a perfect view of the house across the street. It had stopped sleeting; the sky brightened. The sun came out and there he was, my Rudolf Hess, back at his bench. I adjusted the glasses to bring his face under the pilot's helmet as close as possible. He was as beautiful as ever. His lips moved. He was talking to himself, like Mother. I admired him so much I could not tear myself away—until I remembered my promise to Hanna Roth. She answered the telephone herself and said, "I was expecting to hear from you." I loved the tremor in her voice.

As soon as I hung up, I ran to get my new bicycle from the garage, rode it down to the gate just in time to see a black limousine arrive at the Water Castle. Fritz Janicek jumped out, and a medley of men in uniform poured out after him; in their midst I saw the fat Wicked Angel. Fritz Janicek made a great production of unlocking the gate. Then they swarmed up the main path, and I started ringing my bicycle bell. Not one of them turned to look in my direction. I could not see my Rudolf Hess and hoped that he who listened to inner voices and to birds had heard my warning.

Unfortunately, I had not studied the chapter on mass hypnotism in my book, or I might have been tempted to try my powers. The men spread out and darted in and out among the ornamental hedges. I climbed the gate and looked through the opera glasses.

My hero had vanished. I felt much relieved when Hanna Roth drove up in a taxi. She, Frau Traude, and a statuesque woman in a gray fur rushed up the steps. The gate had been left open. Fritz and all his men had entered the house. Hanna Roth headed for the empty bench. Frau Traude helped her to stand on it. Hanna stared up to the sky, waving her umbrella, and there was a buzz of an engine. The plane rose within minutes and circled. Did he wave to me as he took off, or did he wave goodbye to the dwarf, the deserted house, and his would-be assailants?

Fritz and some of the men came out on Resi's balcony, noisy, angry, pointing at the sky. They watched the plane vanish into clouds. Hanna Roth stopped to pick a sprig of forsythia near the empty bench. I waited for her in the street. She did not give me time for more than a curtsy and a "Heil Hitler" à la Hess before she handed me the yellow blossoms and said, "Remarkable child," as she had years ago. I felt as though I had been knighted. The lady in the gray fur had tears in her eyes as she and the others drove off.

The black limousine remained at the gate. Fritz Janicek was still inside the Water Castle when Mama was brought out to enjoy the sun. I stayed high up on a perch Gusti and I had made from old boards, and acted as though I were watching a robin's nest in the big linden tree. Frau Schwester in her uniform and white sweater sat on the sunny bench, knitting and counting stitches. Mama talked to herself when they were alone. Frau Schwester never listened or responded. As far as she was concerned Mama was out to get some fresh air, and talk was a sign of vitality, like an infant's babble. "Ferdl is at Resi's a lot. I know it. I can smell the lavender when he comes home. I guess Resi misses Eugene and Eli and Berthold. I understand. I can't move, but I can certainly figure things out. I have all the time in the world." Her hands fingered the armrest of her wheelchair; a ring sparkled. "Whoever took Puppe crippled me."

Frau Schwester was clacking her tongue, saying, "Ja, ja, we're right on schedule today," as if she were addressing bees in the clover.

"But I'm not angry anymore," Mother went on. "Resi doesn't live like other women. A different man, a different role. It's convenient. I'm not that lighthearted; I just pretend to be like her.

I saw how much Ferdl enjoyed the way she fussed over him, the laughing and teasing. I imitated Resi. There was no one else around to teach me how to be a woman. Not my mama, not Agnes, certainly not the holy nuns. He never knew that I learned to flirt from Resi. It made him ecstatic. Here he had married a sixteen-year-old schoolgirl and she acted like a soubrette. He will never know how frightened I was—not so much of the act of love, but of displeasing, losing him to her. I feel so safe with him. From the moment he walked into the kitchen and into my life, my world became safe as a cloistered garden—except, of course, that I was safe with a man and not just the Lord, like the nuns . . ."

I remembered her words because she spoke so well and made good sense, while everyone prayed for her sanity and treated her like a harmless, helpless, adorable madwoman. She was never left alone during the day. Agnes, her nurse, or a maid sat with Mother when she dozed off after lunch. She slept alone at night and woke up alone in bed to another day of being nursed, pampered, displayed by her husband like a precious, fragile doll, and desired by strangers. She inspired devotion.

❀   ❀   ❀

"I don't want the Gnädigste to see me like this," Vlado said when he arrived at the Meinert-Hof a few days later. He staggered down the kitchen stairs as if he were performing for the military. "Forgive me, Frau Agnes. I had to come here. I don't want my woman to see me like this, either. After all, she is my niece."

Agnes gave him coffee and cake, and I stayed out of sight while he told her how all the young men in his father's village in Slovenia had been locked into the church by the Germans and then burned up. "I used to go there and we'd drink in the vineyards, dance at their weddings." Agnes talked to him softly and told him she understood. The Germans had strung up all the Falkenburg gypsies that hadn't escaped into Hungary across the lake. I stayed in a closet full of jars while Vlado cursed and cried. He was beginning to feel better when Frau Schwester called Agnes to help her carry Mother out into the garden, Vlado forgot his sorrow. He had come to adore my mother and ran up all smiles, trying to cheer her up.

Agnes had to go to the market. The twins were in their room

listening to dance music. Their new radio was a present from the police officer, who was now a corporal stationed in Belgium. I decided to cheer up Vlado and invited him to come and sit in Father's green chair. Then I offered him brandy from Paris and filled a crystal tumbler. After the first gulp, he nodded his approval, grinned: "*Dobro.*" Sitting stiff and upright, he continued to drink as though someone might walk in and take the glass away. His eyes wandered over the Persian rugs, whitewashed walls, peasant furniture.

"It's all old and worn," he complained. "Not fancy enough to make me good and mad. What's the matter with the master? Is he too stingy to put more glitter around?" He became thoughtful. My father, he told me, was a kind man. He paid for Nadica's piano lessons with the best teacher. "My oldest girl has a natural talent. She's different from the rest. Smart, although not as smart as you are." He called me his comrade and saluted me with his fist. I returned the Bolshevik salute with gusto.

He had started to yawl his song of beautiful Slovenia and I was refilling his glass when Frau Schwester came running into the house. "Quick, quick! Herr Vlado, you must come at once." Her veil was askew. Krampus ran around her, barking. "He took her from me, slapped me, made off with the Gnädige. Lieber Himmel!" She tried to pull him toward the door. He hung back, holding onto his brandy.

"Who did what, Frau Bath Schwester?" He sounded more Slovene after his drink.

"Janicek, that horrible man, on the promenade." She tried to make Vlado run, but he kept singing "Beautiful Slovenia" and performing his spastic act all the way up the hill. I raced ahead of them, found the back gate with the spikes open, and ran onto the promenade. The wheelchair had left a trace I could follow, and I turned to the right.

Before I reached the bend where the path joins a narrow road, I saw Mama under a blooming pussy willow. Her hands rested on the wheels of her chair as though she wanted to push off. Fritz in his black uniform knelt before her, sobbing into her green linen lap. His strong fingers were crumpling a pink scarf she had worn.

"My mother. It was all my fault. I turned her into a cripple."

I hung back, saw him shudder. "I was the death of her. She never said a word and worried herself sick. As long as she was there, and she watched, everything seemed to be all right. I thought she understood." He bawled like dirty Gusti; his uniform cap slipped back from his head, the skull emblem gleaming in the sun. Bees swarmed around the blooming pussy willow. One, attracted to the emblem, hovered above his head. He did not notice.

"She had never pushed herself out of her room before. The boys and I were in my room—not too noisy, either. She didn't knock on the door. She must have suspected something after I was dismissed from the school, but she was not prepared. She opened the door and died . . . She died." He bit into Mother's pink scarf and let out a scream. "The first time I saw you in your wheelchair on the avenue, I thought I saw a ghost. I was driving along and I almost hit a tree. *Mutter* in her wheelchair . . . Since she's gone, nothing has been the same." He sobbed without looking up. "Forgive me; you were good to me, on my side. I did clear that Jew-ridden house for you. I'm not done yet."

He raised his head, looked up to her with frantic eyes, and saw Vlado and the nurse come rushing around the corner. Mama gave her wheels a push, and Fritz threw himself down. "Go ahead, push those wheels over my body, push." I knew he was keeping an eye on Vlado.

"He has a revolver!" I shouted.

For a second or two I heard only the hum of the bees among the golden blossoms. Then Frau Schwester grabbed me and pushed me behind her body. Vlado shot forward from the bush.

"With my last breath I'll snap your chicken neck!"

Mama took her hands off the wheels, folded them on her crumpled dress. "Put the gun away, Herr Janicek. You have drunk too much."

He stood up and followed her orders. Vlado grabbed him.

She said, "Nein, nein. Enough." Her eyes moved slowly from side to side, coquettish and scheming. "I don't know what you are talking about, Herr Janicek. You have behaved terribly. Go away and never come near me again, unless you bring back my doll. You wrote the notes; you must have her."

Fritz Janicek made off in small, hurried steps. I stood on a tree stump and watched him stop at the wayside crucifix on top of the hill. He laughed like a crazy witch and waved Mother's pink scarf above his head. Then he ran down the hill.

❋   ❋   ❋

Father came home early. "Just wait!" he yelled as soon as he walked into the living room. "I won't let him get away with that."

Mother was practicing the piano and I pictured Fritz the Professor running away to Schubert's music, waving Mother's pink scarf, with Father chasing him.

"Who are you talking about?" she asked, and went on playing.

"Janicek—that lunatic."

"He is a nuisance," she said, turning the page of music.

Father grabbed her by the shoulders. "Sometimes I wonder whether you really forget or whether you choose not to remember."

"I don't particularly want to remember his ugly face. He is disgusting. Of course, if he were good-looking like you, Ferdl, he wouldn't be such a revolting parasite."

"He drew his revolver," said Father. "What if he had pulled the trigger?"

She shook him off. "Revolver? Why should anyone want to shoot me? Haven't I been hurt enough? Janicek stole Puppe. It's his fault that I am crippled, and he knows it. Seemingly nothing can be done. We must forget. It's better that way." She smiled and looked into his eyes. "I adore this sonata in B-flat, K. 378. It's your sheet music. Your sister Stephanie used to play it with you. She bungled, but you played well, I do remember that." Then she reached for Mozart and played only for him, weaving around him a web of harmonies. Spring flowers shimmered in crystal vases. The fragrance of cooking made me feel hungry. Agnes was making breaded spring chicken with greenhouse lettuce, as a special treat.

Father said, "How well you play," and kissed the ringlets on Mother's nape. He ran off and returned with a violin. I had never heard him play and settled down to listen, like a proud parent. Krampus came and sat with me, ears pricked up. Mother's music pleaded, tempted, teased, and caressed the hesitant violin. When they played for the second time, Father stood close to her and smiled; his instrument began to sing. He had finally forgiven her for the accident and forgotten his frustration and anger about Fritz Janicek. That evening he stayed at home after dinner and held me on his knee. My parents were practicing the Mozart sonata when I went to sleep.

This was the beginning of the evening house concerts. The first one was not planned. It must have been a Saturday or Sunday. I was at home and riding my bicycle around the land at the back of the Water Castle. Sometimes I made believe that Eli was sitting in his room by the window with his schoolbooks. This time I turned the corner so fast I almost ran into the blue car. Hanna Roth sat leaning out of the car window, field glasses trained on a pale blue spring sky festive with flocks of gold-edged clouds. She did not notice me, and I had time to admire her dark-green pot hat. A breeze toyed with a lilac chiffon bow.

I greeted her with a curtsy and a "Heil Hitler." "Are you waiting for Rudolf Hess, Frau Hanna?"

She seemed pleased to see me, but her salute lacked spirit. "I know he won't come back." She kept staring up at the sky, with such fervor, I expected to hear the drone of a plane. Mother was practicing at the open window, and her music drifted toward us in the wind. Krampus was barking in our garden, and birds circled under the fancy clouds.

"I woke up with a start this morning and knew he was taking off. His intention was clear as the morning star. He was leaving his Führer at the mercy of those who compete with each other and deceive him." Tears sprang into her eyes. "I thought he might come here first, out of sheer habit, like a homing pigeon."

"Can you make him come here?" I had read about telepathy and bit my lip, exerting my will.

She shook her head. "It's too late. Jawohl, too late." This was the only time I ever saw her weep, and she wept for a man who did not heed her warnings. In desperation, she lifted the field glasses once more, shuddered as she looked up at birds and clouds, then put them away. "I see him flying into a cage." Mother was playing the Mozart sonata she had practiced with Father. Hanna brushed tears from her face, tilted her head, listening. "How marvelous. I will go to her. Music takes one away from disaster and gives wings." She drove around the corner as though she intended to rise from the ground.

I found her at the piano with Mama. She performed as though not only Krampus and I but a large audience sat listening. Rudolf Hess must have been crossing the English Channel while they played Schubert's Andantino Varie in B Minor with a flourish. Hanna Roth and Mother were still at the piano when Father came home and brought Resi. The concert continued, and by the time Resi sang Brahms's Lullaby, Rudolf Hess must have already performed his masterful landing in Scotland. When Hanna Roth sat down to have a cozy supper with us, he was in captivity.

❀   ❀   ❀

That spring we had house concerts every week. The sliding doors in the front rooms were opened, and I helped to line up chairs facing the piano. Then I would go to the kitchen to help Agnes make sandwiches until the guests arrived. On one of those evenings, I came upstairs and found Hanna Roth standing before the collection of redheaded dolls in the library. Our doctor had had the cabinet moved out of the salon where Mother spent her days.

Hanna, of course, knew those dolls would never remind Mother of Puppe. "Not one of them has any life. A mass production. It's like giving a rhinestone to someone who's lost a diamond." She stepped back, put on her driving glasses, and seemed to be fascinated with the redheaded dolls after all. "Now I know. I see his eyes." She was peering into the reflection at something I could not see. "I see his face. Fancy his sending all these lifeless dolls!" She turned to me. "Don't ask me who did such a mad thing. You'll see him in person before you know it. I promise."

Unfortunately we were interrupted by the Hohentahlers. Grandmama and the Rittmeister had come with them. The Wine Biter and his wife, the German lawyer, Cheese Hannes, and our doctor arrived only ten minutes later. Resi came late with a Luftwaffe officer who was in love with her on one evening and Mama the next during his two weeks' leave. An army colonel recovering from a wound spoke French with Madame and Magda. Later he discovered Nadica, Vlado's girl—the music student—and he stood up in the back of the room with her and the maids during concerts.

This mixed audience, a variety of music lovers, assured an evening without political talk. No one dared express doubt. The war went on. Sons had died or returned maimed. Friends had vanished. The flight of Rudolf Hess had finally come out in the open. No one believed him to be a simple traitor. Everyone was guessing. I had the answer, but could not speak in case I gave myself and Hanna Roth away. Would Adolf Hitler invade England to recapture his Rudolf Hess?

Spring was turning into summer. From the open window, despite the blackout curtains, came the fragrance of early roses and moist grass. The concert this evening began with the Mozart Sonata in B-flat Minor, played by my parents. They had practiced long, and I remember how grand they looked in the lamplight, Mama in a dark dress with a white lace collar and Father in a formal Styrian suit.

When they finished, the applause in the room was echoed faintly by applause from the street. I crept under the curtain and looked out the open window. A crowd of neighbors often gathered to listen in front of our gate. Some of them had stood and watched the Jewish ladies scrub the street and had looked on when Resi was arrested; now they swayed as she sang "Little Brother, Little Sister," from *Die Fledermaus*.

Halfway through the song it suddenly poured, and the street audience dispersed, except for one lone man. He kept pacing back and forth under the trees. The rain subsided, and the moon came out. The man went back and forth from light to shade, from shade to light. I became hypnotized. The white house across the street began to float before my eyes, and the man seemed to stand still. Moonlight turned to snow and dressed the man in white sheets. He slowed down each time he passed our gate. And he limped.

The voice of the dwarf was in my ear: "You will see him before you know it . . ." I slipped away unobserved. Clouds covered the moon again as I went to the gate. The man was walking away from me. Farther up the avenue stood a military vehicle; the gleam of a cigarette showed someone leaning against it, waiting. Dim headlights fell on the restless figure under the trees. He wore the uniform of an SS officer, and his cap was pulled low over his forehead. I ran to him and he turned. I heard a familiar sigh. Clouds parted, the moon shone on his round face, those innocent eyes. He grabbed me with both hands.

"Uncle—" I cried out. He clapped his hand over my mouth before I could say "Eugene." His hand smelled of perfume. "What are you doing here?" I whispered when he took it away. "And in this uniform?"

He drew me under a linden tree. "I'm listening. Is your mama playing the piano? How wonderfully well she plays. I was here last week when she was playing Schubert." He did not mention Resi's singing.

"Why don't you come in?"

"No one must know I am here. I am never recognized in this uniform."

I threw my arms around his neck and kissed his cheek. "Is Eli here too?"

"Eli is in Switzerland." Then he took my hand with one of those beautiful sighs that I had missed so much. "You're surprised to see me in this uniform." Resi trilled and warbled in the distance. "You always wanted to know all the answers. Well, you know how ermines and hares turn white in the winter? I'm blending in."

"Camouflage. Like the time you dressed up as an Arab."

"Not quite," he paused. "Ah, those were the days. Fasching, the carnival, the disguise for romance, love. Now I am in another masquerade. They might waltz me to death. Who knows?"

He could never pass for a German. His words, his perfume, his exotic gentility did not belong on the parade ground or in a war. How could he march, when he always squeezed his feet into small boots? He might have arrived on a flying carpet. His presence brought magic and made my everyday world seem drab. "The moon is too bright," he said. "Like a concentration camp spotlight."

"Have you been in one?"

"I have seen everything," he said solemnly. "But, do you know, they don't really see *me*. What do the Herren see? Money, raw materials, fuel for the war machine." He put his arm around me. "With my help, little one, those murderers are about to make the wrong move."

It sounded like chess talk. "Does Papa know?"

"No. If you are as clever as I know you are, you won't tell him. It's safer for both of us if he believes I'm in Switzerland." We strolled back and forth to the strains of the waltz. "Resi." He pronounced it with a *z*, as he always did, but a new German inflection disguised his foreign voice as the black uniform covered his rounded shape. "She always finds the right song for the right occasion. 'Lucky is he who forgets . . .'"

"You once said that everything is just one big masquerade," I reminded him.

The moon shone on his melancholy face. "Did I now? And you remember." He walked ahead of me. "You know, I'm sad because I have no present to give to you." He took a little flask from his pocket, raised it to the moon, and said, "*Prost*, up there." Then he toasted me, the Water Castle, and the Meinert-Hof. He raised the flask again. "To the woman I love." The song ended; applause drifted toward us, and laughter.

"Resi?" I knew I should not ask.

"I quite adore her. My little white rabbit, hopping here and there and nowhere. No, not Resi."

"You love my mama."

He sighed, and I tried to sigh exactly like him, I liked it so much.

"How can I help it? For her I dressed up as an Arab, just to try and make her laugh. How she would laugh if she saw me like this." His voice was lost as the wind rustled young leaves. Rain once again dripped on us.

"You sent all those dolls?"

"They did not please her. She mustn't know." He took his uniform cap off, shook it, and pulled it down over his forehead. "I feel helpless. Here she is in a wheelchair, and there are doctors in Switzerland who could do wonders. For her I must get the war over with." He drank to that. "For her the Wehrmacht must march and march, roll on in their tanks to defeat. It's up to me to find the money from overseas, to finance this insanity. They will be well equipped to march north toward doomsday."

"Are you an Arab or a Jew, Uncle Eugene?" I whispered.

"A clown," he laughed. "A pet Jew, at the moment. The high and mighty like having a pet Jew—as long as he performs well." He scrubbed his face with both hands, as though he had to cleanse himself of the grime of centuries. "You can't be beaten if you know the opponent's game." He held me against his heart for a moment, and his uniform buttons hurt my arm. He promised to send me a beautiful dress to make up for making me stand out there in the rain and listen to a drunken old man. "A beautiful dress, if it's the last thing I do. And I'll tell Eli I saw you."

I stayed under the dripping trees after his car had driven away. When would he return? I stood waiting like the empty house. I had heard talk of honorary SS men. My grandmother had said that Hitler sometimes presented men he needed and didn't trust with that uniform to secure their loyalty. It was also his way of angering the devout SS, who had gone through rituals and hardship in training for endurance and obedience. Hitler liked to keep rivalry going between his followers, to keep them suspicious of each other, devoted to him. I wondered whether Eugene Romberg had ever met with Adolf Hitler, and I wished I had asked him about Rudolf Hess.

"What are you doing out here?" asked a clipped German voice. "Who were you talking to?"

I recognized the man coming toward me: my Frog Prince. He hadn't changed at all, even wore the same raincoat. I didn't know what to say except *"Guten Abend."*

"Do you know who he is?"

Mother was playing the *Fledermaus* waltz. This time Resi was not singing; perhaps she danced with Papa or one of the officers.

"I'm not sure," I chirped like Resi. "Are you after him?"

He was taken aback. "I was only watching the Romberg house," he said. "Does your father know you're out here in the dark talking to strangers?"

"You're not a stranger," I said in my operetta voice. "You're a prince." I almost said, "Frog Prince."

I made him laugh the way Eli had laughed when he was serious or sad. Suddenly I felt as though he had taken Eli's place, and I took his hand. He escorted me past an old couple with a dachshund, who had come along and listened at our gate. "You'd better go in now; you'll get cold." He watched my performance with the golden keys and laughed again. When I was inside, he suddenly asked, "Was that man really a stranger?"

I ran away without answering. At the top of the steps, I stopped in the moonlight, and like Resi showing off before an adoring audience, I threw him a kiss.

19

A Lullaby at Dawn

I woke up, saw the Water Castle through flimsy curtains at the haze of dawn, and closed my eyes again to allow violins to sing me back to sleep and a vague dream of wild amusement. "*Whang, whang,*" something went. "*Whang.*" I sat up and felt faintly disappointed when I traced the banging to coat hangers on the wardrobe door. No whangdoodle. The draft from the open window sent my freshly laundered blouses into a ghostly dance.

We were packing to go away for the summer. I had been all excited about the mountain farm Father had bought. Now I suddenly wanted to stay on in Vienna and wait for Eugene Romberg. He would bring me presents and Eli. The war in Russia was going well. Hitler would reward Eugene Romberg.

I jumped out of bed and went to the window. Roses shimmered with dew in the courtyard below. Not even the warble of blackbirds, the spring song of all the birds at dawn, could drown out the sound of my dream violins. I imagined I saw lights in the dining room across the street. I told myself it was only the first glint of the rising sun. I couldn't believe I really saw the downstairs lights come on one by one, as though someone was running from room to room turning on lights, pushing back curtains, throwing open windows. Laughter and gypsy music was in the air. The conservatory shone like a lantern. Eugene Romberg had returned! I suddenly had no doubt. Who else would turn on all the lights at dawn?

I dressed in leather pants, carried my shoes downstairs. Fortunately, Agnes was out. Her missing shawl and prayerbook told me that she had left for early Mass. I stuffed bread into my mouth and let myself out. A pale moon lingered in a cloudless sky, like a target for the cupid weather vane. The imp went into a spin as a warm gust of wind drove me on toward the gate of the great house.

A few days before I had watched furniture being carried up the steps. Cleaning had gone on. The porter's wife shook little rugs out on Resi's balcony. Now I wondered whether she would let me in if I woke her up. I tried the gate. By some miracle it had remained unlocked and it yielded. Violins lured me on, past the silver birch I had once seen encased in ice in a crystal garden. A chill ran down my back. In my hurry I had forgotten to pull a sweater over my shirt. But the warm, brightly lit house was waiting.

A squirrel sat on the backrest of the Rudolf Hess bench, flicking its bushy tail. Then it took off and ran ahead of me, leaping from branch to branch. Church bells tolled out joyously. It was Sunday. A special Sunday. The three Graces seemed to dance in a circle among dandelions gone to seed.

When I reached the door, the squirrel went *tchk, tchk, tchk, tchk*; I could no longer see it. The door was locked. I rang. No one came. The violins played on. I rang again and again. Finally I ran to the back of the house, past Eugene Romberg's secret room. The window of Eli's room stood wide open. I whistled one long, three short. I tried again. The answer was a crash—bang! I ducked down behind bushes.

A pink-faced man opened the music-room windows and leaned out in shirt-sleeves. His gold-rimmed spectacles shone in the sun. "It's nothing. Nothing in the garden. It came from upstairs. Our very own poltergeist." He pulled the curtain further back and smiled. "*Schön*, beautiful. Look at that!" He gazed up at the pear trees on the right side of the garden with a dreamy expression. I did not see his gun. It went off like a champagne bottle in the snow. Something fell with a thump.

"Why don't you save your talent for Russia, William Tell?" growled a deep voice.

"Why should they want to send me to the front—or any of the boys? We are artists," the hunter said peevishly.

I did not dare move, in case he shot at me. Carefully I pulled some twigs apart and looked into the music room. Eugene Romberg was not around. He would be with the gypsies in another part of the house. A lady in a long floral dress sat down at the piano and spread her skirt. I knew the dress well and was about to call to Aunt Resi when I noticed the wide shoulders and the cropped dark hair. She didn't look like Resi and she didn't play like Resi. Her big hands thumped away on the piano. Dancing began at once, and wild couples came bounding along doing a polka, although the music was a slow waltz. No one listened to the tune or followed a partner; all of them tried to lead. Ladies danced with each other, tripping on long dresses Resi used to wear. Men danced with each other, too, in Nazi uniforms, half-uniforms, full army uniforms, barefooted, adorned with ostrich feathers. A tall female in a tangerine-colored costume spun around with the hunter.

In the midst of the fascinating, hectic madness, one stout man waltzed sedately all by himself. "Uncle Eugene!" I called. No one heard me. The round man turned toward the light. He was a stranger, young, tired. Coy as a dancing girl, he picked up his uniform tunic between two fingers. "And we must march on Russia," he sang to himself. His voice mingled with high-pitched, wordless sounds. I forgot the gun and wanted to get in there, leap about and shriek, join the fun. The ladies kicked their legs. Some of them wore men's shoes. I loved the way they started grabbing partners, pushing each other away, leaping like circus clowns. A pair of silver foxes with vicious glass eyes dangled over a broad uniformed back.

I stood up in my excitement and wandered over to the left for a better view of the room. My foot stepped on something soft. A dead squirrel, paws stretched out for a final leap, eyes open, only a few ornate beads of blood on the white chest where the bullet must have struck. My hand reached out to touch the bushy tail. I was grabbed up by the seat of my pants. The dead squirrel and black boots danced before my eyes.

"Don't step on the squirrel," I yelled.

"That's what we do to spies!" The voice sounded weak. The hand holding me up felt like cast iron.

"Let me go," I screamed, dangling above weeds. A poison-green glove clamped over my mouth. Resi's glove. I gasped for air, then I bit.

"Lousy boy," he said and carried me upside down, bumping me against the window frame as he climbed in.

Female shrieks, shouts of surprise welcomed him. I was held up for inspection. I smelled wine and cigarettes. The hunter said, "I shot a squirrel, not a boy." He bent over, examined me face to face. "Unharmed," he said.

"Spying on us," said the captor.

"I was not," I yelled. "Take me to Eugene Romberg."

"Who is that?" asked a German voice.

I was dangling upside down, all the blood rushing to my face.

"A Jew, a criminal," said a female.

I felt sick.

"Who are you, boy?" someone asked sternly.

I said nothing.

"Now, we could let him go and have a little hunt. Give him a head start . . ." This was William Tell speaking.

I kicked and struggled.

"Careful, he bites," said my captor. "We'd better show him off."

I dangled above the Oriental runner in the passageway, the blue carpet in the great hall. The red dining room flickered before my eyes when he finally turned me over and dumped me on the table. My foot landed in a dish full of stuffed eggs, my hands in a platter of cold sausage. All around me stood empty and half-empty dishes and wine glasses. The skeleton and head of a carp on a platter hemmed me in; dead eyes stared at me. Violins played on in another room.

"Where did you find him, Liebling?" asked a witch's voice in broad German. "Isn't he just too sweet?"

"I'm a girl."

"Clever of you," said the man I had mistaken for Eugene Romberg. "Girls don't have to go to Russia."

I stood up, and a group of about twenty revelers formed a half-circle around the table. The sun, chandeliers, lamps—all lit up—re-created the brightness of my first day with Eli. A pattern of crimson rectangles showed where paintings of fruit had decorated the red wall. I kept my eyes fixed on that pattern to avoid staring back at my audience, letting them know I could tell they were men—all of them. They had been playing in the attic just like Eli and I once had. We had never been allowed to dip into Resi's stage make-up, though. These men had smeared their faces with it. Perspiration glistened like morning dew and beards sprouted through rouge and heavy powder.

The man in the green gloves stepped forward. "Are you the porter's boy?" he asked.

Heavy, painted eyebrows, a tiny, smeared, dark-red mouth in a big, coarse face, hair like a shaved hedgehog pleased me so much, I almost forgot how mean he was. "I'm a girl," I repeated. "Reyna von Meinert Dornbach Falkenburg."

I heard an ugly laugh. "Nobility?" Violins struck up behind my back. I veered around. There sat Puppe, propped up in Eugene Romberg's chair. Fritz Janicek was bowing to her, then to me.

"I knew it, I knew it—if I turned on all the lights, threw back the curtains, a certain little falcon would fly into my trap."

I screeched. Violins were playing a song full of sadness and pleasure into the doll's china ear. Her party dress was crumpled, a leg stuck out, her braids looked as though they had not been combed for years. All the neglect only served to emphasize the female perfection of the china face; the image of Christina von Kortnai, likeness of my mother. I blamed Puppe for all the evil in my world. I would smash her and escape.

The moment I tried to slip off the table and get closer to the doll, the man in the green gloves nabbed me and put me back as a centerpiece. "You stay where I can watch you."

They were all watching me. Fritz whispered to them, told them about me. Strolling around among them in his black uniform, he adjusted a wig here, wiped rouge off a cheek there, buttoned a shirt. I looked at my legs in leather pants, knee socks. Never again would I be seen like this. I made a second attempt to move closer to the head of the table where the doll sat. "I must go home," I said in my grandmother's voice.

"You must go home," Fritz echoed. "Surely not before the party ends?"

The men stopped talking. One lit a cigarette; another one took off a gray fluffy Hannah Roth hat. They did not like to be reminded that the party would end as night passed into day.

"Let her wait for you, look for you, the way she looks for the doll. I can see her in her wheelchair, staring across the street," Fritz went on. "Ready to punish me with a glance from those incredible eyes. Let her look for me, wait, and watch forever!" He took my mother's pink scarf from his pocket and waved it before the doll until her eyes began to move from side to side. "Fritz is bad, gracious one. Jawohl, the professor is a swine having fun in the Jew house. Ha, ha, ha."

"What's going on here?" A fat figure came tripping into the room in Resi's lilac-colored Biblical dress. "I slept like a baby." He rubbed his eyes, looked around smiling like a pampered infant and dimpled. It was the Wicked Angel. He wore Resi's dress back to front and unbuttoned to leave room for his big belly. Delighted to see me on the table, he clapped his fat hands. "Here you are, my dear boy. I am so sorry. It must be your bed I broke. Did you all hear the terrible crash? You weren't worried about me and Fritz? Austrian beds, you know. Not like the solid stuff we build in the Reich." He looked at me again and smiled. "Beautiful boy," he said. "I love beauty."

"I'm a girl," I said in anger.

"Boy or girl," he waved his hand, "quite unimportant to a connoisseur." He accepted the uproar after this remark, throwing kisses. "Enough, enough! Fritz, Liebling, I know you like to have fun with boys, but is this wise? I mean, one does have to be careful. Little ones do talk." He stood so close to me that I smelled Resi's lavender perfume. Everyone was watching him, and if he moved away I could smash the doll and escape into the garden through the side door at the conservatory. "Come, come, my boy, you must not be afraid. Why are you staring at me like that? Who do you think I am?"

His spit touched my bare knee. I was ready to say anything that came into my head to move him away: "Reichsmarschall."

There was an uproar. They yelled, "Hermann the fat; sweet Göring." The uniform with the silver foxes slid his hand across a furry throat and made the sign of the cross. The Wicked Angel hitched up Resi's dress, hopping around on one leg: "I'm so glad no one can guess, my name is Hermann Göring, yes." I could not help admiring the small bare feet with bunions and manicured toenails. Finally, during the repeat performance, I had a chance to slide back on the table.

Suddenly the hunter pounced on Fritz Janicek and confronted him with his pistol. "Stop him. You hear me! This is an insult. I'm no honorary SS. I took my oath."

The Wicked Angel stood by; beads of perspiration ran down his pallid, smooth cheek like childish tears. Suddenly he straightened, saluted the hunter. "Ready to die for Führer and fatherland." He started to sing: "I had a good comrade, a better you will never find . . ." His magnificent voice boomed in the song "The Good Comrade"; violins played along. The other men sang in harmony: "He walked by my side, keeping pace, keeping pace and step."

I made a careless move and knocked down a tumbler. Only a gypsy saw me, and he was busy filling glasses.

"A bullet came flying, is it for me or is it for thee, my good comrade?" When they came to ". . . shake my hand once more, I am reloading," the hunter finally put his pistol into the holster. "My eternal life is yours, my good comrade, my eternal life is yours."

No one moved. Gypsies dropped their violins. During a silence more memorable than the song, I stood captive and felt the power of this realm of paradox, a world so private only an intruding child could give it momentary reality; it touched my heart.

"We will die," the Wicked Angel cried out, throwing himself against Fritz Janicek. They toppled, recovered.

"Nonsense. The dwarf is a blackmailer. Her warning means she wants this house. And she wants the doll. She is not interested in saving me, or any of us."

At that moment I grabbed the doll's arm, threw her toward the wall. The big man in the tangerine-colored dress leaped like a soccer player, caught her. I jumped off the table. A bowl, plates, and the fish platter came down with me.

"*Halt*," Fritz Janicek yelled as I ran into the conservatory.

They came after me like a pack of hounds. Fear of the hunter made me keep low and slowed me down. Near the swing I tripped over a rake. I was grabbed and thrown into the swing just as the gun went off.

"Why in the devil's name did you have to shoot a parrot?"

"It's worth a lot of money."

"Dirty Jew bird kept screeching *shalom*." This was the voice of the hunter.

The pianist and the man in the green gloves were pushing my swing so hard that I was afraid I might go over the top. The hunter and his trophy, the beautiful red-and-green parrot, wavered down below. A lilac dress flashed by.

"Don't shoot me. Put that gun away. Don't shoot," called the fat one.

"You've always been one of my favorites, Willy," Fritz said. "Give me the gun. We won't be able to keep our club if the neighbors report shooting. We have all been drinking."

My swing went up so high I was almost upside down. I clung to the chain. A palm leaf scratched my cheek. "Stop it!" I yelled. One of the gypsies, the oldest one, came along with a tray full of wineglasses. The men left the swing to take them. I got away; ran toward the aviary, but they were faster. A thin man in a gray, tulle-covered Roth hat caught me.

"What shall I do with this?" He held me by the neck. I struggled and kicked.

Fritz raised the gun in my direction with half-closed eyes, as if he were aiming at a painting with his long-handled brush.

"If you shoot me, the Gestapo will come," I said. "Take you into night fog."

"Just put this parrot into the empty cage," Fritz said.

Birds flapped their wings and twittered as the men carried me, bumping against cages. I struggled, but they pushed me into the empty parrot cage. Parakeets shrieked, empty seed husks flew into my face. The beakproof latch snapped shut.

They shut me in. Their hands could no longer grab me and crawl over me. I saw my advantage at once and sat with my knees drawn up, grinning at them in defiance. They staggered around, although they had not seemed to be terribly drunk before.

"*Achtung!*" yelled the fat one. "Our Führer loves canaries."

Two of the gypsy men, in theatrical costumes, red headscarves, and gold earrings, started to play a tango. One of them sang of glowing poppies and glowing hearts. The oldest served wine in the conservatory. Glasses clinked. Unlikely pairs formed. The dance began. Fritz was in the conservatory, holding the gun in one hand; with the other he was picking dead leaves off plants.

"Fritz, Fritz Liebling!" The Wicked Angel came back to him, whispered something. "We must slip away. We must get away from your wild, wild boys. Dance me away from here. I am afraid."

Fritz took a stiff bow, stuck the gun into a pocket. Then they danced. I marveled at their grace. They seemed to float as they turned and glided so softly in each other's arms. I saw them kiss without losing a single step of their rhythm. Never had I seen anyone kiss with such lust and vigor. I quite forgot I was in a cage.

The other couples had followed the gypsies into the dining room. The tango of the red poppies sounded more and more distant as the gypsies moved further into the house. Fritz and his fat partner moved on slowly and as precisely as figurines on a run-down music box. I had known Fritz Janicek as an avid gardener, a ruthless man, a great teller of gruesome tales, a painter of purple self-portraits, but I had never really admired him until this moment.

Lovers had come to interest me more and more. I had once looked for them under trees when I was out for evening walks with Krampus. When Magda Hohentahler said goodbye to a Luftwaffe officer, I had hidden under a schoolroom desk and watched. The kisses lasted so long, I wondered how they could breathe. Men and women clung together, but Fritz and his partner kissed only once more, then tore apart and ran into a serving pantry which led into the corridor and connected with the rest of the house. The pianist in the floral gown came running into the conservatory, chased by a giant in a ruffled white blouse. He stopped, reached for his head. "I don't feel well," he said. The giant held him up and led him out. I was forgotten in my cage.

I was almost sorry when the carousing moved off. Gypsies now played their own music, soft, as persistent as the dream violins that had lured me across the street. The birds had quieted down. I looked around in the bright sun; they had not been fed, and their water dishes were empty. This put me into a rage. I banged and pushed hard against my cage, and it almost toppled. Then I took a wooden perch and banged it against the latch until it gave way. By the time I climbed out, a single violin played the gypsy lullaby which Agnes had sung for me when she wanted me to go to sleep.

No one sang, no one laughed. I tried the side door, found it locked. I crept through the glass house, peeked into the dining room. It was empty. The doll had vanished. Empty bottles of wine stood on the table. Meinert Nussberger: the label bore the crest of the grapes and the shield. It was so quiet I heard a car drive out of the garage and into the street. Perhaps they had all left. I made my way along the red carpet. When I had walked here with Eli it had been brightly lit. Now it was dark. I tripped over something. A boot. A leg. "No, don't shoot," I yelled.

The hunter had given up his gun. Now he sat in the corner, staring at me with glassy eyes. I stepped over his legs. He did not stir or say a word. I ran on to the big hall, stopped in the doorway. Sleeping carnival figures lay on divans, lolled in armchairs, rested on the carpet. The silver foxes lay on the stairs, and the man who had worn the fur piece looked uncomfortable with his head hanging down, his mouth wide open, snoring with an ugly rattling sound. I wondered whether sleepers in the enchanted castle had snored for a hundred years until the prince came to awake the princess with a kiss.

Not everyone was asleep. One young gypsy stood on the gallery and played a lullaby; the other two walked around picking up empty glasses. The enchantment of the stillness, the sleepers in Resi's silks and feathers, could have been part of one of my strange dreams of the great house. I waited and listened for the sweet song of the violin to come to an end. The hunter had not moved. The dead parrot on a side table reminded me that all the birds would die—they were starving.

I ran back as fast as I could and began to open some of the glass panels, then I opened cages, shook them. Birds flew out. I opened more and more. By the time I stood on a crate to make my escape, the first finches came winging out over the trees. When I reached the main path I heard the parakeets shriek with joy as they flew over the ornamental hedges. African sparrows sat chirping on branches of my silver birch, then they flew off over the open gate in bewildered ecstasy. Not many of them would survive among the wild birds, but at least they would die free.

20

Shadows on Snow

THE BELL RANG shortly after I had crept up to my room. A man said, "You'd better wake him up." He sounded young and German. "And fetch little Reyna—she is wide awake, anyway." It was the Frog Prince. He in his raincoat and Father in a belted blue velvet robe cast nearly identical shadows on the sun-flecked wall in the morning room. The moment I came downstairs they fired questions at me.

"When did you go over there? Did anyone invite you? Have you done this before? Who did you see?" Their two gesticulating shadows loomed over my insignificant silhouette. I jumped up and down to improve on it. The interrogation seemed but a shadow game.

"If you had the so-called club watched, your man should have seen a child wandering in and he should have stopped her," Father said.

"My man was gone for only ten or fifteen minutes. He heard a shot when he returned." The prince crouched down beside me and cast a perfect frog shadow. "You must have been in there when that first shot went off. Who were they shooting at?"

"At me," I said.

"Mein Gott!" Father yelled.

"Who was there—anyone you recognized?"

"Fritz Janicek. And there was Herr Göring dressed up in one of Aunt Resi's dresses. A lot of men dressed up in her clothes and dancing." I left out Puppe, because I had thrown her.

The Frog Prince got up and seemed to be listening to the

cuckoo calling in our woods. "How about Adolf Hitler, Herr Goebbels, anyone else?"

"I used to see Rudolf Hess on a bench."

"Dressed up as a woman?"

"No, silly, as a pilot. He used to fly to the Water Castle before he flew into a cage."

"You're impudent and you are showing off," Father said sternly. "She adores Rudolf Hess, cuts his pictures out of the paper."

They didn't believe me, and I was glad. Hanna Roth had warned me not to talk about the deputy Führer.

"Herr von Meinert." The young German sounded pompous and boyish. "How can you allow your little girl to run around like a street boy?"

"We half-expected two ladies we know well to move in. One of them is a distant relative. It would be natural to go and welcome them."

"At dawn?" The prince moved toward me, and our two shadows on the white wall merged into one stout one. "Listen to me, Kleine, you did not see Hermann Göring dressed up as a woman. You saw some war-weary men and some men who are being drafted having a party, a carnival. You understand? There must be a stout fellow nicknamed 'Hermann' in every squadron, and there are lots of pilots as handsome as Rudolf Hess. You did not see the deputy Führer." He put his arm around me and told Father he had a sister with "blooming fantasies" like mine. "Herr von Meinert, I must ask you to take your family to your new country house at once."

"I see the Gestapo is well informed," Father said. "Is this an order?"

"More than that. I would consider it a personal favor," he said stiffly. "I want her safe."

I leaned against him as I would lean against a tree. The safe, sweet smell of breakfast cooking brought on sudden hunger pangs. The prince stared out of the window at the roses. His face relaxed. His "Heil Hitler" at the door had so much style that I added the flippant gesture to my repertoire at once.

After breakfast, Father took me to the gallery for a handing-over of the golden keys. I remember his silly lecture on the advantages of being a sensible Meinert, a realist. His eyes kept wandering over to the wicker settee where I had seen him and a half-naked Resi under an ermine cloak. "We Meinerts have always used good sense and moderation to stay out of trouble." His ancestors on the walls had themselves portrayed as stout, respectable patriarchs—the way they wanted to be seen—typical Meinerts.

"I like Uncle Ernstl best of all," I told Father when he locked my golden keys into the glass case. "He was different."

"He lived like a king and died a beggar. Didn't have a groschen to leave to anyone," Father replied.

"He left the golden keys." I almost added, "To me."

*   *   *

We departed in the afternoon. My adventure at the Water Castle was not mentioned again. Father stayed in the mountains to settle Mother and me with Agnes, Frau Schwester, and Krampus on the farm. German cities suffered from bombing; Vienna might be next. He decided to leave us at the foot of the Dachstein mountains. We would lack no comfort during the winter; he saw to everything. Electricity was brought up from the village of Oberndorf. Provisions arrived at night in a beer truck. A retired farmer came to work for us and brought white hens, a horse named Heini, a cart, and a snowplow. Father bought a sleigh.

A plumber on sick leave from the army worked for us and spread the word of the crippled lady and a hospital nurse. Soon everyone believed Mother and I had been moved to the mountain farm because we were both consumptive. At the bakery or the general store, villagers stepped aside after a polite "Grüss Gott." They kept a safe distance in church, and no one would take Holy Communion close to Mama. Pfarrer Kronz, Father's kinsman and my teacher, could have disputed the rumor, but consumptive relatives were an asset to a priest who was said to have moved to the village for his health. Actually he had gone into the mountains to avoid arrest. He considered the imprisonment of priests and nuns harmful to the church.

From late autumn until April or May, the meadow farm lay deep in snow. During a storm, only the pointed steeple of the church marked the village. Mountain peaks of the Dachstein rose steeply from the *Alm,* the pastureland above us. The highest mountain crag looked like Fritz Janicek, with a sharp nose and slot mouth, especially from the woods. Pfarrer Kronz came uphill on skis. When it snowed hard, he stayed for a day and played the flute to Mother's harpsichord or read to us. Mother sat at her loom or spinning wheel, keeping busy.

All winter long and even in the spring, when patches of grass began to show, I was on skis. I learned to measure the slope like an artist confronting an empty canvas. Pure air rushed toward me as I raced downhill, shrieking with joy.

After I had made friends with Stopperl, she taught me to yodel and to leap. With her I forgot I had been banished to safety. She was seven years old, tiny, and loved danger. We would watch the folds of snow at the foot of the mountain chain grin at us with thick, ugly white lips. "An avalanche will get us. Swallow us up," I would say. Her red knitted hat would dip down ahead of me, her brown braids flying, as we raced for our lives. She skied on the longest pair of men's skis I had ever seen. Her leather breeches were huge; so was her distrust—everything else about her was small and tough. Mountain ghosts, village boys, monsters, sent us into flight. With Stopperl I would lean against the padlocked gate of an abandoned amethyst mine and listen. She always heard voices; I pretended I did, too.

Stopperl, the child of *die Sennerin,* a traditional cow-maiden, had been born on the Alm, the mountain pasture. From below I could see the tiny Alm hut where they stayed all summer. When the young cattle grazed up there, we heard the sweet sound of their bells. At the end of the summer, Stopperl and her mother decorated the grown cattle with alpine flowers and brought them down to the village. No one had ever seen die Sennerin with a man. Stopperl might have been conceived in a dream, fathered by the wind. The village children teased her, but she could outwit and outski them anytime.

During my second winter in the mountains, church bells often tolled for village fathers and sons who would never return from Russia. Stopperl and I saw footprints going into the amethyst cave and out again. The gate was locked as usual. The ghosts, I pointed out, wore boots. They also carried things. You could see the drag marks. The gate did not yield to my loud "Open, sesame." Stopperl tried to squeeze in but couldn't.

More than once that spring we saw tracks. Then the snow melted. Father came and brought letters from Berthold, with a picture of a Russian bear, drawn for me by an army artist. I wanted to know when Berthold would come home on leave. Father turned away. Frau Schwester and Agnes secretly listened to the British radio broadcasts. It had been a hard winter for our armies in Russia. Father liked to forget the war here in our mountain paradise. Violets, buttercups, primroses, gentian, and alpine roses sprang up in the warm sun. Lambs were born on the neighboring farm. I went climbing with Father, and he took me down to the mountain town of Schladming for my yearly exam by the school principal.

I did well. During my oral exam, I showed off by ending sentences with a dashing "What?" like Berthold. While I was writing I blinked like Eli. I finished off with a Hess scowl during math, and made my exit in high spirits with a Frog Prince salute. Afterwards, Father and I met the barrel Meister for lunch. It was a splendid day and we sat at an outdoor table. The Meister and his father before him had made barrels for the Meinerts. He had helped Father find the farm. His ugliness intrigued me. He had a square face mummified by weather, hair the color of rock. But I never liked him. When he came to see us I stayed in the kitchen.

From our table at the café I had a view of the town square. Women in the local dirndl dresses came and went from church. Across from the church were the town hall and the police station. I became interested when the Meister told Father about a rumor that art objects were being stored in the old mine. A man had been arrested up there, suspected of breaking in. The Meister pointed at the police station, and I saw a face at the first-floor window, pressed against the bars. Whoever was in jail had a perfect view of the beautiful old town. "They say the mine up there is too damp for museum stuff. Everybody's saying they keep gold or the crown jewels up there. The coming and going in the middle of the night makes you wonder. They sleep in the mine." He whispered something to Father. "You wouldn't believe the rumors that are going on. After all, we're close to Berchtesgaden."

Father told me to go for a little walk. I had a lot to tell Stopperl. I found her among cows and their calves. It was late afternoon. Mist was rising in the valley like steam from a pot of witches' brew. We could not see the cave. She squinted and listened.

"It's dead soldiers in that cave. Listen carefully."

I didn't hear anything.

"Do you hear them howling? Their souls fly back to Austria and straight into the cave like bats."

*   *   *

Grandmother come in August. One afternoon when she was in the pantry listening to the radio, I went off and picked gentian in the field above the mine. Crouching in the grass, I saw the flash of black, glossy boots. Men were carrying large flat crates from a truck into the mine. Their cheerless voices echoed from the cave like voices of the dead. I fled.

My grandmother was waiting for me on the hill. She took my hand and told me of the battle of Stalingrad. We carried the gentian to the *Mater Dolorosa* of a wayside shrine. Then we walked through our woods, and I led her to my favorite clearing and seated her on my throne-like tree stump. I often came here to read or to watch a family of deer. She sat up straight and did not say a word. The diffuse light, her dress of unbleached linen, the pallor of her braids and face lent her the monumental quality of great pines and ancient rock.

"I want you to be safe, and yet I don't want you to be unworldly and ignorant, as I was at your age. You are closer to me than anyone else in the world."

I had not realized how much I had missed her until this moment. "Father won't let me go to Vienna because of the club at the Water Castle. He won't talk to me about it. What happened to the men?"

"The men died the morning you saw them."

"You mean they were dead when I thought they had gone to sleep?"

"Poisoned by Meinert wine. Fortunately, the wine they drank had been locked in the cellar of the empty house for years. Your father was questioned; it looked as though he had delivered poisoned wine to his former friend, Herr Romberg. He was acquitted because of his supposed villainy. No one will ever know what really happened."

Something rustled in the blueberry bushes. You could hear the cowbells from the Alm. "I know," I told her. "I think the gypsy musicians poisoned the wine."

"You might be right. After all, gypsies are a target for hatred these days. And hatred reverberates in the soul. We must pray for both the murdered dead and the murderers or their hatred will pass on to us."

My hatred of Puppe had not been passed on by anyone. I changed the subject. "Anyway, some of the men left in a car." I thought I had heard Fritz Janicek's voice in the cave, but it could have been a ghost. "They weren't all dead."

My grandmother came away with the impression that I could not accept the cruel facts she had imposed on me.

At Christmastime she gave Father a box full of old novels for me. I lost myself in those stories written for girls of another era. Stopperl would come and wait at the door; I could not tear myself away. She often gave up and left me sitting at the tiled stove with my book. I read of girls and their sisters and cousins, their governesses, on country estates. There were balls, handsome officers, harmless betrayals, inevitable suitable love matches. Stories as contrived and glorious as imperial Austria, they inspired me to study myself in our spotted mirrors. I let my hair grow and wore ribbons.

As I observed myself more, I noticed others far less and took them for granted. Frau Schwester had received bad news. Her nephew had been killed, not in the war but on home leave, during the bombing of Frankfurt. She went around with red-rimmed eyes. It snowed all day, but I was reading of blossoms. A girl named Ilse von Langscheidt had run away from her governess to meet a young count she loved. I had swept up my hair to look like the picture of her with the count, on his knees proposing. My favorite in the story, the wicked baron, was about to come crashing through the thicket on his black steed, breaking blossoms and hearts. There was a knock on the door, and Stopperl stood there shaking snow off her cap. "Grüss Gott."

"*Servus.*" I did not put down my book.

"You've got to come." It sounded urgent. "Something's going on down there."

"There hasn't been a soul."

"Two sleighs. One inside, t'other one coming up the hill. *Schnell!* Come on."

Snow came at us in the south wind, stinging cheeks and eye-balls as we took the hill in two daring curves, leaped over the hay barn, swooped over a buried fence. Stopperl got ahead of me in a cloud of powdery snow, skating on her skis to gather speed. Suddenly I saw a small pine tree where there had never been one. I christied to a stop. The tree moved and called, "Reyna," and turned into Hanna Roth in a snow-covered dark-green feathered hat and matching cloak. Her style was inimitable.

She curtsied and I returned the curtsy on skis, as though we were meeting at Schönbrunn palace. "How many years has it been? The snow on your curls! No headdress could be more becoming." Snow drifted between us, replacing the veil she had left off. She stood with her back to the hill, staring into the cave. Her sleigh remained at the entrance, and Stopperl was talking to the horse.

If I had not steeped myself in romantic yarns for weeks, the encounter in the snow with Hanna Roth would have baffled me. But events in the stories I had been reading were always accompanied by hail, snow, brilliant suns, full moons, thunder, rain. I was used to the extraordinary. Hanna had me under her spell at once.

Stopperl stayed behind and gaped. I hung onto the back of the sleigh while the horse labored up the snow-covered road. Hanna Roth sat upright in the snow drift, her hands buried in a silver-fox muff. She seemed indifferent to weather and purposeful as any of the people in my stories.

"To see you, my dear, and the child, restores me at once," she said after Mother had—for the first time ever—kissed her cheek. "You are both the picture of health, blooming like mountain roses."

I had overheard women in the village talking about how those with the lung disease were rosy and full of life to the end.

"Ach, it's been too long, far too long, since I have seen you." Hanna looked around the meadow farm and admired the hand-painted old peasant furniture, the Persian rugs on old floorboards. "A regular Meinert-Hof."

"But no Herr von Meinert," Mama said. She was sitting in a high-backed blue chair decorated with flowers and hearts. The chair was on rollers, and she had pushed herself toward the door.

"Herr von Meinert is kept busy," Hanna Roth said, watching Mother's face.

"Resi Romberg is keeping him entertained," Mother said with a pleasant smile. Her fitted dress, braids coiling over each ear like a peasant girl's, emphasized the new and majestic self-containment which baffled Father. She no longer tried to please, yet her presence had never been more pleasing. Whether she sat at her spinning wheel, the loom, or the harpsichord, she remained cheerful and busy.

Agnes and Frau Schwester enjoyed visitors as a welcome change and wanted to help Hanna Roth take off her damp wrap. She said, "None of this fussing. I can't stay too long," and threw her cloak over the muff, keeping her hat on her head. Mother asked her to please stay at least for a few days. She only shook her head. "I have been upset. I am no longer the same." To me she looked quite unchanged. "Here you are, hidden away from the wicked world," she went on. "Blooming, thriving. Ah, they would make eyes in Vienna if you turned up with the child. It does my heart good to see you both so well and contented. In the city everyone is tired, hungry, sick, and weary, while the terrible war is going on. Here you are . . . Ja, Herr Ferdl knows how to arrange things." She walked around Mama as though she were designing a hat for her. "Can you walk?"

Mother pulled herself alongside the table to the harpsichord. "Can I?" She played a sad little tune with one hand. "Will I ever walk again, Frau Hanna?"

"I know nothing!" cried the dwarf, and twisted the dark-green sash on her dress, staring into space. Her lips moved without sound. I was hoping for a trance. She astonished me by making the sign of the cross. "At present I am unable to tell anyone anything." She looked small and unhappy. Melted snow dripped from the feathers on her hat. "Frau Traude has finally been handed the keys to her son's house. Now I hesitate to move in."

"You said you were going to live there one day," I reminded her.

A shudder went through her. She kept looking at Mother as though Mama's loveliness would banish a vision of fearful finality. "Those men had betrayed the ideals of our Führer, disgraced his cause, and they were punished. I had nothing to do with it. In fact, I sent a warning. It might not have been the wine. They could have eaten something poisonous, French paté, cheese from Holland. Food spoils all by itself." I was reminded of the time she had come bursting into the little palace, blaming Mother's accident on Resi and the wind. "If anyone is to blame, it is Janicek. I warned him to get out of that house."

"I don't know what you are talking about. What house? Poisoned wine? Fritz Janicek should be locked up. He is a thief. I'm sure he stole Puppe. No one does a thing about it. He is quite mad."

The dwarf covered her ears and turned to the window. "Janicek. He barred my way when I came to the chancellery to warn my Führer. I had a letter from Rudolf Hess. The Führer would have listened to me. I detest the men who stopped me and insulted me. Now their voices are always in my ear. Day and night, screaming, 'Professor! Professor!' I hear nothing else. I have lost my gift. My ladies come to me and I have nothing to tell. I can hear shattering wineglasses, the soft thud of bodies falling down."

She had forgotten who was in the room with her and stared down into the snow-covered valley. Mama pushed herself alongside the window seat, to put her hand onto Hanna's shoulder. "I blamed myself for the death of my child. Living up here has helped me. Guilt can be self-indulgence. I should know. You end up hating yourself. Dear Hanna, you must hold onto life, as you always did."

"Hold on . . ." Hanna echoed, as if she had heard only the last sentence. "You are quite right."

During lunch, Hanna Roth recovered visibly. She enjoyed the kaiser *Schmarren,* a sweet omelet served with stewing apples from the old apple tree behind our farm. "I'm so glad I came. I feel my head clearing." The wind had sprung up and clouds parted; the weather was clearing, too. I felt as though Hanna had passed her nightmare onto me. I luxuriated in mourning, remembered how funny the men had been when they danced, forgot their threats. I liked them all, now that they were dead.

After lunch, Hanna Roth was in high spirits, but anxious to leave. Her driver had enjoyed a warm meal in the kitchen and sat waiting in the sun. "I'm so glad I didn't turn back when the snow came. I feel such relief. You have done wonders for me." She stood under a baldachin of icicles, throwing kisses to the mountains, Mother, me, even Agnes and Frau Schwester. "You are really away from everything up here, little highness," she said to me with haughty disapproval. I saw the magnitude of my sanctuary shrivel before her. "You should come to Vienna." She sounded well on her way to being her old self, as the sleigh moved off.

"Why should I come back to Vienna, Frau Hanna?" I shouted.

The horse snorted, bells jingled, and the driver yelled, "*Hüh, hoh, hüh!*" clicking his tongue. No one answered my question. I went back to my bench by the tiled stove, ready to pick up my book.

"You'd better ski down after her, Herzerl," Mother said from the window. "The sleigh has turned toward the old mine instead of going straight down. Perhaps the horse has gone lame."

I kept my eyes on the road while I strapped on my skis. The horse moved slowly through the new snow. Now I remembered that Stopperl had said something about another sleigh inside the cave. Hanna Roth had hurried off, spending no more than an hour with us. Her pilgrimage was perhaps not completed. She was up to something. I headed toward the woods and slalomed between the trees. Three avalanche walls protected the entrance to the cave from the hill. Two were buried in a snowdrift. The middle one stood out as a parapet. I hid behind it, crouching low, and watched the cave.

The sleigh came along merrily and the dwarf sat tall, wrapped up in her cloak and blanket, hands inside the big muff. The driver shouted, "*Hoh!*" The horse stopped at the cave. Hanna leaned forward, chin on muff, waiting in the warm mountain sun. Smoke curled from the cave, as though the place housed a sleeping dragon. I heard the snort of a horse, and the horse at the gate answered with a whinny.

"Janicek!" Hanna's summons hung in the air like smoke.

He appeared on command, his long black leather coat trailing behind him as he sank in at each step. He was sipping from a steaming mug. "Go away, dwarf. I owe you nothing."

"Is that so?" she answered, laughing.

"My boys are dead. Thanks to you. Some are imprisoned."

"If I had not warned you, you would be dead."

"You informed," Fritz said, and spewed some of the hot liquid into the snow. "Then you sent the warning. I see through it all. That dream of poisoned wine. No dream. You saw to it; put Meinert up to it." He gulped from the cup, made a grimace as if he were swallowing fire. "I'll kill you!" he yelled, and hurled the mug against the rock wall.

"You are dead if you harm me. I prepared for this journey." Black snowbirds flew up from the woods and uttered cries of lost souls. I wished Stopperl were with me. I had not bothered to wear mittens; my hands were numb with cold in the shade of the wall. I did not dare move out into the sun.

Fritz Janicek was walking around the driver, who sat smoking a pipe, as unconcerned as his horse. "This man can't go back to Schladming." He pulled out his gun. The man, red-faced and terrified, raised his hands.

"He's deaf," Hanna said. "Can't hear a word unless you bellow into his left ear. But he's not blind. Put the gun away or you'll be back in jail."

"Never!" Fritz Janicek waved his gun. "Now they know who they're dealing with. I was set free by the highest authorities. What have you been saying about me on the hill, did you tell her everything?" Hanna Roth ignored the gun and sat leaning forward over her muff, fixing him with her eyes. "Did you give it back to her, or keep it out of spite?" He pointed the gun at her head. "Speak!"

I quietly shaped a hard snowball. Stopperl and I had become expert at hitting small targets. I felt my heart beat in my throat; my neck stiffened. Then the snowball dropped from my hand. Hanna Roth had pulled the doll out of her muff.

"I came to find an answer. Now I know she doesn't need her."

Puppe, dressed exactly like the dwarf, stood propped up on the muff. "She wants the doll. Always wants her," Fritz said.

"So do I," Hanna said with passion.

He lunged forward, grabbed the doll by the neck, and almost pulled the Meisterin off her seat. She screeched. The horse rose up and neighed.

Fritz Janicek laughed like our laundrywoman when she got drunk on Hitler's birthday. The gun went off and he was left with the doll's head. "I'm Salome, I'm Salome," he shrieked, shaking it in the air.

Hanna Roth cowered in her seat with the shattered remains of Puppe. A doll's arm in tattered green cloth lay in the snow. For a moment I thought Hanna had been struck by the bullet. Then she tapped the frightened driver on the shoulder. He yelled, "Huh, huh!" She stayed down low as the sleigh turned around.

Fritz Janicek stuck the gun back into the holster. I watched him undo the doll's braids, kiss the hair. "I missed you so much! I missed the wicked eyes watching me." Trailing the coat behind him, he rushed into the cave. His laughter echoed.

21

Première

I RETURNED to the meadow farm as though I had been to the end of the world. Mother was sitting on the sunny bench by the south wall. Sleigh tracks in the snow showed me the farmer had taken Agnes and Frau Schwester to the village. Mother did not see me; she was scanning the slope below with opera glasses. All the years while she had waited to get the doll back, my hatred of the evil one had flickered cheerfully as an Olympic torch. At last I had seen Puppe dismembered. Alas, fulfillment of passion —hatred or love—never lasts. A cold, dimpled china hand seemed to prod me; shifty violet eyes glared at me. She possessed me. There was no past. Nothing was ever over.

I fled to Mother and she stretched out her arms. "Dear Gott be thanked, you're safe." She startled me with those blue eyes. Her hair flamed up in the sun. A shawl she had thrown over her shoulders embellished her face with touches of purple. I remember her at that moment, as garish and pleasing as one of those holy pictures the mountain peasants paint on glass.

"What happened?" She held me tight. "Fritz Janicek was down there, wasn't he? I heard a shot. Who was he shooting at?"

"He shot Puppe's head off." I heard myself tell her everything, quickly, as a dreamer remembers a dream.

"You were there, and you did nothing to stop him?" Tears came into her eyes. "I always felt if I got Puppe back, things would be the way they used to be. We would get Austria back, return to Father, to Vienna . . ." She looked down at her little black shoes with silver buckles, unsuitable footwear in the snow. "I guess now I'll never walk."

"You will, you will!" I quickly promised, for her bereavement threatened to spoil the execution for me. Far down in the valley, the sleigh crawled like an ant dragging a dead grasshopper. "Hanna Roth once said you'd walk."

"I never want to see Hanna Roth again." She pulled the shawl over her head and sunk into herself, a penitent. "I'll give the doll's clothes to the convent for orphan girls. I want to get it over with. Finally, I think, I've paid up."

Her "You did nothing to stop him" sang in my ears like a trite tune. "Fritz Janicek might have shot me if I had tried to stop him." I did not sound too convincing.

Mother had not heard me anyway. She was looking down into the valley through her opera glasses again. I sat beside her and took her hand. "You are cold." She put her glasses away to rub my fingers. "Funny. They're keeping art treasures down there in the cave, where no one can see them, just to keep them safe." She kissed my cheek. "How lovely you are. What if the war never ends for us? A hundred-year war, thousand-year Reich. We will grow old and die up here where everyone thinks we are diseased. No one ever asks us to come to their house. I see the little village down there, the children. We are outcasts. Your only friend, poor little Stopperl, is one too."

She had finally mentioned the war. It frightened me. I quickly told her we were safe; it was beautiful up here. "One day we will be back in Vienna again."

"Your father should take you to Vienna for a visit. You are not crippled or crazy. You must meet people, see more of your grandmother. I want you to get away from here, for a while, especially from me."

"You must leave, too. What if Fritz Janicek comes up here?"

"He has already been here. He came and promised to get Puppe for me, told me a wild story about his boys being poisoned at the Romberg villa. He had been drinking. He told me about paintings he had stored away for the League for the Protection of German Culture. I think he is mad, but when he promised he would have someone bring Puppe for me from Vienna, I really believed him. How could I have guessed Hanna Roth was involved?" She erased the broken doll she had drawn. "No good worrying your father. We mustn't say a word. I did try to tell

Agnes and Nurse about Fritz. They thought I was having hallu-
cinations. I know they went to the retired doctor in the village.
Now they put some medicine into my Maltaline tonic. I can tell
because I get so sleepy after I take it. Even now. They gave me
some before they went to the village."

"I'll tell Father," I said.

"He would take your word rather than mine, but we must not
worry him. He has lost so many workers. Vlado, that nice man,
has left. Papa must rest when he comes up here. Promise you
won't say anything." I promised. "If Janicek ever comes near me
again, crawling on the floor, trying to kiss my shoes . . ." She
shuddered. Her eyes lit up in a fury, and she swung a crutch and
slashed icicles off a wooden flowerbox. "He won't dare. That
murderer."

      ✿   ✿   ✿

"I want to go back to Vienna with you, Papa," I said when he
came on my twelfth birthday. "I'm too far away from everything
here," I explained, quoting Hanna Roth.

"Since Poldi and Lise have been called away to do war work,
I only have Frau Boschke once or twice a week. There's no one
at the house. I'm in town most of the time. "You'd find it boring."

"Why can't I come now?" I asked again in July. "Grandmama
can take me back with her when she comes in August."

"They have bombed the aircraft factory at Wienerneustadt.
Poldi and Lise survived, but it was hell. You probably don't know
that they have bombed Rome for the first time."

"I do know. Italy has surrendered and declared war on Germany."

"That's no surprise. They turned on us during the First World
War . . . Anyway, if they bombed Rome, they won't spare Vienna."
We were climbing uphill, and he stopped to catch his breath
and look up at the cloudless sky. "Better wait and see." He had arrived in a beer truck in the dark, and I had helped hide it in the
haybarn on our land. Two of his trucks had been requisitioned,
one had vanished; horses delivered beer and milk now in Vienna.

A year went by slowly. I wanted to be thirteen years old and
go to Vienna, and I wanted to be in love like the girls in my story-
books. I grew tall and Stopperl stayed the same. We kept an eye

on the cave, but nothing happened all winter long—except for one murder in the village, when a soldier came home on leave and killed the retired doctor out of jealousy, beat his wife and children, and ended up in jail in Schladming. Soon he was released and sent back to the front, where they made good use of angry young men.

"Vienna has not been bombed," I told Father when he came in 1944 for my thirteenth birthday. He gave in too easily. I should have known he had good reasons for taking me back to Vienna after all this time. He merely said he had a ride in a military limousine for us. This would be a convenience in taking me along to Vienna.

The officer who sat waiting for him at the inn at Schladming did not expect to see him with a girl and seemed taken aback. I hardly recognized him in his army uniform. He had grown a cap of short, thick brown hair. When I was seven I had laughed at him. Now my Frog Prince had turned into a storybook officer.

"Don't you remember my girl, Reyna, Prince?" Father liked the effect I produced from the beginning. He must have relived the days when he was first seen with a tall, redheaded girl in convent-school uniform. "Girls her age look as though they have been stretched on a rack," he said with authority.

The prince jumped up, clicking his heels, and bent over my hand without touching it with his lips. As a Gestapo he had seemed funny; now he was dashing. I resorted to playing the part of Hermine in *The Broken Promise*, my favorite novel. I used Hermine's language of the eyes, staring and smiling, but Father spoiled everything. The prince was saying I had grown up beautifully. Father told him how well I did in my exams, and, as so often when paternal pride reached a climax, he also belittled me.

"Her imagination is still in full bloom, too. She keeps her mama entertained." He put his arm around my shoulder with an embarrassing hug. "You didn't really see Fritz Janicek up there, did you?" I was too humiliated to speak. "And you invented the story about the doll's being broken. I don't object. There has to be an end to that."

I felt so angry with Mother, I said, "Of course I made it up." Either she had chatted away to herself when someone was listening, or she had changed her mind and told Father everything to get his attention.

The prince watched me with his arms crossed as he had years ago when he questioned me about Eli and Eugene Romberg. When we were left alone for a few minutes in the limousine, he said to me, "You really did see that man, didn't you?"

I used the language of the eyes and tried to smile like Mother.

"Where did you learn to smile like that? You don't have to flirt with me. I'm your friend." He squeezed my hand.

I went to sleep on the road, as usual. When I woke up, leaning against the prince, I kept my eyes closed. Father was talking about Cheese Hannes. "It's such a relief not to have that scoundrel breathing down my neck. I am grateful to the army and deeply indebted to you, Arnold."

"Never," said the prince.

They had become friends. I felt both happy and hungry. There was never enough to eat anymore. I went back to sleep and dreamed of delicacies. We had arrived at our gate when I woke up again. Father gave the driver some cigarettes and shook hands with him. Arnold von Lütensteg clicked his heels again and bent over my hand. "I'm sure we will meet again while you are here. There is something I want to tell you . . ."

I did not listen to his tone of voice. In the stories I had read those words had only one meaning. He must have wondered why I blushed and ran into the house so fast.

I had left my old self behind with the snow and the Latin books. In Vienna it was spring. Never had our garden with the old pine trees looked better, or the spring flowers brighter. Father said the house felt clammy and opened windows while I ran around throwing my warm hat into the air and catching it. Finally I was back in Vienna. Father had to leave me for a couple of hours. I hardly heard the key turn in the lock. I was left alone, had the house to myself. Nothing suited me better. I ran to a mirror and it gave me the face of a girl, not a child. A smiling pink face with soft lips, amber eyes, and a cloud of dark hair. What did I care about wars, unhappy people, gray houses, shattered hopes, and dread? I felt inspired by the happy face in the mirror and well pleased with myself in my suit of natural homespun wool. I looked grown-up and tall.

When I stepped back from the mirror, a fragment of the Water Castle—Resi's balcony—came into view. A tiny black figure stood up there: Hanna Roth, in a black lace mantilla. There she stood after all, in possession of the great house. Most everyone in Vienna dreaded the days to come. Hanna and I looked ahead with unequaled appetite for the extraordinary. A pigeon flew to her. She held out her arm, and it landed on her. She took it into Resi's room.

Father had not mentioned the Water Castle, but he had locked me in. I fancied Hanna Roth had seen me with the prince and expected me. The lure of the great house was as sweet as ever. For the first time, I felt confined to the Meinert-Hof, the way Mother used to be, without a key to the door and gate. Afternoon light flitted over oak beams and muted decorations on old hand-painted furniture. At the piano, motes danced in a shaft of light. A white silk shawl of Mother's lay draped over the embroidered bench. I picked it up, held it to my face. The perfume Mother had used years ago, the winter of the last Romberg ball, assailed me. I sniffed the scent on an open book of music history in the library, on sheet music strewn on the brown velvet chaise where Mother had embraced Berthold. A bunch of daffodils thrust carelessly into a Ming vase had lost their delicate fragrance, impregnated by a perfumed hand.

I ran upstairs to the boudoir. The door stood open. Chairs looked dusty and dull. Only a faint outline on the blue wall showed where the clock and the Fragonard had hung. Father had stored valuables in the wine cellar, in case of bombing. The doll's wardrobe and the gilded little chair stood in place. A coverlet on Mother's bed had been crumpled. My fingers traced the embroidered crest of Falkenburg, the falcon perched on the sun —Mother's trousseau linen. The pillow reeked of the same perfume. Someone had invaded the boudoir where my parents once laughed and loved each other and where I had hated the doll.

A comb lay on the floor. I picked it up: brown hair, darker than my own, clung to it. I let it fall as though it had scorched my fingers, then lifted the crystal perfume bottle. It was almost empty. The perfume, like Father's wines, had aged with the years, become potent, less innocent. Through the perfume I discerned the acrid, sultry odor of a stranger. The scent of the perfume thief —an invisible presence—repelled me. Had I not been locked in, I would have fled the house, the street.

The sun was sinking toward the Water Castle. A group of

ladies came bustling down the steps in their fluffy hats, self-important and plump as hens. I picked up my bag full of novels and carried it through the empty, shadowy house to my room. The door stood wide open. I peeked in like a stranger. The bag dropped from my hand. Another me lay in the bed, snoring softly: a rosy face, dark curls spread out on my lace-trimmed pillows. One bare foot stuck out under the tangerine-colored eiderdown quilt. The room was heavily scented, the foot dirty. The picture of the guardian angel still hung above the bed.

"What are you doing here?"

She woke up with a start, stared at me as an intruder, and rubbed her eyes. "Is that really you, Fräulein Reyna? I wouldn't have known you." She stretched and yawned. "Don't you remember me? I'm Nadica, Vlado's oldest one. You must excuse me. I came here yesterday to clean, but I have an exam at the conservatory today. I stayed up most of the night to study and to practice. I came up here to make up your bed. I was so tired, I dropped off."

Vlado's brat had made herself at home at the Meinert-Hof far more easily than her Marxist father. Her clothes lay in a pile on my chair. She slipped out of bed without bashfulness and danced into the bathroom in a pair of Mother's crepe de chine step-ins. Vlado's children must have shared clothes and beds without giving it a thought.

Nadica was as cheerful as her father, beguiling with her high cheekbones and her mother's hair and complexion. I watched her slip into her clothes—or rather, a dirndl dress and Mother's soft white coat. She smeared lipstick over her mouth. "Do you ever wear any? Hitler forbids it, but it suits me." She looked at her watch and said that it was late. "And I never did dust. Could you be an angel and do your father's room? Just this once. Tomorrow Frau Boschke will be here, but she is old and has bad feet." She used my silver-backed brush and comb, grinned at herself in the mirror. Her thick, sturdy legs made me think of a pony as she bent over to put on Mother's silver-gray sandals.

"I don't know where Father has gone. He had to hide, being a Communist. If it weren't for the master, we would all be in the street. He let us stay. Mother runs the vineyards. She's good with the foreign workers. Two brothers are in the army, Gusti in the

Hitler youth. I'm at the conservatory. Your father pays for it. I started coming here to practice the piano and I clean and work in the garden. He often comes to work in the garden with me and . . ."

She gave me a quick, searching look, picked up a briefcase Mother had given to Papa. Then she grabbed my hand, said she was starving, and led me down to the kitchen. We sat down together and feasted on crackling and dark bread. Her mother had slaughtered a pig. They all missed the pig; it had been friendly as a dog. But it tasted so good to have some meat. My father had promised them another piglet soon.

"I've been chosen for the student concert. I want to play better than anyone. Just for the master." She took my hand again when she was ready to leave and led me upstairs like a sister. I enjoyed it all, against my will, until I saw her take my golden keys from her bag. "I'd better hurry or he'll come back and find me here. *Bitte, bitte,* Reyna, don't tell that you found me in your bed." She threw her arms around me and kissed me on both cheeks. "You're so pretty." She locked me in and made her way around the back of the garage, wheeling Poldi's bicycle.

During my stay I resented her, and yet I wanted her to come back—to make free with Mother's piano; dance around in Mother's frothy underwear, perfumed and unwashed; go to sleep in this or that bed under down quilts and wake up smiling in a grim world where the heroic Nazi army blasted its way into this or that country like a mass of dull robbers. The art of taking is delicate. A great thief feels at home in the world of luxury and takes with love, not hatred. The perfume thief had invaded my world like a child wandering through a field, picking daisies. She had helped herself to Father because she needed him and he was hers for the taking.

Vlado had vanished. Had I questioned him, his answer would have been theoretical, just like his notion of sitting in Father's chair. I kept hoping Father would mention Nadica; I never did. But I took her place, became a usurper, and didn't know it.

Two days after my arrival in Vienna, Father decided to surprise Resi and take me to the première of a film she had just made. There was talk of theaters being closed down. Hitler had declared total war, but Resi's film had propaganda value and she had become the Führer's favorite canary. Vienna went in for gala occasions whenever the outlook was grim.

Father led me to the boudoir, to Mother's closet, and picked out the pale green dress she had worn on the last New Year's Eve of Austria. I tried it on while he sat smoking in the alcove. As I pulled it over my head, I could see the tucks and smell the perfume—not as Mother had worn it years ago, but the pungent aroma of the perfume thief. I saw myself in a cloud of shimmering green, submerged in Mother's myth and the secret of the sweet thief. Like Nadica, I pinned my hair back, and this lifted the corners of my eyes.

"Perfect," Father said.

        ✿   ✿   ✿

The night was starless; searchlights patterned the sky like jewels on dark velvet. The glitter in the theater lobby was less discreet. Never had I see such gems, colored silks, flounces, frills. Men jingling with medals wore uniforms or full evening dress. The bell rang before I had a chance to take it all in.

"Perfect timing," Father said. "If it weren't for Reserl, no ten horses could have dragged me here." He whispered into my ear, "I wish they'd all acquired a little taste with all the jewelry, and requisitioned some manners with their high positions."

A poster showed Resi, all smiles, in a dirndl dress. I had seen Resi in one of her early films, on a rainy day at the Water Castle with Eli. She had smiled and sung to an imperial officer until he missed his maneuvers and got into trouble. Then she was seen weeping in a puffy Roth hat, and racing to Schönbrunn palace. There she wept, smiled, and sang for the kaiser until he did his bit to unite the lovers—and bring on the Vienna choirboys.

The wartime film was very much the same; only the uniforms had been changed. The lover, a Waffen SS man, missed his transport because Resi sang and kissed so much. Later he won a battle almost all by himself, and became a hero. He was wounded. Adolf Hitler turned up in the end to reward the handsome officer with a medal and with his girl. It looked as though the same actor had played both the kaiser and the Führer, merely by changing uniforms and replacing side-whiskers with a small black mustache. No one could help loving such a kind face. The choirboys sang.

Resi warbled a final song about the Vaterland: the typical sweet
Vienna girl.

The audience went wild. Cheering and bravos went on until
Resi yielded and sang the song of love and victory onstage, not
once but three times. A large German carried her out and put
her down in the lobby where champagne was being served with
little open sandwiches. The food attracted as much attention as
the star. I did not quite know what to make of it all. Part of me
thought the film, the entire evening, was silly, while my new self
loved the trite romance on the screen and was swept into the
garish excitement that followed—especially when the prince appeared and handed me half a glass of champagne. He said he was
delighted and bent over my hand.

Resi turned, saw me and came rushing to take me into her arms.
She laughed and cried, thanked Father for the surprise, and
scolded him for not letting her know that I was in Vienna. "So
tall, so beautiful and grown-up!"

"Now, don't you drink so fast," Papa told me. As soon as he
and Resi were swept away by her admirers, I gulped in defiance.

The prince watched. He took the glass from me and put it away.
"I have heard a lot about you recently from your mother's cousin."

"Berthold!"

We were interrupted. An early June beetle was flying around
some cut lilac. "You must catch it," Resi was crying. "Please catch
it and let it out, or it will die." Her heroes went rushing around
in the midst of shrieks and encouragement. The prince pulled me
behind Resi's poster.

"Funny how concerned everyone is about a bug, or a pig.
Berthold von Hohentahler got into serious trouble that way." He
put his arm around my shoulder. "This is perhaps not the best
place . . ."

"Where is Berthold, what happened to him?"

"We did not meet under the most favorable circumstances. He
horsewhipped a superior officer in Russia. His war record and his
high position as one of the heroes of the Austrian Anschluss saved
him. And the fact that he had been shot in the arm. I knew him
and was called on as a character witness."

I grabbed his arm, begged him to go on, but there was a big
commotion, applause and toasting as the June beetle was caught
and released into the night.

"Some officers were amusing themselves in a little hovel by taking shots at a pregnant sow. A terrible thing to talk about to someone . . . well, so young. Anyway, Hohentahler horsewhipped them all, and especially the one who started it. That officer turned and shot Hohentahler in the arm; he could have killed him. I went to the hospital. When Hohentahler found out that I was about to go to Vienna on a special mission, he told me all about his friends and relatives. Gave me an introduction to Resi Heller. We talked about you."

"I would like to kill those men!" I could not stop my tears. I fumbled for my handkerchief and couldn't find one. He gave me his.

"I felt the same way," he said in his clipped, formal voice. "But Berthold von Hohentahler is free and will no doubt return to Vienna before long. You will like this, won't you?" My face told him how I felt. "He is a lucky fellow. I'm not that fortunate. I am in disgrace with my family."

"How did you get into the Gestapo?"

"The way your cousin got into the SS. We are the same age. At first I was enthusiastic, but once I got involved, found out what was really going on, I stayed to keep authority from some of those disgusting beasts. When it became impossible for me to play my part deceptively enough, I joined the army. I understand that you are remarkably discreet, and you have courage and are smart. We must not give up."

He refilled my glass and his, and we drank to each other. This time I did not drink fast. All the same, by the time Father came to get me I was leaning against the prince, quite in love, forgetful of Berthold or anything else in the world. The atmosphere had changed. Father led me to the door, and older men eyed me, took my hand and held it. "So good to see your little Fräulein, Ferdl. You are a connoisseur."

Hungry eyes, sticky hands. Then the coat was being placed on my shoulders. "My daughter," Father said.

"I'm leaving Vienna," said the prince. "Think of me kindly."

"You were always on my side," I said.

"That was not difficult. It was always the right side." He clicked his heels and kissed my hand.

"Isn't the prince beautiful?" Resi asked in the taxi. "The kind of face you never forget. And he likes children."

"He likes Berthold, too," I quickly said.

"He told you?"

"He shouldn't have," Father said. "Must be the champagne. We all talk too much."

"Well, I'm not sorry it happened," Resi said. "At least Bertl is out of the war. And he's going to be home soon."

We were driving toward the Opera. "Then you will ditch me for a younger man," Father laughed.

"Look who's talking. You're never happy unless you have a young creature in tow." She drew me into her arms and held me until the taxi stopped on the Ring. It was very dark. Father took a flashlight from his cape. *Bunker* was written in white letters on Resi's apartment house, and an arrow pointed to the left.

"We are lucky to enjoy an evening like this." Father helped Resi out, whispered something, and said aloud, "Kiss your hand, and sweet dreams. A wonderful première, Reserl."

She reached into the taxi and touched my cheek, reluctant to part. "I wonder," she said with feeling, "whose première it really was."

✿   ✿   ✿

"I saw Hannah Roth on Resi's balcony," I said to Father when we were making our own breakfast in the kitchen the next morning.

"She stands up there and waits for her carrier pigeons. The aviary is full of them. She sends them out three or four at a time, in case some of them get lost."

"Where does she send them?" I asked.

"Who knows?" Father laughed. He handed me a boiled egg, put a spoonful of honey into my milk, and seemed quite at home in the kitchen. "I'm in town most of the time. It's easy for me to keep my distance. Of course I prefer having Eugene's mother to that so-called club as neighbors. But there is a lot of gossip and intrigue going on over there. In the morning Hanna's former customers come by streetcar or on foot. In the afternoon the Nazi elite drive up. A regular henhouse. The only men over there are foreign workers. They do keep up the garden beautifully. I sent the ladies some fresh wine, the least I could do after what happened over there."

"Gypsies poisoned the wine."

"That's all over. Best not talk about it, *Kind.*"

I asked him for my keys, and he reached into his pocket and gave me a spare set. I mentioned the golden keys, and he said, "What difference does it make? Now, remember to let me know when you go out. Don't let strangers in. Tomorrow you'll go and see your grandmother and stay for a few days."

As soon as he left, I took a book to the hammock under the trees and daydreamed of Berthold and my Frog Prince until I dozed off. The bell rang at the gate and woke me up. Hanna Roth stood there in a simple dark walking suit and felt hat.

"Dolfi, Dolfi, come here at once," she was calling.

I went to the gate. There was the black cat, sitting on the slope. "Mitzi, Mitzi," I called. My kitten was now a fat old cat, but it came to me and dropped a dead pigeon at my feet.

"Take the pigeon, *Kind*," Hanna Roth yelled. "Hurry, let me in before he makes off with it and devours the bird with its message."

The cat settled down to a meal. I ran to let Hanna Roth in. She rushed toward the cat, grabbed the pigeon, and gave the cat a swift kick. "Bad Dolfi, bad! I warned you to leave my pigeons be." She turned to me. "You don't have to look so shocked, little highness. Pigeons are killed to be eaten every day. You've grown blessedly tall, but don't forget you're still a child. No convent, no palace, no mountain retreat can keep a child from this." She held up the dead bird, as she had held up the remains of Puppe.

"It was you who destroyed Puppe," I said. "Not Fritz Janicek."

She laughed like an aged child. "How many times we acted out the old fairy tales with dolls in my days at the palace! Snow White was poisoned over and over again. Didn't you find those old stories entertaining when you were younger and wiser? And you knew there had to be a beginning and an end to everything. And didn't you like the cruelty?"

She drew me away from my romantic stories, notions of safe romance, and plunged me back into the world of magic, murder, and madness, where witches ran concentration camps and put little ones into ovens and turned them into gingerbread men.

"Ah, there he is, *mein Schöner*. Dolfi, Dolfi, come home!"

The golden-eyed cat stared up into the trees, listening to birds twitter and warble around nests, and ignored her.

"What men and women call love is much more murderous than this." She dangled the pigeon before my face. It looked uninjured. Then she left, and I watched her enter the garden across the street, a tiny dark figure outlined by luminous green. The cat was walking behind her, swinging its tail.

❖   ❖   ❖

Father continued to display me to wartime society. I had no qualms when I wore Mother's dresses. They fitted well since they had been altered for Nadica. I repossessed Father, too—allowed myself to be admired and took the girl's place until no one believed she'd ever existed. "So, the lovely Fräulein is your daughter," his acquaintances said when we met them in town.

"Does Nadica, Vlado's girl, still come to practice the piano when I'm out?" I asked Frau Boschke one day after I had stayed in town with Grandmama.

"Ja, ja, she comes, all right. She's been allowed to come and go. You can't blame her. What with all the young men away in the war, her father vanished away. God knows whether he's still among the living. There has to be a little Liebe. No one knows what tomorrow will bring. You can't blame anyone."

Insidious as the soft south wind, something stirred in our hearts that spring. I was not alone in my yearning for romance and love. Nadica had been at the Meinert-Hof with Father while I went to Resi's dress rehearsal for *The Bartered Bride* at the Opera. Father had planned it that way. He told me Nadica had come to help him plant geraniums. I loved the red flowers, anyway. There was bartering going on in Vienna on every social level. Father needed an afternoon off, needed to be diverted. He worked from seven-thirty in the morning until seven o'clock in the evening.

His social life at night was a diplomatic necessity. The regular table at Wiesner's, I soon discovered, had changed. I missed some of the old faces, but I liked some of the newcomers, who were young men, invalids. One wore an eye patch. There was dancing. No one mentioned the war The Rittmeister danced with my grandmother; his love for her was old, but he gazed into her eyes like a boy. I watched them like a chaperone when he escorted us back to the little palace in the dark. One evening he kissed both her hands in the passageway. And when I turned my back, I saw them in the glass of a clockface, in each other's arms.

They kissed like drowning lovers. Time stood still. Swallows chirped softly in their nests. It amazed me to see old people obsessed with each other as I was with my imaginary lovers.

❀   ❀   ❀

"I have never known the swallows to come back so early," my grandmother said to Father when he came to pick me up one morning. I was planting some geranium cuttings around the stone angel. Swallows darted over Father and the countess as they walked back and forth. Father looked worried. They kept their voices low. Perhaps she was telling Father of her secret plan to kidnap Adolf Hitler. I admired them from a distance. Grandmother had lost weight, and there was a spun-glass quality about her in her light, pleated dress; she seemed to float. Her pale face looked taut, smooth as marble. Father's side-whiskers had begun to turn white at the roots; this set off his pink cheeks. He never showed fatigue.

"He's Frau Traude's son," Grandmother was saying. "She should use the dwarf's influence with the criminals who are in power." (This was the only time I ever heard my grandmother call Hanna Roth "dwarf.") "No one has better connections. She even has undated letters written to her by Rudolf Hess; she showed them to me. This gave me all sorts of ideas. She could be used in my plan. Napoleon was handled well. Murder creates ghosts."

"Let's leave Hanna out of my problem," Father said. "You can't trust her. There is another possibility."

He looked at his watch. It was eleven o'clock. We left in a hurry. He walked with his hands deep in his leather breeches.

"Are we going to see Resi?" I finally asked.

"Ja, Eugene is in trouble. He was arrested in Salzburg. Better than Berlin or München—at least it's Austria—but still no joke. I can't imagine what made him leave Switzerland. Arrested for smuggling. I don't believe it. Resi often sings at Salzburg, and the mayor is her devoted admirer. She might be able to do something. We'll see." He walked fast through narrow streets, avoiding the busy Mariahilferstrasses.

I could no longer hold back. "I saw Eugene Romberg outside our house in an SS uniform. That was before the Russian campaign. He made me promise not to tell you or anyone, said he was helping Germany lose the war by sending them to Russia."

"You should have told me at once!"

"You would have said my fantasy was blooming. Besides, he had been drinking."

"Well, you certainly don't talk your head off like other girls." Father often mentioned girls in general when he had a need to talk of Nadica; he liked her so much. "Not a word about Eugene. I'll handle it all."

Resi's apartment was on the first floor in a grand apartment house directly across from the Opera. Father rang the bell. No one answered. Resi slept late, he said and rang again. While we waited, he wanted to know every word of my conversation with Eugene Romberg.

"He didn't take such a risk to hear Resi sing." Father took the keys from his pocket, and one of them fitted the door. He simply let himself in. "He wanted to be near your mother and hear her play. He worships her."

I had left out Eugene's love for Mama. Romantics don't discuss romance. Father had never stopped loving Resi, either. He had found her the apartment to get her away from Berthold and help her return to the opera before the war. I recognized the rustic benches, a carved umbrella stand in the entrance, and an old loden jacket of his hanging on the coatrack. He liked to wear it as a housecoat when the weather was cold.

He knocked on the door and called, "Schazi!" A radio was playing zither music. We walked into a darkened living room. Papa pulled back the curtains, and the sun shone in like a stagelight. A pink chandelier, white sofa, china wood stove, old and new furniture, and trinkets all clashed and went together.

"It's wonderful here!" I said.

"Resi always collects things." He knocked on the bedroom door. There was no answer, but the sound of soft voices. We went in.

"You could have phoned, Ferdl. You don't just walk in!"

Father sent me out to wait in the entrance room. I took my time while he made his excuses and said he had to talk to her, it was important. "Shut the door, Reyna," he said.

"Never mind all that," Resi interrupted. "Why don't you come back a little later? After all, you don't live here."

"And that is rather fortunate," said a familiar voice. I wanted to run through the door and fling my arms around Berthold; I also wanted to run away. I could see him through clear roses on the frosted glass panel of the door. He had flung a scarlet wool blanket around his shoulders, like the cape the tin officers wore on his father's imperial war maps. He was barefooted.

My father said: "Berthold!" and stretched out his hand.

Berthold produced his left hand awkwardly. "You must excuse me, *bitte*, Ferdl. My right hand is missing." The handshake was brief because the blanket was slipping from his bare shoulders. Father took a step back, then went to him and embraced him without a word. The radio was playing the song of the red poppies, and Zara Leander, a famous singer who sounded like a man, sang of poppies glowing like hearts.

"You'd better get some clothes on, Bertl," Father said in a low voice. "There's someone in the hall."

"Annerl!" Berthold's voice had not changed, nor his enthusiasm.

"Reyna," Father said with pride.

"My little Reyna!" Berthold was rushing to the door.

"Not so little anymore. You'd better get dressed."

Resi laughed, pulling him back into the bedroom. I wanted to flee, but Papa had locked the door from the inside, as he always did, and the keys were in his pocket. When he came to take me into the kitchen to make coffee, he was too overwhelmed by his own feelings to notice my embarrassment. He opened shutters and looked out onto the *Ringstrasse*. A red streetcar was crawling along. Gray people crept about, keeping their heads low like beggars. Only the opera house stood proudly in the sun.

"You probably heard it all, anyway. Resi has a heart of gold. She's trying to comfort Berthold. He's lost his right arm. It is tragic, but he is with us. I know she'll also do something for Eugene."

Later he drew Resi into the music room and they stood at the piano, holding their cups, while the radio announcer talked about treachery in Tunisia. She was crying.

"Don't worry," Berthold said. "Resi cries as easily as she laughs, bless her."

I had rehearsed Berthold's return so often in the mountains that I was unprepared, distant when we met. He had dressed in a hurry, thrown his uniform jacket over his shoulders like a cape to spare me the sight of the missing arm. His face was lined and tired, but the eyes, tousled hair, the familiar gestures reassured me.

"I somehow thought a little girl would come running through the door and throw her arms around my neck. Funny how one believes everyone will wait while one is away, wait growing old, or wait growing up." The room was flooded with sunlight. I recognized a Biedermeier bouquet in a crystal vase. "I can't believe I'm really home in Vienna like this. I can't believe this is me."

He laughed the way he used to, and I had to laugh with him. He reached out with his left hand and pulled me to his side, adjusted his jacket, smoothed over his unruly pale hair. "Are you too grown-up and too beautiful, too disgusted, to give me a kiss?" The fair beard on his cheek scratched my lips. I can still feel the thrill. I could not say a word without giving myself away. If he had listened, he could have heard my heart beat. "You have grown too much. I can't pick you up anymore and put you on my knee. Great disadvantage, having only one arm, what?"

Papa and Resi sat side by side on the piano bench. He was talking to her softly, and while he spoke he stroked her neck. She wore a loose blue velvet robe which reminded me of her Biblical days, her confrontation with Fritz. While Father talked to her so earnestly, she suddenly dimpled, whispered something into his ear, and kissed the bare spot just above his kaiser head.

I looked at Berthold's pale, unshaven face. Just seeing him gave me a thrill of unbearable sweetness I never got accustomed to. He caught me looking at him and hugged me. "Turn the radio off, Reserl, bitte," he said. "I feel so much at peace, I don't want to hear about the war." Sun danced over mirrors, and the pink chandelier threw rosy blossoms onto the wall. Pigeons cooed on the window sill. "Lucky if they don't get eaten," he laughed. "Poor birds. Life's pretty grim in Vienna, but I get restless at the Landsitz . . . I can't imagine your mother in the country, and still in a wheelchair. I wonder what she would say to me now."

"In Carnuntum you once said that Mama and I were part of you, just like your left arm."

He laughed, slapped his forehead, gave me a smacking, familiar kiss. The spell was broken. "Then I have not lost either of you. Heaven be praised. But how on earth do you remember such things? Did I really say that, or did you make it up?"

"I don't make things up." I felt angry because I had invented him for years.

"Well, I think Annerl would laugh at me. She always did. Perhaps nothing has changed, after all. If she only knew how much was at stake. All last year: bombs in overcoats, bombs in brandy bottles, silent bombs, English bombs—such conspiracies. I wanted to help end the lunacy I had helped bring about. Then, after all the bomb failures, it was I who exploded at the sight of a helpless mother pig! It was all worth it. I would do it again. Did I enjoy giving it to them with my whip! I made a fool of myself. The story is out. I'm a marked man, but all at once I have a lot of friends."

"I'm hungry," Resi cried out. "When I get upset I have to eat. I wish we had some fresh rolls. My daily woman is elderly, but she does stand in line at the bakery. I wish I had not sent her away this morning."

"All my fault; let me volunteer." Berthold jumped up, and I stood up with him. He turned to pick up Resi's bread stamps, and the stump of his arm touched me. I shrank away, but he didn't notice. "All these stamps. How dazzling."

She put a finger to her lips. "Shhhh."

I stood at the window and watched him cross the street. He took long strides, and his slightly bent legs made me think of Mother.

"He won't stand in line," Resi said. "He may have lost his arm, but he certainly hasn't lost his charm."

My father laughed and kissed her hand. "I didn't know you to be a poet, Reserl. So many undiscovered talents . . ." He fondled her neck and told her she deserved a medal for cheering everyone up.

In our society, there never seemed to be one man and one woman. The novels I read spoke of the one and only love in life as the key to everlasting happiness. But I knew Resi had changed from the wife of Eugene, a Jew, to the lover of a young duke who was a great Nazi, and back to Ferdl's girl. Now Berthold had returned and she had taken him in. I watched her spread butter on a roll for him as if he were Eli, and she insisted on cooking her last egg for him. Father emptied his briefcase and there was smoked ham and sausage, a feast. We all ate too much starchy food.

Resi had looked a little puffy under the eyes and pale in the bright sun, but as she ate and smiled, turning from Berthold to Father, pouring coffee and saying how lucky she was to have such food and such company, rosiness spread from her décolleté to her cheeks. I could not enjoy eating because I kept thinking of her night of love with Berthold. My romantic notions of love in a gondola or in moonlit rose gardens, everlasting bliss, had been ruined the day Stopperl had pointed at cattle mounting each other and laughed. When I had told her to stop it, she had said, "Why, humping is fun! Everyone likes it." In my daydreams the setting was very important, and I received shy kisses and endless declarations of love from Berthold, Eli, Eugene Romberg, the prince, and Rudolf Hess. In my fantasies I changed lovers more frequently than Resi, but I was shocked by her because she made it all seem ordinary.

"When I saw the black uniform through my peephole, I thought they were after me again," she said.

"I was after you. I was, Reserl," Berthold said. "Everyone is always after you. But I guess I should have let you know I was coming."

"You've never learned to think before you act," Father said.

"That's what makes him irresistible," Resi chirped. "I'm surrounded by too many important and terribly careful men, nicht wahr?"

"Good protection," Father said.

Berthold turned her around and kissed the tip of her nose. "Are you protected or beleaguered?"

She covered the rest of her roll with honey. "What difference does it make?" She ate with pleasure. "I hope poor Eugene is not hungry . . ."

"If he goes hungry in Switzerland, it's his own fault." Berthold did not like to be reminded of Eugene Romberg.

Father got up and sat on the window seat, smoking his pipe. Pigeons circled over the Opera. "I came to tell Resi that poor Eugene was arrested in Salzburg."

Berthold jumped up from the cozy sofa. I did not like the way his stump moved the empty sleeve. "My God, how did that come about?"

"He's been playing some kind of power game. Reyna saw him outside our house in SS uniform. That was three years ago, during a house concert."

Resi was clasping her hands, and tears rolled down her cheeks. "He wanted to be near me. Hear me sing. But why did he get into the Nazi uniform?"

I could have enlightened her.

Father went to fetch a pipe ashtray I recognized. He must have brought it from home with some of the Meinert furniture when Resi moved into the apartment. "You know what it means if he is in the hands of the Gestapo?"

"He isn't, yet. The mayor of Salzburg knows I sing for Hitler." Resi had recovered enough to drink more coffee. "I should go to Salzburg at once, but I have to sing *The Bartered Bride*. If I left Vienna, it would attract too much attention."

"I'll go," Berthold said at once. "I like Eugene. I'll get him out, Reserl. I'm good at pranks like that, what?"

My father scowled. "Your last prank cost you dearly." But he would move the knight to protect the queen.

Never had I seen Berthold in conversation with Eugene Romberg. I knew how uneasy he felt around Father's Jewish friend. He avoided him in the same friendly manner he used around Krampus, my dog: he was not accustomed to small dogs, or Jews. But he would defend a living creature with his life.

"No," I cried out. "I don't want him to go!"

My father looked at me with amazement.

"He shouldn't," Resi agreed. "He's too crazy."

"Then it is up to me," Father said.

"You can't go. You're not even a party member, even if you have everyone believe you are."

"I'm an invalid. I have my uniform. I cut quite a figure, what? No one can doubt me, or refuse me a favor. I can handle it. I have nothing else to do." Berthold sounded too eager.

Resi went to write a letter to the Bürgermeister of Salzburg. Father had to make a phone call to his office. They accepted Berthold's offer, and I could tell that they had planned to send him to Salzburg from the beginning.

Berthold sat down on a footstool beside me. He wanted to know all about my meeting with Eugene Romberg in front of our house. "I know Lütensteg was there. He told me all about you. You don't have to worry about him," he said.

"I never did."

"Do you like him?"

"He is marvelous!"

"How about me? You think I was right to defend the pig, Reyna, don't you?"

I nodded and used the language of the eyes.

"When you were little, you always had a way of making me feel I was marvelous, too. Now I am a ruin. I feel sorry for myself, sorry for poor old Austria. I'm a fool. What we have done in Russia and everywhere else in the name of the fatherland and the Führer . . . Well, we'll pay in the end. I am disgusted. Most of all with myself. I have got to do something, what?"

I flung my arms around his neck as I always had and forgot all my notions of romance. "I love you."

He jumped up and went to the window. I followed and we watched clouds, birds.

"No one has said that to me since I've come home as a cripple."

He no longer towered over me, and I stood tall beside him. "It's only an arm. You can walk. You'll be able to ride. You're not a cripple."

"Not like your poor mama."

"That was not your fault. The wind blew the hat."

He laughed and hugged me. I leaned my cheek against the stump of his arm. He understood.

"Now I feel I've really come home," he said.

"So do I."

We took leave of Berthold at the station the next day, surrounded by soldiers, weeping women, older men leaving for the first time, boys too young to go to war, women and girls waiting for a train to come in, children getting lost and crying. A mob tried to push into a crowded carriage. Berthold kissed Resi very much like the lover in her Hitler film. She smiled through tears. The stationmaster blew his whistle as the last in line, mostly older people with rucksacks, pushed their way onto the train.

"You've got to get on," Father said.

Berthold was standing behind me. "Say it again!"

"It was the wind," I said.

"Not that."

I whispered into his ear, but I think I overdid the language of the eyes. He had to laugh, and kissed me on the nose three times. Then he was gone. The conductor helped to pull him onto the steps of the compartment reserved for the military. The train began to move and he leaned out, waving his SS cap.

"Auf Wiedersehen," I yelled.

Resi sobbed in Father's arms. She stood out on the grimy, dreary platform like a primrose in a coal chute.

"He'll come back," Papa said.

"But not to me," she cried. "He's too young. It's all over."

Freight cars at the end of the train moved past us, carrying coal and military vehicles. One of them was closed but had one small window. I saw a man's face.

"Papa, look, there's Fritz Janicek!"

My father reached into his loden jacket and produced the spectacles he used when he surveyed the vineyards from the bottom of the hill. "Verdammt! There he is. And look at that. Right there, behind him, my two beer trucks." The trucks had "Meinert Beer and Wine" painted on the side in large white letters. "National art recovery society be damned. I have just made a move to get them back. God knows what those men are hauling out of Vienna. That crazy scoundrel is behind the entire thing."

Girls and women were running alongside the train, calling names, words of parting. The engine belched smoke and panted off. I panicked and ran after the train. "Come back, Berthold! Come back!"

He had gone, but the sharp-nosed architect of disaster took notice and waved Mother's pink scarf from the window as he was carried off with Berthold.

22

The Winding Staircase

18 March 1944

High Honored Frau von Roth:

Please forgive a stranger for taking the liberty of writing to you, but I had the honor of making a discovery of great importance to you during my convalescence at Schloss Falkenburg.

I humbly suggest you take the short journey and go to the library and look for the Goethe shelf on the right side near the main entrance. It opens to a winding staircase. You must carry a light.

Heil Hitler!

A respectful wellwisher

"What does it mean?" I asked Hanna Roth after she let me read it. We were in a taxi, on our way to Falkenburg.

She snatched it from me. "Everything, everything."

"You had some doubts at first," Frau Traude reminded her, but Hanna Roth was looking out of the car window at a little girl with a doll carriage. We passed a small park. I felt drowsy. It was early, about nine o'clock in the morning, a day or two after Berthold had left Vienna. I had been standing in line at the bakery when Frau Hanna and her assistant had come along in a battered taxi driven by an old fellow with a broken nose. The engine stalled and the driver got out, cursed at the engine, and punched it to get it going again. Frau Traude clambered out and came to invite me for a morning drive to Schloss Falkenburg.

The housewives around me gave her mean looks because she was so fat at a time when no one had enough to eat.

I did not have to be persuaded to come along, for I was bored and disgusted with the women and all their talk of food: the Sachertorte with Schlag they had eaten before the war and the Sachertorte they would eat again as soon as Adolf Hitler came through with his secret weapons and destroyed the enemies. Hanna Roth, in midnight-blue serge, a dashing hat, and veils held together by a silver arrow, cheered me up. She could hardly contain her excitement while I read the letter. "Have you seen the stairway?" she asked. I had to disappoint her. My grandmother had never allowed me much time to explore the castle. Hanna took the letter and studied it. I dozed off, and when the honking Falkenburg geese woke me up, she was still holding the letter.

In vineyards, garden plots, fields, women stooped at work. Our noisy car made them straighten, shade their eyes against the bright sun.

"All these women," Frau Traude said. "Without men. Widows —nothing but widows." Storks came and went from nests on the gabled roofs of the whitewashed cottages. The road curved down close to the lake, and wind rippled the blue water and fanned my face with moist fragrance. A pair of gray herons stalked calmly across the road, spreading their wings to take off. "Look at that. They know nothing of war or shortages." She moved her eyes like the late doll, and there was resentment in her voice.

I had hardly eaten anything that day and my stomach growled. Frau Traude handed me a cough drop—all she had at the moment. We crossed the road leading to Gasthaus Falkenburg, the inn at the lake. I knew I could not ask Hanna Roth to go there first.

"I stayed at the inn many years ago," Frau Traude said, as though she'd read my thoughts, "just before the First World War. I came to visit the nuns. The almond trees were in bloom, just as they are today, but the weather was not as mild. Your grandfather, Reyna, Karl von Dornbach, was in residence at Schloss Falkenburg. Such goings-on. The music went on all night long, and early in the morning I woke up and saw him gallop past my window, barelegged, in shirttails, and splash straight into the lake. What a splendid figure of a man! I have never forgotten his happily smiling face. No wonder they called him Schöne Karl. There he was on horseback in the lake, having his morning wash, laughing and singing; he threw water into his face, his mouth, gargling and splashing. A typical von Dornbach. To him everything was an amusement, even the war."

"That's why he never came back," Hanna Roth said. "His grand-nephew Hohentahler might not be as beautiful, but he did come back. Now he's off again. Against my advice. I warned his mother. He'll do more harm than good, as usual, with the best intentions in the world. And he'll get away with it."

"He lost his right arm," I said in anger.

"His own fault," the dwarf said without pity.

"Will he come back?" I demanded.

"He'll come and he'll go. That's his style. Like the water of Lake Neusiedel. One century it's there; the next century it is gone, they say, only to return overnight."

The shallow water shone dark blue, like Hanna's dress. A few ducks swam about among reeds. I rolled down the window. Village children were chasing each other around the gallows tree, too young to give it a thought. The gypsy cottages had remained empty. We turned left toward the castle. Starlings perched on the intricate wrought-iron work on top of the gate. For the first time I felt proud of the old family seat. The original simple structure, a square two-story building with wings on each side, had remained gray and untouched by the plump cherubs, gods and goddesses, garlands, and unicorns of the baroque style. I saw it as neither forbidding nor inviting, just perfect, so much more my grandmother's style than the sweet little neglected von Dornbach residence. She stayed away because her father had banished her, but she had defied his memory when she handed the castle over to her frolicsome husband, Karl von Dornbach.

"One day all this will belong to you," the dwarf said. I was shocked rather than pleased. She did not notice, for she could not wait to get into the castle. A potato-faced guard came to the gate. She impressed him with papers and intimidated him with her special Hitler salute. He took his time, and she did not hesitate to use me. "This Fräulein is going to be the owner of this castle one day. We haven't got all day. So you'd better be quick. All we want is a few minutes in the library." He opened the gate, but when she climbed out of the car at the main entrance, he came after us to have a look at her.

"Did you ever see Countess Anna Gitta?" I asked as we walked toward the large reception room.

Her fingers clasped my arm. "Once," she said. "I'll never forget it."

Two officers came along, one on crutches, the other one bandaged under his coat. They stared at us. I knew I had seen the one on crutches before. The dwarf greeted them with her "Heil Hitler." They responded with less fervor and watched her reach up to the door handle to pull it and open the door.

"Did you like Countess Gitta?" I persisted as we came face to face with the portrait of my great-grandmother, Anne-Marie von Kortnai Falkenburg, with her best friend and sister-in-law, the countess Gitta. They wore identical white dresses and garlands in their hair, but that's where the similarity ended. My great-grandmother, the Angel, could have served as an illustration to one of my novels with her soft, sweet face. I quite forgot that this was Christina von Kortnai's sister and Frau Traude's aunt. I was much more interested in the countess Gitta. So was the artist who had labored hard to capture the vitality of that young face; it stood out from the canvas and came at you. A cloud of dark hair emphasized the short upper body of a hunchback.

The room had faded wallpaper, and the desk and chairs must have been put there by the new occupants. My grandmother had sold the old furniture when she had needed money after the First World War.

"You asked me whether I liked her?" Hanna Roth said, without taking her eyes off the picture. "Well, just imagine me when I was eight and the size of a large doll, dressed up for the Christmas party for orphans at the castle. Traude holding my hand and I pulling her; I was so excited. I had never been allowed to come along before, but I knew all about the cakes and candy, the good food and the dolls. I expected to take one back with me, like all the other girls. There in the dining hall, beside the tallest Christmas tree I had ever seen, stood the countess Gitta in a cherry-red dress. She had hair just like yours, only longer. Her handsome brother, Count Otto, was with her, and she kept her arm around his waist as though trying to hold him back. The moment he saw

us, or perhaps that enchanting little daughter of his—your grandmother—he shook her off and walked away. I was fascinated by
the countess and ran to her."

Frau Traude put her arm around Hanna and tried to pull her
away from the painting, saying that losing her childhood friend
could have deranged the countess.

Hanna Roth took a step toward the portrait. "The moment she
set eyes on me, she let out a scream: '*Hinaus,* out, out!'—the way
you might yell at a dirty dog. She pointed at the door and
stamped her feet in a rage. I fled to the library, where the nuns
waited, and they tried to comfort me. Fortunately, the court hatter, Pierre Roth, came with Christmas presents for Traude and
took a great fancy to me. Well, you know what happened. But
none of the affection Madame and Pierre Roth gave me could
make me forget how the count had turned his back and walked
off, and the way the countess, his sister, had yelled when she
saw me. There have been many beautiful dolls in my life—"

"I know," I interrupted. "Even Puppe."

"—but I never forgot the one doll I didn't get when I came
here full of expectations as a small girl." Hanna Roth turned on
her thick heels and hurried into the huge dining hall in the center
of the castle; it was full of mess tables. "This is where the tree
stood, with all the flickering beeswax candles. The fragrance! All
the little dolls tied to the branches . . . That's where she stood,
right under the mural painting of the noble knights."

I considered the picture of jousting knights ignoble. You could
almost hear the clang and clatter of kitchen pots as they struck
one another. I always suffered for the horses, camels, and elephants who were part of the intricate composition.

"You must not upset yourself, liebe Hanna." Frau Traude forced
a cough drop on her friend. "After all, think of the count banish-
ing his own infant, Countess Reyna, just because her mother had
died when she was born."

"The countess Gitta was behind that," I pointed out. "They
called her the Witch. Frau Boschke, the laundress, told me that
she could look into the future."

"*Unsinn,* nonsense," Hanna Roth said, and rushed from the
room, across a passageway, and into the library. "This is where
the nuns sat when I was kicked out."

Count Otto von Falkenburg, my great-grandfather, had created the library for his bride, Anne-Marie von Kortnai, and his sister. The friends had loved to read. The library held a valuable collection of poetry and old family books. My grandmother had kept it locked. Now it was open for the young officers. Walls were lined with books; tall windows facing both the courtyard and the gardens in the back looked inviting, with cozy window seats. I could imagine my great-grandmother and her friend sharing books and reading to each other.

Hanna Roth surprised an officer as she came creaking across the parquet floor on her built-up shoes. She yelled, "Heil Hitler! We don't want to disturb you, but this is Fräulein von Meinert Falkenburg, future owner of the castle. We are here on private business. If you could excuse us for a few minutes . . ." He exchanged a smile with me, saluted, and withdrew.

In the stillness of the room, I could hear the rustle of a petticoat as Hanna Roth turned to the Goethe shelf. "It must be here. Reyna, you're tall. Look at the top." I moved a volume of *Faust*. She reached up and pulled the handle herself. The bookshelf opened to stairs, winding down toward the flower garden.

"You must let me go first," Frau Traude said. "You do have some enemies. And you never know. It could be a joke; it could also be dangerous. We shouldn't have come alone. Please be careful."

Hanna Roth produced a flashlight and her spectacles. As she vanished around the first spiral, her footfalls in the narrow shaft banged like pistol shots. The dank smell of old stone walls seduced me to follow like a blind person, follow where knights had walked in clanking armor, and women who were witches, like the countess Gitta Falkenburg, and heroes who hid away from the world and went mad.

"Wait, wait," Frau Traude clammered, somewhere behind me. The banging footsteps stopped. I heard a rasping, strangled cry and rushed down. I stumbled, recovered, went on, feeling my way blindly along the wall. Then I heard Hanna Roth laugh, and came into the faint light.

"Hanna, liebe Hanna, are you all right?" Frau Traude called from above.

The Meisterin was leaning against the wall on a fan-shaped

landing, her torch trained on a framed picture of a dwarf in armor. The light flickered over the face and I saw dark eyes— her eyes, her smile. The knight had a black beard, short thick limbs. She lit up the breastplate for me: the coat of arms of Falkenburg, the falcon on the sun. This seemed to please her most, although in noble households dwarfs, dogs, cats, monkeys—like the linen, crockery, and silver—bore the crest of the family. The face and the smile worried me, rather than the name printed at the bottom of the picture.

"Count Johannes von Falkenburg, 1768," I read out loud. "We must have had a portrait painter in the family."

Frau Traude had somehow made her way down in the dark. Now she hovered over her little friend, and their shadows on the wall formed a kneeling camel.

"Painter," the dwarf cackled. "Nein, nein. Count Johannes is right here before us. A small knight. Falkenburg men are known to be small." She had the satisfaction of seeing what she wanted to see and no more, finding exactly what she needed to justify herself in days to come. "To think that I have been cheated of my name, my rights, all my life! Just like you, my Traude."

"It's a hoax," I said; but they didn't hear me as they helped each other up the stairs. I hadn't had such wild fun for ages, but the joke was on me. I knew Hanna Roth would use her discovery for all it was worth, even before we looked at the family chronicle on the library table. It was I who saw the book there, conveniently open, exposing the family tree to anyone who wished to study it. I knew the book had not been on the table when we had first come in.

At this moment of gratification, Hanna Roth fumbled with her spectacles, and her gloved hand shook. "There, there, see that? Seventeen sixty-eight, Johannes von Falkenburg." We leaned over the vellum page, but her slightly tainted breath made me draw back. "Johanna von Falkenburg, 1879, linked with Countess Gitta von Falkenburg!"

"She was not married," I said gleefully.

The count was in the middle; his wife, my great-grandmother, on the right; the sister on his left. Under the trio were two offspring, the countess Reyna and her parents, linked with curly lines, and Johanna von Falkenburg, linked with the count and his sister.

"Can brother and sister have a child?" I asked. Stopperl had not educated me on that subject.

"Lieber Himmel." Frau Traude popped two cough drops into her mouth. "You mustn't ever say such a thing. Hanna was born a few months after the count and Anne-Marie von Kortnai were married. Those things do happen; perhaps she was premature, a small child. She was placed at the convent and on this page, put to one side for the sake of discretion and design. There is no doubt that you, Hanna, and Countess Reyna are sisters."

I didn't believe a word of it. "Johannes and Johanna are written with ersatz ink. I know, because I use it."

I was ignored. They didn't want to hear me. When it came right down to it, I was as biased as any Jew-hater: I loved fabulous creatures: unicorns, mermaids, giants, Danube nymphs, dwarfs were my favorite, but I didn't want to have one in my family.

"I'm taking the chronicle to Vienna," Hanna Roth said, and closed the book.

"You can't," I said. "It belongs to Grandmama."

"But *you* could, child," Frau Traude said with a sly smile.

I refused, but she made me laugh. Hanna Roth did not appreciate my amusement. I wanted to stop at the cottage where Agnes's old father lived; she refused. Nor did we stop at the inn as I had hoped. She was in a hurry to get back.

"Everything has changed for me," Hanna said. "One day all this will be worth a great deal. So unspoiled—and the warm climate in this corner of the lake is so delightful." Her expansion plans and her logic showed an affinity with her idol, the Führer. Her roving eye, however, did not notice the large O and 5 drawn in the sand at the gypsy cove. It had not been there when we arrived. Someone had drawn the sign on the wall of St. Stephen's when my grandmother had taken me to Mass; I noticed it here and there in the inner city. She had told me it stood for the Austrian resistance movement: the O for the first letter on Österreich, Austria; the five for the second letter, the *e*, the fifth letter in the alphabet.

My new great-aunt interpreted my silence without any psychic power. "You don't seem to like the idea of having me as a relative, little highness, do you now?" she said with satisfaction.

* * *

Hitler's army marched into Hungary for want of other victories. Hanna Roth turned herself into Johanna von Falkenburg. She lost no time. Within two days, the coat of arms of Falkenburg appeared on top of the gate of the Water Castle. My father had scolded me, called me a goose for getting involved with that mischief-maker across the street. Then, only days later, he actually encouraged me to accept an invitation to the salon. He told me to keep my eyes and ears open, to let him know what was going on over there. It was the end of March, but it should have been April first: Fool's Day.

The temperature had dropped overnight. I had become hardy in the mountains and usually ran around barelegged, but that morning I put on Mother's last pair of silk stockings. The caress and the warm luxury of the silk reminded me of her smile when she had put the stockings into my suitcase. I missed being pampered by the women of the meadow farm. All this was now past and gone. Within two days—ever since Grandmama had had word that Berthold had gone underground, or else crossed the border into Italy—I had decided to work for the Austrian underground movement and become a spy. It was now up to me to find Eugene Romberg.

To be a successful spy, I imagined, you had to feel both daring and a darling of the world. I twisted my hair into a bun, wore the tightest skirt I possessed and a blouse with a scarf. Then I completed my costume with the daisy earrings Grandmother had given me. They were made of pearls and had diamond centers that glittered in the half-dark mirror as I let myself out. I certainly looked more like a descendant of giants than of dwarfs, but the encyclopedia described dwarfism as an inherent trait which can show up after several generations. None of this mattered. Conspirators and spies seldom lived long enough to marry and have children. My father had said the O5 in Vienna were a suicidal bunch. They didn't have a chance. The city was crawling with Gestapo; heads would be rolling. I could see my own head, with the sparkling earrings and the soft hair, on the chopping block, and tears came into my eyes.

My mission would have been more promising if I had been invited to the salon in the afternoon, when Nazi ladies came in droves like pilgrims. I had been invited for eleven o'clock, and this gave me enough time to ride toward the vintners' village and smear a big O5 onto a Nicht Kapitulieren poster. This was only the beginning. I greeted Frau Traude with a brazen "Heil Hitler."

To my surprise she ignored this and greeted me as family, with a kiss. "I could not imagine who that lovely young Fräulein was. You look even more like the countess with your hair up." She wore a voluminous gray smock and sounded amazingly cheerful.

I responded with restraint. The curtains in the entrance room were drawn, and I felt a chill. By a single light at the coatrack I saw the room had been emptied of all furniture. Only the ludicrous picture of Resi posing as a Madonna with a six- or seven-year-old Eli in a christening robe had remained on the wall.

Frau Traude tilted toward me, smelling of chocolate. "I have a big surprise. That's why I asked you to come."

Here she was, bouncy and fat, in Eugene Romberg's house, eating chocolate while he might be starving in prison. "I have a surprise for you, too," I blurted out, forgetting my Mata Hari voice. "Eugene Romberg has been arrested in Salzburg, and no one can find him."

She borrowed the dwarf's cackle as though she had no laughter of her own. "Nonsense. There are so many rumors these days; some are meant to catch traitors. I know better." She reached into her smock pocket, produced a framed photograph, and held it up close to the light. It showed a tall youth in tennis clothes, one foot on the running board of a small sports car. "Hanna says he looks a little like me now—the full lips, the shape of the eyes."

"Eli!" I was shocked, not pleased, to see my friend grown up, ready for a game of tennis, while I was prepared to play away my life to save his father. Only a few days ago the picture would have made me fall in love with this stranger. "How did you get that picture?" I tried to sound casual. "Was there a letter?"

"Not a word; but wait till you see!" She took my hand, hers felt cold and hard as china as she led me through the half-dark, sparsely furnished passageways and rooms where I had once loved to play. She stopped, offered me some chocolate, and when I refused, took the unexpected liberty of pushing a piece into my mouth. "From my son. Swiss chocolate!"

I would have liked to spit it out, but could not resist the delicious flavor. "He paid dearly for this chocolate," I said. "He was arrested for smuggling."

"*Unsinn!* If he had been arrested, do you think they would have sent us the box? Imagine, something for everyone. Silk stockings for your mama. Dress material for you. Shirts for your father, and cigarettes for Frau Resi. All kinds of luxuries for dear Hanna and me. Coffee, real coffee! If he had been foolish enough to carry it across the border himself, they would have arrested him just to get their hands on the box, but it was sent to us."

The empty passageways seemed endless and cavernous. Close to the great hall Frau Traude drew me into a serving pantry, a favorite hiding place when I had wanted Eli to find me. She switched on the light. "Na. Now you can look for yourself."

Tempting packages and clothing in neat piles lay on a lacquered serving table. It looked like a birthday or Christmas before the war. She showed me pink cotton material, a fancy blouse for me, Mother's stockings. And she packed it all into a shopping bag, in such a hurry I suspected she felt sorry to see it all go. Chocolates were noticeably absent.

"Now, when you go home you must take it all and show it to your father, but you can bring back the material. Frau Hanna will have it made up for you into a pretty dress." A gong rang out. "Frau Hanna calling," said Frau Traude.

I detained her. "Don't you see? Someone wants you and Father to believe that Eugene Romberg is in Switzerland. That's why you received all those things. You and Frau Hanna have wonderful connections. They don't want you or Father to do anything for him."

She walked past me. "Hanna would have sensed it at once if anything were wrong."

"No," I said in my deep O5 voice. "She has lost her gift as a fortuneteller."

She turned on me and her eyes moved from side to side, gleaming in the half-dark like the doll's. "Don't ever call her that," she hissed. "It sounds cheap and degrades—not just Frau Hanna, but you. After all, she is your family."

The gong rang out a second time, and Frau Traude went bouncing ahead into the big hall. Cool air met us, smelling of steaming felt, like Salon Roth. The cupola was covered over because of the war. The chandelier was not lit up, but shimmering crystal dominated the twilight. In the days when Resi had come tripping down the stairs, leaving all the doors open behind her, the crystal pendants, alive with dancing lights, had chimed to her songs. The ever-changing decor of urns and vases, hangings and low tables of Resi's Biblical and Jewish days, had now vanished. Titian's mournful prophet had been replaced by the Hitler poster from Salon Roth. The Styrian suit and the green hat with the unfortunate brim the Führer wore looked faded, the face pale. His prophecies for a thousand-year Reich had faded like the poster.

A curtain billowed in the draft from an open window. I heard the faint sound of a piano. Birds seemed to sing along to Schubert. Father had stayed at home to work in the garden and relax. He was not alone. The music stopped abruptly; Father had interrupted Nadica. I imagined them together, and everything bothered me. My hand came to rest on the back of a sofa where Resi and Eli had sat with me on our journey to the Promised Land; it had been re-covered with hairy cloth. My hand shrank back, and goose pimples formed on my arm. Frau Boschke had told me Poldi and Lise now worked in a factory where human hair was made into cloth.

A small table had remained in place to remind me of the Egyptian cat Fritz Janicek had taken. My cat, Hanna Roth's Dolfi, sat in a clearing among hat stands on top of Resi's piano. Eyes closed, head a black mask, he sustained the archetypal pose of the missing effigy. Gilded chairs from the salon lined the music-room walls. Every available mirror had been hung up; I recognized the one from Eugene Romberg's secret room. His coffee perfumed the air; his screens and drapes created a seclusion I took to at once. The adjoining library had been converted into a workroom with sewing machines and irons.

The Meisterin came rushing through the dividing drapes and screens and welcomed me with a curtsy, introduced me to ladies who knew me well while I stood and gaped. She had adorned herself with a wig of white braids and had the audacity to say, "You have transformed yourself, liebe Reyna. With your hair up, you are typically Falkenburg." Her nose jutted out without veils; she was smiling, and like a clown she made me sad. As Johanna von Falkenburg, she no longer held the stage.

I saw a signal pass between ladies who had once played in the dolls' room. Tante Hohentahler sat on the Salon Roth piano stool being fitted with a white felt cap. "Reyna," she said, "you must come and see the general. He always wants to know how you are. You are such a favorite." I found her improved, less nervous. Her eyes danced like Berthold's. "Here we are among ourselves," she lowered her voice. "Bertl would want all of you to know he is not a traitor, but loyal to his Führer. The press did what they could to cover his tracks. I think I can trust everyone here to keep quiet. My only son has gone behind enemy lines, risking his life as a double agent."

Berthold would never have left Austria without Eugene Romberg. They were safe, I told myself. Some of the ladies jumped up and went to the duchess to embrace her. "Of course, of course," said Grandmother's friend, Tante Hermine. "His English, so perfect. He has such an ear for languages."

"They say there are female generals in the American army. And who wouldn't be taken in by that von Dornbach charm?" Frau Traude made herself heard. She was filling cups.

"Dear Hanna," Berthold's mother exclaimed. "You watched him and his sisters grow up. I had to tell you the truth. I knew how it would hurt you to listen to the afternoon ladies and read in the paper that our Berthold is a traitor."

I saw a look of conspiracy pass among the ladies, but Hanna Roth was staring at a Japanese screen. "I saw dragons in a dream, birds with flaming wings . . . heard monstrous cries and thunder. I know mein Führer will attack with secret weapons before the cherries turn red." I knew she had invented the dream. Her eyes were fixed on the dragons and cherry blossoms on the screen. "You wait and see. There will be thunder and fire, buildings will fall apart and splatter as if they were made of marzipan." She spoke in her own voice, licked her lips at the vision of sweet disaster, and quite forgot to be a Falkenburg. Her vision captivated me, as it had years ago on my birthday, when she had predicted the Opera would fall.

Berthold's mother was the first to get up and leave. I jumped up and gave Frau Traude the impression that I couldn't wait to make off with my treasures. She walked to the door with us, carrying the shopping bag for me. At the door she reminded me to come back soon and be measured for my new dress.

Tante Hohentahler put her arm around my shoulder as we walked toward the gate. "I used to think you should have been a boy, but I was quite wrong. I missed you when you went away, we all did, especially the general. Berthold adores you."

"You were fooling Frau Hanna," I said. "You can't make me believe Berthold is a double agent."

"But Frau Hanna believed it, and she will tell the afternoon ladies every word I told her. This will not only cover his tracks, but get the Gestapo off our backs. They have come to the Landsitz to interrogate us. We might have been arrested. Now we will be safe, too." She lowered her voice and looked around. The garden was empty. "It's your grandmother's idea. We wouldn't bother coming all the way out here just for hats." She let go of my arm and her hands became restless, fingering her new white cap, pulling blossoms off a quince bush. We came to the silver birch from my crystal garden.

"Are you an O5?" I asked. She did not answer, and scattered the red petals. "How about Grandmama?"

"Shhh, do you want to have us all killed?"

"No, I want to help."

"You help by staying out of it and never mentioning it again. One word would be enough to have us wiped out. Here we have Communists, Socialists, Catholics, Monarchists. One group doesn't know what the other is doing. Only Catholics and Monarchists get along, because we want an independent Austria. The vital leaders were rounded up before the war. In other occupied countries, young men are part of the resistance; ours are all away, and we don't even have a foreign language to protect us."

"There is the language of intrigue at Café Weisner."

She grabbed my arm. "You must stay out of it. Never talk to anyone." She looked around again. We were alone but not unobserved. On top of the gate, on the crest of Falkenburg, sat the cat—all puffed up, fluffy, and round-eyed, transformed into a black owl. "We are of the same family tree. A branch or two might be lost, but we must not be cut down. You must not get yourself and us into trouble. Just keeping your grandmother company and being seen with her and your father is good and helpful. No one would suspect you." We walked out together and I banged the gate shut. The cat did not leave its post. "You know where you belong, and you can be proud of that."

I smiled my O₅ smile. The glorious sense of danger as part of the underground transformed me, as ice had once turned to crystal the furthest twig of a certain young tree.

23

Dragon's Kiss

DRAGONS OF BLACK CLOUD unfurled to bursts of thunder and shrieks of hell. The Hanna Roth prophecy had turned around on us. Flaming wings fanned a morass of sky. "Ach, how horrible. How beautiful," I cried and jumped up and down holding onto the handlebar of my bicycle. There is a bit of a Nero in all of us.

I had been drawing an O5 on the board wall of a shoemaker's hut when the *Flieger* alarm began. Instead of seeking shelter, I had pushed to the top of Meinert Hill. I fancied myself a female knight in a white knitted dress which had shrunk into a tunic. Vienna lay at my feet. Towers, rows of houses, lines of trees, palaces and parks, church steeples: forsaken city of dreams.

A plane fell from the sky: a winged creature aflame, with a tail of smoke, tumbling down, swallowed by the gray Danube, sinking to the realm of silence, where the King of the Danube held court among giant carps and small water nymphs.

Bombs struck the river. Just below the hill a dog howled and flak guns went *ratatata*. I leaped into the saddle and took off like a bedeviled Joan of Arc, downhill toward something green-and brown-spotted. But stopped too late and smacked into the truck. Someone picked me up.

"*Verfluchtes Mädel!* Can't you look out? We're loaded with ammunition for the flak." A Luftwaffe man, young, in a fury, with eyes of steel. "Goddamn you! What's the matter, are you blind and deaf?" Without warning he grabbed me, pressed his hard, dry mouth against my lips. I felt his teeth; his hot tongue unfurled and pushed into my mouth. I choked, struggled, bit, kicked. Then I was free and on my bicycle.

They laughed behind my back. "Better learn while there's still time," he yelled after me.

The truck drove toward town. I headed the other way. Close to the Meinert chapel, explosions shook the ground. I fell again. The truck had blown up. I knew it as I lay there. My assailant had been blown to hell. My lips scorched by my first and loveless kiss, I said, "I hate him." Then, as I fled into the chapel: "God forgive."

Out of habit I went to get a candle. My hand shook, and I had trouble lighting it. I made the sign of the cross and kneeled. Never had I come here alone. I could not pray. My head felt as though it might explode, and covering my ears increased the roar and brought on a dizziness. My scraped knees and my arm burned. I jumped up, ran back to the holy water, and washed my face and mouth in a fury. Nothing could wash away the degradation of the dragon's kiss. Never again would anyone touch me like that. I sank into the prayer bench in a huddle of confusion. The assault on Vienna became linked with my personal insult.

Someone had left a bouquet of yellow roses in a potbellied jug at the altar; they drooped, and some petals had fallen. Roses Mother loved, among the old images of unholy and holy suffering. The Madonna was too pink, the Jesus heart too red. An acrid smell of new paint took me back to the gardener's cottage: the easel, the inevitable unfinished self-portrait beside a fragment of mirror. A fierce purple face depicting Fritz Janicek listening to the radio. And the Führer's voice shouting, threatening his enemies, accompanied by the snap of a trap, the squeak of a field mouse at the end of a maze. The smell of paint had remained the smell of death.

Dragons whirred through my mind, turning into blue-eyed men. Heavenly powers had failed me. I gathered myself with all my might and tried staring into the candle to put myself into a trance: "Appear, appear . . . Rudolf Hess, Eli, Prince Arnold, Eugene Romberg, Berthold, Berthold—come!"

The door creaked and my body went limp, not in a trance but in terror. My eyes stared back at me from the glazed jug. Something light stirred behind my reflection. I could not move my head; my neck had turned into a steel rod. Soft footsteps approached. My heart throbbed in my throat. "Berthold!" I yelled.

"This time I seem to be the intruder," said Fritz Janicek.

My supernatural power, in calling all my loves, had invoked the devil. I crossed myself, retreating to the stone relief of the slaughtered infants. Fritz Janicek had materialized near the holy-water font with a bouquet of yellow roses.

"To think I should have chosen this week to come to Vienna and this day to bring fresh flowers for her altar!" He seemed to have shrunk since he had destroyed Puppe. "My form of worship. I touch up the paint for her, no matter what happens." He walked around the old chapel slowly, gathering up fallen petals, then he took the drooping roses from the jug. As soon as he turned his back to fetch some water, I ran to the door.

"*Halt*, stop!" he shrieked, and barred my way. "You must not run away. You must stay and finish your prayer. She would want you to pray at this moment. Just like my mother. Go and kneel down!"

I had never been afraid of Fritz, and I refused to listen. He forgot his command and turned to arrange flowers. Filtered light fell onto his rouged cheeks and lips. He had adorned his own face as lavishly as the Madonna, the green Christ, and all the saints.

"What are you gaping at?" he hissed. "Kneel!"

"You shot the doll to pieces."

"Then she knows, she knows. That witch told her!" He had held his black uniform cap under his arm. Now it dropped to the floor, and he didn't bother to pick it up. He was wild with delight.

"Wait till Mother hears about the letter you sent to Frau Hanna and how you fooled her with that painting at Falkenburg and forged the family tree. Mother will never forgive you."

He whipped a dagger from his uniform belt and brandished it so wildly I did not know whether he would stab himself, sacrifice me, or throw it like a dart into the bleeding, flaming Jesus heart. "I should kill that freak, that murderess!" he screeched in a hoarse, high-pitched voice. "No one has to fool that dwarf. She deceives herself and everyone else every day, and that includes mein Führer." He brought the dagger down on the stems of the fresh roses and notched them with vicious stabs. Then he stuck them into water with the care of a gardener.

"She is clairvoyant," I said. "She warned Adolf Hitler to save his life."

He glared at me, cross-eyed in his fury, cursing me in Latin. "To think she was allowed to have my boys killed! A dwarf, a cheap sideshow comedienne. Where was her vision, na? She planned it, she loved it, that murderess."

I could not forget the men in Resi's clothes, singing "Good Comrade" with patriotic passion. "I am truly sorry," I said.

"Sorry! I hope that house was struck by a hundred bombs and she is burning up in it right now. Hahaha, hahahaha!" Hatred turned his jagged profile with painted cheeks and lips into a heathen mask. He had made himself as garish as the old carved figures of saints. There was no end to his talent for destroying what he embellished. Turning Hanna Roth into Johanna von Falkenburg had been a master stroke. He had ruined her image, but did not know how much harm he had done—especially to Mama —or he would have been pleased, not angry.

On one knee before the altar, arranging fresh roses, he was saying, "Perfect, perfect, rare. So hard to find!" Transformed by pleasure, he leaned over to smell. He kissed a flower and trembled. The half-open rose seemed to incline toward the man as to the sun. I was forgotten. I could have run, but I stayed to behold the most unlikely and tender act of love. He kissed the rose again, holding the stem gently. Caressing the center with his tongue, he penetrated. Man and flower turned to stone. His shudder ran down my back. He moaned, released the flower, and it stood fresh, as though it had been touched by a butterfly. "Ah, holy one, terrible one, my red-haired goddess, I worship you and I hate you with all my heart."

His devotions were interrupted by the sound of an ambulance racing along the road. "Get out of the chapel," I said in Mother's nasal tone of voice.

To my surprise, he picked up his hat and the dead flowers and went to the door. "Tell her, tell her, there are yellow roses at her altar. Tell her all about Fritz."

❈   ❈   ❈

"Tell me about Vienna," Mother asked on the morning after Father and I arrived at the farm. We were alone, sitting in the sun, but I could not talk about Fritz; I never told anyone. Had I tried to describe to her the man kissing a rose, she would have thought I had dreamed it all up. I could not even make her see the Sleeping Janicek, that jagged white mask of his profile up among the snow-covered crags of the Dachstein mountains.

"How was it?"

"Exciting," I said.

"Exciting?" Wide-eyed and eager for excitement, she stared down into the valley and then up the slope to where Father had reached the edge of the woods on his skis. He had told me to keep her company while he went off—to unwind, as he put it. "It's hardly exciting for your father in Vienna. The worry of hiding our car and as many trucks as possible. On top of everything, he has had to move Vlado's wife and her brood into our house."

"At least it won't be requisitioned for bombed-out families."

"And he will have someone to keep house for him and cook. Frau Boschke is too old, and she talks too much. I just hope the children are not going to annoy him."

Nadica in my room and at Mother's piano belonged to another world. Mother wanted me to speak. I could not say anything. It was too hot for her delicate skin, and she sat in the shade of the balcony. You could hear the crackling and whispering of the spring thaw under the crust of crunchy snow. A delicious clean chill, even in the sun, made me tingle with pleasure, and I could not wait to get onto my skis for a downhill run.

"Would you go in, Reyna, and tell Agnes to turn the radio down? Frau Schwester is a little deaf, and it's much too loud."

"But there's no one around."

"Someone could be hiding in the stable. People have been shot or locked up for listening to foreign stations. You don't have to look shocked. I have had a few visitors recently. I know about the war and what is going on."

I stayed in the pantry long enough to hear about the German defeat in Odessa. When I came out, Mother was standing up on her crutches, peering up the hill. "I just saw a girl on skis, dressed in leather breeches, the way your father liked to see you when you were little. She even looks like you. He'll be surprised if she catches up with him on the other side of the woods. Is there anyone like that in the village?"

I could only shake my head. I hated my father.

"Well, there are all kinds of refugees from the cities up here and down in Schladming. How I wish your grandmother would have come away with you! Since she has those bombed-out nuns staying at the little palace, she could easily leave Vienna for a while."

I had dreamed of the countess turning to stone on the bench overlooking Schönbrunn park. I could not move her. "She won't leave."

"Is she terribly upset?"

"She doesn't seem to be. She draws during raids."

"Horses?"

"Wild horses." Stallions from her sketchbook had thundered through baroque clouds in my dream.

"Then she is upset," Mother said.

"I wanted to stay with her." I made a silent vow to take my stand with my grandmother at the little palace when the time came.

"I can understand that." Mother sounded so sad, I was glad when the *Waldhofer* son from the neighboring farm came dancing past us on his one leg with superb grace. He yodeled as he passed. Mother smiled and waved, but shadows of fatigue showed she had not slept well. The face looked small, the eyes huge.

During the night, Mother woke me up by hobbling on her crutches to the top of the stairs. She called, "Ferdl! Ferdl!" He did not come up. "Just an excuse. Your truck is well hidden in the haybarn. You just don't want to be with me!" I did not hear his response. It put her into a temper. She pounded back to her room, banged the door, locked it. I heard something drop, probably the crutches. "Liar, liar!" she yelled. I heard her sob.

After she had cried herself to sleep, I got up. Outside, a big dumpling of a moon glazed treeless slopes, and lunar light carved out the indigo shape of the woods. I opened the window and sniffed the fragrance of moon on snow, enjoyed by night creatures. I felt sharp hunger pangs and would have crept down to the kitchen, but Father was asleep in the living room, snoring evenly on the padded bench beside the tiled stove.

I had never liked it when my parents had kissed and fondled

each other in front of me, but now I worried. Especially when Father went off into the village that morning right after breakfast and would not let me come. I watched him strap on his skis.

"Are you meeting someone?"

"Jawohl," he said.

I tried to divert Mother with the story of Hanna Roth and Frau Traude while he skied away from us. He broke the rules: stood up straight, never gathered too much speed, and never fell. I told her how they had loaded their car with hatboxes on top, the cat in the back window, and a convoy of Nazi ladies following in their cars. People had come rushing out of their houses to watch; some waved as if it were a parade, others were angry. There was no fuel and most vehicles had long ago been requisitioned. Mother kept watching as Father disappeared.

"They all go to Salzburg, closer to their Führer, away from the bombing." She did not hear me.

I told her I was going to look for Stopperl and followed Father. The church bells were ringing. It was some kind of Nazi holiday. There was no school that day in the village. Pfarrer Kronz had gone to visit a priest in the valley. He wanted me to be free like the other children and enjoy my father's visit. I followed Father like a spy. My skills of investigation, however, were hardly put to any test. As soon as I met up with Stopperl, she told me that Father was at the Gasthaus with a doctor, a German, who had come away from the bombing and was writing a book.

Father introduced the famous man to me as Herr Dozent when he brought him to the farm. I remember him as a fish in human form. "The Fräulein daughter is well developed. Thirteen, I understand?" When he was taken upstairs to examine Mother, he gasped and panted, muttered "Enchanted, honored," and undid his shirt button. The room was unheated, warmed by the sun shining onto the bed where Mother sat in a transparent green robe, tearing at her long hair with brush and comb. She didn't need the mantle of flaming red hair to keep her warm; she was in a hot fury.

"I don't know why my husband has troubled you, Doctor. I'm quite well, no matter what they say in the village. I have been injured by a fall from a horse and I can't walk and I am a crazy Falkenburg."

The Dozent kept Frau Schwester in the room during the examination. Father waited downstairs. After about ten minutes, the big pike came down and accepted a glass of Enzian schnapps, a gentian brandy. I had foreseen this and had locked myself into the toilet.

"I see no sign of hereditary dwarfism. The limbs are very long. Only the hips are narrow, but this is not uncommon at all in women of her class. Difficulty when it comes to delivering an infant is not confined to dwarfs."

Father had laughed at Johanna von Falkenburg and agreed with me it was an elaborate hoax. He had teased my grandmother when she admitted Falkenburgs had often been small. Now he had this doctor look at my mother, and perhaps glance at me, for signs of dwarfism. The obsessions with race had affected even my clever father. The emperor Meinert, proud to have married a Falkenburg Dornbach, was now looking for "bad blood" like any little Nazi. He needed a good reason for putting Mother and me aside so he could devote himself to the intruder.

I followed the Dozent on skis and cut him off at the wayside shrine with a christie. We were standing above the village. The houses had balconies, and the shingles on the roof were patterned with rocks. Before long, flowerboxes with geraniums would appear. Smoke was rising from chimneys. He took in the scene, then he gave me the fish-eye. "You have a question, mein Fräulein?"

"Will my mother walk again?"

His cold eyes appraised me from my ski trousers to the top of my curls, as though he were taking measurements. "My field is genetics."

"What's that?"

He pointed at a few black-and-white cows at a farm. "See those animals? Small heads, short legs, long bodies. When properly bred, they will produce good, predictable calves. Well, it's the same with us. There are inherent traits. Is that clear?" He was obviously used to delivering lectures, but he gasped. The thin air, he explained, bothered him. He did not feel well at such an altitude. I wished him to the bottom of the Danube. "Now, if you married a good German, tall, fair, like your parents . . ."

"I won't give birth to a dwarf." My departure did not give evidence of breeding. I took off and went down in full schuss. High above me war planes flew in formation over the mountains: enemy fliers—English, American, or free French—with bombs for Vienna. Men with eyes of steel, hard mouths, dragon's tongues. Our swollen mountain stream went rushing under the bridge and gushed into a basin as a small waterfall. During the summer, Stopperl and I used it as a *Sprudel* bath; splashing about, we had learned to swim in the icy water.

Stopperl had reported that no one had been at the mine while I was away. I skied down. She was right: no sign of tracks in the soft snow. I took my skis off and climbed the gate; nothing had changed. I saw crates at the back. Just as I picked up my skis, I saw a man on a brown horse ride slowly uphill. Neither the horse nor the rider was young. He wore a brown suit with plus-fours and a cap, a costume tailors used to call *echt* English before the war. The man sat straight and stiff in the saddle, staring up to the farm. He did not see me, but I had a good look at the broad face with the dueling scar. All men who bore "student scars" looked the same to me. This man's was particularly ugly. His fight to defend honor or add injury to insult had left his right cheek split in half. I admired that.

Keeping well behind him, I followed. The brown nag was tied at the barn post. By the time I came around the corner, the stranger had Mama crushed against his imitation tweed, his mouth glued to hers. I was there in a second, swinging my ski poles.

"Let go, let go!" I yelled.

Mother appeared as untouched as the yellow rose in the chapel, quite untroubled. The man, bald as an egg without his cap, said, "Die Gnädigste sent for me."

I knew him by the hoarse whisper, the urgency of a man at a confessional. Years ago I had overheard him when he felt compelled to talk of a girl he had saved from a concentration camp, only to destroy her. "She preferred death to me." And Mother had invited this sinner.

The pantry radio was on, but not too loud. Agnes was singing in Hungarian in the kitchen. Suddenly the radio stopped talking. Father came running out. "How dare you!" He was about to strike the man.

Mother said, "No, Ferdl. I sent word to Schladming and invited him. He was waiting to see me when you arrived. Some of the men you brought to see me when the war began are now coming back to visit. I asked him to come, just as you invited that girl who looks like your daughter. And if he kisses me, who cares? At least he doesn't think I have the plague."

24

De Bello Gallico

ON JUNE 4, 1944, Anglo-American forces took Rome. On the sixth, the Allies invaded Normandy. A bomb went off under Hitler's conference table on the twentieth; he survived by a miracle. While all this was going on, Pfarrer Kronz made me study for my yearly exam, and I had to review *De Bello Gallico*. If anything could ever counteract the weeks in Vienna which had turned me from a fanciful dreamer into a self-styled conspirator, translating the pedantic accounts of dull victories and occupation, written in a dead language by boring old Caesar, would certainly do it.

De Bello Gallico lay on my lap. I sat on my balcony with my feet propped up, well hidden by blooming geraniums. We had lived through weeks of dank, eerie weather when Resi arrived unannounced from Berchtesgaden. She no sooner sat down to tell us how she had sung for the Führer himself and cheered him up when the sun came out. "When angels travel, the sun laughs," she said, and made herself at home.

After lunch Frau Schwester had washed Mother and Resi's hair in rainwater. Now they sat in the yard below, letting it dry in the sun. Mother, reclining in a deck chair, let her blazing mane hang down to the alpine green grass. Resi lolled on a blanket, sipping buttermilk. Flowers dotted the slope. I have never forgotten that moment, the stifled excitement in their voices, the talk of love and men. All that remains of Latin is my hatred of *De Bello Gallico*.

"You could call it an obsession," Resi was saying. "Less than

love—perhaps more. I really don't know. I have been to the Berghof often enough to know how to get along, have some fun, and
look out for myself. How could this happen to me? We had not
exchanged a single word, not even after I had sung. It was early
in the morning. There was an alarm. Adolf Hitler himself ordered
me down to the shelter. Now I'm beginning to wonder whether
he didn't arrange it all. No one else was called to the *Bunker*.
They all stayed in their rooms. But then, they'd drunk so much.
What with toasts to the new bomb—and there was a toast for
Hanna. Did you know that she sent Hitler a carrier pigeon with
a note before the invasion? 'Watch Normandy.' He keeps it in
his pocket."

"What happened in the shelter?" Mother asked.

Resi took her time, sipped her buttermilk. I could not hear
what she was saying until she got excited. "Not handsome, no
charm, no feelings, but such strategy."

"I understand," Mother said. "Something strange like that happened to me too. The man is despicable."

"You!" Resi sat up and clapped her hands.

"I would never have allowed that man near me if Ferdl hadn't
brought a girl and kept her in the village."

"I know about her," Resi said with disdain. "Doesn't mean much.
He really cares only for you and Reyna. I should know!"

"I had other reasons for being mad at him. So I sent for that
man. The scoundrel grabbed me. Never has anyone kissed me like
that. A horrible man, but if he had come back . . ."

"I would have gone to the end of the world with my monster,"
Resi said.

They whispered. Then Resi ran inside and came back with a
fox fur, a short, hooded jacket: loot from Hitler's Berghof, a present for Mother. She showed her the Paris label. Later she rubbed
Mother's legs with skin tonic, tickled her feet. "If you can move
your toes, you can walk," she said.

After supper, Mother accompanied Resi on the harpsichord.
Pfarrer Kronz was with us. "Do you really have to go back to
Vienna tomorrow?" Mother asked her.

"I must," Resi said. "I'll be moving to Salzburg soon."

I cornered her and asked her to take me back to Vienna. I
wanted to stay with Grandmama. She smiled and said she was

so glad I was safe, and my place was with my mother.

My life seemed very dull after she went away. I had gone to Vienna with fantasies of love and returned to the farm with fantasies of Valhalla that were hard to sustain. I would stare down into the valley, ready to die as a knight, an Austrian. I needed a comrade under my command. Late in August, after the Allies had taken Paris, I bribed Stopperl with a smoked sausage.

"You swear to be an O5?" We were leaning against the Alm hut. Frau Schmiedl, Stopperl's mother, was churning butter.

Stopperl took a good bite from the sausage. "All right." She squinted up at me. Her face had acquired a wizened look beyond her years; she had not grown much. "If Hitler is caught and put on that island, will there be chocolate, raisins, and all the sausage you want?"

"Certainly."

"Then I'll help." The barrel kept turning inside the hut. We were waiting for a piece of black bread with fresh butter. We were always hungry. "Will all the boys come back?"

"The ones that are not dead," I said.

"The dead ones are back. I can hear them at night. They howl in the old mine."

"There's nobody down there. You said so yourself. If it's anyone, it's some drunken Nazi."

We proceeded to chalk O5 signs onto slabs of rock on the Alm and down at the entrance to the mine, and we used chalk coal on the back of the bowling alley. Rain must have washed some of the letters away. On her last day on the Alm, Stopperl helped me to carry and roll heavy rocks, to form a huge O5 on the highest meadow. It was cold and dark. While we worked it started to snow, and before we had finished the rocks were covered over.

"I want to go back to Vienna," I said. "I don't want to study all winter when I should be with my grandmother, helping to stop the war." I whispered to my comrade a secret plan. We would use Resi to lure Adolf Hitler into a trap.

"And I want to help, too. I'm coming with you," Stopperl said.

"I don't want to be buried in the snow up here," I said, imitating Mother.

Stopperl looked impressed. Snow came down in heavy flakes.

She shivered in one of my old dresses and crossed herself. "Snow in August, shrouds in March," she said.

*   *   *

After the Russians took Budapest and their tanks rolled toward Austria, the radio kept playing Wagner's *Götterdämmerung*. Nazis executed anyone suspected of resistance. During that time Pfarrer Kronz forced me to study and gave me assignments when he went down to the valley. He was gone a great deal. Soon after my birthday, he caught me drawing a huge O5 in the soft snow. His blue eyes dark with anger, he erased the sign with his skis. "*Kind*, child, you don't know what you're doing. They have been known to round up an entire village for just that. They're running scared, and this makes them more reckless than ever. Now that the end is near, the godless ones want to take us down with them. Those who are trying to prevent useless bloodshed are hindered by your kind of childish prank."

He had never railed at me like that. "Are you an O5?" I asked. "Is that why you go down to the valley so much?"

"I am for God and I love Austria." He put his arm around me and pointed at the thick folds of snow at the foot of the Dachstein. "We must pray. Just look up there, that mass of wet snow. Unless the temperature drops, it might all come down on us."

Much of my life had been spent at the foot of the mountains, and each time there was avalanche danger we kept the dogs in. Even a bark could set one off. "The snow comes down further south," I said. "Never here."

I tried to question him about the resistance movement as we walked side by side, making new tracks, but he spoke of our duty as Christians. At the shrine he stopped for a moment of meditation. What good was tearful prayer, waiting? The faded fresco, the *Mater dolorosa*, faced the valley. Eyes stared in terror from the pale face. "Why on earth didn't Mary do something to get Jesus away, like the Jews who left Austria?"

"The Son of God could not run away from his assailants."

"He knew his mother would be in misery. He could have performed a miracle to save himself for her and his friends, instead of having himself crucified, making everybody feel guilty for hundreds and thousands of years."

"We all have to die. And if our death can help others to live a more worthy life, we are blessed. The death of Jesus was sanctified."

I could well contemplate my own heroic end without considering anyone, because death was something that happened to others. At the age of fourteen I felt immortal. A chill of doubt came over me. "You are not going to be a martyr?"

He laughed like a boy. "I'm a country priest and a teacher. God's worker, not a saint."

He blessed me, and I watched him ski down toward his little house at the edge of the village. The air felt moist. A cock crowed. I suddenly remembered a big O5 I had drawn on the other side of the woods. My skis hissed like angry snakes as I traversed uphill. I obeyed my spiritual father, but I was tired of being a child, a schoolgirl. I was growing; a knitted cuff had had to be added to my ski trousers. My stomach always growled with hunger.

Snow had fallen during the night, and footprints of small rodents and hares crisscrossed tracks I made earlier in the day. The eighty-year-old Herr Förster, a mountain spirit with a white beard, was having a hard time guarding the woods from hungry poachers.

I came out above the Waldhof and quickly erased my O5. The sign Stopperl and I had made with rocks lay under twenty feet or more of snow; the Alm hut was buried. Down below, at the Waldhof, snow melted during the day and turned to ice at night. Smoke rose from the chimney in a straight line, and the Waldhoferin was hanging sheets and bright aprons out on the balcony. The farmer's wife saw me, yodeled, and waved. Then she came out in the yard and waved a letter. I skied down.

A small boy had brought the letter addressed to my mother. Sepp, the Waldhoferin's son, had skied down into the valley and the Walhauser, her husband, had gone down with our horse, Heini, to pick him up. "With that old horse they'll be slow getting back." Everything about this woman was round. Her dark hair sat on top of her head in a tight ball. I did not like her last remark. Old horses were slaughtered and eaten. The look in her button eyes told me that we had better get Heini back to the meadow farm.

I hurried home and found Mother in her wheelchair by the window. She looked lovely in a drab green skirt made from a blanket and a black quilted jacket, fitted in dirndl style to keep her warm. I was struck by her restiveness. A faraway look in her eyes told me she hardly listened while I talked of the horse. I took the letter from my pocket.

"Give it to me!" She strained forward, eager and long-necked as a goose. As she snatched it from me, Dostoevski's *The Idiot* fell from her lap. She ate little, gave me most of her food, and had gone on a steady diet of Dostoevski. Just as the Russians had invaded Austria, she had allowed her very soul to be invaded by the Russian author. I believe she sought answers in novels that merely raised questions and reflected the inner torment she tried to suppress. "Purple ink!" she cried out.

"Like the notes you got after Puppe was lost."

She did not hear me and burst into the wild gurgling laughter of her younger days in Vienna. "Listen, listen:

"To you, oh Juno
Scorched by scorn
Of your unearthly eyes
I make my sacrificial offering
And lay my tribute
In the vale of darkness
At your marble feet
To you, oh Juno!"

She shook with laughter, and tears ran down her cheeks.

I took the letter and recited the poem, hand on heart. By the time I had read it twice and knew it by heart, she had stopped laughing. The Falkenburg frown appeared between her eyebrows.

"I think Fritz Janicek wrote this and all the notes you used to get about the doll." I could not get her to respond, and words came tumbling out of my mouth. The anonymous letter to Hanna Roth, my trip to Falkenburg, the dwarf in armor—I told her everything, and she remained amazingly unimpressed.

"Hanna never got over playing in the dolls' room at the palace. She knows how to look out for herself, and you can't blame her. When she knew that Hitler was taking over Austria, she became an Aryan. It suits her to be a Falkenburg now that the Nazis are finished. She could have written that letter herself, arranged it all."

"Only Fritz could write the Juno poem, and it's the same hand-writing and the same ink. He wants you to know it's his."

She became thoughtful, took the poem back from me, and studied it. "You might be right. 'Offering' can only mean he has brought me the doll."

"He shot her to pieces," I said.

"You were behind the avalanche wall. It could have been any redheaded doll. Hanna would never let anything happen to Puppe."

"I know it was Puppe," I said.

" 'Vale of darkness . . .' He has the doll in that mine." She pushed herself toward the door, then back to the window. She picked up her field glasses. "Have a look. The marks of snow chains are on the mine road. He must be waiting down there, the rogue."

I told her of my meeting with Fritz Janicek at the chapel, but she had wheeled herself to a dark spotted mirror and was study-ing her smiling, radiant face. "Ever since Reserl was here I've felt I would walk again. Do you know what it would mean if I got the doll back when everything else seems so hopeless? You must take me down in the sled chair."

I would not have listened to her entreaties if she had not taken me by surprise. All at once she grabbed hold of a shelf and raised herself from the chair. For the first time in seven years she stood up without help. I rushed to her, for she was trembling. "No more marble feet. No more marble feet," she said through clenched teeth. When she heard Agnes and Frau Schwester, she let her-self sink back into her chair. "What will they do if I get Puppe back and walk again? You are growing up. They won't have you anymore, but they could always fuss over me, poor old things."

After our meager lunch of potato soup and a dessert of stewed apples, Frau Schwester and Agnes went to do the dishes and listen to the radio. "Come on, let's go out," Mother whispered. "They'll think nothing of it on such a lovely day."

I liked the conspiracy, and Mother's happiness was infectious. I jumped on the rung of the sled chair and we took off. She steered with the rope and I used my foot as a brake. She turned her head, all smiles, rosy, with sparkling eyes, and cried, "Faster, faster!" At the bend of the road we almost toppled. "Isn't it fun, isn't it great?" Strands of hair curled around her face. She pointed at the sky like a young child. "Look, look—a falcon."

Stopperl had taught me to look out for bad omens. The falcon from the crest of Falkenburg had dangled Puppe in my childhood dream. "I want to go back. Fritz might be drunk. He paints his face and he's crazy."

"I don't care. I want to go on to the mine. You've got to take me."

I reminded her of my English and geography lessons at three in the afternoon. She said we would be back in half an hour and this would give me plenty of time. She closed her eyes against the sun. "Push me, Herzerl, come on."

When we heard the air-raid alarm, she covered her ears. "It's faster to go to the mine, than back up the hill. Besides, the chances are they won't come this way at all."

I pushed as hard as I could. We were only twenty feet from the mine when the squadron thundered through the valley, shattering the sunny peace of spring; roaring and clattering, they circled over the old churches of Schladming, then up over the mountain road, the hay barns half-buried in snow, a small farm, and the snow-covered fields of the meadow farm.

"Hurry, hurry!" Mother cried out. "Leave me at the wall. Run! Take shelter!"

The squadron leader circled below the mountain peak, the Sleeping Janicek. Then the bombs dropped. I shoved Mother toward the gate. It yielded. At the first explosion she threw herself forward. An almighty blast drove us into the cave and sent me tumbling onto a crate. The weight of the world held me down. Then the monstrous white lips above the village opened and spewed snow, rocks, trees, a door, loose logs, a pig. Everything turned white; the meadow farm faded like an old photograph. The village vanished.

"Mama, Mama!" I yelled. "What happened, what happened to it all? Mama! Mama!"

White as the snow queen, she came staggering toward me. We clung together, and the empty sled chair flew past us and crashed into the rock wall. She shook and her teeth chattered as her lips shaped the word: *avalanche*. A wig of snow sat on her braids. She pointed at the entrance to the mine. Her hand looked green in the eerie light. We watched the snow pile up, listened to the gushing like the sound of a gigantic waterfall. "How will we get out?" she asked.

"You're standing up. You can walk—you can walk! The bombs started the avalanche, but we're all right."

Mother gripped my arm, and her hand felt like ice. "Wait, I hear someone. Professor Janicek, is that you? Do you have my doll? Where are you?"

It thundered, and we were thrown against a truck. Through it all, as I clung to the side of the truck, I heard someone moan. Mother was trying to pull herself up into the back. I held onto her. "Let go," she yelled. "If I fall in I might crush Puppe."

"Wait, just wait. You can walk again; forget the stupid doll."

The mountain god had calmed down, but not my mother. I kissed her, pleaded. She kept on shouting for the doll. The miracle had happened; she had found the power to walk. Now she had lost all reason. As she struggled away from me, pulling herself up, she wiped the snow off the side of the truck. "Meinert Beer and Wine," I read in the half-dark.

"The doll. Puppe, where is Puppe?" Mother yelled.

Then I heard it. "Dolls, dolls . . ." echoed a man's voice.

"Stay back," I said. "It's a foreigner."

"Janicek, Janicek, who have you brought here to watch me die?" the weak voice moaned.

Father had kept flashlights and a first-aid kit with brandy in every truck. I climbed into the cabin, fumbled in the dark, and there they were, untouched. I even found a package of dry biscuits. Mother's clamor bounced back from the rock wall and brought snow down from the top of the rock tunnel. I found her standing at the back of the truck. A man lay in the corner, and his stench held me back. In the dim light from the weak flashlight battery I saw a black beard. He was chained down and in rags.

He opened his mouth like a hungry bird. "Water . . . water."

I went to him and fed him snow, put brandy into the bottle cap and held it for him to let him sip. He took a few crumbs of biscuits. "The key, the key. In the corner."

After I had unlocked his chains he raised a thin claw of a hand, opened it as though he had something to offer, something to give. I knew that hand at once.

"Eugene Romberg, Uncle Eugene!" I kissed him and drew back,

overcome by the putrid odor of his body. He was smiling. Carefully, I raised his head and upper body. Bruises and sores covered his neck. He was hot with fever. I did not know I was weeping until I tasted my tears. My hand shook and I spilled brandy.

Hours seemed to pass before he opened his eyes. He stared past me at Mother, who had come to kneel beside him. "Holy Madonna. You have come to save me in my degradation." His eyes never left her face.

She sat back on her heels pouting. *"Pfui,"* she said. *"Ugh."*

I shone my light on her face. Her eyes were moving from side to side. Fritz had not brought Puppe. Instead, he had left her a dirty, sick man. She felt disgust, and as angry as I had been when the cat had dropped a dead bird at my feet.

25

Saintly Sinner

EUGENE ROMBERG HEARD Mother's voice, not her disgust. She took the dim light from me to search the truck for the old doll. Her face, lit from below, glorified by shadows, appeared to him disembodied, a vision of deliverance. "Angel, angel," he said.

As for me, a sip or two of brandy and I was ready to explore the cave. Above piled-up snow and chunks of ice at the mouth of the grotto I saw a ribbon of deep-blue sky. I went to look for a shovel and found the old mine office, a rock chamber enclosed by planks. An acrid smell of paint took me back to the gardener's cottage. I was not surprised to find an easel with a mud-colored Janicek self-portrait in one corner. Facing it on the board wall hung the likeness of the Wicked Angel Fritz had painted on the Semmering. The room was equipped with cots, blankets, and quilts. I found an oil lamp, an alcohol stove, canned meat, wine, schnapps, stale bread, and coffee. Radio and electrical equipment sat on a table in the right corner.

We could survive there for a week or two. I went to cover Eugene Romberg with a quilt. His eyes opened. "Elijah, Elijah," he said. He had come to resemble Titian's haunted prophet with the ragged beard. I led Mother to a cot, moved mine next to hers to keep warm. Then I went to sleep.

When I woke up and heard voices, I thought I was dreaming. Men entered with shovels, ice picks, and lanterns, casting gigantic shadows onto the snow-covered rock wall: the Waldhofer; Sepp's friend Johan, who had lost fingers in the war; Widegger, an old mountain guide with bushy eyebrows and the face of a mummy;

brownshirts in ski boots, who were strangers. I ran to thank the men. They backed away. Had they come to look for treasures and found us? At first I could not understand the reproach in their eyes. Somehow they blamed us, the city folks, for being safe inside the mine while their own kin lay buried under the avalanche.

The SA men walked around the truck, talking in undertones. "Meinert Wine and Beer," I heard them say.

"My father's truck was requisitioned," I said.

They examined the fuel tank and came across the National Socialist Art Recovery sign. "What the devil is that?"

I tried to explain, but they had raised their lanterns and found Eugene Romberg. "Who's that? God-awful stink of dung and schnapps!"

"Do you know that man, Gnädige?" asked the Waldhofer.

"Of course not." Mother wrinkled her pretty nose. "He smells awful. A sick man." She regarded unhealthy people with distrust.

"What's going on here? I thought die Frau was an invalid. She's standing up—." One of the brownshirts, who looked like an old fox, held up his lamp. "Ahhh, look at that!"

While they stood around, my mother and the Waldhofer explained to the strangers who she was; I climbed onto the truck to watch over Eugene Romberg. The odor of his body, the brandy I had spilled, and the smoke from the lamps made me ill.

"Come here," called one of the men in a deep voice. *Here, here* reverberated from the mine shaft. "Radio equipment. A spy nest"—*Nest, nest,* went the echo.

The SA regarded us with suspicion. "The radio and pictures belong to Fritz Janicek," I said.

"The Fräulein's right," said the Waldhofer. "That Janicek was locked up for a while, accused of stealing paintings from the museums. It turned out he took the pictures to store them away for some important man."

They came back and surrounded the truck, enclosing Mother.

"Herr Janicek used to work for us a long time ago," she said. "He stole my doll. A family heirloom. He lured us down here, promised to give her back."

"*Zum Teufel!*" yelled the old guide, swinging his ice pick. "What do you think this is Frau! Dolls, heirlooms—half the village folks are dead and buried by an avalanche!"

"American swine unloaded their bombs on the Dachstein and brought the mountain down on us."

The Waldhofer jumped up on the truck and took my arm. "Your Hof stands free. Gott be thanked. We're all right, too. All those who ran to the church when the Pfarrer rang the bell were saved. He was in there when the bombing started." The church stood protected by houses on the hill and avalanche walls.

"How about Stopperl and the Sennerin?"

The Waldhofer looked at me with the shy, kind eyes I liked in his son. "I wouldn't know. Some skied down to town."

"Angel, angels' voices," Eugene Romberg murmured. Stopperl would have taken this as an omen. My heart sank.

"You, Fräulein. Do you know this stinking drunk?" asked the foxy old SA.

"I don't know this man," I said in good faith. For who had ever really known Eugene Romberg?

He spoke of angels as they cursed and loaded him onto a stretcher; he looked up at the stars before he lost consciousness. It was a clear night. We progressed slowly. No one spoke as we climbed through the snow on the narrow path the men had dug. It was like a funeral procession. Never had the farm on the hill looked more beautiful. The old apple tree, usually protected by the house and barn, stood so deep in snow it looked like a shrub.

"Some have all the luck," said a bitter voice behind me.

"Perhaps it's more than just luck. Someone could have signaled those hell-birds." This was one of the brownshirts.

"Shut your trap," snarled the Waldhofer. "You know that's crazy. They just like to unload what's left over before they fly back."

I turned around and faced our accuser. "Do you think I'd want my friend Stopperl dead? Or any of the villagers?" I screamed into his stupid old face. The daggers in his eyes told me our rescue was more dangerous than being trapped.

The men dug a path through the courtyard. Agnes and Frau Schwester came out to help. I threw my arms around the women, gave myself up to kisses and tears, and warned them not to say a word when they recognized Eugene Romberg on the stretcher.

Krampus almost gave us away. Leaping through snow, the Pekingese came to greet us and jumped onto the stretcher. Yelping with joy, he licked the face and hand of the man who had fed him delicacies and made so much of him during winter walks before the war.

"What have we here?" grumbled the guide. "Do you feed a pet monkey while we starve?"

Agnes interrupted and said there was soup on the stove, would they care to come in? Most of the men refused. Mother wanted to give them money.

"What good is money now?" said a voice from the dark. "A full larder is more important."

The Waldhofer and Johann had some soup; then they, too, hurried away.

        *   *   *

Windows facing the mountains had been smashed. Agnes had to close the shutters. Frau Schwester, in her old, patched nurse's uniform, went to work. "Look what they've done to you, my beautiful clean Herr." She clacked her tongue. "What a job I have, cleaning you up in this cold place." I wished she wouldn't wash and perfume him so much and would keep him warm instead. I saw him shake with fever until the high, blue-painted bed trembled. He wore Father's striped pajamas and lay in the bed Father had used during his last visit. Eugene Romberg stared up to the ceiling, looking for the face he had seen in the cave. Mother never came near him.

All morning long, church bells rang and the bells of the two churches in Schladming answered. The dead had to be taken down into the valley for burial. Survivors dug them up. During Mass, shovels stood lined up beside skis. I prayed that Stopperl had skied down into the valley with her mother when the bombing began. I wanted to help dig out the village. Pfarrer Kronz stayed by my side when I went to work where Stopperl's house had been. I struck a dead man's arm wearing a gold watch. I never found out who he was. My teacher sent me home.

His own home lay under snow, so he stayed with us. In the evening he sat with Eugene Romberg. Mother wandered around, rummaging through drawers, lining up old dolls' hats I had never known she had with her. She grumbled like a spoiled child. "Where is everyone all the time? Agnes, Frau Schwester—what is going on? There's a box of old photos I want to find." Now she was able to walk again, she found herself ignored and neglected. "There! Look, Reyna!"

She held a photograph of Hanna Roth dressed as a coachman in a fancy little carriage drawn by goats. The Meisterin had her fixed smile. The face had been rounder then. She held a whip and wore a bowler hat. All around her sat solemn little girls in white, holding big solemn dolls dressed just like them. One of the Belvedere sphinxes sat above the path. "She was never poor, never rich, always a freak, and she knows how to amuse and get pleasure out of life. I'll bet she already has a Salon Roth in Salzburg, and no matter what happens she will come out on top and outlast anyone." Mother rearranged dolls' hats. "I think we have to leave this place. We could go to Salzburg. We must try to reach Father. If he knew I was walking, he would come. If Hanna moved to Salzburg, it must be safe there." She opened the shutter and leaned out in the sun. "Look, the snow is melting again. The road should clear if this keeps up."

I shuddered and walked away. She seemed to have no idea what lay under the snow. No one talked to her about bodies. She did not seem to give it a thought. "I don't know why we have to take a sick stranger into our house," I heard her say. "No one seems to have time for me."

❋   ❋   ❋

The man on the high bed was a stranger. An eternity of suffering lay between us. Where had he come from? What had happened to him? Had I been allowed to question him, he would not have heard me anyway. I peered through the half-open door. I wanted to go in, hold up my wrist, show Eugene Romberg that I was wearing the diamond-studded watch he had given me. I wanted him to know me.

A candle burned on the bed table. A simple wooden cross hung on the wall. I smelled incense. The bearded face propped on three pillows stared into space like the prophet Jeremiah. The mouth opened to make a prophecy, but there was not a sound. Pfarrer Kronz was giving Eugene Romberg the last rites. I did not know it. I was spying on death. Eugene Romberg closed his eyes and lifted his hand, casting a long-necked shadow on the white wall. An empty hand sustained a gesture of offering. Then his mouth closed, and he smiled his old apologetic smile. He had no more to give to me—to anyone on earth. His hand fell onto the quilt and lay open as he gave himself to God.

Never again would anyone slip a gold coin into my pocket, give me a ring with a ruby heart, a leather coat lined with fur, books, games, a diamond-studded watch. I realize now that he gave me those trinkets, as he called them, because Mother would have none of his bounty. Nevertheless, I had thrived on his constant admiration and encouragement. Now he had left me. A door had closed in my face.

Mother and I were not supposed to know what was going on. No one mentioned the man in the spare room, but most of the food during our meager evening meal ended up on my plate. I ate fast. During the night I felt sick. Eugene Romberg wandered around in my dream, dressed as the Arab in a white sheet.

In the morning I woke up and heard voices in the yard. I looked through the shutters. The body, wrapped in white sheets, lay strapped to a flat sled. Johann held the rope with the three fingers on his right hand, pulling the sled past the barn. I smelled bread baking. Mother was already playing the harpsichord, repeating a sad, sweet song over and over again. If she did not know who had died in our house, why did she play the Hebrew song Resi had practiced for her concert and never performed? To this song of ancient hope and never-ending sorrow, Sepp on his one leg and Johann danced the body down into the valley. Each of the mountain boys tried to take the more difficult terrain, and this gallant rivalry reminded me of Father with his only real friend, Eugene.

Light snow had fallen during the night, barely enough to blur the track left by the sled. I found myself humming the Hebrew song as I skied into the valley to send a telegram to Father. All at once I understood: Mother had played a requiem. Not selfishness, but some deep-rooted concern for me made her deny death and suffering in the Grimm's fairy-tale world of ours, just as she had left out the hungry giants who devoured little people when she used to read to me. She chose not to subject our threatened household to her grief. I remember her sitting on the bed with dolls' hats, holding the photograph of the dwarf in an attempt to draw me into the magic and fantasies we all needed to survive and to go on dreaming of the "happily ever after."

I threw myself into the downhill run, forgetting to keep low like Stopperl, a master at controlling speed. A rock got in my way. I rolled over in a perfect somersault, got up unhurt, and brushed the snow off Resi's fox fur. Stopperl had taught me to ski fast without falling. She believed in omens. Did my fall mean she was dead? I could not believe it. She had to be in Schladming.

Halfway down the hill I found the dead falcon, one wing buried in snow. Its feathers shimmered, and the golden eyes glinted like the glass eyes of a stuffed bird. I stroked the soft feathers under the sharp beak. The falcon had died with outspread wings; it had been circling above the woods just before the avalanche. I picked it up because it was beautiful. Stopperl would like to see it. I bent my knees, swooped over the icy slope of the lower hill, turned toward the gold-green willows at the cemetery, and crossed the bridge where our mountain stream runs into a creek and becomes a torrent.

I leaned my skis against the wrought-iron gate but carried the bird with me. The graveyard was empty. A man sang as he dug a grave; candles flickered. Snow had dusted wax roses, pine wreaths, and the makeshift crosses on new graves. The man saw me come toward him, jumped out of the pit, doffed his green hat. He had a large Austrian goiter and appraised me with pop eyes. "Heil Hitler." He saluted my fancy fur. In a coat like that, I had to be a Nazi.

"Heil," I responded—in case *he* was one.

"How can I serve, Gnädiges Fräulein?"

I hesitated, felt my throat constrict. "You know the Frau Schmiedl from the Alm and her girl?"

He leaned on his shovel, "Ja, ja."

"Have you buried them?"

He took a sheet of paper from his droopy leather pants. I kept the bird behind my back, waited and prayed.

"Not yet. Not on the list. But you can't tell until we get a thaw. They expect me to work like ten men. My helper has already ruined his back. When they kept bringing them down, the ground was soft. Last night it froze. Herr Gott, who do they think I am? When you can't even get a piece of meat." He picked up his spade. "Looking for anyone else?"

"The man from the meadow Hof."

"I should have known." Weariness vanished. "The nameless one?"

"The nameless."

"In the third row. Had my orders to leave it unmarked. Keep my mouth shut."

I thanked him and walked toward the new graves; he came along. His eyes never left my face as he talked about food he couldn't get, especially pork. Someone had broken into our larder the night before. Pfarrer Kronz had cornered the thieves and told them to get out, to shut up with their fantastic accusations. He refused to tell me what they had said, but I had heard my name.

"Place of honor. Right in the middle of the row." The man pointed at a high, snow-covered mound. "And plenty of room for visitors when the time comes . . ." He glared at me, and I began to wonder whether he was crazy. I knew I had to be careful, and kept shifting the dead falcon out of sight.

"So you say you don't know him. That's smart. Who would have believed he would come here to die? I've seen them come and seen them go up that mountain. Always in the dark. 'Watch that grave, Hirsl,' the police said. I need no pistol. The old spade is good enough."

I reached into my pocket like a real Meinert, smiled a false smile, and gave him a few bills with my one hand. Money didn't really mean much anymore, but I got rid of him.

"A *Dirndl* like you coming to the grave—I hope it happens to me when they put me under the ground. In the end it doesn't matter who you are." He went back to his digging; only his head and shoulders protruded from the pit. He accompanied the rhythm of his spade with a rather suggestive milking song, yodeling at each refrain. If Fritz Janicek had identified the dead man, the grave of a Jew would hardly have had a place of honor in this graveyard.

The raucous song and the sound of rushing water tormented me and tore at my happy memories of Uncle Eugene. He would have put his plump hand onto my shoulder: "Don't worry, mein

Kinderl. What would you like? What can I give you?" I secretly wore the watch he had given me. The glorious Dachstein towered above the meadow farm where he had died. He had known the luxury of giving, and in the extraordinary, the bounty of each day, he would always live. I had no flowers, no wreath or candle. Quickly I laid the falcon on the grave and ran.

Smoke rose from chimneys as I entered the town square, carrying my skis on my shoulders. War had come to our mountains, but Schladming remained untouched. Sturdy pink-faced women stood outside the bakery with bread stamps and baskets. They wore their winter dirndls with colored aprons and shawls, patiently waiting for fresh rolls, the end of war, the return of their men. Two women came down the church steps. I had to say "Grüss Gott" before I was recognized in my fancy coat. They whispered behind my back. I turned around and asked whether they had seen Stopperl. They shook their heads.

The Protestant church bell struck the half-hour, then the *Pfarr Kirche* bell, the Catholic church bell, in its high tower. Half past eleven. I should have gone to the post office before it closed at noon to send the telegram to Father: "Village destroyed by avalanche. Cannot remain here. Please come." Instead I wandered around looking for Stopperl's red woolen hat among children in the street and in the schoolyard. In one of the classrooms, children were repeating the words of "The Good Comrade" after a teacher. Boys my age were now armed to fight and die in Hitler's war. Stopperl would stay away from school if she possibly could.

Her mother sometimes helped out as a chambermaid at the Hotel Post. A military car stood in front of the hotel, just like last year. I crossed over. So certain was I that my Frog Prince had come, I did not notice how everyone in the square had turned to watch me. I went to the window. A man in a black uniform sat at the table. I dropped my skis, and they fell with a clatter. I ran into the dining room, pushing past the headwaiter and jostling the drink waiter.

"He's dead! He's dead!" I yelled at Fritz Janicek.

A fountain pen fell from his hand, and purple ink splattered over the white tablecloth. He had been writing, perhaps another poem for Mother. I was holding a ski pole. He grabbed it and drew me closer.

"She was there. She was there, wasn't she? They were in the mine together during the avalanche!"

"She didn't know him."

"You're lying. She must have known him."

Waiters closed in on me. Fritz waved them away with the tired gesture of an aged diva. His receding hair was tinted red and clashed with petunia-pink lips and cheeks.

"What a stroke of fate. If I had only waited. If I had seen them together." He studied me as though I were a beetle in the garden of his evil schemes. He was up to something. "He wanted to save the artworks and see her once more." I heard a false tone of reverence I could not understand. He hated Eugene Romberg. "She will not fall into enemy hands, nor will the Velasquezes, the Brueghels. Janicek will see to that!"

His melodrama entertained me as much as ever. I did not notice the gendarme until I was grabbed from behind. He was a small man with a large gray mustache and a red nose.

"Go easy," Fritz said. "This is precious bait. You must keep her locked up until I get back." He seemed to have forgotten that he himself had been accused of stealing artworks and had been put into jail. He picked up his pen and went back to his writing as I was led away.

"You don't have to hold onto me," I said to the gendarme. "I won't run away."

"I've got my orders."

"Are you going to lock me up?"

He said nothing.

Women with baskets, some of them leading toddlers by the hand, fell in behind me. Schoolchildren came running with bags strapped to their backs. The town idiot, Goldegger, related to the mayor and spared from Nazi "mercy death," could always be found among the children. Goldegger was a strong man and carried luggage for tourists in the summer. He liked to carry the drum he played on Sundays in the town band. Now he was beating it, shouting.

"Stop that, Goldegger, or I'll lock you up!" yelled my captor.

Children and a mangy dog, who all loved Goldegger, surrounded him and me.

"I forgot my skis at the hotel," I said, and turned to get away.

At the end of the small procession I saw a red hat: Stopperl, carrying my skis. I ran to her.

"Where have you been? I'm so glad. I'm so glad you're all right." I hugged her. She smelled pleasantly unwashed, of hay, woodsmoke, and cinnamon, and like a wild creature she shied away from being touched.

"I missed it all. *Mutter* and I were down here." She sounded disappointed, reproachful. "How did you catch him?"

"Let's go now. Let's move!" said the gendarme.

Stopperl stayed by my side, carrying my skis. I had the poles. "They all know about it," she whispered. Her red hat sat at a piratical angle; she blew a long, lank strand of hair from her face. "When they said you'd chained a man up in the mine, I knew you'd done it." She gave me an angry look. "You promised to let me in on it. To think he's been coming to your *Mutter* all the time and you never let on!"

"*Schluss*, enough of that whispering," said the gendarme. He waved some old people aside, and they too fell in behind me.

Did they all believe that I had caught Hitler? Catching Adolf had been one of Stopperl's favorite games this winter, along with running away from imaginary storm troopers, Russians, and mountain ghosts and chasing will-o'-the-wisps. Surely no one would believe her.

"You didn't talk?" I whispered.

"I told *Mutter*."

The Sennerin must have told the story at the hotel where she worked and at the tavern where she drank. The rumor no doubt spread within an hour. Children kept getting in front of me, leaning over and staring up into my face. I had come to understand the local dialect through Stopperl. Women behind me were talking of all the gold hidden in the mine and pictures worth billions—all of it for "her and him."

"Crazy about her all those years, and all he got out of it was bleeding lungs!" They referred to blood in the snow.

"Who would believe it? Hitler buried in Schladming . . ."

"Lived like a saint. Fat chance. Could have had his pick. But they say those with the lung disease . . ."

"And she'd sworn to stay in that wheelchair until he came."

"So they've done him in, the rich folk."

Millions of unloved women loved Hitler. He was to meet his end in a million guises.

A scuffle took place as women, children, the idiot with his drum, and even the dog pushed into the police station and filled the small square room. It could have been the living room of a farm, with wood-paneled walls and white, well-scrubbed floorboards. The police chief, knarled as an old tree, retreated behind his desk. The foxlike SA man from our rescue was with him. "Hands up, O5!" He pulled a revolver. "Back, back."

"Don't be daft," said the police chief. "Put that thing away."

"Mein Führer might be dead and murdered. We'll carry on!"

"Come off it!" the chief hissed through a space left by two missing front teeth. Goldegger was beating the drum again. "Out, raus. All of you, out, before someone gets shot."

Stopperl held her ground. "I've got her skis." She gave me a look of envy as she was pushed toward the door. "I drew some of the O5 signs, too," she yelled, and was ignored.

Through the open door I saw Fritz Janicek driving off. The SA man ran out, waving his arms: "*Halt!* I requisition the car as evidence!"

Janicek drove around the corner and headed toward the road by the river, the willows. He would soon pass the cemetery, the unmarked grave. I could well imagine his splenetic satisfaction. Every word he and I had exchanged had been overheard by waiters. It all fitted in with the story the Sennerin had told in the taproom. No one wanted to listen to my denial. Had I not bribed the gravedigger? The dead falcon I had put on the grave spoke of my demented state of mind. I obviously knew the "painted monkey," as they called Fritz Janicek among themselves. The town had once gained in self-importance when they had kept that one in jail until Hermann Göring had given the order to set him free. They had everything to gain by locking me up now. Did some of them dream of an execution? I pictured myself and Mother, everyone from the meadow farm, in front of a firing squad.

Stopperl's mother walked in, swinging her hips. It was I who had taught Stopperl to draw O5 signs, she declared. I could hardly deny this. Her girl, she said, was too young and hadn't known what she was doing.

No one considered Stopperl too young to be believed when it came to the story of Adolf Hitler's death. Nor did anyone consider that I was too smart to signal the enemy bombers and bring destruction to my own home for the sake of killing one dying man.

I stood accused, yet was admired. The mountain folk knew the Nazis couldn't last any longer than this year's snow. And when it was all over, Hitler's grave in Schladming would bring thousands of tourists. Let the radio and the newspapers say the Führer was in Berlin. According to the old schoolmaster, that man was a double. By the time I had come down to send the telegram to Father, all of Schladming must have believed that Hitler had been Mother's secret lover; all at once, they remembered seeing cars and trucks go up the mountain road in the dark without headlights.

A mirror behind the large desk had taken the place of a Hitler portrait. You could see the dark mark of a larger frame on the wall. The Ober Inspector had some foresight. He also knew how to handle the SA. "This is top-secret, Herr Gruppenführer. Panic might break out if word gets out that Hitler is dead. You are the one to get them all to shut their mouths while we investigate."

I saw my own face in the mirror—a lot like grandmother's when she had been young. What if she heard that I had put Adolf Hitler in chains and let him die? With my pink cheeks, I did not look much like a folk hero—or like a murderer.

I was taken upstairs by the gendarme and locked into jail, where I had once seen Fritz Janicek behind barred windows. The square below had emptied. It was lunchtime. I sat down on the bed. The room was unheated, but Resi's coat kept me warm. Half an hour passed. I heard footsteps. The gendarme unlocked the door and handed me bread and ersatz coffee. I could not get him to tell me what was going on. After he locked me in, I ate and lay down.

Stopperl yodeled in the square. I went to the window and felt like Richard the Lionhearted, whose faithful minstrel had come to sing at the dungeon. My friend stood below my window making signals, pointing at herself, at me, and up either to the mountains or to the heavens. Her mother came, grabbed her, and pulled her away. I kept waiting.

It was almost dark when the gendarme came back. He led me down the steps and out the back door. The inspector and the mayor himself were waiting; they smelled of beer. "There're those who'd cut you in a thousand pieces for what they say you've done," said the mayor.

"I've done nothing!" I called out.

"That doesn't make a speck of difference."

"Come then," said the chief of police. "We'll take you round the back lane to the tavern." He threw a cloak over me. "No one can say we didn't do what was right. No one will know you're there." The bearded mayor owned the tavern.

We stomped through the muddy snow, keeping under the trees. Near a smelly outhouse we stopped. A couple of men came out and went back into the tavern. We used the back entrance. I was led up the stairs to a simple unheated room and locked in. The mayor returned and gave me hot broth, a hunk of dark bread, and cheese. I ate with relish.

A pattern of edelweiss, gentian, and alpine roses on the wallpaper fell into straight lines in either direction, relieved only by damp stains. The sickening symmetry of garish flowers crisscrossed my mind and held me captive until I switched off the light. I sat in the dark. The hot soup had warmed me. As evening came to the tavern, I almost felt the heat rise from the crowded taproom with its cursing, laughing peasants. I heard snatches of the milking songs, arguments.

My room overlooked the east side of the tavern. I opened the window and heard a pig grunt in a shed. Chickens awakened and cackled in alarm. A woman in a long apron came out of the coop, carrying a couple of them by the legs, and went into the kitchen. A cockerel crowed three times. I was locked up like a chicken or a pig.

I leaned out of the window. Fruit trees in the garden reached up toward the last azure light of the evening sky, full of sap in preparation for spring. I breathed in the loamy sweetness of grass emerging from snow. A sense of relief came over me. My predictable days had ended. I was locked in and felt free, elated rather than afraid.

Fanatical Nazis would always behave as though another misdeed would justify all they had done through the years, and they might kill me if they only half-believed the story of Adolf Hitler. The myth of the Führer dying in chains could only be sustained

if I was dead and buried. The look of envy from my friend Stopperl, glances of esteem from the women, the sound of Goldegger's
drum, had raised me to the status of a folk hero, a saintly sinner.

My cheeks burned. I watched the clouds part to a waning moon,
a single bright star. My star. Me, the girl Falkenburg who had
chained Adolf Hitler up like a rabid dog. Bewitched like one
accused of witchery, my heart beat wildly. Down in the tavern,
feet stomped, hands clapped and slapped leather breeches—the
dance began. I fell onto my bed and sank into a dreamless sleep.

26

Escape to Nightmare

"WAKE UP, FRÄULEIN, wake up!"

He tore me from deep sleep, where I drifted through endless white corridors lit by the flare of northern lights, brilliant, glacial. "Is it you, Eli?" I said, in the Water Castle of the snow queen.

"It's only me, Johann."

I sat up and snow fell from my coat. He was standing at my bed. The northern lights were a flashlight attached to his belt. The floor, the chair, my bed cover were all sprinkled with snow.

"Hurry," he whispered. "Sepp's waiting. We want to take you out of here. Good thing you left the window open." He had come with the long ladder country boys use for *Fensterln*, "windowing." Courtship begins with pebbles thrown against closed shutters and a serenade. If the girl opens the window or shutter, the boy will climb to the top of the ladder.

My escape down the ladder would have been amusing if it hadn't been for my heavy ski boots and my worry that Johann in his heavy boots, holding on with his mutilated hands, might fall. Halfway down, the flashlight fell from his belt and sank into the new snow.

It had stopped snowing, but the ground was well covered. The pungent smell of the outhouse and dung heap met us as we carried the ladder toward the back lane. We banged into a shed, and a pig grunted.

"Go back to sleep, pig!" Johann said, and it was quiet. "Pigs are real smart. Did you know that?"

I felt as though all this had happened before. From the moment I woke up I had a sense of inevitability I could not explain. A sleigh stood waiting, and the horse, dark as a shadow against the snow-covered bushes, pawed the ground. Sepp took my hand and pulled me up. The two men put me in the middle and spread a blanket over us. I hid myself under my fur hood and felt invisible. A few snowflakes drifted about. Sepp drove through fields until we reached the river. Willows hung heavy with snow, and as we crossed the bridge the wind whipped a branch against my cheek. The dark horse snorted when Sepp slowed it down at the graveyard. We made the sign of the cross.

"So we brought Adolf himself down on the sled? Isn't that a lark!" Johann laughed. "We, the two cripples."

"Did Stopperl tell you?" I asked.

"She did that, all right," Sepp said. "Almost didn't believe her when she said they'd locked you up at the tavern. She'll tell you anything. We all know that. Easy to fool the Schladmingers." Rivalry between mountain folk and the town must have existed for centuries.

The sleigh went *shhhhh, shhhh* as it sank through snow onto the frozen mud. The sky was dark, and light came from the ground. I suddenly felt tired. We drove on in silence, and the sky became as luminous as a mountain lake. My star seemed to follow us.

I might have dozed off if an old man at a wayside farm had not accosted us. He was walking back to the farm from an outhouse. When he saw us he ran out onto the road, swinging his lantern. He was a mean-looking old fellow in a nightshirt and coat. "Young devils! Wenching around instead of driving the Russians out of Austria!"

Sepp turned the sleigh and stopped short in front of the old fellow, waving the stump of his leg. Johann held out his hands. "You fight the Russians—it's your turn now!" The old man fled.

"No one likes to look at us," Johann said.

"I do," I said. "You are heroes. And you ski even better than Stopperl."

Johann turned the talk to Stopperl, and they both laughed and called her a cannon, the highest praise for a skier. "She'll win a few races when she grows up."

We drove on over the last snow of the season. A night bird

shrieked. We did not speak. Another night closer to German defeat. We knew it.

"Where are you taking me?" I finally asked.

"To the priest in Landeck," Sepp said.

"Pfarrer Kronz's friend?"

"He'll see you're safe," Johann said.

"I must go to Vienna," I said. "Did you bring me clothes?"

Johann pointed at a rucksack. "All we could take." They had skied down in the dark and borrowed the sleigh from the old veterinarian, a friend of the Waldhofer's. "I'd like to see the Bürgermeister's face when he wakes up!" They laughed. "He'll think you can fly, Fräulein," said Johann.

The wind whipped clouds from the moon and carried darkness toward the mountain peaks. Snow sparkled on hedges. In the soft light I saw the cheerful faces of my rescuers. The tassels of their woolen ski hats danced in the wind. Pride made them feel whole again, not mere Ostmark peasants crippled in the German war. Pranksters make good heroes.

In the east, the horizon showed the sheen of predawn. Courage, like fear, is infectious. I listened to them swap stories of wartime escapades: a hedgehog in a German captain's bed, a clandestine meeting between a young German lieutenant and a scarecrow dressed up in a fur coat and a hat with a veil. We laughed together, ate apples and bread they had brought along. A mongrel came barking from a wayside homestead. Sepp cracked his whip, and the dog turned back.

Few dared offer shelter to a fugitive in those days. Fortunately, I did not look like one. Pink-cheeked, young, dressed in the French fur, and the company of two young men, I arrived at the Pfarrhaus before five in the morning. The priest's home sat behind an old church with a new, pointed steeple. The door to the church stood open, and candles flickered at the feet of a Madonna. Young pines grew around the two-story house. It had wooden balconies, beehives in the back.

It was much too early. I rang the bell timidly. The door opened at once. We found ourselves face to face with a molelike housekeeper in a gray smock. Her dark, beady eyes were set close together, and she looked me up and down while we exchanged our "Guten Morgen."

"You come back at a decent hour if you want to get married. This is not the time to disturb His Saintliness."

Priests in Austria are addressed as *Hochwürden,* Your High Honor. Just as I was beginning to wonder whether my teacher's friend was saintly because he was dead, a door opened and firm footsteps were heard. "No wedding." I suppressed the giggles. "Pfarrer Kronz is my teacher. I had to flee."

The housekeeper said, "Shhhh. Shut your mouth!" and pulled us into the house, locking the door. "Hochwürden, it's one of those."

The priest wore his vestments and carried a black overcoat and a large silver crucifix. He impressed me as youthful and powerful, with wide shoulders, a square chin, a broken nose, and penetrating eyes. "Reyna von Meinert, please come in!" He had a gruff, harsh voice.

His study reminded me of the police station, with wood-paneled walls, uncomfortable chairs and benches, and his method of questioning us reminded me of the Gestapo and the SA at the Tanten-Haus. I felt myself stiffen, as though he too were trying to ferret out a hidden friend.

The housekeeper never left her post in front of the door. No servant I had known had ever behaved like this. "Speak up now; who was it that locked you up? Be quick about it!" she yelled at me when I faltered. "Better get the two peasant boys out of here before the sun comes up and melts the snow. Better they're not missed."

The little mole of a woman seemed to be in charge when it came to practical arrangements. She would not let me step outside the door when Sepp and Johann left. I shook hands with them. "His Saintliness" gave them a brusque blessing. As soon as the sleigh moved out onto the road, he and the servant went to work and shoveled snow over the tracks. It looked as though they had done this many times before.

When they came back, I wanted to ask all kinds of questions, but instead I had to answer an interrogation about the artworks in the mine, the SS man Fritz Janicek. I had to explain why I needed to go to Vienna at once. It did not sound convincing. The Russians were marching on Vienna and I wanted to go there with a pack on my back.

The priest was looking out of the window with a watchful expression. His broken nose and strong chin made a powerful silhouette against the golden light of the rising sun. "Ja, ja. I've no choice. I must send you on to Vienna to your father and grandmother."

"The sooner the better," said the servant. "We can't keep anyone here. Not now. A priest was shot by the SS last week. He had taken in a foreigner, and the man was careless and left a pair of fancy reptile-skin shoes behind. His name was inside them." I could guess the name of the owner of those elegant small shoes.

"I leave the child in your hands," the priest said to the servant.

"The four o'clock train," she said.

The priest and the servant belonged together. His yielding up of power was not weakness but strength. They were equally cautious and intrepid. When I came away with the servant in the afternoon, I was well fed and I had rested in a sun-heated little room under the eaves. The priest had blessed me. They had added to the food in my rucksack, made me put money into a cloth bag around my neck. I had had to memorize names of priests and convents, in case I got stranded. My coat was turned inside out to be less conspicuous.

The servant took me to the junction. We waited behind trees in the woods. There she sang the praises of "His Saintliness," told me how he risked his life to help others. "If it weren't for me, he would no longer be among the living."

A short freight train came along before I had a chance to ask her whether the "Saintliness" with the broken nose had ever been a boxer. She waved her gray head scarf, and the train stopped at the junction. She handed the engineer a package, then she took me to the end of the train. The two guards hoisted me in, and she handed them a package and a bottle. "To Vienna," she said, in such a manner that it wasn't clear whether she meant the packages or me. She signaled with her scarf, and the train moved on. "God protect you!" she shouted, and it sounded like an order.

The guards said, "A good woman; we've helped her out many a time. Always helping someone out. Can't promise nothing. Verdammt. Blasted miracle if we get through to Vienna. At times we're stuck for a day or two until they fix the rails."

They locked the door, settled down on a box that could have been a coffin, and warmed their hands on a small kerosene lamp. In the half dark I found a seat on a crate. One of the men did all the talking; the other was more interested in the bottle.

"He was bombed out," said the spokesman.

"But I slept through it all," said the one with the bottle. "I had put my mattress under the bed. The house came down. I was all right."

When the train entered a tunnel and waited for warplanes to pass, he threw himself down and held his ears. After the train went on, the two men took turns drinking until they sank down on their cots and started to snore. I went to sleep among a pile of grain bags.

When I woke up, the train had stopped. Flak guns rattled in the distance. The guards got up.

"Are we in Vienna?" I asked.

"What do you think this is, the Orient Express?"

We listened to the guns. "I hear no bombs," said one of them. "Wonder what they're shooting at?"

They passed the bottle back and forth, offered it to me, and almost dropped it. Someone was banging at our freight car. They raised guns. "Off with you, or we'll fire!"

"Don't shoot, don't shoot! Open up!" a woman clamored.

They opened up and I held the lantern. It was a woman wearing several coats, a head scarf, and a Tyrolean felt hat with a feather in it. She hoisted a suitcase tied up with rope in my direction.

"Here, help me, boy. Help me get to Vienna and I'll give you all chicken and beer."

The guards pulled her up and she collapsed among the grain bags, breathing hard. When the train began to move again, we settled down to chicken and beer, some of my bread, and the woman's story: "My sister was bombed out. A beautiful dancer at the Maxim. She never liked my poor mother, so she moved in with this widower. No longer young, but rich. Used to make copies of museum pictures. Owns five houses."

With food and drink, Austrian comfiness, *Gemütlichkeit* took over. "What does she need my mother's flat for?" the woman said. "Never even went to see her or gave her any food. This winter killed the old people off. *Mutter* always said I would get the flat, furniture and all . . ."

The beer and the woman's voice made me drowsy. I went to sleep and dreamed about the wine Biter.

An air-raid alarm woke me up. "They're going to bomb us!" howled the woman. An explosion shook the carriage. The guards opened the door, yelling, "Raus, out." I jumped with my rucksack. The woman handed me her heavy suitcase and jumped, landing on top of a man.

"Dumb cow! Want to kill me?" It was the engineer. He picked himself up and told us the track had been bombed. The planes had now moved on to destroy a railroad bridge.

It drizzled. I felt the warm Föhn wind. We had left the snow behind. The train had stopped on a hill among trees. Fires burning in Wiener Neustadt lit up the sky. I must have been dreaming about the war, for I felt I had seen it all before, and the shabby, shadowy people who sprang up around us seemed long familiar. They bartered and bargained with the engineer and the guards. Explosions sounded far away. The flak stopped. Before I was fully awake, human ants dragged long logs toward the road and made off with grain bags.

I shouldered my pack and followed them to the road. A man put down his bag not far from me and pulled a motorcycle with sidecar out of the bushes. I ran to him. "If you take me to Vienna," I said, "my father will give you anything you want."

He held up a light to look me over. Goggles and a cloth helmet hid his face. He grinned. "Who might your father be, boy, that he can give me anything I want? Göring, Goebbels?"

"Wine, Beer, and Milk Meinert," I said with pride. Stopperl had warned me about strange men in the dark. Better he took me for a boy. "You'll see, he'll give you anything!"

He put the grain into the sidecar and fastened the top. "Well, get on the back. You'd better hold on. Can't stop if you fall off." As we drove away, the woman in the two coats came running after us, shouting, "Take me along!" She was left behind. "To the devil with you!" she yelled after us.

I held onto the leather back of the stranger and closed my eyes. The rucksack pulled on my back. I felt grit in my mouth. The wind carried the stench of burning. I was a girl in trousers again. But there were advantages this time.

"Is this Vienna?" I yelled, after an eternity of discomfort.

"Jawohl. Fine mess. Hold on. Have to go fast. Not safe to slow down!"

He sounded as though he were glad to have me along on his ride through this netherworld. I never learned his name. He was young to be out of uniform, and expert at getting in and out of Vienna, it seemed. A smuggler? The innocent drama of those who had led predictable lives had ended. Disaster had forced everyone to improvise. Neither saints nor sinners, men, women, children like me had been forced to play the parts of heroes and villains.

"Hitler's said to have taken a panzer division out of Berlin to defend Vienna," shouted the driver. "But God only knows . . ."

We entered a Vienna in the midst of disaster. I saw the ruin of a factory, the wing of a warplane.

"Where is your father?" yelled the driver.

"In the ninth district." I gave him the address.

"Hope we'll get through!"

"We will." I believed it.

A man in boots and two women wrapped up in blankets came away from a doorway and tried to stop us. "*Halt*. Where did you get the gasoline?"

"Hold on, boy!" The driver swerved around them at full speed, over a curb. I screamed and laughed as though I were on a roller coaster in the Prater, far too excited to worry what would happen to me. We raced along bomb-torn side streets, past dark houses with broken panes, half-houses, boards, fallen bricks. The sky cleared; I saw the waning moon, turned to look for my star, and almost toppled. Through dust and rubble, I felt the magic of Vienna, city of inspiration, obsession, greatness, imperial city without empire, fortress with no other fortification than its hungry, grumbling, selfish Viennese punsters, notoriously unreliable when deprived of good food and good music.

I heard the sound of a piano. A song from a musical: "Fortune will stand at the door . . . at the White Horse Inn." A piano had been moved out of a windowless café. People sat around it on chairs and boxes, talking, singing, drinking wine. They raised their glasses as we came along; they were shouting, "*Prost, prosit. Prost* Stalin!"

"*Prosit* Stalin!" I yelled as we zoomed by. I was singing the silly song at the top of my lungs when we turned left at the next corner and came to a halt at a roadblock.

Old men in steel helmets, little boys in Hitler Youth uniforms, a policeman: no one bothered with a Hitler salute. The boys were pitifully thin and wild-eyed with fatigue. We had to show identification. The policeman looked at mine with interest, shined a light into my face. "Fräulein von Meinert. What are you doing out on the road like this?"

The motorcyclist appraised me. They all stared. I felt inspired: "My sister is bombed out—a beautiful dancer at the Maxim. She never liked my poor mother." I thought my imitation sounded perfect, and as long as I kept my eyes on a swastika armband I could keep from giggling. Why shouldn't I help myself to the woman's story? No worse than helping yourself to a bag of grain. Certainly more fun.

"What's the Maxim?" asked one of the boys.

"Naked girls dancing, boy," said a fat-faced man.

I blushed for my invented sister as we drove on.

"Why didn't you tell me you're a girl?" asked the driver.

I didn't answer.

"You did all right. If it weren't for you, they would have searched the sidecar. I'd like to meet that sister." We passed a damaged church. People were kneeling at the altar, and a few candles were lit. "Does your father have gasoline?" he asked.

I assured him that Father had everything. Quickly I said two silent Pater Nosters, one for Father, one for Grandmother. The last time we had heard from Father, Vienna had suffered one of its worst air attacks. He was working at his office at night when it was quiet. During the daytime bombing he slept in the cellar of the building as much as he could.

We reached the Ringstrasse, and the motorcycle skidded on damp cobblestones.

"Look at the poor Opera!" yelled the driver.

The walls of the great house had tumbled. Hanna Roth's prophecy had come to pass. People stood around it in the dark, mourning. A foul odor of decay hung in the air, a smell of death. By some miracle, Resi's apartment house stood; the other buildings facing the Opera had fallen. Now the pack on my back felt as though it had been filled with lead. I could not possibly hold on anymore. My neck and arms ached.

A church bell rang out at the Schottentohr. Stopperl would have called this a good omen. Then we passed through the stench of broken gaspipes. I covered my nose with one hand and almost toppled, grabbed the driver's arm. He cursed like a Viennese. We reached the ninth district. One more turn. He knew the city well.

The schoolhouse at the corner had collapsed. One wing of the beer warehouse had fallen. The office building, garage, stables, remained. We drove into the yard.

"The horses, the dear *Pinzgauer!*" I jumped off and ran to the wagons. Patient horses stood in the dark, waiting for their load of milk. An amazing sight. The workers gathered around me.

"My papa, is he here?"

"Who may he be?" an old man said wearily. "You can ask Herr von Meinert; he has a list of those of us that remain."

I almost fell around his neck. "*Danke schön.* Thank you!"

"It's the Meinert girl," the driver said.

I was running toward the office building, and a woman followed and handed me a little lantern. "For God's sake! I'd like to see his face."

"Don't forget my gasoline!" yelled the motorcyclist.

I ran up the stairs. My heavy boots clattered over the stone floor. There was no need to knock. A gray-haired man in a black suit tore open the door and came out holding a gun.

"Where is—" I began.

He put the gun into his pocket and opened his arms. His face and hair looked as though they had been dusted with ashes. I had never seen him without his kaiser beard. Candles flickered on his desk. He looked hollow-cheeked. As he held me and smiled, color rushed into his face, his eyes sparkled. "I know you miss my beard. I'll have to grow it back. And I'm too thin. I'll grow fat again. You'll see. Where is Mama? How is she?"

Finally my rucksack came off my shoulders, and at the same time the weight of my worries left me as I began to talk. I felt warm and relaxed. A log was crackling in the slow-burning tile stove.

I forgot all about my driver until he came knocking at the door. He received everything he asked for: a canister of gasoline, sugar, eggs, bread. Father kept food stored in a wall safe in the cellar, his shelter. He sat down on a cot with the man and they talked in undertones. When the driver left, Father told him to come back when things became normal again.

"Hard to imagine when that will be," said the man, and hurried away. He had remained faceless in his cloth helmet and goggles, but I remembered his fine teeth when he grinned. And his voice had a certain gruff dignity.

Survival, Father explained to me, was now the biggest problem. He wished to supply milk in Vienna for as long as he possibly could, yet Mother was his main concern. He stared into space while he ate. The death of his friend Eugene, my escapade and rescue, the mine with the art treasures, Fritz Janicek—all figured as he sat in thought, as if he had to play a game of chess against destiny itself.

He made me lie down on the sofa in his office, bending over me to cover me with the old fur rug from our car. Tears rushed into his eyes. "There was a young girl in my life. A music student. She is dead. Killed by the one bomb on our avenue. Vlado's girl. I took the family into the Meinert-Hof to keep strangers out. It happened in the afternoon, after the all-clear had sounded. She was standing in the middle of the street with a soldier on leave. A *Streifer*, a single plane, came along and dropped a bomb." He went to his desk and refilled his glass. "Nothing left but a crater and a silly old straw hat of your mother's."

I remembered Hanna Roth's warning. "When did this happen?"

"In September. The doctor's house across the street was hit at the same time. All of them are dead. He was the street warden. A dreadful man, but all the same . . ."

"Nasty little Herbert?"

"Dead."

"The Romberg villa?"

"Untouched. A few windows blown out at our house, too."

He put another log into the tile stove, sat down beside me, stroked my hair, watching over me as my eyes closed.

27

The Last Stand

FATHER AND I WALKED to the little palace in the morning. He carried my rucksack and talked. In the Burggarten he showed me a bench where he had once sat with Mama when she had been my age. He took me past the coffeehouse where he had met with Resi before she became famous. We walked past ruins and stopped at a boarded-up jewelry store. "I bought a little piece of jewelry here not long ago." His face told me that the girl he had given it to was dead. He took my hand. "If we didn't remember and hold on to all that is gone, how could we hope?"

We walked through narrow streets, saw a saddle shop, a town house ornate with tritons. "Our city was built to please the eye, to amuse. A city for love, music, not war. Why should anyone want to destroy it? Or bomb innocent people?"

I could have said: we attacked their land, and destroyed their cities killing girls like Nadica. Instead I diverted him and asked for an apple from the rucksack. The closer we came to Grandmother's street, the more slowly we walked. I tried to make him laugh with stories about Stopperl. He told me about Krummerer as a defender of the city who had vowed to protect the little palace.

Before we reached the corner, we had begun to tease each other. I kept asking myself, is she alive? Does the little palace stand? Is there something beyond—this day, this minute, this me? Neither of us wanted to go on around the corner. We turned into a pair of clowns, teasing and insulting each other as never before. I don't remember what made us laugh so hard. Dilemma is the essence of Viennese wit. Like any clowns, we turned fear and misery into mock combat. I pulled Father's cloak; he pretended to give me a slap. We performed, we laughed at ourselves.

I reached for his hand, in the end. Slowly we turned the corner. "There it is." He beamed. "And the Hohentahler house as well."

"And one day Berthold and the Hohentahlers will come back. And Eli will come back to the Water Castle, and Resi, too." He returned my smile. For a minute we stood lost in hope.

"Right now a lot of scum lives at the Water Castle and the Hohentahlers'. They are said to be bombed-out people. Who knows? A sorry lot. Your grandmother had the nuns living with her. Officially they are still sharing the little palace with her. In this confusion no one has time to inform; perhaps they're afraid to. You must not be surprised to find the countess changed." He went on talking about the wonderful nuns, who had repaired locks, boarded up the downstairs windows, and left my grandmother elated and full of hope. He produced a bunch of keys to unlock the portal. Then he told me about my grandmother's maid, who was terrified of the bombs. The countess had had to send her to the Hohentahlers. Now there was only a cleaning woman. "I don't go home. Vlado's wife is there, but . . ." His calm voice bothered me. Someone was digging and the shovel scraped, grated.

"Did you love the girl better than me, Papa?"

He hunched over the keys, as though he had trouble unlocking the gate. "What on earth brought that on?" He sounded tired. I felt ashamed and did not look at him when he held the gate for me. "I never thought much about it. Now that you ask me, I would say she simply tried too hard to be like my wife and ended up being less than an adopted daughter. She had become an obligation. A gifted girl. I did not feel as close to her as I should have because of her class—her upbringing, her mother. I thought I would find it convenient having the mother in the house to cook and clean. The situation became repugnant. Although they all kept out of the way, I came to spend most of my time in town. The girl took up with other men, perhaps to make me jealous. I had not seen her for weeks when the bomb killed her." He turned around and locked up from the inside.

"You're locking Grandmama in, just like Mother when she was at home."

He drew me to him. "I'm an old donkey. Obsessed with trying to keep those I love safe." We both laughed. I felt better. The magic of the old courtyard with its shrine, stone angel, and early spring flowers growing in the grass made me forget all my anger.

"I wanted to come back here," I told him. "Somehow it feels safe."

"An illusion. Foreign workers are loose. There is a lot of looting. Your grandmother does have keys, but she's inclined to leave everything open; an old habit. She was always taking a chance. I will have to leave you for a few days. It might be better if you could take charge of the keys."

I asked him whether he was going to Mother. He did not answer me, and went on to tell me how the countess had walked all the way to the Palais Auersberg in the middle of an air raid, to meet with some of her friends. "Highly dangerous." Fortunately, Krummerer followed her. Pulled her into a bunker."

"The Puppen detective?"

"I helped him out. He is counting on me when all this mess comes to an end. In the meantime he is reliable. Your grandmother goes around all dressed up these days. She could have been robbed if he hadn't been there. You must see that she goes down to the shelter during raids. Don't let her take the boards off the downstairs windows. She worries about the swallows getting in to nest when they return. It's been a cold spring, and if those birds have any sense they'll stay away."

"Could the war be over in time for them to nest?"

"God only knows." He picked up my bag, and we crossed the old courtyard. The last light fell onto the white stucco façade of the little palace. Angels, scrolls, baroque garlands made the old building appear fragile, although it could well withstand wars. Just like my grandmother.

Father rang the bell before he let himself in. The passageway was dark with the window boarded up. I switched on the light. "I stored all the clocks in my wine cellar." I resented the change.

The countess Reyna appeared at the top of the marble stairs, dressed in a full-length claret-colored gown and matching cloak. She glittered with gems. "Reyna!" she cried, and put down the painting she carried. I ran into her arms and found myself enfolded in her fur-lined cloak, enveloped in the faint fragrance of violets and that dank odor of cellar rooms and stone, an aroma of the past.

"You look as though you were off to a court ball, Mama," my father said in a jovial tone. "Everyone else is getting more and more shabby; you, more and more fancy."

"My old court costumes were designed to keep me warm at the Hofburg and Schönbrunn palaces. Those icy passageways and chilly reception rooms were almost as bad as it is here now. Agnes used to scold me for keeping all my finery from Worth. Now that I live mostly in the basement and cellar rooms, I'm glad I did."

I missed her serenity. She looked flushed, excited. "When everything is dark, one has to be festive. Nicht wahr?" she said. I had to agree. "Diamonds are best worn in the half-dark and in private, anyway. Then they sparkle like stars." I fingered her moonstone necklace. "This used to belong to the mother I never knew. I wear it as an amulet."

A few years ago, I would have been delighted to see her wearing a tiara worth a fortune, and all her diamond pins. Now I had to get used to her new ways. We had both changed.

She went on to explain how she finally had to fetch her kaiser. It was no longer safe to leave the picture upstairs. That shifty-eyed cleaning woman talked so much about looting, and then, we might expect night bombing. She sighed. "How I wish the nuns could have stayed."

My father carried the painting for her and studied it. "Annerl thought I looked just like him. I'll never forget her face when she saw me walk into the kitchen that first day. She held up her dolly and said, 'Look, the kaiser.'" On the way down to the kitchen, his beautiful hand with its long, tapered fingers caressed the thick walls. "I always enjoy coming down here. They really knew how to build in the days of the Kaiserin."

The kitchen was full of upstairs furniture and pleasantly warm. Father let himself fall down on the bench and lean against the tiled stove. "This is where she sat in her school dress." He stared into space and pulled on his graying side-whiskers. "I'm in love with that memory. I always will be."

Grandmama was trimming the wick on a little lantern. "Memory. Ja, ja. I wander through empty rooms. They seem full of the past. I was beginning to feel like a ghost here all alone."

She touched my cheek and grew pale, suddenly old, like the faded silk chaise, the sofas and padded chairs. I felt drawn to her, treasured her at such moments when she faded before my eyes. My hand would caress the back of the old chaise, my fingers run over the keys of the instrument that Mozart had played when he was a boy. "I'm glad I could come," I said.

Father led the way down to the laundry room, the "wash kitchen." He showed me the huge copper kettles, the maid's bath, which had to remain filled with water. One had to be prepared. He was glad my grandmother always kept the plumbing in good condition; he took it upon himself to check the toilet. It had been repaired. Sacks of coal and wood lay piled up beside the brick stove, which heated water when the linen was boiled. Cooking utensils sat on shelves above the sink; dishes were lined up on a bookcase. A small table and chairs stood near the stove, and a harp had been stored under the tiny slit of a window which was level with the flagstones of the courtyard.

My grandmother's sketchbook lay open on the table beside a half-empty bottle of wine and a glass. She had drawn a prancing horse. I remembered her drawing horses one day in the past spring when we had sat in the courtyard. A parade of Hitler Youth had marched past her open portal. We had talked about Mother. The horses on her page began to go wild, rearing up on their hind legs. She drew one stallion leaping.

"Mother can walk again," I now told her.

"I knew it, I knew the day would come! Dear Father in heaven be thanked!"

My father and I looked at each other and silently agreed to leave it at that. She asked a great many questions and hardly noticed that we did not answer them. The way she tripped around the room, smiling, pleased and eager to please, reminded me of my mother.

Soon we all sat at the little table by candlelight, eating bread and country ham and drinking Father's wine. "We'll never run out of wine," said the countess, "even if we run out of water. Your father has filled my wine cellar. Well, the czarina used to bathe in sparkling wine." She took it for granted we would both stay with her. There was plenty of food stored down below in the cellar.

"It's good to see you eating something, Mama," Father said.

"It's Reyna and the happy news." She jumped up and pulled a sheet off the pipes. There hung a collection of her old gowns, costumes for our voyage into the past. "Now that you've grown tall, there's enough elegance here for both of us. I do not like to see my granddaughter in black trousers like a Bolshevik girl— such charm hidden under this odd bulky coat!" I was wearing the fur inside out. My grandmother raised her glass. "Let us drink to elegance. What is elegance but the right dress for the right occasion? Before we know it, all the church bells will ring out and our crown prince will be here." We clicked glasses.

She had been drinking rather quickly. I had finished my glass of wine and found myself drawn into her mood, ready for anything. Grandmother said she wanted to take the kaiser down into the cellar where he belonged.

"Where is the cellar?" I asked.

"Where no one will find it," Father said.

A slightly tattered tapestry from Schloss Falkenburg had been hung in the recess of the laundry room. I became intrigued with this copy of the famous portrait of Otto the Brave and was marveling at the lifetime of stitching when the countess, with the kaiser picture, dipped under it. You could not have seen the cellar door because it was part of the paneling. When she opened it, I was amazed at the wide staircase and the stucco ornaments beyond. My grandmother, in her long dress and cloak, rushed downstairs with the heavy painting and would have fallen if Father had not lunged down past me and caught her. They were waiting at the foot of the stairs to see my face. I stopped, dumbfounded.

"Where am I?" I asked.

In dimension, the vaulted, shadowy space resembled the Capuchin crypt; the Habsburg burial vault below the church of the Capuchin monks. Only this had been arranged for life underground, not for burial. The Oriental rugs from upstairs created an impression of warmth. The cellar was dank and cold, yet full of yellow blossoms in crystal vases. Forsythia had been brought indoors to bloom early. A large bouquet stood on the medieval table from Schloss Falkenburg. The straight-backed old chairs—at least ten of them—and a fine white tablecloth: everything had been prepared for a grand occasion.

Six underground chambers ran into each other for the length of the building. The storage pantry and a large wine cellar extended under the courtyard. Smoked meats, eggs, potatoes, turnips, carrots, cheese, dark bread, a large variety of preserved foods stored in the icy pantry were worth more than all the valuables from the past. One could almost say a ham was worth its weight in gold in those days.

I was born to great families, good health, property, even a little madness to help me enjoy it all; this hiding place meant more than anything else. Here you could really vanish from the face of the earth. The nuns must have decided they should not remain in safety but minister to the afflicted in the war-torn world. Here they must have worked like a small army of men, trapping mice and rats, carrying Grandmother's furniture down. Her high bed and night table occupied a small private chamber where firewood had been stored. They had installed additional lights. Neat rows of cots showed where they had slept, and a makeshift altar showed where they had knelt and prayed. Only a simple cross remained. The sisters had taken their holy images to comfort the sick and dying.

Grandmother placed the kaiser portrait on the altar and busied herself with sprigs of yellow blossoms, candles. Her restiveness made me uneasy. I went to look around, and Father showed me the pantry. In the wine cellar he held a lamp up to a massive oak beam. "Napoleon be damned" was carved in the middle. The date: 1805.

"An old hiding place," he said. "The nuns won't talk. Your grandmother's old servant never opens her mouth. No one knows of this place. Better than the Führer's bunker. Everyone knows where he is."

"Not really," I said. "Hitler is wherever anyone wants him."

He laughed, put his arm around me, and by the way he talked of an invasion I knew at once he would be gone for more than a day or two. "The radio will tell you when to come down here and wait it out. In case of any danger, stay in the laundry room. Keep the kitchen locked and bolted. The portal, despite all the fancy carving, was built to keep out intruders." He tried to persuade himself that we would be safe, yet a simple ladder would get anyone over the palace wall and into the courtyard. "Don't worry if your grandmama tipples a little. Heat her wine when you are down here in the cold. Water it whenever you can. I have paid someone to watch this place."

"Don't worry so much," I said later, when I kissed him in the courtyard. Night had come. "We'll be all right."

"I'll come back as soon as I can." He locked up.

I listened to the key turning in the lock, his footsteps as he walked away. All certainty went with him. A few minutes later, my grandmother said, "We're locked in. Where did I put my keys? I know I had them." I looked for her keys, found them on a side table. "You keep them, Herzerl." She called me "little heart," just like Mother when she wanted me to do something.

The daily woman stopped coming after two days. "I never liked her, Herzerl," said the countess. I took over the work with enthusiasm and inexperience. The stove had to be lit, potatoes boiled. I learned to prepare simple meals. My days in the kitchen with Agnes had taught me a lot. Our waking hours and meals depended on air raids.

I remember running along the passageways, up and down stairs in the half-dark, finding windowseats, old books, a dedication on yellow paper in an old travel book: "With everlasting love from your Dorothea." I found dust, spiders' webs, a red uniform hat with moth holes, a feather fan, unwashed glasses.

This was before Easter. Russians in a newspaper I found in the kitchen looked stumpy, smiling, innocent as the seven dwarfs in my old picture book. My grandmother switched the radio off. I heard of rape, plunder, and violence when I went to the bakery, as though it did not concern me. I had no time to worry or think. When my work was done, I took off my Bolshevik trousers and changed into a long gray velvet court gown decorated with braids of the same fabric on the skirt and sleeves.

"He proposed to me the day I wore it," my grandmother would say. "Your grandfather always wished I had more color. He would have adored you."

Our food was badly prepared, but the ceremony was exquisite: silver, china, crystal, and my grandmother's stories. She ate little, but enjoyed her wine and my company on her excursions to the past.

Before Easter we still ventured out, to church in Mariahilf, or to the milk store, the bakery. We sat in the courtyard in the evening when things were calm. The bell at the portal was out of order. Grandmother listened for her friends. They would stand outside the wall in an alley and whistle the first four notes of the Austrian anthem. She could not whistle, and before I had come she had answered the signal on a little silver pipe. Now I replied and let them in.

On such an evening, Grandmother and I sat on the bench beside the stone angel. I had carried out wine, glasses, and walnuts from the Meinert gardens.

"Stop fidgeting," she said. "I know you're waiting for your father. I myself hope he is in the country with my Ann Marie and stays there. He has been through so much. He had a sad loss this autumn."

"His girl was blown up." I sounded quite like Stopperl.

My grandmother turned her proud head. "We must pray for her soul," she said meekly.

"She took Mother's things. Father gave her my keys—"

My grandmother interrupted. "And that was all she ever had. Someone else's father, another woman's husband. Worn garments. Nothing of her own. Your father did give her the chance to study music. I went to her concert. Don't look so surprised. Did not Empress Elizabeth go to the theater to see a certain actress who played such an important role in her life? She called her 'the friend.' Dear Katerina Schratt—such a comfort to His Majesty, Emperor Franz Joseph, and therefore a friend to the empress." The countess raised her glass, and the jewels glittered in the candlelight. "Come, we must drink a little toast to all the Katerina Schratts of this world. Women who sustain great men."

I obeyed without enthusiasm, but my interest was aroused. There had been that shadowy path at Bad Ischl which led from the kaiser residence to the Schratt villa. We clinked glasses. Secretly, I drank to the man who sustained the countess: the Rittmeister, her faithful friend. A male version of Frau Schratt, now imprisoned in a concentration camp.

"Let us drink to the return of the Habsburgs!" She put down

her glass, and her loose sleeve caught on a rusty nail. "Here I am, the last of the Falkenburgs. To think that he banished me. Lived only for his horses and the sister. Never served his emperor. A disgrace. Now it is up to me." She talked of her father every day. "How could he hold my birth against me?"

"It was Anna Gitta, the witch." I made myself heard. "She was behind it all, I'm sure. I think she made him put you into the convent when your mother died."

My grandmother ignored my comment. "I had the most loving attention from the nuns."

"They tied you to your bed at night to make you tall and straight."

"They did. And I grew tall and was always admired for my upright posture. Bless the sisters. The body and the mind require discipline."

The sisters seemingly had not succeeded with Hanna Roth, who was not much of a Christian and had never grown at all. I ate nuts and heard my grandmother go on with the story of her Aunt Christina as I listened to the twitter of birds in the bushes. I heard the story over and over again: Christina von Kortnai took my grandmother from the convent, ran off with her to infuriate Count Otto, her brother-in-law. My grandmother always went over familiar ground before she ventured out into the more intricate details of those stories of the past. Then she contemplated. "No matter how I felt about traveling with Aunt Christina—she traveled like an actress with all those trunks, the doll—I did get to see the world. Your parents never cared much about going abroad."

"I thought you would have preferred to stay at the convent."

"I did want to return there many times. Let me see now, how did we get to the convent? Ja, ja. Your father, my father—your grandfather. Now you are old enough to understand. My husband, Karl, was left on his own a great deal, just like your father. I refused to stay at Schloss Falkenburg. He loved it there. Took good care of the estate and the stud farm. Just like your father with your mama in the country, he had to find some consolation. I was glad he did. Don't you think we should be grateful that your father had company? The Meinert family has dwindled, too. His sisters are in England. Only a few old uncles. Of course, your wonderful teacher, the priest. No one here in Vienna. He saw a great many people, went to the Opera, the theater—played chess. We had dinner together quite often, he felt so lonely. I was glad when he found this protégé."

I had no time to respond. We heard the whistle. I ran to unlock the portal, looked all around. There had not been an air-raid alarm since morning. People strolled through the street, whitefaced as convalescents. I waited.

"No one here, Grandmama," I called.

"Please lock up at once!"

A tall officer in front of the cinema stared at me. The theater had been closed with all the others by the end of the summer. A poster and pictures in a glass case remained from Resi's last film. I liked to walk past there and look at those pictures. Perhaps the officer felt the same way. He stood near the glass case in the recess of the entrance. I could not see his face.

"Lock up!" my grandmother said.

"Anyone could have whistled a bit of the anthem," I pointed out.

"Four notes?" She emptied her glass. We went inside and I locked up. "Green Thursday, tomorrow. I don't even know whether we should go to church."

✿   ✿   ✿

On Green Thursday Agnes had always baked something sweet to add to the customary vegetables. I missed the meadow farm and felt sad without my mother on this day. Whenever I felt downhearted I washed clothes. After the delight, the luxury of scarce soapsuds, I now made my way to the attic and the washing line. I liked to get out onto the flat part of the roof, for I craved heights after my years in the mountains. I could hear the tickle grass, and dry weeds on the roof rustling in the wind.

My grandmother had gone to her room after lunch and I had a chance to turn on the radio while I washed. "That lying voice of a stranger" she hated so much had said that we would throw the Soviet army back at Wiener Neustadt. I looked toward the distant hills of the Vienna woods, dark hills against a golden spring sky and the dark shingled roofs of the city, chimneys with little caps; a multitude of sentinels. What would happen, and when?

My grandmother had expected Tante Hohentahler yesterday.
I couldn't imagine the duchess whistling outside the palace wall.
While I hung up a damask tablecloth, someone at Berthold's open
window put bedding out to air. Strangers lived over there, bombed
out families. Perhaps the general would return with maps of this
war, and Hitler's army would be made of tin, winning the war
we were now losing. The last stand in Vienna wearied me. I
wanted something to happen.

Birds twittered and warbled in the palace courtyard. A few
surviving pigeons circled a school roof; most of them had been
eaten. I thought it was thundering when I heard the first Russian
guns. The rumbling took on a pattern. The beginning of the end.
I actually felt glad.

Each time the guns rumbled, children down in the street yelled,
"Boom, boom, boom!" I suddenly wanted to go down into the
street. I ran downstairs past Grandmother's room. She sat at the
window, and her gown looked pink in the rosy light reflected
from the walls. Only one small table and one chair remained there.
She had a sketchbook on her knee. I looked over her shoulder.
The horse she had drawn stood waiting, head held high, as though
it had heard the guns and might shy.

"Guns." She turned the page. "Coming closer. I can feel them
like my own heartbeat." She started another drawing. It looked
like the same horse.

I left her, ran down, let myself out, and locked her in.

"Boom, boom, bang! You're dead," cried the children.

The officer stood at the theater exactly where I had seen him
the day before. He stepped out of the entrance as soon as I appeared. I recognized him, waved, and ran across the street. He
clicked his heels: formal, typically German. My Frog Prince. Thin,
shy. Addressing me as Fräulein von Meinert.

I had rehearsed such meetings while washing dishes, or just
before I went to sleep in the cellar. In the beleaguered city my
fantasies returned to all my loves. Resi on the poster, advertising
her film of war and romance, all smiles, blonde curls, and dimples, inspired me. I laughed and threw my arms around the neck
of my German hero. A typical Vienna girl, a tease, a rogue, I be-
stowed on him—Eli, Rudolf Hess and Berthold—my version of
a dragon's kiss. I felt his mouth: smooth, firm, yielding like ripe

fruit. A bitter taste. His lips opened. I felt him say, "How sweet." Sweet as a ripe peach, sun and snow, was the first taste of pleasure: a delicious certainty. My brazen gesture and the endless thrill of his almost wicked innocence.

"I am so pleased," he said foolishly.

I treasured this phrase as though I had heard Schiller or Goethe speak to me. How could I have regarded him as rather ugly? I had never seen anyone so proud and kind. His fair, taut skin felt like satin as he leaned his cheek against mine.

"You're too young," he said. "I saw you yesterday in that beautiful dress. You seemed grown-up. And I thought of you all night while I stood out here."

"You stayed here all night?" I loved the idea.

A mother walked by with the two small children and gave me a nasty look. I wore pants and stood in a doorway with a German officer. One of those.

He held me tight until she was out of sight. "Now they hate us Germans. She hates you for kissing me."

Resi's poster face smiled over his shoulder. I felt the devil in me. "In Vienna we kiss all the time," I chirped.

He gave me his calm, unsmiling attention, and through the mask of his earnestness I saw fatigue. He had stayed up all night outside my door. I kissed his cheek, felt his fair beard.

"You laugh at everything in Vienna. Make the best of a rotten world. I can't give up and laugh. If I had given up, I could not have warned your aunt, the duchess, yesterday. She was followed."

"Did she come and whistle?"

"Foolishness. Why couldn't she just ring the bell?"

"It's not working."

"You must talk to the countess. We are trying to make peace. There are those who are trying to get through to the Russian generals and negotiate, stop the bombardment. The Monarchists could spoil everything. Russians don't trust them. If they get the impression the O5 are royalists, Vienna doesn't stand a chance. Could you explain this to your grandmother?"

We stood with our arms about each other like lovers while he questioned me about food provisions, our hiding place. I put my head on his shoulder and admired his perfectly shaped white ear.

"Stay in the cellar. Lock yourself in," he said, while his eyes told me he wanted to keep me out here.

"We'll be all right." Futile searchlights patterned the sky. Someone coughed at an open window.

"Are you afraid, Reyna?"

I shook my head.

He kissed my hair. "Too young."

"Don't keep saying that. Mother met Father when she was fifteen. They married when she was sixteen."

"You not only kiss, but you propose marriage to a German Gestapo?"

"Ex-Gestapo, Prince. What made you a Gestapo?" I asked.

"One thing led to another. I was only a boy, in love with my sister's English governess, a very religious girl. Quite plain, but she undressed at her open window in the summertime. After Hitler came into power, she married a pastor. I felt jilted and joined the Nazi party to shock her. I wanted to get away after I had finished one year of university. The Gestapo recruited me for all the wrong reasons. I could make bad things look decent with my honest German face. In Vienna I found out what they were up to." He cleared his throat. "The English girl wore a pin. Three monkeys. 'Hear no evil, see no evil, speak no evil.' I would like to send her a new one. My monkeys would hear, see, and speak of all the evil, at the right moment, to the right people. That is my duty as a German."

While he spoke, Easter bells began to ring out. You could no longer hear the distant guns. Women hurried past. A priest came along and stared at us over the rim of his glasses.

"The Gestapo took Grandmother's old love," I said.

"I know. One of my men at headquarters was able to advise him secretly to confess, any wild confession. It worked. They sent him to a camp. At least he has a chance."

"I think he'll live and come back, because he loved her so much."

We turned to each other and listened to the bells. I leaned against the Resi poster, and we kissed. It was like rushing downhill on my skis in the sun, gathering speed, gaining momentum. The bells stopped ringing, and we heard the guns again.

"You must go," he said.

I ran off. At the portal I called, "Auf Wiedersehen," as though I would see him again in an hour or a day.

He stood stiff and upright as a sentinel as the guns thundered. When I looked down to the street from Grandmother's room, he had vanished. A small man in green knickerbockers sat on a field stool reading a paper. Herr Krummerer had taken his place. I laughed, but my eyes filled with tears.

28

The White Horse

I CLOSE MY EYES and I can smell beeswax candles, taste tart wine, and hear the rumble of the *Unwetter*, the tempest, as Countess Reyna called the noise of combat in the streets of Vienna. She faced me at the dark, narrow table in the cellar room. Candlelight danced on her crystal glass, the golden wine, and in her eyes. We felt the earth tremble when Russian tanks rolled through the narrow streets. It hailed explosives up there. Where we sat it sounded as though a drunken cook had spilled all her dried peas and was throwing pots and crockery onto a tile floor. My grandmother ignored such misdemeanors as though she were deaf.

I can hear her say, "Some good came from every bad thing that ever happened to me. At this point, everything exists in the order of importance and delight. There is no past. However, there are moments of hatred—definitely from Lucifer."

We drank to each other, and we smiled, for we belonged together as the past and present belonged during the good, the bad, and the terrible days of the last stand. "Lucifer was once an angel," she said. I didn't know what she meant.

Hidden under the ground, we shared a journey which cannot be measured in days, miles, or years. No watch or clock ticked. My grandmother burned our calendar to revive the fire in the brick stove. When the lights flickered and went out, she remarked that she would miss hearing Mozart on the radio, but not the voice of the lying intruder who kept on telling us we could win the war and must fight on for the Führer and the Vaterland.

I remember singing "Must I go, must I go away from this town,"

Schubert's song of the wanderer, while we filled every tub, bucket, basin, pot, and even empty wine bottles with water. My grandmother joined into the song I had sung with Eli and Resi on our journey to the Promised Land. No sooner had we finished the song than the tap went dry with a drip, drip, drip.

We no longer knew day from night, or one day from the next. During the worst of the Unwetter, time had no meaning. The weeks that passed can, however, be divided into days of the sketchbook horses and the horses my grandmother drew on old newspapers when the last drawing paper had been used up. I was far more interested in words than in pictures at the time. The madness of a newspaper headline—"April 1, 1945: Hitler Declares Victory. President Roosevelt Ailing"—impressed me more than the noble head and wild sadness my grandmother portrayed in her Lippizaner stallion on those pages. By the time the Russians had entered Vienna, the American president was either dying or dead.

"He knew how to train them to obey any order." I thought she was talking about Adolf Hitler until she went on. "*The horse* obeyed *him* to the end. I can still feel *him* riding toward me, his only child. The last Falkenburg. The nuns said *he* didn't see me. I saw him use his whip, forcing the horse on to trample me to death." She never called the count Father.

"He didn't see you; he had his mind on something else." I remembered not to say Great-grandpapa.

She never listened when she sought an answer to the questions that tormented her soul. "Once the nuns had to pull me out of his way. They saw me just in time. They considered it their duty to take me to Schloss Falkenburg, and I was quicksilver the moment I arrived. The sisters should see me now. I feel paralyzed whenever I set foot in Falkenburg. Anyway, that day I had been playing on the high hurdle, leaping down from it into tall grass —a game they did not like because it made my skirts fly up, and they considered this undignified. The nuns were about to reprimand me when *he* came along on the horse." She sighed. "I feel as though I were still lying in the grass with him coming at me on that white horse. It would have been natural for me to jump up and get out of the way, but I lay there in front of his hurdle, let him gallop toward me, and thought to myself: if he kills me, he'll fry in hell and I will float around among God's angels with my own mama."

Her voice would be accompanied by the *brrmmm, brrrmmm, brrm,* the meat-grinder sound of tanks above the ground. "Now I know that this was the devil in my own heart." She searched for the truth, searched for her father as she took me back to her early days. Pink spots appeared on her cheeks, and she stared into space like the visionary who had claimed to be her half-sister.

She insisted on going up to the laundry room right there and then. As soon as we entered, we heard a loud *ping* from the old harp, as if some invisible hand had plucked a string. I had carefully covered the slit of a window, which was level with the ground. We stood hand in hand in the light of a small lantern.

"I see a chink of light. I must see the daylight." She removed the cardboard. "Never mind the *ratatat* and the banging and bashing out there, we will regard it as fireworks for our little celebration. Put a log on the fire."

She slipped behind the screen which served as our dressing room and bathroom, fumbled around among old hatboxes she had stacked in that corner behind a standing mirror. I heard her laugh the way I often laugh. When she came out, her attire had acquired a distinctly Russian flavor. A tall beaver hat, dull with the years and reeking of mothballs, sat on her head at a rakish angle. Her eyes, sparkled. "Here, here, *pour vous!*" She handed me a tall black fur hat.

I wore trousers and Resi's fur inside out, day and night, to keep warm in the damp cellar. Now I tucked my hair into the hat. Grandmother took both my hands and smiled at me. "You look like a Cossack." We laughed and could not stop laughing. Never again would I hear her laugh so freely. "Fetch one of those precious cans of goulash and a bottle of your father's 1920. A superb vintage. Victory is ours. Didn't you hear the *ping* of the old Habsburg harp? Isn't there a lull in the Unwetter? Can't you feel it? I believe Crown Prince Otto has entered the city with the Russian army. He is a born diplomat. We must be prepared to welcome the prince."

"Grandmama, the Russians are Bolsheviks, and they hate all royalty."

She had drunk almost a bottle of wine while she had been drawing in the cellar. Her mood had changed, and she looked forward to a great new Austria. "The Russians are royalists in their hearts. I know it. When I traveled in Russia with my great-aunt, Christina, wolves ran after our sleigh, and we wore these fur hats. She took the whip from the driver, leapt onto one of the horses like a Cossack, and rode us out of the woods and away from the wolves. I had to hold the wretched doll. When we entered the village, peasants came running out to see her riding like a man in her skirts and sable cloak. 'Long live the czar,' they yelled. You can't tell me that they hated him. Our crown prince is a born diplomat, I always said so. He will lead the Russian generals into Vienna." She raised her glass.

We feasted in the warm laundry room, indulged in old wine and new fantasies. My head began to spin, or I would have remembered my promise to Father and my Frog Prince when the countess asked me to unlock the door. We had become accustomed to the sound of guns, had drunk more than usual, and were "animated," as we put it in Vienna. It was so pleasant to feel as though the tempest had subsided, as we walked arm in arm from room to room in our Russian fur hats.

In my grandfather's closet we found a cavalry sword with gold tassels and a hunting horn inscribed "To my little friend Karli, from old Uncle Rudolf." My grandmother slung the horn over one shoulder. I wore the sword. "Imagine, 'Nazi' was the nickname they used for Crown Prince Rudolf, poor fellow. My Karl had his shortcomings, but he adored the Crown Prince."

"Did the Crown Prince shoot himself and Fräulein Vetsera, or were they murdered?"

She sighed. "Who will ever know?"

It was amazingly quiet. We heard a fly buzz. Silence made me uneasy, and my grandmother always talked more when she felt unsure. She went on with the story of Crown Prince Rudolf: how they had taken him away from his mother, stuck him into uniforms, when he could hardly walk. He was handed over to a fool of a military tutor who took him to the Lainzer animal park and yelled "wolf" to make a man of the four-year-old. If he had never been allowed to be a boy, how could he ever have grown up and become a man and an emperor? Our present Crown Prince had been well educated in a most sensible fashion. "He will save our Austria, and Vienna will again be the heart of the civilized world," she concluded as we walked down the stairs to the darkened corridors with the empty swallows' nests.

"Listen." I grabbed her arm. "What is that noise?" Wood cracked and splintered. Someone was prying boards loose from a window.

"We have intruders," the countess said calmly. "We will defend this palace and the honor of the house of Habsburg."

If we had not drunk that final toast before we had come up the stairs for our promenade, I might have held her back. It looked as though a bear or a wolf was forcing boards and pawing its way through the broken panes. A furry brown arm, then a thick leg came through.

"I'm stuck," said a coarse female voice. "I'll cut my bloody head off." The boards gave way and fell. Two other women waited to get in. They carried sacks. You could only see their uneasy eyes; all the rest was wrapped in scarves and rags.

My grandmother marched toward them and raised the old hunting horn to her lips: *Waahooo, aohaooo.* I rushed after her and drew the sword. To lift it above my head, I had to use both hands.

"Death to the enemies of God and the new emperor!" yelled my grandmother.

I lunged forward, and the heavy sword dropped and hit the fallen board as I took my place by her side. She was holding the small inlaid mother-of-pearl pistol I had admired years ago.

"Back, back, run for your life! There are Russians in the palace. Ukrainians!" The woman tried to get back out through the window, and her brown fur stuck. "Don't shoot, don't kill! My father is White Russian. *Stoi, stoi.* Don't chop my head off!"

"To the devil with you," I heard myself scream, like a Russian, as she squeezed herself out, ripping her clothes.

The women fled toward the wall, clambered up a ladder with their bags and sacks of loot.

"I would have killed them," my grandmother said. "There is a lot of hatred in me. Do you hate anyone, Kinderl?"

I preferred not to answer this question. I had hated Puppe with all my heart. Otherwise, I was always a fickle hater. "I don't hate the Germans, although they got us into all this trouble." I worked at hammering the board back in place with the heel of my boot. "I told you about the German prince."

"What prince?"

"You know, Arnold von Lütensteg. I told you he was watching out for us. I saw him outside the gate. He told me to keep you in the cellar. Father said the same thing." I took her arm, and we went down to the kitchen where Father had first seen my mother. He was more than likely at the farm with her now.

"Lütensteg is handsome in an odd sort of way," Grandmother said. "He struck me as a confused young man. Such fine manners when he came to question me. German *Uradel*, a prince of the old blood, in the Gestapo?"

"Secretly helping people. I think he is wonderful!"

"Of course you do. You'll think many more young men are wonderful. And I hope they'll all be princely fellows. I remember an evening at Schloss Esterhazy . . . I was in love with three princes."

We were interrupted by the clang and clatter of the Unwetter and went down to the cellar. My grandmother picked up some old newspaper: "Führer orders military, industrial, transportation, and communication installations and all stores in Germany to be destroyed with help of Gauleiters." Her stallion pranced over the page.

"What was it like that day when you were in love?"

"About this time of the year. A very mild spring. I wore the gray velvet you like to wear, my hair loose in the style of the empress Elizabeth, and like her hair—and yours now, in the candlelight—it had a red sheen. I wore lilies of the valley during the concert." She put the horse away and sat smiling in a sunny landscape of her past.

"The three princes, were they all of the old blood like Arnold von Lütensteg?"

"When it comes to *Libeleien*, matters of the heart, we create our own nobility. Two of them were aristocrats, and in the end I married the most handsome of them all. Funny that you should bring that up." She drained her glass, but I had watered the wine. Her hands trembled with girlish emotion as she poured some more. Intoxicated with the fragrance of the lilies of the valley she had worn, she tilted her head. "Lallala, la-la-la-la." She was humming a Brahms Hungarian dance. "He sent me a note: 'I make music for you as long as I live.' He was a musician, my prince of princes. A true artist. He conducted the orchestra with such passion that the audience wept. When he took up the violin, beautiful as a wild bird, his eyes beseeched me and the violin sang only for me. I could not stay in my seat, and ran out into the greenhouse. I knew he saw me go out, and I knew he would follow."

"Did he kiss you?" I asked. There was a terrific bang somewhere above us, like the dropping of a huge iron pot.

The countess seemed to be deaf to the Unwetter, as to my curiosity. "He loved me as only a great artist can love. A perfect moment. Complete self-forgetfulness. One enshrines such joy. How fortunate I am to have had such a first love. He had to return to Vienna. I remained hidden among hothouse roses and gardenia shrubs. Karl von Dornbach found me there in tears. He kissed my hands. 'I know how you must feel,' he said. 'It is terrible to separate after you have loved for the first time. But you can't marry him. Why don't you give me the right to cheer you up?' He had been watching me and knew everything. By the time the sun came up, I was weeping like a child, and he held me in his arms, teasing and laughing. He had unruly flaxen hair, just like our Berthold. I tried to run away. He hid behind petunias and sprang out at me in his blue uniform, twirling me around among falling flowerpots. 'How about grouse and champagne for breakfast, schöne Reyna?' He pulled his mother's emerald ring from his pocket and slipped it onto my finger." She held up her hand to the candlelight and I admired the ring.

"Were you ever sorry you couldn't marry the prince of princes?" She shook her head. "I should have married the third one." "The Rittmeister?"

Tears came to her eyes. "My beautiful Karl and I parted. It was perhaps my fault, too. He married a Falkenburg; he married the estate, the horses he loved. He wanted it all. I was not enough. He said *Lebwohl*, live well, not auf Wiedersehen, when he went away to the war." She looked at me and smiled. "Ja, we did part as lovers. 'If I am killed,' he said, 'don't marry again.' I can hear his laughter now. Sometimes in my dreams he stands there in his uniform and laughs at me because I took him seriously."

"You should have married the Rittmeister," I said.

"No," she said, and refilled her glass. "It would have ruined everything. Karl knew that. He called me a nun at heart. His ravished nun. All these foolish things." She hummed the Brahms Hungarian dance. "In fairy tales and silly novels there is always just one prince, in life—your life, certainly—there will be more than one."

"I know that," I said.

More and more frequently I had to turn my grandmother's contemplations to love to help us both forget the war and the loneliness of our last stand.

Whenever there was a lull in the clatter and banging, we went upstairs as far as the laundry room to warm ourselves and wash in a small amount of water. We brushed each other's hair, sprinkled it with violet water. I braided hers because her fingers were stiff and rheumatic from the damp cellar. Sometimes we ate at the little table beside the Habsburg harp. I felt uneasy that day.

I should have known the countess felt slightly feverish. She looked tired, downhearted, and seemed restive for the first time. I kept the keys, otherwise I would not have been able to deter her from going to the attic to raise a white flag and the old imperial double eagle; one to appease the Russians, the other to welcome Otto von Habsburg.

"Will this Unwetter never end?" she said. Her fur hat sat on her braids at a rakish angle. She always carried her little pistol in her pocket, and I worried that she might fall and shoot her own leg. The hunting horn remained slung around her shoulder. My sword was always by my side. "Why don't we have a little hot wine? I'm cold." Her delicately veined hands trembled over a satin eiderdown she had gathered around her. She seemed to feel better after I brought her the hot drink, some dark bread, and some cheese. By now, everything had a moldy flavor.

I sat down beside her on a padded bench and we shared the quilt as though we were off on a winter's journey. "Tell me about your aunt Christina," I asked. "What was she like as a girl?"

I thought it safe to revisit the von Kortnai estate with its lichen-covered stone walls, the beautiful redheaded sisters: Anne-Marie, who would marry my great-grandfather, and Christina, who was always a little mad. I already knew they had both loved him.

Each time my grandmother talked of the sisters I learned a little more, and so did she.

Christina—indulged by her father, the Hungarian Baron—rode like a boy. Day and night she would be on her fierce brown pony, darting in and out of woods to get away from the groom; she startled wild ducks, gypsy lovers by the lake, with her red locks flying around her round face. She was a mischief-maker. Obsessed with her handsome neighbor, Otto, she hid behind the poplars to watch him walking with her older sister. Secretly she followed him when he rode his stallion: the Horse—*das Pferd*—nameless as the doll Puppe. She would gallop across his bridlepath, disguised by flowing capes, masked as a highwayman. Or she would hide in a tree and pelt him with unripe apples, making his horse shy. Once she went to the Falkenburg stables dressed in white muslin, all ribbons, flowers, under a parasol, to pet the count's horse—and made off with his saddle, hiding it in the bushes. Had Otto looked at her, he would have found her by far the more fascinating beauty of the two sisters. Christina, my grandmother believed, would have been his match.

My grandmother's retrospective journey took the form of a housecleaning: she looked at events she could not simply dismiss and rearranged them in her mind. I listened to my grandmother as I had once listened to Eugene Romberg and never interrupted except to help her along. "How about the sculptor, Antonelli, the one who made Puppe?"

"Sheer defiance," the countess said. "I never thought of it until now. She never cared about any of those men who fell in love with her. She remained obsessed with the count, demented with jealousy. Her adventures, her travels with the doll and with me, were much the same as the apple-throwing. She hoped he would hear about her antics and come after her. That way she would get him away from his tyrannical sister. But he never even reprimanded her as a brother-in-law, when she caused the scandal with the sculptor. She did succeed in the end, though, by taking me from the convent. This, at last, infuriated him. Not that he cared about me."

She clasped her hands as if she had to hold onto herself tightly. "I tried to win his heart for the last time that Easter. I failed, disgraced myself. This made me eager to go with my aunt Christina; I was ready to leave the convent. The nuns had taught me to believe in love and forgiveness, so on that Easter Sunday I had gone to Falkenburg with a reed basket full of flowers. I went running down the back stairs from the library and startled him and Aunt Gitta in the herb garden."

"Did you notice the painting of a dwarf in armor?" I asked.

"I was far too anxious to look at any painting. Besides, it was dark. My only light came from open doors. Never again have I set foot in that winding staircase, or in the herb garden. It is now all overgrown—a wilderness." She stopped talking, trembled, and pulled the quilt around her.

"And then what happened?" I asked.

"I ran to them and said, 'Happy Easter.' I held out the basket and was about to tell them that I had woven it and had gathered the flowers myself. The countess Gitta, with bushy dark hair hanging down her back to hide her deformity, always dressed like a child and had the voice of a nasty infant. 'Keep her away,' she squeaked. 'Look how big she is. That's what killed my lovely Anne-Marie, my sweetest friend.' I was twelve years old, tall like you, Reyna. The count glared at me with detestation. I flung the basket at them. It hit her. Flowers spilled out and I trampled on them."

The smell of burning interrupted us. I jumped up and ran to tend to the alcohol stove. Our spiced wine had boiled away. As soon as I had repaired the damage and refilled our glasses, I asked, "How did you find out he killed himself?"

Her need to talk won over her reticence. She drank before she went on. "The family doctor wrote to Christina and told her every detail in a long letter. He always wrote to her. After she had left the village she used him as a go-between, since he tended to the Falkenburg household. It was he who must have treated her when she had the measles or fell off her pony, and he watched her grow up into one of the beauties of her time. She always turned to him when she faced serious trouble."

"You mean, when she gave birth to Traude?"

The countess gave me a sharp look. "I was as inquisitive as you are, meine Leibe—never as brazen. It's wearing pants that makes you so pert." She fingered a diamond pin shaped like a horseshoe which her aunt Christina had given to her. "She loved me and she hated me. Life with her was never dull. I refused to ride with her, but we climbed mountains, swam, went to theaters, the opera in Rome and Paris. She never talked to me as I talk to you. She turned to the doll on the day I handed her the letter. Everyone thought Puppe belonged to me, although she carried her. They believed I liked having a doll dressed like my aunt. That morning, Puppe and my aunt wore hats made by Hanna trimmed with ostrich feathers."

The countess described the doll sitting in her gilded chair in the hotel room overlooking the churning green water. (Her aunt and the doll always wore cream or white dresses when the weather was dreary.) It rained as it can only rain in Nice, she told me, and the window was open. I imagined the doll rocking back and forth, the scheming eyes moving from side to side in the sirocco. My great-aunt had run out on the balcony, tearing the letter into small pieces and throwing it to the wind. "Damned sisters," she had yelled, "mine and his!"

"She grabbed Puppe, created to look like her twin," said Grandmother. "She talked to the doll, not to me, raging against the doctor who had no doubt loved her as hopelessly as she had loved Otto all those years. The doctor had never married, and he told her the truth about the count, hoping to finally cure her of that obsession. It was too late. She held onto her love as the count had held onto his dead sister."

"He locked himself up in a room with her," I said, "refused to have them take her away after she died. The doctor and the priest came, but he got away." I was thinking of Father holding Eli and leaping from the Tanten-Haus and added, "He wrapped her up in a bedspread, jumped from the balcony. Then he flung her onto the saddle of the horse, rode it up Falkenburg, and forced it to leap toward the sinking sun. They crashed into the quarry."

"You seem to know more than I do," said the countess. "I was told that Aunt Gitta died of a fever and he rode out in his grief and broke his neck. Who gave you this vivid description?"

"Frau Boschke, our laundress."

"From laundrywomen to royalty, everyone talked about and improved on his death, and they will not let the story end, any more than they will the tragedy of Crown Prince Rudolf at Mayerling," my grandmother said. "Self-murder, which we all contemplate in some form or other, is the one assassination those who live on can rarely survive. Crown Prince Rudolf died . . ."

"With his love," I filled in.

"His death was a bitter accusation and stirred up young assassins in the Balkans, everywhere. It led to other atrocities."

"The murder in Sarajevo. Hanna Roth says it all happened because Archduchess Sophie did not wear the yellow hat that Hanna had made for the occasion."

My grandmother gave me a look of gentle reprimand. "Under normal circumstances, under the monarchy, Hanna would never have gone beyond the nursery and playrooms where she belonged, playing her games with children. The need for wizards and fortunetellers among the men who have led us to disaster is only natural. They are men of uneasy consciences, and their hearts are set on the future because they cannot look back. Hanna Roth has used them and she has been used. They have to justify their misdeeds by looking ahead to new spurious victories. A true Austrian must look back. We must look back, acknowledge any wrongdoing in our heritage and in us; this is a form of confession, a cleansing of the soul which helps us to face each day with hope, prayer—not vengeance."

During a few minutes of silence we both drank and listened to the sound of the avengers. My old whangdoodle was on the rampage. "Don't worry, Grandmama. Soon it will all be over."

"Our Crown Prince will enter Vienna."

I smiled and thought of my Frog Prince.

"Austria will be Austria again," my grandmother said.

"Everyone will come back to Vienna." I raised my glass, and we drank to my parents, the Rittmeister; and I secretly toasted all my loves, including Hanna Roth. I felt certain they would all survive and return. My one worry was Rudolf Hess.

My grandmother felt thirsty. After she had put her glass down, she stroked my unwashed curls. "I talk to you because I believe one day you will figure things out. I talk to you because no one ever talked to me when I was your age. It has taken me all my life to know how guilty my aunt must have felt for running away from the count instead of going to him as a woman in love."

I took up my glass and felt proud of having run across the street, as a woman in love, and kissing the prince.

"I can see my beautiful aunt leaning over the balcony into the wind after she had torn up the doctor's letter, crying, 'The horse —poor, poor horse!' She darted back into the room, ignoring me, and snatched up the doll, ready to leap. It took all my strength to pull her back. I locked her into the room. After that she was never the same. She had to take me back to Vienna for the settling of the estate. I had become an heiress. Pauline von Kortnai, an aunt, became my guardian. She had been a lady-in-waiting to Empress Elizabeth. Christina had embarrassed me more and more, yet I was sorry to see her leave Vienna. She wanted me to kiss the doll and say 'Auf Wiedersehen,' and I laughed at the idea. This offended her so much, she never came to my wedding or your mother's christening. When she did return to Vienna to die, she had nothing to say to me."

"But she took a fancy to Mother because Mother had red hair," I said. "Must have been crazy."

My grandmother became so annoyed she dropped her spoon. "That is not so. My aunt called for lawyers and was of clear mind when she left everything to your mama. She saw herself in that little girl."

We had, in a sense, arrived at a destination. The countess looked slightly flushed, and I felt agreeably warm. She reached for her praline box; it was, of course, empty. I kept taking my watch off and putting it on again. My grandmother paced back and forth. "It has to end soon," she said. "I don't hear the guns anymore. Before long I'll just have to open the shutters and allow the swallows to return." Then she said, "I want to go upstairs to the kitchen to see my furniture and sit at the tile stove to warm up. I can't draw down here, my fingers get too stiff."

We went upstairs. The next horse she drew, a horse leaping, went into the tile stove. She stopped drawing after she had warmed up, and her eyes were closed when she said, "Listen, listen, Reyna. Do you hear horses' hoofs?"

I had come to see everything through her eyes, feel as she felt, and did not pay much attention to the clatter of hoofs on stone. The faint cry of a woman's voice could have been Great-Aunt Christina bemoaning the death of her beloved mad count, my great-grandfather. I did not go to the window until I heard women crying for help. Nor was my sympathy aroused when I looked through the wrought-iron grill and saw the woman who had tried to break into the little palace running from a young soldier in a gray, unfamiliar uniform. He laughed as he ran after her. His round, boyish face reminded me of Johann. A round fur hat slipped to the back of his head. A suitcase tied with ersatz string slowed him down. "Frrrau, Frauuu. Uhrrr, Uhrrri!" he shouted.

I liked this man, the first Russian I saw, but could not understand why he wanted watches. He already wore several of them on both arms, strapped over his uniform sleeves.

The woman in the brown fur fled from him on short bent legs like a frantic bear. I had read in Herodotus that Greek sailors in the fifth century fancied apes and took them for women. Russian soldiers, I speculated, might like women who resembled bears.

Just as the soldier caught up with the fugitive, she threw her bag at him and yelled, "Uhr, Uhr!" He did have the sense to prefer a watch to the ugly looter. Down on his knees, he emptied her bag; candlesticks, silver spoons, a cashmere scarf fell onto the cobblestones. He pushed three fingers of his left hand through a silver napkin ring while the woman climbed a ladder, dragged it up over the wall, and fled.

"Don't take the ladder, Rose. Don't leave me!" yelled another female. I saw her, half-hidden by evergreens and shrubs at the side of the stoop. Another boy in a fur hat was pinning her down. Only about eight or nine meters to the right, below my window, he lay on top of her, a rider taming an unruly horse. Her feet kicked and trampled the snow.

Soldiers on leave had persuaded girls to lie down with them in our woods near the meadow farm. Stopperl and I had fun startling them. I never really saw what they were doing. I would not have been shocked in the least by what I now saw if an alarm clock the soldier wore around his neck had not gone off. The soldier jumped up, forgot his pants, cursed the clock tied around his neck, couldn't get it over his head or break the string. He stared in horror at the brass bell on top designed to ring forever, burst eardrums, stop and start again like Gestapo torture, jingle in the brain: a secret weapon, German clock, made to murder, enemy of the Soviet Union—monster.

The fur hat, machine gun, pants bunched over boots added to

the freak show of his half-nakedness. So did the female sitting on her haunches, struggling with rags and glaring at the man in an amazement I could well understand.

At the pit of the Russian belly, between thighs of a marble Greek god, hung a furry pod. A long pink rod stuck up from it as though it did not belong, displaying a parasitic life of its own.

I had never seen a naked man in this state—only horses in the field. With the logic of a child I saw the Russian as unique: half-beast. I could not help feeling sorry for this pale country boy afflicted with the alarm clock as well as this deformity. He bit through the string and flung the clock away. The struggle to get his pants over his protrusion almost made him give up. He was about to go back to the stoop, the woman, when the alarm started up again. The woman got away to the coach house.

The soldier with the loot bellowed, held up a small gold watch. The clock kept ringing while the comrades rolled on the ground, through puddles, fighting for the watch. I was too absorbed in their pelting, vicious attack on eyes, noses, and that hidden thing I had seen to notice my grandmother, until she said, "If the woman gets into the coach house, she can squeeze out the back window and get away." I wished she had not seen any of the fight, or heard the snapping and yelping.

Yaahuo, hauo, auuuuuh: the old hunting horn howled like a hound in hell. I fell against the wall with fright. Nothing could ever prepare one for the imperial hunting horn. Her fur hat tilted to one side, glittering with gems, the countess kept blowing the horn. I could not stop her. The soldiers fell apart. Too startled or too drunk to trace the sound, they sprayed bullets all around. Finally they attacked the portal, the lock. *Aouhhh, aouha* went the hunting horn. They fled.

A small gold watch lay on the cobblestones among scattered loot—a schoolgirl's watch. Not fancy like the one Eugene Romberg had sent to me from Switzerland. Later I would pick it up, broken, bent. "To Lotte on her tenth birthday from *Grossmutter*." One watch of thousands, or perhaps millions, of girls' watches the *Sodalteskas* fought for. Did they ever look at the engravings—to daughters, nieces, on birthdays, name days, for graduation—after they had shared a girl my age or a grandmother and fought to kill among themselves for a little watch?

"Grandmama, put your horn away. Put it away. They'll come back!" I tried to pull it from her hands. She held on.

"Take up your grandfather's sword, against evil!" she commanded.

We were both overwrought from drinking hot wine. I obeyed her order, but she stayed me, grabbed my arm. "Horses' hoofs, a horse!" she said. "The horse." The horn sounded off triumphantly.

The response came at once. The howling and barking of every hound of the hunt came toward us, louder and louder the yelping and snarling. They leapt onto the wall—soldiers in gray with an exotic touch of purple. Crouching, crawling, prowling, they surrounded the stone angel, the shrine, the old trees, and barked. A few sparrows flew off.

"Turks, Mongolians, the heathens!" The countess rushed at the kitchen door. It was locked. "Open up, for God's sake, open!"

I did not obey. She leaned against the wall, fingering her rosary. One of our panes had been hit by a stray bullet, and the heavy curtains rippled in a gust. The sun came and went like the electric light in the cellar just before the power failed. I encircled her with my arms.

"Listen to them howl and bark," she said. "No longer human. Lieber Gott in heaven protect our young emperor among the heathens."

A burst of sniper fire came down over the wall. One of the soldiers raised his machine gun and aimed at the Hohentahler mansion. Little men, not much larger than the general's tin soldiers danced on the roof, waving a swastika flag. Two explosions, a flash of lightning—the men, the flag, and half the roof had gone.

At that moment, a white horse trotted into our courtyard, swinging its long tail from side to side as though it might perform a quadrille.

"The horse," I said.

"*His* horse," said the countess.

The stallion wore a saddle and a bunched-up blanket. After the explosion, the blanket sat up and turned into a rider worthy of such a horse: a face as smooth and pale as an almond, large eyes of dark agate, a gray uniform with pale purple trim. He controlled the trembling beast. The men on the wall yelped and barked. He pranced about with a faint smile, as though he had come invited, an honored guest from the Orient.

He raised his right arm. A dozen watches sparkled in a spotlight of April sun. The barking stopped. I forgot that he might break into the palace, do us harm. So did my grandmother. She stared at him and let the horn fall down. A prince from the stories of the Arabian nights. He wore his fur hat like a crown.

Smoke and dust from the Hohentahler roof drifted down over our courtyard. He turned his horse and it waltzed as he shouted an order. I misunderstood his gesture, for he never stopped smiling as he confronted the smiling angel. Then he barked three times. The gun was in his hand. He fired the first shot at the angel's breast. As if a stone angel had a heart! The second shot splintered the halo, the smiling lips, putting an end to cheerfulness.

Soldiers on the wall then fired, aiming carelessly, hitting the shrine, stucco rose garlands, a stone wing. The officer on the white horse threw back his head and laughed a loud bark upon seeing a Cupid's head roll into a birdbath. Old ornaments, created to please, to divert, were under attack. The horse turned its head from side to side, pawed the ground. Mad with terror and restraint, it rose on its hind legs, stayed there, trained to sustain this pose, in pitiable confusion.

My grandmother was praying, her eyes half-closed, lips whispering words I could not hear. Then the praline box and the rosary fell from her hands. I was shoved aside forcefully. She stood at the window, aiming her pistol. She had lived gently, according to her faith, in her conspiracy to restore the empire. Yet all these years the pistol of the murdered empress had remained loaded and ready.

Had the Mongolian rider seen Countess Reyna von Dornbach Falkenburg at that moment, he would have found her as inviting a target as the stone angel. She stood tall, stiff, her head held high, slightly inclined.

"Don't shoot!" I called to her. Soldiers out there kept firing in all directions. "Stand back!"

Her arrogant bearing contrasted with an expression of submission and humility. She followed the command of some inner voice, met the challenge of the rider on the white horse—assassin of the angels. Her arm, hard as stone, thrust me aside. Nothing could touch her in this state of violent elation.

The target had to be larger than life, the threat universal. "Poor horse, poor horse, poor horse!" This was no longer my grandmother. It was the voice of Christina von Kortnai. I dared not approach. She faced death in that saddle: the death of the house of Falkenburg, the Austrian empire. She ripped the curtain aside, fired three times—at *him, him, him.*

The rider fell. Soldiers dropped from the walls and gathered around him. A scuffle followed for the wristwatches, the sack of loot left by the woman. The horse reared up, throwing back its head. It was no Lippizaner. I saw it now. It had some gray mottling, although it had looked white in the sun. Then it trotted out into the street, a very ordinary horse.

"The horse is saved, the horse is saved," the countess cried, and fell to her knees. I dropped down beside her. She had not been struck by a stray bullet; her knees had given way. I pocketed her gun. Two of the Mongolian soldiers looked at the palace and seemed to be on their way to the door. A sniper bullet made them veer around, crouch. Dragging the fallen rider, the troop retreated as they had come, barking.

The countess sank down on the bench and shivered by the warm stove, clutching at her heart as though she had been wounded and were bleeding. Her wound, in a sense, had been a mortal one.

"Reyna, Reyna. Just like the hunter stalks and becomes like the beast he hunts, I have become like *him.*"

I held her and knew she had a bad fever. Her teeth chattered. "It wasn't you," I said.

She closed her eyes, and for a long time I heard only the log crackling in the fire. Shots had moved off into the distance.

"I abandoned him," she finally said. "Now I see everything differently. He had entrusted me to the nuns. Wanted me safe. I never attempted to meet with him when I grew up into a young girl. Who knows, had he seen how much I looked like him, he might have yielded. This might have saved him."

I repaired the curtain and helped her down the stairs into the cellar, covered her, and gave her aspirin. "Everything is going to be all right. I know it. The war will soon be over. The swallows will return. Everyone will come back to Vienna." I sounded like Hanna Roth, for I believed in my own prophecy. My grandmother did not hear me. I hoped she would go to sleep and went to sit at the dark table where I sit now. I can still hear her beautiful voice. She accused herself for having been meek when she should have been forceful. Forceful, finally, when she should have been meek. What inherent madness had made her see the man on the white horse as an apparition, an assassin, when he shot at weathered stone? She said she had waited for this moment as any Falkenburg waited to shed all doubts, all fears, in a moment of diabolic violence against the enemy.

I believe my grandmother, Countess Reyna von Dornbach Falkenburg, fired the three bullets at the devil, as Martin Luther threw his inkwell against a white wall, aiming at Satan and leaving behind a black mark of fear.